Two Novels

CHARITON'S
Callirhoe

AND

XENOPHON OF EPHESOS'
*An Ephesian Story:
Anthia and Habrocomes*

Two Novels from Ancient Greece

CHARITON'S
Callirhoe

AND

XENOPHON OF EPHESOS'
An Ephesian Story: Anthia and Habrocomes

Translated, with Introduction and Notes, by
STEPHEN M. TRZASKOMA

Hackett Publishing Company, Inc.
Indianapolis/Cambridge

14 13 12 11 10   1 2 3 4 5 6 7

For further information, please address
Hackett Publishing Company, Inc.
P.O. Box 44937
Indianapolis, Indiana 46244-0937

www.hackettpublishing.com

Cover design by Brian Rak
Interior design by Elizabeth L. Wilson
Composition by William Hartman
Printed at Sheridan Books, Inc.

Library of Congress Cataloging-in-Publication Data
Chariton.
    [De Chaerea et Callirrhoe. English]
    Two novels from ancient Greece : Chariton's Callirhoe and Xenophon
of Ephesos' An Ephesian story : Anthia and Habrocomes / translated,
with introduction and notes, by Stephen M. Trzaskoma.
        p. cm.
    Includes bibliographical references.
    ISBN 978-1-60384-192-4 (pbk.)—ISBN 978-1-60384-193-1 (cloth)
    1. Syracuse (Italy)—Fiction. 2. Caria (Turkey)—Fiction.
3. Slaves—Fiction. 4. Love stories, Greek—Translations into English.
5. Greek literature—Translations into English. I. Trzaskoma, Stephen.
II. Xenophon, of Ephesus. Ephesiaca. English III. Title.
PA3948.C3E5 2010
883'.01—dc22   2009040580

ΤΗΙ ΔΑΦΝΗΙ ΤΗΙ ΕΜΗΙ

CONTENTS

Acknowledgments   viii
Introduction   xi
Note on the Texts and Translations   xxxiv
Maps   xxxviii

Callirhoe   1
An Ephesian Story:
   Anthia and Habrocomes   129

Select Bibliography   182
Endnotes   189

ACKNOWLEDGMENTS

The appearance of excellent critical editions of the Greek texts of the two novelists translated here was reason enough for me to want to spend more time with these authors, and I want to thank Bryan Reardon and James O'Sullivan for the tremendous advance they've made with their editions on the scholarship of these works. I am also grateful to Bryan for his correspondence and encouragement on this project. That he himself is a translator of Chariton and that this book could be seen as competition for one of his own should be ample proof of his magnanimity. Brian Rak, my editor at Hackett Publishing, mused aloud about doing something to plug the "Greek novel gap" in Hackett's catalog at just the right moment in 2007 for me to take him seriously. For his excellent timing and his able guidance—and for putting up so graciously with too many minor delays and one big one—he has my gratitude. Thanks also to Liz Wilson and everyone else at Hackett who helped bring the book through production, as well as Bill Nelson for the excellent maps.

I was extremely fortunate to have Joel Relihan of Wheaton College (Norton, Mass.) as a reader for the press. Though it is cliché to say so, it is also quite true that he went above and beyond the call of duty. He read the translations with extraordinary care and improved them in countless ways. His critiques also helped me out of several jams when I had thrown up my hands in frustration about how best to render something. By curious coincidence, I first studied these texts under his direction while I was in graduate school at the University of Illinois in the early 1990s, and it was a true pleasure to be reunited with him in this fashion after so long. My enduring interest in the Greek novels is surely due at least in part to his wonderful teaching.

My colleague at the University of New Hampshire, R. Scott Smith, served as an unofficial second reader, and his input was literally invaluable. Colleagues and friends who will candidly tell you when you've goofed should never be undervalued. Jeffrey Henderson of Boston University was working on his own translation of Xenophon of Ephesos as I was preparing mine. When we learned of our mutual interests, he was kind enough to suggest we exchange versions (his has now appeared, combined in a single volume with Longos' *Daphnis and Chloe*, in the

Loeb Classical Library), and I have repaid his kindness by shamelessly stealing a few phrases from him. Harbour Fraser Hodder copyedited the manuscript and improved it in many minor ways in the process. It goes without saying that any errors and infelicities that remain are entirely my own and not those of the helpful people named above. I should also mention my gratitude to Bruce Swann, Classics Librarian at the University of Illinois at Urbana-Champaign, who helped me track down some particularly obscure scholarship on these two authors.

A great deal of translation took place at the Fondation Hardt in Vandoeuvres, Switzerland, in August of 2008. The excellence of that idyllic institute and its library is matched only by the helpfulness and hospitality of its staff. A Summer Faculty Fellowship from the Graduate School and a travel grant from the Center for Humanities of the University of New Hampshire made the trip to the Fondation possible and provided early support for the project as a whole. I ought also to mention James Connolly, Michelle LeBlanc, Ashley Lord, Devon St. Cyr, and Sean Tandy, the students in my Advanced Greek course on Chariton in the spring semester of 2009 at the University of New Hampshire. Their genuine enthusiasm for the novel, their own translations, their remarks, and their questions helped shape the current book in surprising ways (surprising to them not least because I never told them I was preparing a translation for publication). I thank them for their conversations and their heartening devotion to a supposedly dead language. I did much of my work on this book at Me & Ollie's café in downtown Exeter, New Hampshire. For making so little money off of so frequent a visitor, they deserve at the very least this plug.

Two deaths marked the preparation of this book and will forever be associated in my mind with it. As I began thinking seriously about the project in December 2007, my maternal uncle Conrado Manuel Lozano passed away; then my cousin Eddie Williams died in August 2009 just as I was putting the final touches on the manuscript. *Que en paz descansen.* They are missed and their memories are cherished by those they left behind; it is of utterly no consolation that their passing gave me an interesting distance from which to reread Northrop Frye's *The Secular Scripture: A Study of the Structure of Romance* and the arguments of B. E. Perry and B. P. Reardon for the emotional and social function of stories like *Callirhoe* and *An Ephesian Story* in their original contexts.

Not all of my mental associations with this volume are so unhappy, of course. A case in point: This book is dedicated to my wife, Laurel. She earned it for reading through both translations (twice!) and for putting up with my punctuating our home life for over a year with constant questions about whether this sounded OK or whether that sounded too corny or didn't she perhaps prefer this other phrase. Her apparently inexhaustible capacity to humor me is a wonder of nature, and I hope that I never have cause to find that it is, in fact, exhaustible. For her beauty and brains she deserves the honor (such as it is) of the dedication, and for so much more, but it would try the patience of the reader for me to catalog her virtues. Let it suffice for me to make this declaration publicly: Should it ever happen that I become the object of the affections of a sex-crazed barbarian woman or be kidnapped by pirates or sold into slavery—or even all three at the same time—I vow to remain faithfully hers. (And let's hope that's enough to make her forget that the gift for a tenth wedding anniversary isn't supposed to be a book dedication.)

SMT
Exeter, New Hampshire
4 September 2009

Addendum: While this volume was in press, the sad news came that Bryan Reardon had passed away on 16 November 2009. Bryan was an eloquent advocate for the study of the ancient novel, an exacting critic, and simply a wonderful human being. As did so many others, I had my first exposure to Chariton via Bryan's 1989 translation. It was my privilege to enjoy his friendship and support in more recent years, and I profited enormously from his generous willingness to continue sharing his expertise and ideas long after his retirement—to the very end of his life, in fact. It would be difficult to exaggerate his contributions to the field or his influence on me.

INTRODUCTION

Toward the end of the first century BC or the beginning of the first century AD, a small tremor struck the literary landscape of the Greek and Roman worlds. It was so small that it was widely ignored at the time, though many centuries later it would contribute to a complete reshaping of western literature. As the Roman Republic gained total dominance over the Greek world and was transforming itself convulsively into an empire, authors began for the first time to write in a genre that would one day come to dominate literature almost entirely—the kind of extended fictional narrative in prose that we now call *novels.* They would continue to do so until almost the end of the western Roman Empire in the fifth century AD. The genre, however, never attained wide literary respectability or visibility in the marketplace of ancient artistic forms, and as a result, the rise of the novel as the dominant literary form of the modern world did not spring simply, quickly, or directly from these first novels. Instead, the subsequent story of the novel would be one of revivals. Several of the later ancient Greek and Roman novels circulated during the middle ages and had a significant influence on the development of fiction in medieval Byzantium. Another rediscovery—this time in western Europe during the Renaissance—contributed to the fashioning of new prose vernacular literatures and the rise of the modern novel. This role in subsequent history should command our attention, but ancient novels are also worth reading in their own right.

Applying the term *novel* to these ancient texts is not entirely uncontroversial. Many modern critics, preferring the term *romance,* have a particular view of what novels are or the conditions under which they arose that excludes the ancient exemplars from membership in the genre. To these critics, books like the two included in this edition should not be called *novels* either because they were written prior to the development of certain historical conditions held to be necessary for the rise of the novel (conditions that were in place, for example, by the time Cervantes wrote *Don Quixote,* Defoe wrote *Robinson Crusoe,* or Richardson wrote *Pamela,* and so on), or because they lack some key feature, usually psychological or social realism, thought to be essential to the genre. Some who prefer the term *novel,* on the other hand, often do so to avoid any negative association with medieval and renaissance romances, which have been viewed by some as inferior modes of narrative. In any case, *romance* and *novel* are categories of modern not ancient literary criticism, and they are notoriously difficult to define and apply even to more recent texts.

As it turns out, the distinction between novel and romance exists in English but not in most other modern European languages, and this often remarked fact is perhaps a strong indication that even if romance and novel are not the same thing precisely, at least they overlap. Erwin Rohde, a giant in the field of the study of these texts in the nineteenth century, had no trouble referring to them as *Romane,* the German word that covers both romances and novels. In English, however, the name novel has been comfortably applied to them only for the last several decades. This development was intimately bound up with efforts of scholars to raise the profile of these texts and claim for them simultaneously a place in the mainstream of classical studies and a relationship to modern novels, which were the subject of increasingly innovative theoretical approaches to literary criticism. Those efforts can now be declared an unqualified success. From the perspective of someone at the end of the first decade of the twenty-first century, it is obvious that the wide scholarly neglect that prevailed almost wholly until the 1960s has been replaced by intense interest and inventive analysis. Instead of a few articles per year, scholars now have to keep up with dozens, as well as collections of essays and, increasingly, book-length treatments. One consequence of this success is that the terms *novel* and *romance* tend to be used interchangeably to refer to these Greek texts. This practice also reflects common sense. When the works of Tolkien—which for some strict constructionists of genre must be labeled *romances*—can be regularly referred to as *fantasy novels,* and detective stories—another category of the romance—are now called *mystery novels,* to insist on denying the possibility of *ancient Greek novels* seems overly fastidious. As for romance, it need not be bound strictly to form—it is a mode of literature bound up with the particular deployment of certain kinds of themes—so there is no very good reason for denying that the ancient novels are romances, centered as they are on these very themes. It is all well and good to distinguish ancient novels/romances from Harlequin-style "romance novels," but avoiding the term romance entirely separates them also from Sidney's *Arcadia* and Shakespeare's romantic comedies, works with which the ancient romances share much aesthetically and intellectually.

It is generally agreed, however, that we have five complete novels from ancient Greece. The two translated here, *Callirhoe* by Chariton and *An*

Ephesian Story by Xenophon of Ephesos, are usually acknowledged to be the earliest and have been dated anywhere from the first century BC to the second century AD. The three later examples are *Daphnis and Chloe* by Longos, *Leucippe and Cleitophon* by Achilles Tatios, and *An Ethiopian Story* by Heliodoros. The dating of these three texts is also notoriously vexed, but Heliodoros is certainly the latest (from either the third or fourth century AD) and Longos and Achilles Tatios both probably belong to the second century AD. It is easy to see a family resemblance among all the novels despite their being spread over three or four centuries. In addition to being written in prose and at a length significantly longer than what we would call a short story, each centers on the trials and tribulations of a romantic couple. In each novel this couple is heterosexual, of extraordinary physical beauty, free and well-born, (more or less) Greek, and (sooner or later) married. The general pattern involves separation of the lovers, adventures in faraway lands, and a reunion with a happy ending. Because of those happy endings and the accompanying fidelity of the main couple, these have been designated *ideal romances,* a designation that has sometimes been more confusing than helpful ("ideal" being often conflated with "perfectly representative"). Informally, they are sometimes referred to as "the Big Five."

So far the picture seems reasonably clear, but this is not precisely the case. The Big Five are far from the only works of extended prose fiction from this period. There are a variety of other prose literary works from the same era that share some of the characteristics of these novels though to different degrees and in different combinations. In Latin, for instance, we have the fragmentarily preserved *Satyrica* (or *Satyricon*) of Petronius, probably from the first century AD, which is so different from the Greek novels that it has for the last century been seen as at least a partial parody of them. Its homosexual love triangle and interest in urban low life in this view is a calculated inversion of the love stories found in the Greek novels. We also have Apuleius' *Golden Ass* or *Metamorphoses,* an elaborate Latin variation of a Greek narrative involving a man who is turned into a donkey. We have one surviving Greek example of this story in the *Ass* (Greek *Onos*), which was once thought to be by the second-century author Lucian. The real Lucian has given us what is sometimes called the first example of science fiction, his *True History,* which describes, among other adventures, a trip to the moon. These are merely a few examples of fictional prose from the period of the Roman Empire, but they give some sense of the vitality and diversity of which imperial authors were capable. We also have a variety of fragments of other prose fictional writings, usually quite short and preserved in quotation and on papyrus, that add to the complexity of sketching an overall picture of what was available to an ancient reader and how we should imagine all these texts are related to each other.

Calling the Big Five novels *ideal,* therefore, has helped to create the notion that somehow they represent the main, core development of prose fiction, though this was not the sense in which the label was first applied. The other fictional works, both preserved and fragmentary, must then be viewed not only as quite distinct in form and function but even as a set of fringe works. But just as the tendency in earlier decades was to loosen the terminology of the novel to include the five Greek romances, so now the trend in scholarship is to acknowledge that it may make more sense to view ancient prose fiction broadly enough to encompass all of these writings. If the genre of the modern novel can encompass works as diverse as *Pamela* and *Gulliver's Travels,* perhaps we should be able to wrap our minds around *Callirhoe* and *True History* as texts that somehow belong together. Thus another Latin text, *Apollonius King of Tyre,* though later than all other Greek and Latin novels by a century or more, is now usually termed a novel. And the biggest blockbuster of all was the *Alexander Romance,* a heavily fictionalized account of Alexander the Great that was translated into many languages (Latin, Armenian, Syriac, etc.) from the original Greek. It lacks love interest almost entirely, but its Greek versions are clearly related to other Greek prose fiction and they fall easily into a widely defined notion of romance/novel. Of course, there are also plenty of works of fiction in prose from the Roman imperial period that are not novels, but in those cases we usually have something more than the erotic core missing. Many lack a coherent overall narrative, or are simply too short, or have utterly no interest in character.

Ancient writers were fully capable of engaging in sophisticated literary criticism and classification, and yet they never strongly acknowledged the emergence of these new forms of literature. The established genres of epic, tragedy, comedy, lyric, history, philosophy, and the like were conventionalized at a date significantly earlier than the texts we are dealing with here. When new forms arose, they were essentially ignored by the literary establishment. We never, therefore, get a scholarly or theoretical treatment of novels by the Greeks or Romans themselves, something we have or hear about for many of the traditional genres (think of Aristotle's *Poetics* or Lucian's *How to Write History*). As has frequently been noted, there is not a single word in either ancient language that corresponds to either *novel* or *romance,* much less both.

The Ancient Novel and Its Ancient Readers

The lack of a word for *novel* in Greek or Latin does not mean that the ancients did not *read* these novels. Their very existence is evidence to the contrary—as is their relationship to each other. The Big Five are so similar to each other that we can speak confidently of their conventions; it only follows that there must have been an audience of some size capable of expecting and recognizing those conventions. The later novelists show knowledge of the earlier novels not only through broad similarities of plot, but also through specific allusions. The Roman novelists Petronius and Apuleius play openly with the conventions of the Greek romances, which lends additional weight to this point. Further proof comes from the several scraps of the novels of Chariton and Achilles Tatios that have come down to us on papyrus discovered in Egypt (along with one fragment of Heliodoros). These scraps indicate that the novels were in circulation, at least in Egypt—although we have no great reason to think Egypt was unusual in this regard—and were being recopied for new readers for some time. In late antiquity especially, other writers began to show the influence of the novelists. In the letters of Aristaenetus (fifth century AD), for instance, we see imitations of the novels of both Xenophon of Ephesos and Achilles Tatios. A Christian historian in the fifth century tells the story that Heliodoros became a Christian and eventually a bishop—obviously *after* he wrote his novel—and similar stories are told of Achilles Tatios. These (pseudo?) biographical details would never have been created or promulgated unless there was good press to be had in remarking on the authors' conversions. But perhaps some of the strongest evidence we have for the success of the novels lies in Jewish prose narratives and in early Christian writings. Scholars in the last decades have begun the productive work of tracing how these narratives relate to the Greek and Roman novels. Most obviously, the lives of martyrs often follow stereotyped plots and narrative structures with a clear relationship to the non-Christian erotic novels (sometimes with a virgin's love of Christ replacing the sexualized love of the couples in romance, as in the *Acts of Paul and Thecla,* for example).

We can be certain, then, that these novels were being read, but the evidence is generally late and often indirect. It also raises another question: *who* read the novels? It must be said at the start that this is hardly a matter of settled opinion. Initially scholars looked to the rise of novels in the modern world, especially sentimental romance novels, to provide an analog. They noted what they considered to be the obviously low quality of the texts that had come down to us and felt these were clearly no match for the epics, tragedies, and other classics of antiquity. So they assumed that the ancient novels could only have been written for a nonintellectual, female, and even barely literate audience—the sort of audience they imagined for modern romantic fiction. But times have changed. In the 1960s B. E. Perry, though still relying on analogy with the rise of the modern novel, conceived of an audience, distinct from the elite, born from the increasing literacy rates of the last centuries BC with the increasing size of a world now dominated by huge kingdoms and empires rather than local city-states. B. P. Reardon would refine this notion and write of the novels as a literary counterpart to the search for personal meaning and fulfillment that we see increasingly in the religious and philosophical spheres of this period. These are elegantly argued positions, particularly because they neatly address not only readership but also the impulses behind the very origin of the new literary form, yet they constitute merely one set of possibilities out of many.

More recently the strongest arguments have been advanced for a mostly elite audience. This is where literacy was concentrated and where literary production was eagerly consumed as part of a cultural system of self-definition and a renaissance in Greek culture (more on this later). Scholars taking this position have noted in particular the literary relationships the novels have with other works from antiquity. With the exception of Xenophon of Ephesos, who refers to famous episodes and plot elements of classical literature only obliquely, the other novelists indulge constantly in allusion and imitation of everyone from Homer and the tragedians to classical historians such as Herodotus, Thucydides, and Xenophon (of Athens). Their novels thus seem designed for an audience who would be able to recognize these intertextual relationships and incorporate their import into an interpretation of the novels. Literacy, though spreading, was still confined to a small portion of the Greco-Roman world, and the only audience who could reliably be expected to recognize even a quarter of the references was the highly educated elite, not the merely functionally literate.

An interesting but inconclusive approach to the question is the study of the physical remains on papyrus of the novels—in this case not just the Big Five, but also scraps of other texts that for one reason or another scholars have identified as novels. These analyses have shown that the novel papyri are of high quality (they are written on high quality papyrus by good scribes), essentially the same as other papyri of classical literary authors. This, combined with their relative rarity, suggests that they found an elite audience—economically elite, anyway, not necessarily an intellectual elite.

Another strand of investigation has reopened the question of whether women formed an audience for the ancient novel. These inquiries are not based on the prejudices of the nineteenth and early twentieth centuries but on the internal evidence of the novels and on a more sophisticated approach to issues of gender in the ancient world. Elite women were beneficiaries of increasing literacy at this period in antiquity, which is reflected in the several female characters in the novels who are shown writing or reading. The novels frequently valorize the female heroine over the male hero. These heroines can, therefore, be seen as role models designed to appeal to a female audience that could identify with them—though they can be just as easily seen as projections of male idealizations of feminine virtue and thus aimed at a male public.

In all this, there is one group we can identify as readers with certainty: the novelists themselves. Though our biographical information is limited, we can begin with the author we know the most about: Apuleius is well-known to us, particularly through the autobiographical elements in his own work. His *Golden Ass* from the second century AD reworks the rather simplistic kind of story found in the Greek *Onos* into a tremendously sophisticated Latin novel, and there are hints that he knew Chariton's *Callirhoe* quite well. He was not a woman, was not necessarily young when he wrote, does not seem to have been poor in spirit or cash, and was not a Greek (though he was provincial Roman of native North African stock). Instead, he was one of the most highly regarded intellectuals in North Africa with something of an international reputation, educated in Athens and other centers of learning, a self-styled Platonist philosopher, and a famed orator. Our other Latin novelist, Petronius, if he is the Petronius most scholars currently take him to be—that is, the *arbiter elegantiae* ("Arbiter of Taste") of Nero (reigned AD 54–68)—obviously knew something of Greek romances if, as some suggest, he was parodying them. In this case, again, we have an educated man, not a youth or a woman, hardly poor, it would seem, in any sense, and a member of the most powerful circle in the Roman empire. Even if he is a different Petronius, no one can come away from reading the remains of the *Satyrica* without certainty that its author is not only a Latin stylist of the highest order, but also the beneficiary of an excellent education in the Greek and Roman classics. The other novelists frequently show their dependence on earlier novelists as well. Chariton and Xenophon of Ephesos demonstrate that one must have known the work of the other, though there is some question of which direction the influence runs, a matter we will return to shortly.

All this need not lead us to the conclusion that we must support those scholars who argue that the audience, intended or actual, was only the highly educated elite of the empire. This is simply one audience that can be identified, and we might best think of it as one end of a whole range of *audiences*. And when we factor in the element of time, we face yet another difficulty. What is popular literature in its own day can transform into a classic in short order. One need only look at the works of Charles Dickens and Dashiell Hammett, to take two very different modern examples. What literary snobs of one generation sneer at, those of another might praise as high art. Once we acknowledge the certainty that parts of the educational and economic elite were reading these texts, the more difficult task is to show who did *not* read these texts. Aside from the illiterate, who were the vast majority of the population of the ancient world, anyone with a basic education would have found the early examples of the ancient novels accessible, and even the illiterate might have heard the novels read in private or public settings, a kind of early "audio book" experience. On the other hand, we have no strong evidence for such performance readings of the early novels, and in any case the later novels of Achilles Tatios and Heliodoros would have been significantly tougher for an uneducated audience to appreciate because of their ornate rhetoric and recondite vocabulary. This difficulty would have been especially compounded in the setting of a public reading, where one could not go back and chew over a difficult passage.

Perhaps the best way to proceed is to acknowledge the broad middle ground that has arisen because of the scholarly stalemate over audience. First, a literary work's audience is not necessarily the audience imagined or intended by its author. Witness all the adults in our own time who happily imbibed the first of J. K. Rowling's *Harry Potter* books, which was squarely aimed at children, or those who devoured Stephenie Meyer's *Twilight Saga,* which was intended for a teenage audience, or the devout Catholics who read Dan Brown's *Da Vinci Code.* As a corollary we might also take it that the audience is not necessarily uniform either. The barriers to entry to reading at least some novels were set low. The prose form and the relatively simple style of the early examples are approachable by just about anyone. Thus it is perfectly possible that even if we tend to agree with one analysis or theory, we should end up checking "all of the above" on the test: Women, men, rich, poor, old, young, insecure provincials, confident elites, barely educated, and highly literate—why not allow ourselves an inclusive uncertainty and hope for more evidence? Proving that one sort of audience read or could have read the novels is one thing, but such an argument can never prove that another audience did *not* read them. The realization that the novels—even amongst themselves—may have had different readerships should also urge caution. How can we possibly be sure that Xenophon and Achilles Tatios were appreciated in the same way by the same people, and what does it gain us to frame the question that way?

The Same Old Story?

One might easily conclude from these remarks that the Big Five are quite similar works of literature. Boy and girl meet. Boy and girl fall for each other. Boy and girl become separated and face trials and tribulations. Boy and girl are reunited and live happily ever after. This may be true on a basic structural level, but even a cursory reading shows the manifold ways in which this basic structure can be varied by the five authors. Looking to cinema for an analogy, we might note that it is easy to reduce, say, many Kung Fu movies—or romantic comedies or Westerns or action movies or whatever—to a core stereotypical plot. (We can begin each in turn: Student's master is killed by an evil Kung Fu master who possesses apparently unbeatable technique. A high-powered executive whose only interests are money and power finds him- or herself put into a situation of close interaction with a free spirit. A boy's pa is killed on the farm by a man in a black hat. A group of incredibly well organized and technically savvy terrorists seize control of an airplane or building.) Aficionados, however, will quickly note that the best of these films generate interest through an artful alternation of faithfulness to and deviance from a given genre's essential but often indefinable core. That core must be strong enough for audiences to recognize it when they see it represented, as it is this recognition—along with a memory of the range of things that go hand-in-hand with a film of a given genre—that enables an audience to know what to expect of a film, and to see how it relates to others of its kind. Once the genre has been firmly established, it can often be merely nodded to—if even that—so long as enough features remain to tie the film to others in the genre. But every so often we even see a complete explosion of form.

The two novels translated here seem most closely to reflect the structural core of ancient romance. "Seem," I say, because it is difficult to define such a core based on a mere five examples. If we had only five Greek tragedies by five different authors instead of the thirty-one we actually have (all by just three playwrights—Aeschylus, Sophocles, and Euripides), how different would our view of Athenian drama be? But we cannot throw up our hands in utter despair, and when we look at those features that the other three of the Big Five exhibit, as well as the

characteristics of romance that Petronius seems to parody, it is easy to
conclude that Chariton and Xenophon are good representatives of a new
kind of fiction focused on requited love and adventure. Yet no scholar of
the ancient novel is so wedded to his or her overall picture of the genre
that they would be disappointed if ten more Greek novels discovered
tomorrow confounded it.

Both *Callirhoe* and *An Ephesian Story* describe the adventures of a
teenaged heterosexual couple, of extraordinary physical beauty, free and
well-born, from a Greek city-state. In each novel the couple is married
in their home city, then separated. They undergo a series of adventures
(pirate attacks, being sold into slavery, being buried alive, being crucified, and so forth) narrated in a basically linear fashion over large
geographic distances and times, during which their faithfulness to each
other is tested severely. In the end, there is a reunion, and they live
happily ever after. The other three Greek novels dispense with specific
aspects of this narrative structure. For instance, in the later Greek novels
the couples marry not before the separation but after the reunion, and
their marriages are the primary focus of the happy endings. If Chariton
and Xenophon's novels are taken as truest to form, it is not difficult to
find many more examples of how the other romances drop or deempha-
size aspects of the type.

Just a few examples will suffice. Longos' setting is not the urban
world of the city-state but the pastoral countryside, and his couple,
though well-born, do not know their true origins. The adventures and
tribulations are also severely circumscribed. They take place entirely
within a few square miles and are sort of *bonsai* versions of those in the
other novels, carefully pruned so that they are recognizable as miniature
versions of the genre's typical escapades. A pirate attack early in the novel
thus ends abruptly with the capsizing of the ship by some well-trained
cows and the hero Daphnis, who had been made prisoner by the pirates,
escapes, then returns to his beloved. Conventionally, of course, the pirates
ought to make off with Daphnis, separating the lovers and occasioning
elaborate exploits abroad, as happens in *Callirhoe* and *An Ephesian Story.*
In Achilles Tatios' *Leucippe and Cleitophon,* the hero resists all attempts
on his chastity—at least he does right up to the moment when toward
the end he throws it all over to sleep with Melite—who is, in modern
parlance, something of a "cougar" (if a bit young for that designation). In
Heliodoros' novel the heroine is not Greek after all, but the anomalously
white child of the black king and queen of Ethiopia, a child who was
exposed at birth because of her skin color.

Because of the differences apparent between Chariton and Xenophon
on the one hand and the later novels on the other, it has become

increasingly common to divide the Big Five into two groups, the "pre-Sophistic" and the "Sophistic" novels. Chariton and Xenophon are put into the category of "pre-Sophistic" novels because of their simpler narrative structure, their overall attitude, and most of all because of their language. Beginning slowly in the first century BC, a movement called Atticism began in literary and educational circles in the Greek world. Its adherents sought a return to a more correct and classical form of the language based on the classical Athenian writers of the fifth and fourth centuries BC (Attica is the region where Athens is located). The trend gained steam over the next two centuries, and by the mid-second century AD, it was predominant among most of the elite. At the same time, a class of professional intellectuals, orators, and writers—called Sophists—arose in the economically and culturally resurgent Greek eastern half of the empire. The period of this flourishing, let us say the mid-first century AD to the third century AD, together with a concomitant revival of Greek learning has been dubbed the Second Sophistic ("second" because an earlier set of Sophists had dominated the intellectual currents of the fifth century BC). These developments are an area of intense interest among classical scholars at the moment, and the later three novelists have profited from that interest because they overlap with the Sophists not only chronologically but also in their florid rhetoric, strongly Atticizing language (striving for a supposed purity found in earlier Athenian, or Attic, writers), and ostentatious intellectual elaboration. Thus the division into the Sophistic Longos, Achilles Tatios, and Heliodoros on the one hand, and the pre-Sophistic Chariton and Xenophon, who share none of these features and seem to predate the triumph of Atticism and the trends of the Second Sophistic, on the other.

As a result, the label pre-Sophistic sometimes stands in for "primitive." There are serious problems with this. Although Chariton shows no influence of full-blown Second Sophistic rhetoric or other showy elaboration, his novel is far from simplistic or primitive. His language is not fully Atticizing, for instance, but it does show an educated and judicious use of Attic forms throughout. Xenophon's novel, by contrast, is simpler both in terms of its language and its narrative features—it is the perfect example of what Northrop Frye terms "'and then' literature," since it uses as a structure merely one episode strung after another. But the urge to create too neat a picture from too little evidence must be resisted. The features we identify with the Second Sophistic were powerful influences on literature of the period, but by no means universally triumphant. Neither did they attain dominance overnight or everywhere simultaneously. Atticism and other features of the cultural trend seem to have been, in particular, a mark of membership in the cultural elite but also one open to negotiation. An author not interested in playing that particular game of identity politics might happily dispense with such niceties. We can find instructive the practice of Christian writers of the middle and late empire. The apologists and intellectuals are engaging their polytheistic counterparts and often follow the same literary fashions. Those of the same period writing saints' lives and martyr accounts for popular audiences, by contrast, regularly write in a linguistic register close to that of Xenophon or Chariton.

Who Was Chariton? Who Was Xenophon?

We know more about Chariton than most of the other Greek novelists. That's not saying much. Chariton begins his novel with a biographical statement. In imitation of early historians such as Herodotus and Thucydides his first two words are his name and his city of origin, Chariton of Aphrodisias (*Chariton Aphrodisieus*). So we have a name and a location, the city of Aphrodisias in southwest Asia Minor. He also gives us his profession—a *hypographeus,* a job title that lacks precision, but one we might call an amanuensis, secretary, or clerk—and the name of the man he works for, the orator Athenagoras. This is tantalizingly specific, but not of much actual help since we have no other record of this Athenagoras. The job Chariton mentions required a certain level of education, and to judge by the range of literary allusions he deploys, he seems to have had the full course of rhetorical training. But we have no hint of when he lived or how old he was when he wrote the novel or why he wrote it. We do not know if he wrote anything else, though some scholars have suggested that he may have written one or other of the fragmentarily preserved novels, such as *Chione* or *Metiochos and Parthenope.* Both of these may be of a similar date and show some similarities in language, but their remains are so small and the similarities so broad that the hypothesis of Chariton's authorship is at present nothing but speculation.

Only a single text from antiquity may refer to our author by name. Philostratos, a writer of the third century AD, composed and published a series of letters, one of which (*Letter* 66) reads: "To Chariton. You suppose that the Greeks will remember your words [*or* writings *or* speeches] when you die. But as for those who are nobodies when they are alive—what would that make them when they are not alive?" The date of the letter is centuries after most supposed Chariton lived, but this is no obstacle. Philostratos' letters are literary productions, not personal correspondence, and he writes several to others who are dead. It is tempting, therefore, to read this dismissive assessment as directed at our author. If it is, it would imply that Chariton was being read widely enough in the third century to merit the attack, and it also would show quite clearly the opinion of at least one member of the intellectual elite about the novel's literary worth. Still, as tempting as this is, without some further corroboration the notion that Chariton is being addressed must remain nothing more than a possibility.

Of Xenophon of Ephesos we know even less. The *Souda,* a tenth-century medieval Greek encyclopedia, has an entry on him that reads, in its entirety: "Xenophon, Ephesian, historian [*or perhaps* writer of stories]. *An Ephesian Story,* which is a love story about Habrocomes and Anthia in ten books. Also, *The City of the Ephesians* and other works." This is the one and only mention of our Xenophon by name, and it tells us very little. The most important element is its mention of "ten books." Our current text of *An Ephesian Story* is divided into five books, a discrepancy to which we will return in a moment. We ought to be very suspicious even of the basic information here. The entries in the *Souda* before and after this are for "Xenophon of Antioch" and "Xenophon of Cyprus." Both of these figures are also said to be *historikoi,* that is, historians or writers of stories, who wrote love stories, the former *A Babylonian Story* and the latter *A Cyprian Story.* Thus the name of our author, as with the others, is probably a frequently adopted pseudonym taken from the more famous historian and biographer Xenophon of Athens (fourth century BC). Our novelist's supposed city of origin may be nothing more than an extrapolation from his novel, which begins and ends in Ephesos and is about Ephesians.

Pinning Down Dates for the Ancient Novels

One factor contributing to our inability to come to firm conclusions about so many aspects of the novelists and their place in literary history is the lack of solid external evidence for dating them. Because the authors are otherwise unknown to us, we must attempt to triangulate their dates using language and style, cultural references, and their relationships to each other. We are lucky in the case of Chariton to have some fragmentary scraps of his novel preserved from ancient copies on papyrus found in Egypt. These can be dated by the handwriting to approximately the end of the second century AD. This establishes a reasonably firm later limit, but any attempt to estimate how long it would take for a novel written in Asia Minor to find a readership in Egypt is doomed from the start. So we must turn to internal evidence from the text itself. This can be reasonably conclusive in some cases, but it is of limited worth in this context. Chariton refers in his novel to items of Chinese workmanship and to apples as prizes in the Pythian Games. This gives us nothing more than an approximate date after which he had to be writing, say the middle of the first century BC, because we know only the approximate dates that the Chinese became known in the Greek and Roman worlds and that apples were introduced as prizes. Scholarly estimates have ranged from the first century BC to the second century AD, and we are still searching for the clue that will allow us to solve the mystery. In the meantime, studies of the language have contradicted each other and are based on sometimes shaky methodological grounds, some supporting an earlier date in the range, some a later one. All that can really be said of these is that an author of some literary ambition, which Chariton certainly is, probably is not very late into the second century AD or beyond, because he shows very little engagement with the linguistic, rhetorical, and intellectual trends of the Second Sophistic—unless he had some purpose for consciously neglecting these trends that we can no longer divine.

One piece of evidence mentioned in almost every discussion of Chariton's date is the appearance of the word "Callirhoe" in the last line of the first *Satire* of the Roman poet Persius. Persius ends his poem by talking about the sort of people who will not be his readers, people who could not appreciate his highbrow art, and finishes up with: "In the morning I give these people the list of upcoming shows, and after lunch I give them Callirhoe" (Persius, *Satires* 1.134). Persius died a young man in AD 62. If this Callirhoe is our *Callirhoe,* then we know that Chariton's novel was available and circulating by the reign of Nero, the same period in which Petronius' *Satyrica* was parodying ideal romance. Not surprisingly, those who favor an early date for Chariton tend to find this an attractive prospect, while those who favor a later date do not. In truth, interpretation of the passage is vexed even before we consider its implication for the novels. The word I have translated as "list of upcoming shows," *edictum,* could be several other things, not all of which have anything to do with public entertainment. Callirhoe also looks to be a literary title, but there are other possibilities. (It has even been suggested that Persius is referring to some well-known prostitute.) The reference is certainly obscure to us, even if Persius seems to have expected that his audience would readily understand it. The medieval commentaries on Persius, which take much of their material from late ancient sources and admittedly can be notoriously unreliable, supposed it was some kind of dramatic performance, perhaps a pantomime, a popular kind

of music- and dance-centered drama that began to become widely performed in the first century BC. Perhaps we can imagine a pantomime
based on the novel, but then the picture is no longer quite so neat. In
short, the word in Persius is probably not a reference to Chariton's novel.
There is a chance that it refers to a related or derivative work (if derivative, Chariton must be quite early), but the case is very far from proved,
and we are best off not putting too much faith in it.

When we turn to dating Xenophon, we are in even worse shape. In
terms of external evidence, we have none. Internally, the text is difficult
to judge. The language could fit comfortably from the end of the first
century BC to the end of the second century AD. Distinctly datable
cultural and historical references are rare and open to debate. The most
well-known is the reference in Book 2 to a character who is the "magistrate in charge of keeping the peace in Cilicia" (2.12). This has been
plausibly connected to the historically attested title *eirenarchos* ("Peace
Officer") in the area. Certainly, the character in question seems to be
doing a job similar to that of a real *eirenarchos,* and the language used
of him is vague but compatible with how others refer to that office.
Unfortunately, the only thing we can really say is that the office was
established at some point before AD 117 and endured for centuries, so
a date for the novel from the late first century BC to the early second
century AD is possible. This is not, however, a positive argument for
putting forward any particular date; it merely does not rule out certain
dates.

What about the texts' relationship to each other? There are many
parallel features of our two novels. Even beneath the level of overall
structure, where parallels are quite strong, we can note that both heroines are entombed alive, both heroes are crucified, and so forth. At
the level of language, we also have a few places where the two show
distinct similarities. It has generally been felt that these coincidences are
so close that they cannot be due to their generic affiliation or to their
dependence on earlier novels. In this way of thinking, either Xenophon
read Chariton or vice versa. For those scholars convinced by any of
the meager evidence for dating presented above, the matter is relatively
straightforward. Someone persuaded that Persius is referring to Chariton
around AD 60 and that the Cilician *eirenarchy* was established not too
long before its first attestation in AD 117, will think the mystery is no
mystery at all. Chariton, in this view, must have been writing before
Xenophon, and Xenophon is, therefore, the imitator.

Anyone with less firm convictions must look to other methods of
analysis, none of which is going to produce an absolutely certain result.
A case has been made that Xenophon is the imitator of Chariton because

of the latter's relative sophistication. In this view, Xenophon deploys the themes, tropes, and vocabulary of Chariton in a noticeably derivative way. This argument might be countered by noting that it is perfectly possible for a "better" writer to improve upon the work of a "worse" one. In fact, we have an example from this very genre and time period: Apuleius' *Golden Ass* is a brilliant reworking of something like the clearly inferior Greek *Ass*.

Many people believe that the strong influence of historical writing on the novelists (some of the earliest fragmentary examples like the so-called *Ninos Romance* from the first century BC are overtly historical) is a clue. The more historical a novel looks, the earlier it is likely to be, so Chariton, whose language is heavily influenced by historians, and who sets his novel at a particular historical moment, must be earlier, and Xenophon, who is free from these features, is later. J. N. O'Sullivan (1995) has recently put up strong resistance against this argument. He contends that the genre was likely to have arisen from simpler tales of oral storytellers, and Xenophon shows the strongest affinities with that style of narration and method of composition. The very frequent repetitions of certain phrases by Xenophon ("one of the most powerful people" in 1.1, 2.13, etc.) are for O'Sullivan compelling evidence for an author connected to a living tradition of formulaic storytelling, and this is a more interesting explanation of such features than the assumption that Xenophon was working with a strikingly limited vocabulary. Chariton, in O'Sullivan's view, then becomes an elaborator of the simpler form, more strongly moving the genre into the territory of respectable literature. E. Bowie (2002) has recently constructed a picture of the genre coming into existence at a particular time and place—southwest Asia Minor in the mid-first century AD—and Chariton is prominent in that picture as a founder of the form. It should become apparent that these sorts of argument stem from an overall view of the genre and its origins rather than from any single piece of evidence. This leads to interesting and integrated conclusions, but a cautionary tale can be found in the earliest modern study of these texts. Erwin Rohde, in 1876, without benefit of the later papyrus discoveries, developed a theory of the origin and development of the genre that required Chariton to be late—in fact, the very last of the extant novelists . . . of the fifth century AD! All it took was one scrap of papyrus to prove that Chariton must have written by AD 200 to vault Chariton from the end of the line to near the beginning. Rohde's thesis came crashing down. Without further evidence, it may be best to accept the uncertainties we face, continue to tease out patterns in the evidence, refine our arguments, but acknowledge that all of the conclusions of these approaches should be seen as mere hypotheses of greater or lesser force—and that no one has yet put forward a compelling case for reading or interpreting these two novels differently on the basis of any supposed priority.

Xenophon's Novel: The Whole Story?

One particular controversy affects almost every aspect of how we approach Xenophon's *An Ephesian Story*. As mentioned, the medieval encyclopedia the *Souda* describes the novel as being in "ten books." Our text of Xenophon contains only five books, however, and the fourth of these is quite short. The number in the *Souda* may be simply a mistake. Numbers are frequently corrupted in Greek manuscripts, especially because letters of the alphabet were used as numerals. One strand of modern criticism has seen the number as an indication of something else: abridgment. According to this possibility, which was first raised by Rohde in 1876 and became the dominant though not unchallenged view for the next century, at some point in antiquity an epitome, or a sort of ancient *Reader's Digest* abridged version of the novel, was produced. The main structure of the book was left intact, but secondary episodes and most of the details were omitted entirely or reduced significantly in size (Books 1 and 5 were seen as relatively untouched, with Books 3 and 4 showing the strongest evidence of shortening). The unbalanced pace, minor inconsistencies, leaps in narrative logic, and uneven elaboration of language in the novel were taken to be evidence of the epitomist at work.

There are still advocates for this view, but the pendulum of opinion has been swinging the other way for the last several decades—perhaps not coincidentally the period in which the fortunes of the novels have risen in scholarly circles. T. Hägg in the mid-1960s (now translated; see Hägg 2004b) effectively demonstrated that, although the novel could be an epitome, the case for abridgment as it had been set forth was weak at best and incoherent at worst. In the intervening years no champion has subsequently taken up the challenge of renewing the arguments for epitomization more strongly. Moreover, O'Sullivan's recent demonstration of the strong ties between oral storytelling and the style of *An Ephesian Story* provides a persuasive alternative origin for those features that have most caused critics to declare them the results of the epitomist's hand. One need not follow the rest of O'Sullivan's argument about the date of the novel or the development of the genre as a whole or the priority of Xenophon over Chariton in order to accept his line of reasoning on the matter of abridgment. As with so much else, the question is simply unsettled at present. Though opinion is running against the epitome theory, there are clear examples of works of ancient fiction being abridged, expanded, and otherwise altered quite radically (the many forms of the *Alexander Romance* provide the best example of all three of these processes).

A.K.A., or, The Ancient Novels and Their Names

The titles of the novels have been transmitted generally in two forms. Sometimes these are combined into a single title. First, a geographic or descriptive title. Xenophon's novel is called *Ephesiaca,* or *An Ephesian Story.* Heliodoros' novel is called *Aithiopica,* or *An Ethiopian Story.* Longos' novel, on the other hand, is titled after its subject matter, either *Poimenica* or *Aipolica* (*A Shepherds'* [or *Goatherds'*] *Story*). Second, there is a concurrent tradition of titles involving the names of the main characters (sometimes with the man first, sometimes with the woman first). Xenophon's novel is not just called *Ephesiaca* in the manuscript, but also *Anthia and Habrocomes.* In combination, it is called something like *An Ephesian Story: Anthia and Habrocomes.* Longos' novel is better known as *Daphnis and Chloe,* and Heliodoros' is both *Aithiopica* and *Theagenes and Charicleia.* Achilles Tatios' novel has this sort of title: *Leucippe and Cleitophon.* Chariton's novel, like Achilles Tatios' book, is never referred to by a geographic or descriptive title, but it is also something of a special case. The manuscript consistently refers to the novel as *Chaireas and Callirhoe,* but one of the papyri contains the end of a book and the subscription refers to the novel as simply *Callirhoe.* This, combined with the novel's last sentence ("So much have I written about Callirhoe") has led some to believe that the original title was the name of the heroine alone, and that is the title adopted by the latest edition.

Some scholars have analyzed the titles and concluded that those containing the character names are original and the geographic or descriptive titles are secondary. There are problems with the argument, including fragmentary prose fiction from antiquity where the names are only of the geographic type, such as *Phoinicica* and *Babyloniaca: A Phoenician Story* and *A Babylonian Story,* and inconsistent and chronologically divergent evidence. But it is not necessarily an unimportant or even irrelevant question. Consistent patterns of titles would indicate a consistent generic affiliation in the minds of the authors. If these authors writing love stories named their stories in the same way, after their characters, say, as opposed to other writers of prose fiction, who followed a more eclectic system based on descriptive factors, it would show that they thought of themselves as producing a distinctive sort of work. On the other hand, if the diversity of titles is original, it has been suggested that this may indicate a coalescing of the genre under the influence of several earlier genres with varying titling conventions.

The Ancient World and the Worlds of the Ancient Novel

Chariton sets his novel at least four hundred years before his own time, at some point within a generation of the crushing defeat of the Athenians in their invasion of the island of Sicily (415–413 BC) during the Peloponnesian War (431–404 BC). Whether his novel is a historical novel or not depends upon one's definition of that subgenre. He clearly deploys a great deal of historical detail in creating his setting, and his main characters, though not really historical, are related to and interact with famous historical figures of the period. Callirhoe, the heroine, is the daughter of Hermocrates, who led the Syracusans in defeating the Athenians. Artaxerxes, the king of Persia in the novel, is based on the real Artaxerxes II of Persia, who ruled from 404–358 BC. But even scratching the surface reveals that Chariton is not being very accurate in his history. Historically, Hermocrates died in 407 BC, three years before Artaxerxes came to the throne, but in the novel they are contemporaries. The historical Hermocrates did have a daughter and she did marry a man named Dionysios, but that Dionysios was a Syracusan tyrant not a rich Milesian, and the daughter (who is not named in the sources) did not live happily ever after but committed suicide after being savagely sexually assaulted by soldiers revolting against her husband's rule (this is all we know of her, and it comes entirely from a short passage in Plutarch's *Life of Dion* 3.1–2).

There are several possible explanations for this mélange of history and fiction. First, Chariton may not have known his history all that well. This seems impossible, however, in light of his thorough familiarity with the classical historians. Second, Chariton may have been trying to be evocative rather than exact with his history. The details do not matter so much as long as the setting puts a not-too-fussy reader into the right frame of mind. Third (and most plausibly, I think), Chariton may have deliberately confounded the truth of history. He knew his classical historians well, and his imitation and manipulation of them in his own text indicates he expected at least some of his readers to have a similar level of familiarity. Certainly even a rather poor student of history will recall that when Chaireas in Book 7 comes to the city of Tyre and captures it, his exploits are not only modeled on those of Alexander the Great (who captured the city in 332 BC in one of his most famous victories) but actually undercut them. Alexander's great engineering feat and the focus of the surviving narratives of his siege of Tyre, that is, his building of a causeway to connect the island city to the mainland, turns out to be irrelevant or even a lie. If Chariton is to be believed, 70 or 80 years earlier Chaireas found the city *already attached by a causeway*. It is not that we are to see Chariton as seriously attacking the historical reliability of the Alexander historians, but he is playing with ideas of fiction and truth, novel and history, and makes them central to his novel's conception. One of his favorite words is *paradoxos*—paradoxical, unbelievable, unexpected, surprising—and the things we "learn" about history from the novel are part of his program of the paradoxical.

Xenophon's novel, by contrast, is strongly ahistorical, so much so that its dramatic date is impossible to determine. Some details may fit a Roman-era setting rather than an earlier Greek one (the titles and duties of some officials), but there is no mention made of Rome. Other details, if taken as meaningful, point to a specifically pre-Roman setting. For instance, the capital of Cappadocia is identified as Mazaca not Caesarea, as it became known in the Roman Empire, or even Eusebeia, as it was known in the first and second centuries BC. There is no real way to reconcile all these details. Alexandria is said to be the capital of Egypt, so the story is theoretically set at some time period after Alexander the Great, who founded that city in 331 BC. Perhaps that is the best that we can say, and it is possible that Xenophon strove to create a vague unmooring from historical time.

Texts and Intertexts

Intertextuality, the notion that texts are related by readers to other texts they already know, is an area of strong interest in studies of the Greek novels. Authors can, of course, also write their texts in ways that consciously and unconsciously (through allusion and imitation, for instance) bring those connections into the foreground, and *intertextuality* as a term is commonly extended to this process as well. One of the most obvious features of the later so-called Sophistic novels of Longos, Achilles Tatios, and Heliodoros is a very strong allusive streak. Xenophon is, in fact, remarkable for an almost utter lack of allusion. *An Ephesian Story* does contain episodes, motifs, and broad themes that are related in some sense to earlier literature. In the most famous instance, the heroine Antheia is at one point married off to a peasant. She shares this fate with Electra, in the mythological tradition the daughter of Agamemnon and Clytemnestra. Euripides introduced in his tragedy *Electra* this crucial detail: after her father's murder by her mother and her mother's lover, she is married off to a peasant to punish her and get rid of her. These heroines are clearly related, but how? Did Xenophon read Euripides' play? There is no play on the language of the drama to indicate that is the case, and no other parallels are drawn. Does the motif come to Xenophon through a general knowledge of myth, or a particular storytelling tradition, or a summary of the tragedy rather than through Euripides directly?

Chariton is usually held to be in a middle position between the intertextual primitiveness of Xenophon and the insistent urbane sophistication of the later novelists. *Callirhoe* is quite full of reminiscences of Homer, Thucydides, Xenophon (the Athenian), the orator Demosthenes, and other writers of the Greek Classical era. Contrasting the footnotes to Chariton and Xenophon in these translations—where, in addition to clarifying basic cultural and geographic knowledge, I have tried to show where our authors may be echoing or alluding to earlier literature—will show just how little the latter quotes classical writers and how very frequently the former does. Chariton's deployment of those allusions, despite their frequency, has often been seen as a kind of window dressing rather than integral to his narrative, and in any case, notably less intricate and stylish than the intertextual play of the Sophistic novels. I would argue rather that we have significantly underestimated both the amount and sophistication of Chariton's purposeful intertextuality, and that he is much closer to the later novelists than to Xenophon in this regard. The notes in this translation indicate several more imitations and echoes of earlier literature than are usually remarked for Chariton. Not all will be accepted as such by everybody—these matters are always open to interpretation and further analysis—but most are quite clear and have escaped notice until now, primarily because scholars did not believe that there could be any more there beyond what had already been found. Some of these allusions are both quite important and quite unmistakable. One example will suffice: at the end of Book 3 at a moment of high drama, Chariton cites most of two lines of a speech in Euripides' *Heracles*—when Heracles has come out of his madness, realizes that he has killed his own wife and children, and contemplates suicide. The moment in Chariton has been read by one critic, at least, as rhetorical exaggeration. The citation, however, is *verbatim,* and its reference to a famous moment of heroic destruction and potential self-destruction causes Callirhoe's whole speech to take on a very different tone, particularly in the midst of her own deliberations about child-killing and suicide.

The most obvious citations in Chariton are to the *Iliad* and *Odyssey* of Homer. These would have stood out to an ancient audience because of their archaic vocabulary and poetic meter, but they are rarely introduced or commented upon. Chariton also frequently cites the historians Xenophon of Athens and Thucydides. Their language was clearly a model for him, but he also fashions some of his themes and episodes on their histories. None of these allusions is overtly made—the narrator never identifies them with "as Thucydides says" or a similar phrase. The audience is expected either to recognize the nods to these earlier writers or to pass over them. Those readers too uneducated or too forgetful to catch these would in most cases not even pause, but the narrative is enriched for those who can spot them. The Athenian historian Xenophon's *Anabasis* and his *Cyropaideia* are particularly important models for Chariton, particularly the latter's subplot involving the tragic lovers Pantheia and Abradatas. The historian Herodotus is occasionally echoed, and it seems very likely, given Chariton's playing with the motifs of Alexander's siege of Tyre and defeat of the Persian king, that he is using some specific history of Alexander from the Hellenistic period (the time after the conquests of Alexander but before Rome's total dominance), though if so, it is now lost to us. Most Hellenistic prose is lost to us, but it seems logical to assume that if we had more of it we would be able to trace more of Chariton's debts. He alludes to the classical Athenian orators Demosthenes, Aeschines, and Isocrates with some frequency. New Comedy is another source, but we cannot trace its influence very clearly since most of the plays have been lost. Still, it is possible to identify some citations of Menander, the most famous and influential author of that genre, from what remains of his work.

This summary has concentrated on the specific verbal allusions to earlier authors, but there is also a more general influence apparent from these earlier genres on Chariton's novel. The later books, for instance, take on strong historiographical overtones when the subject turns to military matters, and the courtroom speeches show Chariton's rhetorical training.

Reading the Ancient Novel Today

Opinions about the Greek novels (including those offered above) are often strongly held. Yet I have tried in this Introduction to avoid arguing for my own views except where I believe we might benefit from an opportunity to broaden our thinking. After all, one of the most refreshing aspects of reading the ancient novels, whether as scholar, student, or general reader, is that they come with far less received wisdom—fixed scholarly ideas that can hedge in, or otherwise inhibit, reader responses—than epics, tragedies, political speeches, histories, and other more "classical" genres of classical literature. One consequence of the current lack of consensus around so many issues relating to the ancient novels is that new evidence or recognition of a previously overlooked detail or a persuasive theoretical approach can shift the ground considerably; there is still much to be learned, even if great strides have been made in situating these early narratives in the literary history of prose fiction. In recent decades approaches based on modern literary theory—especially gender theory, narratology, and reader-response theory—have opened up these texts in various ways, as has the continued application of traditional philological approaches, where much still remains to be done. The Bibliography contains many studies in English since the 1970s. Those, in turn, will lead to more specialist bibliographies and to scholarship in other languages, the study of the ancient novel being a highly international business.

The aim of an edition such as the present one, however, is not to summarize such bibliography, much less propose exclusive lines of interpretation, but above all to present the texts themselves—primarily in a way that facilitates a reader's direct and immediate contact with them and, secondarily, in a way that provides broad context for such contact. In this case, moreover, we are dealing with two works that still can and ought to be read and responded to as literature, rather than merely as data. *An Ephesian Story* is no masterpiece, but it has its share of charms, and as an action story it is hardly matched in antiquity. *Callirhoe* is above all a wonderfully constructed story whose complexity is belied by its apparent simplicity. One of its most obvious virtues is the sensitive treatment of its main characters, particularly Callirhoe herself. Boxed in little by little, she behaves as no other ancient heroine does—not even her sisters in the other ancient novels. There is remarkable originality there, as elsewhere in the ancient novels, even if that originality is sometimes difficult to see because we are viewing it in the light of two thousand years of romantic conventions.

NOTE ON THE TEXTS
AND TRANSLATIONS

We are lucky to have two excellent recent critical editions of our authors. For Chariton we have B. P. Reardon's edition, *Chariton: De Callirhoe narrationes amatoriae* (München/Leipzig: KG Saur, 2004). For Xenophon there is J. N. O'Sullivan's *Xenophon Ephesius: De Anthia et Habrocome Ephesiacorum libri V* (München/Leipzig: KG Saur, 2005). The present translations are based on these editions. Both of these editions are considerable advances on their predecessors, and for that reason I have stuck quite closely to them. I have noted any deviations in the technical endnotes (marked in the text by *), which gloss those places where I followed another scholar or the infrequent occasions I offer a conjecture of my own. These two texts contain some lacunae—gaps where we have lost material and the editors have not ventured to fill them—and in those cases I have often taken another scholar's reconstruction, even when I am not completely convinced by the reconstruction. This has not been possible in all cases (and those where it was not are marked to show the gap), but I thought it would be less jarring for most readers to have fewer of these lacunae left to mar the translation. The frequent cross-references to the two novels are by book, chapter, and section (e.g., 2.2.4) of the Greek texts. The translations themselves, however, show only the numbers for book and chapter to reduce clutter.

These two novels survived antiquity in a single copy, bound together in the same manuscript, a reminder of how close we came to losing them completely. There are a few small fragments of Chariton preserved on papyrus from antiquity, but they only serve to show how generally unreliable the single manuscript we have is and how flexible the textual tradition could be in the case of a work of literature such as this. Scribes seemed to feel less compunction about making small modifications to what they were copying as they saw fit when the text was a piece of prose fiction instead of a more prestigious literary form.

Compared with the Sophistic novelists (such as Achilles Tatios) and much of the rest of imperial Greek prose, these novels are written in a relatively straightforward style. That is not to say that the styles of Chariton and Xenophon are identical. Chariton's language is professional and direct, with the occasional flourish. The style is relatively uniform throughout, but it does take on the coloring of the action. Courtroom speeches sound like the courtroom; battlefield speeches sound like those we find in military writers; laments sound a bit like Greek tragedy; and so on. In vocabulary and syntax the language is a highly literary version of the Greek common dialect (the so-called *Koine*) with an admixture of Attic (the dialect of classical Athens), without the tendency to hypercorrectness seen in more fully Atticizing authors. In English terms, the equivalent is a correct but not overly aloof or formal register, with the occasional slightly old-fashioned or esoteric word thrown in and, in the other direction, the occasional everyday phrase deployed that a stuffier author would have avoided. To give some idea of the effect, were Chariton a writer of English today, he would end sentences with prepositions without a second thought, split infinitives when it sounded more natural to do so, and not be overly concerned about every *who* and *whom*—but on the other hand he would never use *whom* incorrectly when he chose to use it, and he would not commit egregious solecisms. He would sound educated, in other words, but not fussy. His language would be natural, but it would be literary, not the language of the street. A pedant judging his Greek by the classical standards of Plato and Xenophon of Athens, who lived centuries before him, will judge him as falling short of those standards, but for a contemporary audience he was writing good Greek. At the same time, a reader expecting the verbal fireworks of the later Sophistic novelists and their interest in rhetorical ornamentation will be disappointed. Chariton's hallmark is an admirable restraint.

Xenophon is a very different writer. He is direct and simple—*blunt* is perhaps the better word—in an almost unrelieved fashion. The first book shows more rhetorical elaboration than the other four, and the scenes of lament show more ornament than straight narrative; but even in these places the language is relatively plain, particularly when compared to the Sophistic novelists. Sentences are piled on one after another, often with little more than a string of "ands" tying it all together. His vocabulary is generally more limited and more repetitive than Chariton's, and his style is much less literary—so much so that even when he does use a more literary language, it comes across in context as muted or even awkward. On the whole his writing shows more affinities to less ambitious *Koine* prose, such as that found in most of the Greek *New Testament*, than it does to Chariton's or that of prose historians such as Dionysios of Halicarnassos (first century BC) or Polybios (second century BC). He rarely strives for unusual effects of language, and is more likely to dip into a blunt lower register than to soar into ornate or formal eloquence (again, the laments are an exception). All of these features, it must be said, make his language quite suited to his story, which is leaner than that of Chariton. Action and episode are Xenophon's bread and butter, and a more elaborate style would be at odds with the direct punch of the story. He has sometimes been accused of simple incompetence, but J. N. O'Sullivan, Xenophon's editor and most assiduous student, has given us another way to look at this kind of narrative by arguing strongly that its features—particularly the repetition of both phrases and overall scenes, simple linear plot, and recapitulation—are a conscious product of Xenophon's closeness to the traditions of oral storytelling. *An Ephesian Story* is the equivalent of a rip-roaring action film based around a strong love story. Just as we would do *Star Wars*—and ourselves—a disservice by focusing on how far short it falls of *The Godfather,* we miss the point if we compare Xenophon's novel to the literary masterpieces of classical antiquity.

I chose a contemporary American idiom to render these novels, but not *too* modern. I started out by preparing some sample translations to find the right tone, and went straight for an updated, breezy but knowing tone. These initial translations were more insistently colloquial and nonliterary than the final versions. Why the change? In those early efforts I soon found a growing gap between the content and language of the stories and the language of the translations. Inevitably, irony would creep in as I read them—and I do not mean the sort of dramatic irony that Chariton exploits quite effectively (Xenophon utterly lacks irony of any sort). This approach made the authors on the one hand more accessibly familiar, but it also constantly seemed to be apologizing for the originals, begging the reader's pardon for their not being more modern, less sentimental, and in greater accord with our expectations in the first place. The translations subtly suggested that the originals were beneath them. I was taking an approach that would have worked very well for the later Greek novels and the Latin novels of Petronius and Apuleius, all of which fit more easily with modern sensibilities (and irony!), but I found that it transformed the novels of Chariton and Xenophon in odd ways. That, I realized, did both my authors and my readers a significant disservice. These are (arguably) the earliest extant novels in western literature, and translating them to suppress some of the very things that make them distinctive to a modern audience seemed to miss the point. In the end, I hope I have successfully followed a middle way and produced English versions for a contemporary audience that are readable and appealing, but also give a strong sense of how these authors come across in the original Greek.

I have been inconsistent in the transliteration of Greek personal and place names, though not randomly so. In general, I have favored a system closer to the Greek (Chaireas instead of Chaereas), though C stands for Greek K everywhere. I have, however, never grown accustomed to certain names in this scheme (for instance, Aischylos, Thoukydides) and have reverted to the traditional Latinate transliteration in these instances (so Aeschylus, Thucydides). I trust this variation will not cause serious trouble for the reader.

All translations of ancient texts in the introduction and notes are my own unless otherwise specified.

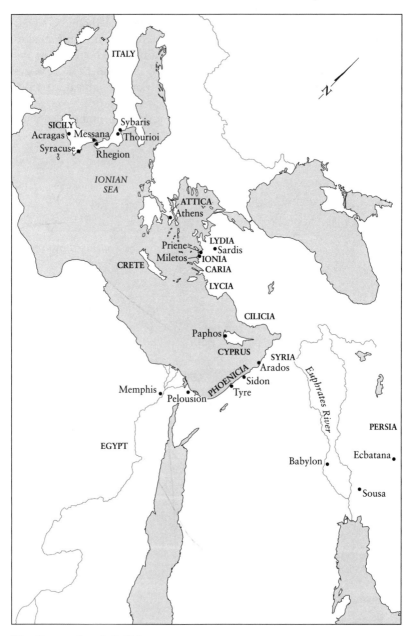

The Geography of *Callirhoe*

The Geography of *An Ephesian Story*

Callirhoe

Book 1

[1] I, Chariton of Aphrodisias,[1] the amanuensis of the orator Athenagoras,[2] will tell the story of a love affair that took place in Syracuse.

The Syracusan general Hermocrates,[3] the one who defeated the Athenians,[4] had a daughter named Callirhoe.[5] She was a marvel of a girl, an ornament of all Sicily. Her beauty was not mortal but divine, and not that of a Nereid[6] or a mountain Nymph but of Aphrodite herself.* Report of the extraordinary sight spread everywhere. Suitors poured into Syracuse, heads of state and sons of tyrants,[7] not only from Sicily but also from mainland Italy and the non-Greek peoples on the mainland.* Eros,[8] however, wished to bring together a couple of his own choosing. There was a handsome young man, Chaireas, who was more handsome than all the others, on par with Achilles, Nireus, Hippolytos, and

---

An asterisk (*) indicates that a technical note on a given passage of the translation or Greek text can be found in the endnotes.

1. Chariton's first two words in the original Greek, his name and city of origin, are perhaps designed to recall to a reader's mind the openings of the histories of Hecataios, Herodotus, and Thucydides, which begin the same way.

2. A common name, though this Athenagoras is otherwise unknown.

3. A historical figure, best known for his role in the Peloponnesian War (431–404 BC, fought between Athens and Sparta but involving the whole of the Greek world), but he did not survive to see the end of that conflict. He was exiled from Syracuse after a military reversal and killed in an attempt to return to power in 407 BC—before the apparent dramatic date of the novel.

4. During the Sicilian Expedition (415–413 BC), a major phase in the Peloponnesian War. Our prime source for this period is Thucydides' history of the war, the sixth and seventh books of which describe the Athenian campaign in Sicily.

5. The historical Hermocrates is known to have had a daughter, though her name is not recorded. As with the date of Hermocrates' death, Chariton has no interest in sticking to the letter of history. The real daughter, according to later sources, was raped during a rebellion and committed suicide.

6. In Greek myth the Nereids were sea nymphs (minor goddesses), daughters of the sea god Nereus, who were renowned for their great beauty.

7. Part of the local coloring. The Greek cities in Sicily and southern Italy were particularly associated with rule by local strongmen, or tyrants, though the word did not necessarily have the negative connotation it now carries, because that form of government remained common there after it had faded elsewhere in the Greek world.

8. The Greek god of love and erotic attraction. Son of Aphrodite, goddess of love and sex.

3

Alcibiades as sculptors and artists portray them.[9] His father Ariston[10] was the second most important man in Syracuse after Hermocrates, and there was so much political ill will between them that they would sooner have made a marriage alliance with anyone besides each other. But Eros loves a challenge and delights in winning against the odds. He looked for his opening and found it.

There was a public festival of Aphrodite,[11] and almost all the women went off to her temple. Callirhoe had not previously appeared in public, but her mother took her out because her father* urged her to pay reverence to the goddess. At that precise moment Chaireas was walking home from the gymnasium, shining like a star, the flush of the wrestling yard standing out against the pale radiance of his face like gold on silver. So by chance they ran into one another at a narrow bend in the road and met, the god orchestrating this encounter* so that each could see the other.* Swiftly they aroused in each other a passion of equal intensity, remarkable beauty meeting its match.*

Stricken, Chaireas barely managed to make it home, like a hero critically injured in battle, ashamed to fall but unable to stand. The girl fell at the feet of Aphrodite's statue and kissed them, saying, "Mistress, give me this man you showed me as my husband."

Night fell, and it was terrible for them both, for the fire burned hotter. The girl suffered worse because she could say nothing, afraid her secret would get out. But Chaireas was a noble and proud young man, and when his body started wasting away, he got up the courage to tell his parents that he was in love and would not survive unless he married Callirhoe.

His father groaned when he heard this. "Then I've lost you, son! It's obvious Hermocrates won't give you his daughter when he has so many rich and royal suitors for her. You should not even *try* to compete or we'll be publicly humiliated."

---

9. Achilles and Nireus were in the mythical tradition the two most handsome Greek warriors in Troy. Hippolytos, the son of Theseus, was another mythical figure of legendary good looks, whose stepmother Phaidra fell in love with him. Alcibiades was a historical figure from fifth-century Athens. He was renowned for his extraordinary good looks and appears frequently in historical writings as well as in some works of Plato as a member of Socrates' circle.

10. Another unhistorical detail based on historical fact. Ariston, a Corinthian, aided the Syracusans during the Sicilian Expedition and is singled out as the best naval steersman on the Syracusan side by Thucydides.

11. Goddess of sex and love.

After that his father tried to comfort the boy, but his son became so distressed he would not even leave the house for his normal pursuits. The gymnasium missed Chaireas and was practically deserted, for the other young men thought the world of him. So they snooped around until they found out why he was sick, and everyone felt pity for a handsome youth who was willing to risk death for the passion of a noble soul.

A regularly scheduled assembly meeting took place, and the people, once they were seated, started off by shouting one thing and one thing only: "Noble Hermocrates! Great general! Save Chaireas! This will be the greatest of your victories. The city requests the favor of holding the wedding today of a couple worthy of one another."* Who could describe that assembly, where Eros was the demagogue? As a patriot, Hermocrates could not refuse his city in its hour of need, and when he gave his consent, all the citizens rushed out of the theater. The young men went off to find Chaireas, while the council and magistrates followed Hermocrates. The wives of the Syracusans also came to his house to give away the bride. The wedding hymn was sung throughout the city. The streets were full of garlands and torches. The front doors of houses were sprinkled with wine and perfume, and the Syracusans celebrated this day with greater joy than they had the day of their victory over the Athenians.

The girl, unaware of all this, had thrown herself onto her bed and covered her head, weeping quietly.

Her nurse came to her bedside and said, "Get up, child! The day we've all been praying for so much has come. The city is giving you away to your husband!"

Her knees gave way, as did her dear heart,[12] for she did not know who she was marrying. She swooned suddenly and darkness poured down over her eyes.[13] She nearly breathed her last, but those who saw her thought this was just modesty. After her servants got her dressed quickly, the crowd made room at the door, and the groom's parents brought him in to the girl.*

Chaireas ran up and kissed her, and Callirhoe, recognizing the man she loved, lit up, growing bigger and brighter, just as the flame of a lamp lights up when it is about to go out but more oil is poured in.

---

12. "Her knees . . . dear heart": The first of three citations by Chariton of a common formula in Homer (*Iliad* 21.425; *Odyssey* 4.703, 23.205; and elsewhere in slightly different form).

13. "poured down . . . eyes": The wording here (and again at 4.5.9) is inspired by a Homeric formula (*Iliad* 5.696, 16.344, 20.421; *Odyssey* 22.88). There are even closer imitations at 2.7.4 and 3.1.3, and another variation at 3.9.10.

When she went out before the public, the whole crowd was gripped by amazement, just as when Artemis[14] appears to hunters in the wilderness. Many of those present even fell to their knees in reverence. Everyone looked at Callirhoe in admiration and offered Chaireas their congratulations. In the songs of poets the wedding of Thetis on Mount Pelion happened the same way.[15] But just as they say Eris was present on that occasion,[16] so too a resentful divinity was to be found on this one.

[2] Once the suitors lost their chance at marrying Callirhoe, they felt a mixture of disappointment and anger. Before this they had been competitors, but now they had the same thought—that they had been insulted—so they got together for a joint planning session. Envy[17] was enlisting them in the war against Chaireas.

The first one to get up was a young man from Italy, the son of the tyrant of Rhegion,[18] and he gave this speech: "If one of us had married her, I wouldn't have gotten angry. It's just like in athletic competitions.[19] One of the contestants has to be the winner. But when the guy who didn't do a bit of work to get the girl is picked instead of us, I won't put up with the insult. We're the ones who stood at her front door, getting no sleep, chatting up babysitters and maids, sending presents to nurses. How long have we been slaves? And the worst part of it is that we came

---

14. Artemis was, among other things, the goddess of the hunt and was closely associated with wild areas. Her virginal status made her a common point of comparison for young women in Greek literature. She was also particularly notable for the frequency of her epiphanies to mortals.

15. The wedding of the sea nymph Thetis to the mortal Peleus occurred on Mount Pelion and is often viewed (aside from one minor blemish, detailed in the next note) as an occasion of perfect happiness and beauty.

16. On the occasion of Thetis' wedding the goddess Eris, or Strife, caused Hera, Athena, and Aphrodite to quarrel over which of them was the most beautiful, a contest ultimately decided by the Trojan prince Paris. In exchange for marriage with the most beautiful woman in the world, Helen of Sparta, Paris cast his vote for Aphrodite. His choice ultimately led to the Trojan War.

17. Pthonos, deified personification of ill will or envy.

18. Modern Reggio di Calabria. The city was a frequent rival of Syracuse and had allied with the Athenians during the Sicilian Expedition. At the dramatic date of the novel (i.e., the time in which the novel is set) Rhegion was not ruled by a tyrant, though earlier it had been.

19. "It's just like . . . competitions": A common phrase and point of reference. It seems to originate in the classical orators, but it is difficult to say whether Chariton was inspired by any single instance, for example that in Aeschines' *In Ctesiphontem* 206, a speech he elsewhere imitates.

to hate each other because we were competing in love. But this penniless playboy,[20] inferior to all his royal competitors, takes the crown without breaking a sweat. Well, his prize better not do him any good. Let's make sure the marriage means death for the groom."

All were in favor of this with one exception—the tyrant of Acragas[21] spoke against it.

"It's not because I have any goodwill toward Chaireas that I oppose the plan. It's because I'm thinking more cautiously. Keep in mind that Hermocrates is not someone you can take lightly, so open warfare[22] against him is impossible for us. Far better to fight a battle of wits. After all, we get our power as tyrants more through cunning than brute force. Elect me your general in the war against Chaireas and I promise to break up his marriage. I'll get Jealousy[23] ready to fight against him. She'll take Eros as her ally and cause some serious damage. Callirhoe may be even-tempered and unfamiliar with malicious suspicion, but Chaireas isn't. He grew up in the gymnasium. He knows all about youthful indiscretions. It'll be easy to make him suspicious and cause him to fall into the trap of a lover's jealousy. Besides, it's easier to approach and talk to him."

The words were barely out of his mouth when they voted for his plan and put him in charge of getting it done. They thought he was just the sort of man to hatch whatever plot was needed.

Here's how he began his scheme.

[3] It was evening and someone came with the news[24] that Chaireas' father Ariston had fallen from a ladder out in the country and had very little hope of surviving. When Chaireas heard this, even though he loved his father, he was hurt even more by the fact that he would have to leave by himself, since it was not yet possible for him to travel with his new bride.[25]

---

20. The Greek word, *pornos,* in its strict sense refers to Chaireas as a male prostitute.

21. Modern Agrigento. This city remained neutral during the Sicilian Expedition. It was all but wiped out by the Carthaginians in 406 BC and did not regain prominence until several decades after the dramatic date of the novel.

22. "open warfare": A phrase recalling one from Herodotus 6.77.

23. Zelotypia, personification of jealousy.

24. "It was evening . . . the news": The first part of this sentence is an imitation of a famous and oft-quoted passage in Demosthenes' speech *On the Crown* 169. Another imitation is found in 8.1.5.

25. The implication being that it would not have been proper for a woman so recently married to move freely outside the house.

That night none of the suitors were bold enough to openly bring a group of people to party at the house, but furtively, secretly, they came and planted evidence that it had happened. They draped the front door with garlands, sprinkled perfume around, spilled enough wine to make the ground muddy, and dropped some half-burned torches. Day broke,[26] and everyone who passed by stopped out of a shared sense of curiosity. His father had improved, so Chaireas was hurrying to be with his wife. When he saw the crowd in front of his door, at first he was surprised, but once he learned the reason they were there,[27] he ran inside like a man possessed. Finding the bedroom still locked, he pounded urgently on the door. When the maid opened it and he rushed to Callirhoe, his anger changed to grief and he ripped his clothes and wept. When she asked why, he could say nothing, neither able to disbelieve what he had seen nor believe what he did not want to. He trembled with confusion, but his wife had no idea what had happened and begged him to tell her why he was upset.

His eyes bloodshot and his voice rough, he said, "I'm crying because of my rotten luck. You forgot me so quickly." Then he took her to task for her carousing.

She, being the daughter of a general and full of spirit, was angered by the unjust accusation. "No one came to my father's house to carouse. Maybe your front door is used to people carousing at it, and the fact that you've gotten married has upset your lovers."[28]

With that she turned away, covered her face, and let forth streams of tears.[29]

But making up is easy for lovers to do, and they happily accept any excuse from each other. Changing his tune, Chaireas started saying what he thought she wanted to hear, and his wife quickly welcomed his change of heart.

This made their love burn stronger, and both sets of parents felt they were truly blessed when they saw how much their children were of one mind.

[4] After his first plan fell apart, the man from Acragas next undertook a more aggressive one. This is how he set it up.

---

26. "Day broke": Perhaps a reminiscence of Aristophanes, *Ploutos* 744.

27. "at first . . . once he learned": The wording is reminiscent of Xenophon, *Cyropaideia* 5.4.7.

28. Callirhoe refers to older male lovers.

29. "streams of tears": The wording has a tragic ring. Compare, for example, Sophocles, *Antigone* 803, and Euripides, *Heracles* 450.

There was a member of his entourage who was a smooth talker, fully endowed with every social grace. He told this man to play the part of a lover: he was to meet Callirhoe's personal maid, the servant she held in highest esteem, and pretend to be in love with her. It took him a while, but he reeled her in with nice gifts and by telling her he would hang himself if he did not obtain his desire. A woman is easy prey when she thinks she is loved.[30]

After making these advance arrangements, the producer of the drama found a second actor. He was no longer looking for one as charming as the first but a cunning man who could talk convincingly. He rehearsed with this man everything he had to do and say, and then sent him on his mission to Chaireas, who suspected nothing.

The man approached him as he was hanging around the wrestling yard and said, "I also used to have a son your age, Chaireas. He really admired and liked you. Now that he's dead, I think of you as my son. In fact, you, when you have good fortune, are a common good[31] for all Sicily. So give me a bit of your time and I'll tell you about a serious situation. It affects your whole life."

With these words that scoundrel threw the young man's soul into turmoil and filled him with hope, fear, and curiosity. But when Chaireas asked the man to speak, he hesitated, giving the excuse that now was not the right occasion and they should wait until they had more time. Chaireas was now convinced that it was something really dire and pressed him harder.

The man took him by the right hand and led him to an out-of-the-way spot. Then he furrowed his brow and looked truly distressed, his eyes even tearing up a bit.

"Chaireas," he said, "I hate to break it to you, but something horrible is going on. For a long time I've avoided saying anything, though I wanted to. But now that you're being publicly humiliated and everyone is gossiping about your troubles, I can't stand to keep quiet. I just don't like troublemakers, and I'm especially fond of you. So you have to know. Your wife is cheating on you. And I'm ready to show you her lover in the act so you'll believe it."

Thus he spoke, and a black cloud of grief covered him; taking dark dust in both his hands, he poured it over his head, sullying his fair

---

30. The thought and wording are reminiscent of a fragment of Menander's lost play *Naucleros* (fr. 250 KA).

31. "you, when . . . are a common good": A reworking of Menander fr. 765 KA ("This is the common good: when a good man has good fortune").

countenance.[32] For a long time he remained in a daze, unable to work his mouth or eyes, and when he managed to collect his voice, it was not his normal one, but a mere whisper. "It's a wretched favor I'm asking you—to become an eyewitness of my own woes. Show me anyway, so I'll have a better reason to kill myself. I won't hurt Callirhoe, even if she is doing me wrong."

"Pretend that you're going out to the country," the man said. "But when it's fully dark, watch your house carefully. You'll see her lover going in."

They agreed on this plan. Chaireas sent a message (he could not even bear the thought of going in the house himself) that said, "I'm off to the country." Meanwhile, that scheming liar set the stage. When evening came, Chaireas went to spy, and the man who had seduced Callirhoe's maid scurried into the alley. He acted like a man trying his best to go about his business unnoticed, but he was actually doing everything he could to be noticed. He had slicked his hair back, and his curls were dripping with perfumed oils. He had put on eyeliner, a soft cloak, and fancy sandals. Heavy rings glinted on his fingers. Then he looked all around as he approached the door and gave the usual signal by knocking lightly. The maid, herself a bundle of nerves, quietly opened the door halfway, took him by the hand, and brought him inside.

When Chaireas saw this, he could no longer contain himself. He ran to catch Callirhoe's lover in the act. The latter, however, hid near the courtyard door and immediately left.

Callirhoe was lying in bed, missing Chaireas. She was so miserable that she had not even lit a lamp. There were footsteps. Callirhoe recognized her husband's breathing before anyone else and happily ran to him. He was unable to find the words to yell at her but, overwhelmed with anger, he kicked her when she came near. His foot struck the girl's diaphragm in just the right spot and stopped her breathing. She collapsed, and her maids picked her up and laid her on the bed.

[5] Callirhoe lay unconscious, not breathing, looking to all the world as though she was dead. Rumor, bearer of bad tidings, spread through the whole city and stirred up lamentation throughout the streets all the way down to the sea. On all sides the dirge could be heard—the situation resembled the sack of a city.

---

32. "Thus he spoke . . . fair countenance.": This whole sentence is a citation of Homer's *Iliad* (18.22–24), the moment when Achilles learns of the death of his friend Patroclos.

Chaireas, his heart still seething, locked himself inside and tortured the maids for information, beginning and ending with Callirhoe's favorite.[33] By the time he had finished burning and cutting them, he had learned the truth, and then he was filled with pity for his dead wife. He wanted to kill himself, but Polycharmos stopped him—Polycharmos was his best friend in exactly the same way that Homer made Patroclos Achilles' friend.[34]

When it was day, the magistrates convened a court for murder, speeding up the trial out of respect for Hermocrates. In fact, everyone in the whole city converged on the marketplace, and each was shouting something different. The unsuccessful suitors egged on the crowd, especially the man from Acragas, who was openly smug at having pulled off a deed no one would have thought possible.

But then an odd thing happened, something that has never happened in a courtroom. After the charge had been read out, instead of defending himself, the murderer used all of his time on the water clock[35] to accuse himself more bitterly. He was the first to cast a guilty vote. He made no mention of the mitigating circumstances in his defense. Not the slanderous gossip. Not his jealousy. Not that it was an accident. He just begged them all, "Execute me publicly by stoning—I have removed from the city its crowning glory. It would be too humane to just hand me over to the executioner—that's what I would deserve if I had killed Hermocrates' maid. Find a cruel and unusual punishment. I'm a worse criminal than those who rob temples or kill their parents. Don't bury me. Don't pollute the earth. No, cast my impious body into the sea!"

When he said this, a lament erupted as everyone forgot the dead woman and pitied the living man. Hermocrates was the first to rise to Chaireas' defense. "I feel certain this was the result of an accident. I can see those who are plotting against us, and they won't have the satisfaction of gloating over *two* corpses. And I won't cause grief for my daughter, even if she is dead. Often I heard her say that Chaireas' life was more important than her own. So let's stop his pointless trial and

---

33. The private torture of slaves by their masters for information was considered a legitimate and lawful, if severe, practice.

34. In Homer's *Iliad*, Patroclos, son of Menoitios, was Achilles' inseparable companion. His death, and Achilles' reaction to it, is the climax of the epic, but their friendship is said to have been so strong that it continued after death. Chariton has already referenced the relationship through a citation of Homer *Iliad* (18.22–24) above in 1.4.6.

35. Prosecution and defense speeches were strictly limited in duration. The *clepsydra*, or water clock, kept track of the time.

turn our attention to her unavoidable funeral. Let's not abandon her to time. Let's not disfigure her body through delay. Let's bury Callirhoe while she's still beautiful."

[6] The judges voted for acquittal, but Chaireas would not acquit himself. Instead, he longed for death and tried every way he could to end it all.

Polycharmos saw that it was pretty much impossible to guarantee Chaireas' safety, so he said, "You're betraying the dead girl! Won't you even wait to bury Callirhoe? Will you entrust her body to the hands of others? Right now you should be making sure she's buried with expensive gifts and preparing a funeral fit for a princess."

This speech won Chaireas over by giving him something to strive for, something to concern himself with.

Who could fittingly describe that funeral? Callirhoe lay on a golden bier, wearing her wedding dress, more striking and lovely than in life, so that everyone thought she looked like Ariadne asleep.[36] The Syracusan cavalrymen—they and their horses in full regalia—rode in front of the bier. After them came soldiers carrying the standards from Hermocrates' victories. Next were the council and, in the midst of the common people, all the magistrates formed an honor guard around Hermocrates. Ariston too, though still ailing, was being carried along. He called out to Callirhoe as his daughter and his lady. After these came the wives of the citizens, dressed in black.

Then there was a royal fortune's worth of goods to be put in the tomb. First, the gold and silver from her dowry. Then beautifully elaborate clothes (Hermocrates had sent along much from the spoils he took in battle). Gifts from relatives and friends next. After all these followed Chaireas' wealth. If it had been possible, Chaireas would have wanted to cremate all his possessions to accompany his wife in death.

The Syracusan ephebes[37] carried the bier, and the citizens followed them. They all lamented, but Chaireas could be heard lamenting the loudest. Hermocrates had a tomb near the sea, magnificent enough to be visible even to sailors far off. The rich abundance of gifts filled this

---

36. In myth Ariadne was a Cretan princess who ran off with the hero Theseus after he killed the Minotaur in her father's labyrinth. During their journey she was abandoned by him while she slept on the island of Naxos. This famous sleep was a popular artistic and literary motif.

37. *Ephebes* were young men enrolled in a city's training system for citizens. Emphasis had originally been on military training, but soon a broader civic, social, and educational preparation became a regular feature and eventually eclipsed the earlier purpose.

as if it was a treasure house. But the manner in which they decided to honor the dead girl set in motion a series of greater troubles.

[7] There was a man named Theron,[38] a cunning and evil character, who sailed the seas as a criminal. He had some thieves anchored in the harbors disguised as regular sailors but organized as a pirate crew. He happened to be present at the funeral and laid his eyes on the gold. That night he lay there unable to sleep and talking to himself. "Wait. I risk my life battling the sea and killing living people for next to nothing when it's possible to get rich from one dead woman? Let the die be cast![39] I'm not going to miss out on the profit! But now who should I recruit for the job? Think, Theron. Who do you know that's right for it? Zenophanes from Thourioi?[40] Smart, but spineless. Menon from Messana?[41] Gutsy, but a double-crosser."

In his mind he went through them and checked them one by one as if he was trying to find counterfeit coins. He rejected many, but he thought a few were right for the job. So at dawn he ran down to the harbor and looked for each of them. Some he found in brothels, some in bars—a fitting army for that kind of general. He told them he had something he needed to talk to them about and took them behind the waterfront.

He started this way. "I've found a treasure, and out of everyone I've chosen you as partners. There's plenty to go around, and it won't even require a lot of work. Just one night can make us all rich. We know all about the kind of work it'll take. It's the kind fools criticize, but shrewd people profit by."

They got right away that he was going to tell them about a bit of piracy or grave-robbing or stealing from temples. "Quit preaching to the converted. Just tell us the job and let's not miss our chance."

Picking up from there,[42] Theron said, "You've seen the gold and silver of the dead woman. We're alive. We deserve it more. I think we should

---

38. Haemus, a bandit in Apuleius' *Metamorphoses,* calls himself the "son of the famous thief Theron," and that may be a nod to this character.

39. Although famous now as Caesar's utterance upon leading his army across the Rubicon, this phrase is a proverbial quote from a fragmentary play of Menander (fr. 64 KA).

40. Modern Thurio in southern Italy.

41. Modern Messina in Sicily.

42. "Picking . . . there": A Homeric transitional phrase, though it becomes relatively common in Greek prose by Chariton's time. Chariton uses it twice elsewhere (5.7.10 and 8.7.9).

open the tomb at night, load up the ship, and sail wherever the wind takes us to sell our haul in another country."

It sounded good to them.

"So now let's get back and act normal," he said. "When it's fully dark tonight each of us should head down to the ship and bring a crowbar with him."

[8] That's what they were up to. Meanwhile, Callirhoe's condition was undergoing a second revival. Through lack of nutrition there occurred a relaxation of her paralyzed lungs, and eventually she gradually began to breathe again. Then she began to move her body one limb at a time. When she opened her eyes, she had the sensation of waking up and called for Chaireas, assuming he was sleeping next to her. When she could hear neither her husband nor her maids and everything was empty darkness, shuddering and trembling overcame the girl, unable as she was to comprehend the truth. Getting up slowly, she put her hand on the garlands and ribbons, which made the gold and silver clink. There was the strong smell of aromatic herbs. And then it came back to her—the kick, the resulting fall. Eventually she figured out that they had buried her because she had been unconscious.

She cried out as loud as she could, shouting "I'm alive!" and "Help!"* After she had yelled over and over with no result, she gave up any hope of being rescued. She put her head down on her knees and wailed, "What a disaster! I've been buried alive though I've done nothing wrong. I'm dying a slow death. They're mourning for me when I'm perfectly fine. Who will send a message? And what messenger is there to send? Chaireas, you did me wrong! I blame you—not for killing me, but for being in such a hurry to hold my funeral. You shouldn't have buried Callirhoe so quickly, not when she wasn't even really dead! Then again, maybe you're already thinking of remarrying."

[9] While she was busy with this jumble of laments, Theron waited until exactly the middle of the night[43] and went to the tomb without making a sound, the oars barely touching the water. After getting out of the boat the first thing he did was instruct his crew as follows. He sent four to be lookouts. If anyone came to the tomb, they were supposed to kill them if they could, and if not, they were to give a signal to let the gang know they were coming. He, with another group of four, went to the tomb. He ordered the rest (there were sixteen of them in all) to stay

---

43. "waited until . . . night": The phrasing looks to be inspired by Thucydides 2.3.4, "waiting until exactly the crack of dawn," which is more closely imitated by Chariton at 3.3.1.

on the ship and keep the oars poised above the water so that if something unexpected happened, they could quickly grab the men from land and make their getaway by sea.

When they started to use the crowbars and pounded harder to break open the tomb, Callirhoe was filled with every emotion at the same time: fear, joy, grief, astonishment, hope, and doubt. "What's making that sound? Is it a spirit coming for me in my misery, the way they usually come for the dead? Or is it not a noise, but the voice of the gods of the underworld summoning me to them? More likely it's tomb-robbers! Yes, this has been added to my misfortunes. Wealth is no use to a dead person."[44]

As she was working this out, the first pirate was inching his way in headfirst. Callirhoe fell to her knees in front of him. Her intention was to beg him for help, but he shot back out in terror.

Trembling, he told his companions, "Let's get out of here! There's a spirit guarding the stuff inside. It won't let us in!"

Theron laughed at him, calling him a coward who was deader than the deceased. He then ordered someone else to go in. When none of them could bring themselves to do it, he went in himself, holding his sword in front of him. Light glinted off the steel, and Callirhoe feared that she would be killed, so she moved herself to the corner and from there began in a tiny voice to beg. "Whoever you are, take pity on a woman who was pitied neither by her husband nor her parents. Don't kill her when you've saved her."

Theron grew bolder and, being quick on the uptake, figured out what was really going on. He gave it some thought. At first he decided to kill the woman, thinking she would get in the way of the whole operation. Soon, however, motivated by profit, he changed his mind and told himself, "Think of her as part of the grave goods. There's a lot of silver in here. A lot of gold. But the woman's beauty is worth more than all of it." So he took her by the hand and led her outside.

Calling his accomplice over, he said, "Here's the spirit you were afraid of. Some pirate you are—afraid even of a woman! So it's your job to keep her safe because I want to give her back to her parents. As for the rest of us, let's get the stuff that's stashed inside out here. Not even the dead woman's guarding it now!"

---

44. "Wealth . . . no use": A thought that accords in sentiment, though not in precise phrasing, with Aeschylus, *Persae* 842, "wealth is of no help to the dead." See also the note to 3.3.11, where Chariton's wording seems to reflect Aeschylus' language more closely.

[10] After they filled their ship with the loot, Theron told the guard to stand a little ways away with the woman, then opened debate about her fate. There were differing opinions on the matter at opposite ends of the spectrum.

The first man to speak said, "Comrades, we came for other things, but what Fortune[45] has turned up for us is better. Let's make the most of it. We can do this without taking any risks. I say we leave the stuff in the tomb where we found it and give Callirhoe back to her husband and father. We'll say we were anchored near the tomb in our usual fishing spot when we heard a voice. Motivated by compassion, we opened the tomb to save the woman who'd been shut up inside. Let's get her to swear she'll back up our whole story. She'll be happy to do it as a favor to the charitable gentlemen who saved her life. Do you know how much joy this will bring to the whole island of Sicily? How many gifts we'll get? And at the same time, we'll be acting in a way that people find moral and the gods find pious."

Just as he was finishing this speech, someone else spoke against him. "You're out of line and out of your mind. Are you really telling us we should start leading lives of virtue now? Is it robbing a tomb that's made us into upstanding citizens? Are we going to show pity to a woman whose own husband didn't show her any? He killed her! Sure, she hasn't done us any harm, but she will, and in the worst possible way. First, if we give her back to her family, it's unclear how they'll feel about what's happened and it's hard to believe they won't suspect the real reason we came to the tomb. And even if the woman's relatives are so grateful they don't press charges, the magistrates and the people themselves won't let tomb-robbers off the hook, not when they bring in the proof of their own guilt.* Maybe someone's going to say we'd make more money if we sold the woman. After all, she'll fetch a high price on account of her beauty. That's dangerous too. See, gold can't talk and silver won't say where we got it from. We can make up a story about them. But loot with eyes and ears and a tongue—who could hide that? After all, her beauty isn't even the normal sort we could hide. 'She's a slave.' Is that what we're going to say? Who's going to believe that after getting a look at her? So let's kill her here and now. Let's not go hauling our accuser around with us."

Many of them agreed with these arguments, but Theron supported neither proposal. "*You* are inviting danger, and *you* are losing profit. As for me, I'll sell the woman before I kill her. When she's being sold,

---

45. Tyche, the divine personification of fortune or chance.

she'll keep her mouth shut out of fear. Once she's sold, let her accuse away—we won't be around! After all, we lead a life constantly on the move.* Now let's sail. It's almost day."

[11] Once out at sea, the ship moved briskly. After all, they had not set themselves any particular course, so they weren't fighting against wave and wind. No, every wind was a favorable one and stood at their stern.[46] Theron tried to keep Callirhoe's spirits up by fooling her with elaborate fabrications, but she understood her situation and that her "rescue" was anything but. Because she was afraid they would kill her if she got angry, she pretended to have no idea and to believe him. Telling them she could not stand the sea, she kept her head covered and wept.

"Father, on this sea you defeated three hundred Athenian ships, but a little boat has kidnapped your daughter and you can't help me at all. Now I'm being taken to a foreign country and I'm certain to be a slave despite my noble birth. Maybe an Athenian master will buy Hermocrates' daughter. How much better it was for me when I was lying dead in the grave! If nothing else Chaireas would have been buried with me. But now we have been separated in life and in death."

While she made this lament, the pirates were bypassing small islands and cities since their cargo was not for those lacking means. No, they were looking for rich men. They anchored off Attica[47] in the shelter of a breakwater. There was a spring right there with lots of clear water and a nice meadow. They brought Callirhoe off the ship here and told her she should wash up and take a bit of a break from the sea. They wanted to keep her beauty fresh.

When they were by themselves, they discussed where they should head next on their journey. One said, "Athens is close. It's a big, rich city. We'll find a horde of merchants there and a horde of rich men. Think of yourself looking at all the men in a marketplace—that's how many whole cities you'll see in Athens."

They all liked the idea of sailing to Athens except Theron, who was not happy about the city's meddlesomeness. "Wait. Are you the only ones who haven't heard what busybodies the Athenians are? They're a chatty people and they love to go to court. In the harbor there are informers all over the place. They'll ask us who we are and where we're bringing this cargo from. They're malicious. Suspicion of the worst sort will get the better of them, then it's straight off to the Areiopagos[48] and

---

46. "stood at their stern": The words are taken from Thucydides 2.97.1.

47. The region of Greece around Athens.

48. The "Hill of Ares," which served as one of Athens' courts of law.

officials who are tougher than tyrants. We should be more afraid of the Athenians than the Syracusans. The place for us is Ionia.[49] Yes, wealth fit for a king floods down into it from Asia and its people love luxury and mind their own business. And I expect we'll be able to make contact with some of the local luminaries."

They brought water aboard and got provisions from some merchant ships close by, then sailed straight for Miletos.[50] On the third day they landed at an anchorage about ten miles outside the city, just the sort of spot for them to lie low in.

[12] There, Theron told them to take some poles from the ship and build Callirhoe a shelter and provide her with anything to make her comfortable. He did this not from love of his fellow man but from love of his own gain, thinking more like a merchant than a pirate.

Theron himself took two of his companions and ran over to the city. He did not want to make an open search for his buyer and have everyone talking about his business, so he was trying to make a quick sale on the sly without any middleman. That proved difficult to do since his merchandise was not suitable for many people and certainly not for some person off the street. No, it called for a rich and royal man, but he was afraid to approach people like that.

As he lost more and more time, he could not keep putting up with the delay. When night came, he was unable to sleep and talked to himself. "You're an idiot, Theron. For this many days already you've left gold and silver in the middle of nowhere, as if you're the only pirate out there. Don't you know that other pirates sail the sea? And besides, I'm afraid our own men will sail off and leave us behind. It's not like you recruited the most moral men so they'd keep faith with you. No, you got the most unscrupulous men you knew. You have to get some sleep now, but when tomorrow comes, run down to the ship and throw that annoying woman into the sea. She's brought you nothing but trouble. And never again get yourself any merchandise you can't get rid of easily."

He fell asleep and had a dream that his doors were locked, so he decided to hold out for one more day.

Since he did not know what else to do, he sat in a shop, his heart utterly dismayed. Meanwhile, a crowd of people was passing. There were free men and slaves, and in the middle of them a man in his prime, dressed in black and looking despondent.

---

49. The Greek region along the western coast of modern Turkey. At the dramatic date of the novel it was part of the Persian empire.

50. One of the most important Greek cities in Ionia.

Theron stood up—human nature being full of curiosity—and asked one of the people with the man, "Who's he?"

"I guess you're a foreigner or come from far away if you don't know Dionysios. He's the richest, noblest, most cultured man in Ionia. A friend of the Great King."

"So why's he wearing black?"

"Because his wife is dead. He loved her."

Theron was even more interested in the conversation now that he had found a rich man who liked women, so he did not let the man he was talking to get away.

"What position do you hold with him?"

"I'm the manager of all his affairs. I take care of his daughter for him. She's just a baby, and now she's lost her poor mother before her time."

"What's your name?"

"Leonas."

"Well, Leonas, it's a lucky thing we met. I'm a merchant and I'm currently based out of Italy, so I don't know anything about Ionia. A woman in Sybaris,[51] the richest woman there, in fact, had a really beautiful maid. She put her up for sale because she was jealous of her, and I bought her. So be the one to profit! Makes no difference whether you want to keep her for yourself as a nurse for the child—she's educated enough—or you think she'd make a good gift for your master. It's better for you if he has a slave. That way he's not bringing a stepmother into the picture for the girl you take care of."

Leonas was happy to hear this and said, "One of the gods must have sent you to be my benefactor. I tell you, you're offering me in reality what I was dreaming about. For now, you've got to come to the house and become my friend and guest. As for the question of whether the woman's a piece of property suitable for the master or for us slaves, that'll be settled by her looks."

[13] When they got to the house, Theron was astonished at its size and opulence. It had been built to host the Persian king. Leonas told him to wait while he first took care of his master, then he got Theron and took him to his own apartment, which was very much like that of a free man. He gave orders for a meal to be laid out. Since Theron was a cunning man and clever at adapting to every occasion, he joined Leonas at the table and buttered him up with toasts to his health, partly as a demonstration of his magnanimity, but more as a confirmation of their

---

51. A city in southern Italy famed for its luxury. Its presence in the story is another anachronism, since it was destroyed in 510 BC and later refounded as Thourioi.

partnership. As they ate, they talked a lot about the woman. Theron praised her character more than her beauty, aware that what is out of sight needs to be argued for, but seeing is believing.

"So let's go and you can show her to me," Leonas said.

"She's not here," he replied. "We steered clear of the city to avoid the customs collectors. The ship is anchored about ten miles away."

He described the location, and Leonas said, "You anchored on our land! That's even better! Fortune was already leading you to Dionysios. So let's go out to the country. That way you all can rest up after your voyage. The villa that's near there has been richly furnished."

Theron was overjoyed at the thought of having the sale take place in the middle of nowhere as opposed to the marketplace and said, "Let's go early in the morning. You go to the villa, and I'll go to the ship. I'll bring the woman to you there."

They agreed on this plan and went their separate ways after shaking hands on it. The night seemed long to both of them, one eager to buy, the other to sell. The next day, Leonas sailed up the coast to the villa. He took money with him so he could make a down payment to the merchant. Theron went to the promontory and found his accomplices very worried about his whereabouts. After telling them about the deal, he began to sweet-talk Callirhoe.

"Daughter, I really wanted to take you back to your family right away, but I was stopped from doing so by the sea because there was a headwind. You know how well I've taken care of you. And the most important thing: we made sure you kept your virtue. Chaireas will get you back and no one will have laid a hand on you, all because of us. We got you out of the tomb as safe as if it was your bedroom. Now we have to make a run all the way to Lycia,[52] but there's no point in you suffering for no reason. Not with your horrible seasickness. So I'm going to leave you in the care of some trusted friends. On my return I'll pick you up and make absolutely sure that I get you back to Syracuse after that. Take whatever you want from your things. We'll keep the rest safe for you."

Callirhoe silently laughed at that, though it pained her greatly, and she thought him a complete idiot. She knew by now that she was being sold, but she supposed that getting sold offered her better chances than her "rebirth" had, eager as she was to get away from the pirates.

"Thank you, father," she said, "for the kindness you have shown me. May the gods grant you your just deserts. I think it's bad luck to use the things that were buried with me. You keep them all for me. A little

---

52. A region to the southeast of Miletos.

ring, which I wore even when I was dead, is enough for me." She then covered her head. "Take me wherever you want, Theron. Any place is better than sea or tomb."

[14] When Theron got near the villa, this was his plan of attack: he uncovered Callirhoe's head and let her hair down, then opened the door and told her to go in first. Leonas and everyone inside were suddenly struck with astonishment—some thought they had seen a goddess, some even knelt in reverence to her. There was, you see, some talk of epiphanies of Aphrodite in that part of the countryside.

They were still astonished when Theron came in behind her and went up to Leonas. "Get up and receive the woman. She's the one you wanted to buy."

The result was joy and amazement on the part of all. They put Callirhoe to bed in the finest of the bedrooms and let her have some peace and quiet. She needed a long rest after her grief, trouble, and fear.

Theron shook Leonas' hand and said, "I've fulfilled my side of the bargain. Keep the woman for the moment—you're my friend now, after all. Go to town, get the copies of the registration, and then pay me whatever price you want."

Leonas wanted to reciprocate. "No, no. I also trust you with the money now before the contract's signed." At the same time he wanted to make a down payment, afraid Theron would change his mind. He knew there would be a lot of people in the city who would want to buy her. So he brought out a talent of silver[53] and forced Theron to take it. He took it, but he acted as though it really was not necessary.

Leonas tried to get him to stay for dinner as the hour was late, but Theron said, "I want to sail to the city at nightfall. We'll meet tomorrow at the harbor."

They parted ways after that. Theron went to the ship and ordered his men to weigh anchor and get underway as quickly as possible before they were discovered.[54] While they were making a run for it to wherever the wind took them, Callirhoe was alone, and now that she had the opportunity, she bemoaned her fortune.

"Look! Another tomb! Theron has locked me in this one, and it's lonelier than the first. My father and mother could have visited me

---

53. A high sum (a talent is 6,000 drachmas) for a down payment on the purchase of a single slave.

54. "before they were discovered": The phrase is found several times in Thucydides (3.30.1, 4.70.2, and 8.42.1). Looser echoes appear in Chariton at 2.10.8 and, more distantly, 3.6.5.

there, and Chaireas could have shed libations of tears. I would have felt their presence, even though I'd be dead. But in this place who will come when I call?

"Resentful Fortune, you've been pursuing me on land and sea. You haven't had your fill of my troubles. No, first you turned my lover into my murderer. Chaireas, the man who had never so much as struck a slave, dealt a fatal kick to me, the woman who loved him. Then you put me into the hands of tomb-robbers. You led me out of the tomb onto the sea and brought on the pirates, and they're worse than the waves. Is this why I possess my celebrated beauty, so that the pirate Theron might get a high price for me? I've been sold in the middle of nowhere. I wasn't even taken to a city like any other slave. Fortune, you must've been afraid that someone would see me and decide I was nobly born. That's why I was handed over like any old piece of property to . . . I don't know who. Greeks? Barbarians? More pirates?"

As she struck her breast with her hand, she saw the portrait of Chaireas on her ring and kissed it. "Chaireas," she said, "You have truly lost me now that I've been separated from you by so great a calamity. And while you mourn and regret and sit by an empty tomb, confirming my faithfulness after my death, I—Hermocrates' daughter, your wife— have been sold to a master this day."

Sleep eventually came upon her as she was lamenting in this way.

Book 2

[1] Leonas ordered Phocas, the estate manager, to take good care of the woman. He himself left for Miletos while it was still dark, eager to give his master the news about the new slave in the belief that it would provide him great solace amidst his sorrow. Leonas found Dionysios still in bed. Distraught with grief, he hardly went out of the house, even though his city missed him. Instead, he spent his time in his room, as though his wife were still with him.

When he caught sight of Leonas, he said to him, "This was the only good night's sleep I've had since the poor woman's death. I saw her clearly in a dream, more striking and lovely than in life. It was as though she was with me and I was awake. I dreamed it was our wedding day. I was bringing her home from my estate by the sea, and you were singing the wedding hymn for me."

As he was explaining this, Leonas cried out, "Master, you're fortunate both in your dream and in real life. You're about to hear me explain what it was you saw." He began to tell his story. "A merchant approached me with a beautiful woman to sell. To avoid the customs collectors he'd anchored his ship outside the city near your estate. I made arrangements with him and went off to the country. When we met out there, we actually sealed the deal. I gave him a talent, and he gave me the woman. But we need to have the sale registered here legally."

Dionysios was pleased to hear of the woman's beauty—he really was fond of women—but not so pleased that she was a slave. He was the descendant of kings, excelling the whole of Ionia in dignity and sophistication, so he thought it beneath him to share a slave's bed.

"Leonas," he said, "it's impossible for a person to be beautiful unless he or she is born free. Have you not heard from the poets that beautiful people are the children of gods and thus are far more likely to be children of noble mortals? Of course she impressed you out in the middle of nowhere—you were comparing her to the peasant women. Still, since you've bought her, go on downtown. Adrastos will handle the registration papers. He's an expert at the law."

Leonas was happy to be disbelieved, since the surprise would add even more to his master's astonishment. But when he went around all the harbors of Miletos, and the merchants' tables, and the whole city, he could not find Theron anywhere. He made inquiries with merchants and sailors, but no one recognized the name. When he was truly perplexed, he took a boat along the coast to the promontory and went from there to the estate, but he was not going to find Theron—he had already sailed. Eventually, dragging his feet, Leonas went back to his master. When Dionysios saw his glum look, he asked him what had happened.

"I've lost you a talent, master."

"It happens," said Dionysios. "It will teach you to be more cautious in the future. Anyway, how did you lose it? Or is it just that the new slave has run off?"

"She didn't," he said. "The seller did!"

"Obviously he was a dealer in stolen slaves and he's sold you someone else's slave. That's why he did it in the middle of nowhere. Where did you say the woman is from?"

"Sybaris, in Italy. Sold by her mistress out of jealousy."

"Find out if there are any Sybarites in town. In the meantime leave the woman where she is."

So Leonas went away for the moment, troubled that his initiative had not turned out successfully, but he kept his eye out for an opportunity to convince his master to go out to the estate. His one remaining hope was for Dionysios to get a look at the woman.

[2] The peasant women* went in to see Callirhoe and immediately began to fawn over her like a mistress. Plangon, the estate manager's wife, a no-nonsense type, spoke to her.

"Child, of course you miss your own people. But you should think of us here as your family too. Dionysios, our master, is a good and kindly man. You're lucky the gods brought you to a good house. You'll be right at home. Now, it's been a long voyage. Wash the grime off you. You've got maids to help you."

It took a while, and she was reluctant, but Plangon got her to go to the bath. Once there, they smoothed oil on her skin and fastidiously wiped off the dirt. They had marveled at her face and thought it divine while she had her clothes on, but they were more astonished once she took them off.* Her skin at once shone palely, reflecting the light like marble. But her flesh was so delicate they were afraid that even to lay a finger on it would leave a severe wound.

In whispers they spoke to one another. "Our mistress was famous for her beauty, but she would've looked like this woman's slave."

Their praise distressed Callirhoe, and she had a hunch where it was leading. After she had bathed and they were styling her hair, they brought her a clean outfit, but she said that they really should not be treating a new slave like this.

"Just bring me a slave's tunic. After all, you all outrank me."

So she put on a tunic that happened to be lying around. Even that, however, suited her and had the effect of a fancy gown, becoming radiant with her beauty.

Once the women had gotten something to eat, Plangon said, "Come to Aphrodite's shrine and say a prayer for yourself. The goddess shows herself there, and it's not just the local people who worship her. People come all the way from the city. She especially listens to Dionysios, and he has never passed her without visiting."

Then they told her about the goddess' epiphanies, and one of the peasant women said, "My lady, you'll think that you're looking at a statue of yourself when you see Aphrodite."

When she heard this, Callirhoe's eyes brimmed with tears, and she said to herself, "What miserable luck! Even here Aphrodite is the god responsible for all my troubles.[55] But I'll go—I've got a lot of things to complain to her about."

---

55. "responsible . . . troubles": The words recall those of Lysias 1.7 ("the one responsible for all my troubles"). See also Chariton at 3.8.3, 4.2.7, and 6.6.4.

The shrine was near the villa, right by the main road. Callirhoe knelt in reverence and grasped the feet of Aphrodite's statue. "You were the first to show me Chaireas. But though you united us in a beautiful marriage, you didn't preserve it. And yet we revered you! Since you've willed it so, I beg one favor from you: make me attractive to no man now that I've lost Chaireas."

Aphrodite refused this prayer, for she is Eros' mother, and she was orchestrating yet another marriage, one which she had no intention of preserving either.

Away from pirates and the sea, Callirhoe began to regain her singular beauty. The peasants were astounded to find she looked lovelier with each passing day.

[3] Leonas found a suitable opportunity and put forward the following proposal to Dionysios. "Master, you've not been to your seaside estate for quite some time now, and the situation requires you to make a visit. You need to inspect the herds and crops, and the harvest is rapidly approaching. You can also enjoy the luxury of the house that we built on your orders. It will also be easier for you to bear your grief there, with the delights of the countryside and the management of the farm to distract you. And if you think one of the cattle herders or shepherds is doing a good job, you can give him the new slave woman."

Dionysios liked this idea and set a definite date for their departure. Word went out, and they got everything ready—drivers their carriages, stable hands their horses, and sailors their boats. Friends were invited to go on the trip, as was an entourage of freedmen, for Dionysios was at heart a generous man. Once everything was ready, he ordered the baggage and most of the party to be brought by sea and the carriages to follow after he went on ahead. He thought a large procession inappropriate for a man in mourning. First thing in the morning,[56] before most were aware of his departure, he and four of his men mounted their horses. One of them was Leonas.

While Dionysios was riding out to the countryside, Callirhoe wanted to go back and show reverence to Aphrodite again, for she had seen the goddess in her sleep the night before. She was standing there praying when Dionysios dismounted from his horse and went into the temple ahead of everyone else in his party.

---

56. "First thing in the morning": A transition found twice verbatim in Thucydides (4.71.1 and 7.80.5) and many more times in slight variations in that author. It seems characteristic of that historian's style, though in imperial Greek it begins to be widely imitated. Chariton uses the phrase again at 3.2.14.

Hearing footsteps, Callirhoe turned toward him. When Dionysios caught sight of her, he cried out, "Be merciful, Aphrodite! May your appearance be a blessing to me!"

Leonas caught him as he was about to fall to his knees. "Master, this is the new slave. No reason to be upset. And you, woman, approach your master."

At the word "master" Callirhoe hung her head and shed a stream of tears,[57] at last coming to realize what it meant to lose her freedom.[58]

Dionysios slapped Leonas and said, "Could you be more sacrilegious? Do you speak to the gods as to mere mortals? You mean to tell me this woman was purchased with silver? Well, no wonder you didn't find the man who sold her. Have you not heard what Homer teaches us? 'And the gods make themselves look like strangers from other lands and inspect both the outrageous and the just behavior of mortals.'"[59]

Then Callirhoe said,* "Stop mocking me and calling me a goddess. I'm not even a happy mortal!"

But her voice seemed divine to Dionysios as she spoke, for it sounded musical, with a tone like a lyre. Flustered and too embarrassed to say more, he went off to the villa, already burning with love. A little while later the rest of his party arrived from the city, and rumor of what had happened swiftly spread. Everyone hurried to see the woman, pretending they were showing reverence to Aphrodite. Callirhoe was mortified by the crowd and had no idea what to do. Everything was foreign to her and she could not even see the familiar face of Plangon, who was busy welcoming her master.

The hour grew late and yet no one came to the villa. They all were standing at the shrine as if that was where they had been invited. Leonas figured out what had happened, went to the sanctuary, and brought Callirhoe out. That was a perfect example of the fact that some are royalty by their very nature, like the king in a beehive,[60] for they all followed her instinctively, as if she had been appointed ruler by her beauty.

---

57. "stream of tears": For the tragic tone of the phrase, see note to 1.3.7.

58. "at last . . . freedom": A slight reworking of Aeschines, *In Ctesiphontem* 157 (echoed again by Chariton at 4.2.4), a notable passage cited in Greek rhetorical handbooks.

59. "And the gods . . . mortals": A citation of Homer, *Odyssey* 17.485 and 487.

60. "That was a . . . beehive": The image and some of the wording here is from Xenophon, *Cyropaideia* 5.1.24. Chariton may also be thinking of Xenophon, *Symposium* 1.8: "Anyone who saw what was going on would have drawn the conclusion that beauty is something naturally royal." The ancients were unaware of the gender of the queen bee.

[4] She went back to her usual room. Dionysios, on the other hand, had been wounded. But, being a cultured man who made a particular point of showing courage, he tried to conceal his wound. Not wanting to look pathetic to his slaves or juvenile to his friends, he toughed it out through the whole evening. He thought he kept it hidden, but he was actually more obvious about it because he was so quiet. Taking a portion of his dinner, he said, "Have someone take this to our new visitor. Tell them to say it's from Dionysios—not from her master."

He kept the party going as long as he could. He knew that he was not going to be able to get any sleep, so he wanted to be awake surrounded by his friends. And after it grew late and he had ended things, sleep eluded him. He was right back in Aphrodite's temple, remembering everything: her face, her hair, how she had turned, how she had looked up, her voice, her appearance, her words. Her tears set him aflame. That was a perfect example of a struggle between reason and emotion. For even though he was drowning in desire, being a noble-minded man, he tried to keep himself afloat.

He lifted his head, as if he was holding it above a wave, and said to himself, "Dionysios, aren't you ashamed of yourself? You are the first man in Ionia in virtue and repute. Satraps[61] and princes and whole cities admire you. And you're suffering a schoolboy crush. You've fallen in love at first sight. And while you're in mourning, no less, before you've finished paying respects to your poor wife's spirit. Is this why you came to the country? To get married in your mourning clothes? To a slave? Probably someone else's slave, too. You don't even have her registration papers."

But Eros was playing to win despite Dionysios' careful thinking. He took the man's self-control as an insult, so he stoked the fire hotter in a soul that was trying to reason philosophically about a matter of love. Dionysios, no longer able to stand debating with himself, sent for Leonas, who knew the reason for the summons as soon as he got it, but pretended to be ignorant.

With feigned distress he asked, "Why are you awake, master? Could it be that once again you are overcome by pain for the dead woman?"

"For *a* woman, yes," said Dionysios, "but not for the one who has died. Because of your kindness and loyalty, I have no secrets from you. Leonas, it's all over for me, and you're to blame for my troubles. You brought fire into my house—no, into my *heart*. And the mystery around the woman is also disturbing me. You give me some hogwash about a

---

61. *Satraps* were the provincial governors of the Persian empire.

merchant. You don't know him. You don't know where he's from. And you don't know where he's gone off to. Who, if he had it, would sell a beauty like hers in the middle of nowhere for a talent when it's worth the king's fortune? What god deceived you? Think! Go back over what happened. Who did you see? Who did you talk to? Tell me the truth—you didn't actually see a ship?"

"I didn't see it, master. I only heard about it."

"There you go. One of the Nymphs or the Nereids has risen from the sea. Even the gods are caught up in certain crises of fate that compel them to associate with mortals. So poets and writers tell us."

Dionysios was happy to give himself reasons to extol the woman and think of her as too majestic to mingle with mere mortals.

Leonas wanted to cheer his master up, so he said, "Let's not worry about who she is. I'll bring her to you, if you want. Don't suffer with the thought that you don't have the right to make love to her."

"I won't do it," said Dionysios. "Not until I learn who the woman is and where she's from. So tomorrow let's get the truth from her. I don't want to have her brought here. If I do, she'll get the impression we're forcing her. No, bring her to where I first saw her—we'll have our conversation at Aphrodite's shrine."

[5] That was settled, and the next day Dionysios took his friends and freedmen as well as his most trusted slaves (that way he would have some witnesses) and went into the sanctuary. He had taken some care with his appearance, dressing himself with a modest elegance since he was about to meet the woman he loved. He was naturally tall and handsome, and, above all, looked dignified.

Leonas got Plangon and also the maids that Callirhoe already knew and went to her. "Dionysios is a most just and law-abiding man,"[62] he said. "So come to the temple, my lady, and tell him the truth of just who you really are. You will not fail to get any help that you justly deserve. Simply be straight with him and don't hide any of the truth. That's the best way to make him feel compassion for you."

Callirhoe went reluctantly but felt cheered that at least their meeting was to take place in the temple. When she got there, they all marveled at her even more than before.

Dionysios was struck speechless. The silence dragged on interminably, but he finally spoke up. "My lady, you know all about me. I am Dionysios, the leading citizen of Miletos and of practically the whole of Ionia. I've got a reputation for piety and compassion. You by all rights

---

62. "a most just . . . man": A citation of Xenophon, *Cyropaideia* 1.6.27.

should also tell us the truth about yourself. The men who sold you said you were from Sybaris and had been sold there because of your mistress' jealousy."

Callirhoe blushed and hung her head. Quietly she said, "This is the first time I've been sold. I have never been to Sybaris."

Dionysios looked over at Leonas and said, "I told you she wasn't a slave. I predict that she is, in fact, noble. Tell me everything, my lady. First of all, tell me your name."

"Callirhoe," she said—even her name pleased Dionysios!—but she would say nothing about the rest. When he kept asking her, she said, "Master, I beg you to let me keep silent about my lot in life. What happened before was a dream, a fairy tale. Now I am what I have become: a slave in a foreign land."

As she said this, she tried to hide her tears, but they streamed down her cheeks.[63] That caused Dionysios to weep, along with everyone standing around. You would have thought that even the statue of Aphrodite herself looked gloomier than before.

Dionysios pressed her, prying even more. "I ask this as a first favor from you:[64] tell me your story, Callirhoe. You won't be telling it to a stranger—people can also share a kinship based on character.[65] There's nothing to be afraid of, not even if you've done something terrible."

Callirhoe got angry at him. "Don't insult me. I can prove that I've done nothing wrong, but since my past is more distinguished than my current fortune, I don't want to appear to be stretching the truth. And I don't want to tell a story that would seem incredible to those who don't know the facts. My current situation makes my past seem unbelievable."

Dionysios was amazed at the woman's strength of character[66] and said, "Now I understand, even if you won't tell me. But tell me anyway. You won't be telling us anything about yourself as extraordinary as what we can see. All the famous stories are less impressive than you."

---

63. "she tried . . . her cheeks": An imitation of Xenophon, *Cyropaideia* 6.4.3 (also imitated by Chariton at 5.2.4).

64. "I ask . . . from you": There is a possible echo here of Aeschines, *De Falsa Legatione* 171.

65. "kinship based on character": For this concept compare Isocrates, *To Demonicus* 10.

66. "amazed . . . strength of character": Perhaps there is an echo here of Ctesias (*FGrH* 688 F 1b, cited at Diodorus Siculus 2.6.9). Another possible echo can be found in Chariton 7.3.6.

Eventually she began to tell her story. "I am the daughter of Hermocrates, the Syracusan general. After I lost consciousness from a sudden fall, my parents gave me a rich burial. Tomb-robbers opened the mausoleum and found me once again conscious. They brought me to this place and in an isolated spot Theron handed me over to Leonas here."

She told him everything, but kept silent about Chaireas.

"So I beg you, Dionysios—for you are a Greek from a charitable city who knows what being civilized means—do not turn out to be like the tomb-robbers. Don't rob me of my country and my family. You're a rich man. For you it's not a big deal to let a slave go. You won't lose what you paid if you return me to my father. Hermocrates is no ingrate. We admire Alcinoos, and we all approve of him for sending his suppliant Odysseus back to his country.[67] I too am your suppliant. Save a captive who has no one in the world. If I cannot live as the well-born woman I am, I choose a free woman's death."

Dionysios was weeping as he listened to this, ostensibly for Callirhoe, but really for himself,[68] for he realized that he would not be fulfilling his desire.

"Callirhoe, don't worry," he said. "Keep your spirits up. As Aphrodite here is my witness, you won't fail to obtain what you request. In the meantime, you'll be treated in my house as a lady rather than a slave."

[6] She left, convinced that nothing would happen to her against her will. But Dionysios, still pained, went to his own room and asked Leonas to come alone.

"I'm out of luck on every count. Eros must hate me! First, I've buried my wife. Second, the new slave wants nothing to do with me. I was hoping she was a gift for me from Aphrodite.[69] I was imagining a life for myself more blissful than that of Menelaos, the husband of the Spartan woman—for I can't imagine even Helen was that beautiful.[70] I'm done for. The same day that Callirhoe leaves here, I'll leave this life."

---

67. Alcinoos, king of the Phaiacians, had one of his ships convey Odysseus back to Ithaca in Homer's *Odyssey*.

68. "ostensibly . . . for himself": A reminiscence of Homer, *Iliad* 19.301–302 (also imitated at 8.5.2).

69. "was a gift for me from Aphrodite": For the phrasing and the image of a woman— Helen, which sets up the following comparison—as a gift from Aphrodite compare Euripides, *Iphigeneia in Aulis* 178–81.

70. The irony is not that Menelaos was not happy—his happiness was proverbial—but that Dionysios is more a Paris than a Menelaos, though an unintentional Paris.

At this Leonas gave a shout. "Master! Do not curse yourself! You're the one in charge here. You have power over her. She'll do what you decide whether she wants to or not. I bought her for a talent."

"You bought her? You wretched, wretched man. She's well-born! Haven't you heard of Hermocrates, the general of the whole island of Sicily? His achievements are legendary.[71] The Persian king honors him and treats him as a friend. He sends him gifts every year because he defeated the Athenians, the enemies of the Persians, in a sea battle. Will I be a tyrant over a free person? Will I, Dionysios, who am famed for my self-control, force myself on an unwilling woman? A woman who not even Theron the pirate forced himself on?"*

He said this to Leonas, but even so he did not despair of winning her over, for Eros is naturally full of hope, and Dionysios was confident that he could realize his desire by taking good care of her.

So Dionysios called Plangon and said, "You've given me ample proof of your diligence. Now I entrust to you the greatest, most valuable of my possessions—the foreign woman. I want her to lack for nothing. I want her in the lap of luxury. Think of her as your mistress. Care for her. Dress her. Make her friendly to me. Praise me constantly in her presence and explain what sort of man you know me to be. And make sure you don't call me 'master.'"*

Plangon understood her orders, for she was naturally astute. Without drawing any attention to herself, she put her mind to the problem, very motivated to solve it. She went to Callirhoe, but she did not tell her she had been ordered to serve her. Instead, she showed her normal kindness and wanted to be trusted as a confidante.

[7] Then the following happened. Dionysios kept lingering in the country, offering different pretexts for doing so at different times. In reality he was neither able to leave Callirhoe nor willing to take her back with him, for when people saw her, her fame would spread. Her beauty would subjugate all of Ionia and rumor would advance inland, all the way to the Great King.[72] While he was stalling, he began to inquire more closely into the affairs of the estate, and he found some minor fault with how Phocas, the manager, was running things. The extent of his criticism did not go beyond words, but in it Plangon saw her chance. Feigning panic* and tearing out her hair, she ran in to Callirhoe and grasped her by the knees.

---

71. "His achievements are legendary": The phrase is reminiscent of Herodotus 7.1.1.

72. The military vocabulary and specific verb (*anabaino* "to travel up from the coast" or "advance inland") evoke the *Anabasis* of the Athenian historian Xenophon.

"Mistress, I beg you," she said. "Save us! Dionysios is furious at my husband. It's the way he is—he can be as harsh as he is compassionate. No one else can save us. Only you! Dionysios will gladly grant you the first favor you ask of him."

Callirhoe was reluctant to go to him, but with the woman begging and pleading, she was unable to say no, obliged from the outset by the kindnesses shown to her by Plangon.

So in order not to be seen as an ingrate she said, "I too am a slave, with no right to speak up. But if you think I can actually do something, I'm ready to add my appeal to yours. I pray we're successful."

When they got there, Plangon ordered the man at the door to take word in to their master that Callirhoe was there. It happened that Dionysios was overwhelmed by misery, even wasting away physically. So when he heard that Callirhoe had come, he was dumbfounded and a mist poured down over his eyes[73] at the shock.

Eventually he pulled himself together. "Have her come in."

Callirhoe stood near him, hanging her head. At first she blushed deeply, but after a bit she spoke up anyway. "I am grateful to Plangon here, for she loves me like a daughter. I beg you, master, do not be angry at her husband. Grant him his safety." She wanted to say more but could not.

Dionysios caught on to Plangon's ruse. "I'm angry, all right. No one in the world could have stopped me from killing Phocas and Plangon after what they've done, but I'll gladly spare them for your sake. And Plangon, you and Phocas better remember that you've been saved thanks to Callirhoe."

Plangon threw her arms around his knees, and Dionysios said, "You should fall at the knees of Callirhoe. She's the one who saved you."

When Plangon saw that Callirhoe was delighted and very pleased at his generous gift, she said, "Well, you ought to tell Dionysios how grateful we are," and gave her a push just then. Callirhoe stumbled a little and clutched at Dionysios' hand. As if it was inappropriate, of course, merely to give her his hand, he pulled her close and gave her a kiss. Then he immediately released her so there would be no reason to suspect his subterfuge.

[8] Then the women departed, but the kiss worked its way deeply into Dionysios' system like a poison. He could neither see nor hear. He

---

73. "a mist . . . his eyes": A slight modification of a Homeric formula (*Iliad* 5.696, 16.344, 20.421; *Odyssey* 22.88) echoed elsewhere by Chariton (1.1.14, 3.1.3, 3.9.10, and 4.5.9.)

was under assault on all sides, unable as he was to find a remedy for his love. Gifts would not do it, for he could see the woman's proud spirit. Threats or compulsion would not do it, since he was convinced she would choose death before submitting to force.

He felt that Plangon was his one source of aid, so he sent for her. "Your opening maneuvers have gone well," he said, "and I thank you for the kiss. It is either my salvation or my destruction, so figure out how, one woman to another, you can get the upper hand over her, with me as your ally. You should keep in mind that your freedom is your reward, along with something I'm convinced is far more appealing to you—the life of Dionysios."

With these orders Plangon brought to bear all of her experience and guile, but Callirhoe was unassailable from all directions and remained faithful to Chaireas alone. Callirhoe, however, was outgeneraled by Fortune—it is only this goddess that no human reason can prevail against. She loves to win, and nothing is beyond expectation when she is involved. Accordingly, that was when Fortune brought about a breakthrough that was not just unexpected, but incredible. It is worth hearing how she did it.

Fortune laid a plot against the woman's faithfulness. Back when Chaireas and Callirhoe made love for the first time in their marriage, they had matched each other in their eagerness for pleasure. The equality of their desire made their lovemaking fruitful. And so just before her collapse, she had conceived, but because of the dangers and the hardship that came afterward, she did not immediately realize she was pregnant. It was now the start of her third month, and her belly was beginning to swell. Plangon noticed it in the bath because of her experience with pregnancy, but she did not say anything right then because there were so many maids around.

During a quiet moment in the evening, she sat next to Callirhoe on her bed and said, "Child, I have to tell you—you're pregnant."

Callirhoe burst into tears. Bawling and pulling at her hair, she said, "Fortune, you have added this on top of my tribulations: I am to give birth to a slave." She struck her belly and said, "Poor thing, before being born you've already been buried. You've already been given into the hands of pirates. What kind of life are you coming into? What kind of future am I bearing you for? You're without a father. Without a city. A slave. You must die before you are born."

Plangon restrained her arms and promised that the next day she would procure for her an easier way to abort the baby.

[9] When they were both by themselves, they thought about it in different ways. With the unborn child to advocate for her, Plangon felt that

a perfect opportunity had arisen to secure love for her master. A hostage had been found to use as a bargaining chip. Motherly love would overcome wifely fidelity. She worked out how to sell it convincingly.

Callirhoe, meanwhile, at first wanted to destroy the child. She said to herself, "Am I to bear Hermocrates' grandchild for a master? Am I to have a child with no one knowing who the father is? Some malicious person will probably say, 'Callirhoe got pregnant while she was with the pirates.' It's enough for me alone to suffer misfortune. There's no reason for you to enter into a miserable life, my child—a life you were bound to depart once born. Die free, untouched by troubles. I don't ever want you to hear any part of your mother's story."

But then she changed her mind, and pity for her unborn child filled her. "Are you planning to kill your child? You're the most godless of women! Are you crazy? Are you thinking like Medea? No, I think you're even more savage than that Scythian woman.[74] Her husband was her enemy, but you're planning to kill Chaireas' baby and leave behind no reminder of your celebrated marriage. What if you have a son? What if he's like his father? What if he has a better fortune than me? Is a mother to kill a child saved from the grave and from pirates? How many children of the gods and of kings do we hear about being born in slavery only to later recover the status of their parents? Zethos and Amphion, and Cyros![75] Child, you will sail on my behalf to Sicily. You will find your father and your grandfather, and you will tell them your mother's story. A fleet will sail from there to rescue me. You, child, will reunite your parents with each other!"

As she thought about this all night long, sleep gradually came over her. A vision of Chaireas appeared, like unto him in height and fair looks and voice, wearing garments like his on his body.[76] Standing near her, he said, "My wife, I entrust our son to you." He wanted to say more,

---

74. Medea, in the version of the myth popularized in Euripides' *Medea*, kills her children to take revenge on her husband Jason for planning to put her aside and marry another woman. Strictly speaking, Medea was from Colchis (at the eastern edge of the Black Sea) not from Scythia (closer to central Asia), but the point is to emphasize her barbarian origins.

75. Zethos and Amphion were sons of Zeus by the Theban woman Antiope, who was forced to abandon them. They were raised by country folk, but later they were reunited with their mother and ruled Thebes. Cyros (the Elder) was the first emperor of Persia, who likewise was abandoned but eventually reunited with his family and ascended the throne.

76. "like unto him . . . on his body": A citation of Homer, *Iliad* 23.66–67, where Patroclos' ghost appears to Achilles.

but Callirhoe sprang up, wanting to embrace him. Believing that her husband had given her advice, she decided to keep the child.

[10] When Plangon came the next day, Callirhoe revealed her decision to her. Plangon did not fail to point out the problem with her plan. "My lady, it's impossible for you to raise a child in this house. Our master is in love with you. Out of decency and restraint, he won't force himself on you if you're unwilling. But he'll be too jealous to let you raise a child. He'll think it an insult if you yearn strongly for a man who is not here and reject him when he is right here. I think it would be better for the child to die before it's born rather than after. You'll spare yourself pointless labor pains and a futile pregnancy. I'm being honest with you because I care about you."

Callirhoe was crushed to hear this.[77] She fell at Plangon's knees, pleading with her to help her find some plan that would let her keep her child. Plangon refused again and again, putting off her answer for two or three days. She fired the girl up and reduced her to begging. Now that she was more trusted, she first had Callirhoe swear that she would reveal the plan to no one. Then Plangon furrowed her brow and wrung her hands. "My lady, the biggest of problems work out right through big thinking. I'm going to betray my master out of my affection for you. You must realize that one of two things has to happen. Either your child must certainly die or it must be born the richest child in Ionia and heir to its noblest house. And your baby will bring happiness to you as its mother. Choose whichever you want."

"Just how much of an idiot does someone have to be," Callirhoe answered, "to choose child-murder over prosperity? But it seems to me that you're talking about something impossible and beyond belief. You'll need to explain it more clearly."

Plangon asked, "How long do you think you've been pregnant?"

"Two months," she said.

"Then time is on our side. You can make it look like you've had Dionysios' child two months premature."

At this Callirhoe cried out, "Better the child die!"

Plangon pretended to go along. "You've got the right idea in preferring an abortion, my lady. Let's do it. It's less dangerous than trying to trick the master. Cut every last tie to your noble birth. Give up hope of

---

77. "Callirhoe was crushed to hear this": The Greek is literally something like "Callirhoe listened grievously," an imitation of Xenophon, *Anabasis* 2.1.9, where the Greeks hear the news that Cyros (the Younger) is dead, they are trapped in the heart of the Persian empire, and the king demands their surrender.

going home. Come to terms with your present bad fortune and become a slave in every way."

When Plangon suggested this, Callirhoe was not at all suspicious. She was a highborn girl with no experience of slaves' trickery. But the more Plangon urged an abortion, the more Callirhoe came to pity her unborn child.

"Give me a chance to think about it. The choice is between the two things I value most: my fidelity or my child."

This time Plangon praised her for not making a choice hastily. "It makes sense that the scale could go either way. One side holds wifely faithfulness; the other motherly love. Still, there's no time for a long delay. No matter what, you have to choose one by tomorrow—before your pregnancy is discovered."[78]

They agreed and went their separate ways.

[11] After Callirhoe went upstairs to her room and closed the door, she held the portrait of Chaireas against her belly and said, "Look, there are three of us: husband, wife, and child. Let's have a meeting to plan for our common good. I'll put forward my opinion first. I want to die the wife of Chaireas alone. This—not to know the touch of another man—means more to me than my parents, my home, my child.

"Now you, child. What do you choose for yourself? To be killed by poison before you see the light of the sun? To be cast out along with your mother, perhaps not even deemed worthy of burial? Or to live and have two fathers, one the leading man of Sicily, the other of Ionia? When you grow up, you'll easily be recognized by your relatives—I'm certain that when I have you, you'll look just like your father. You'll sail home on a Milesian trireme[79] for all to see, and Hermocrates will be glad to have his grandchild back—by then you'll be ready to become general yourself. You cast your vote against me, child, and won't allow us to die.

"Let's ask your father, too. Actually, he's already told us. He himself came to me in my dreams and said, 'I entrust our son to you.' I call you as a witness, Chaireas—you are giving me away in marriage to Dionysios."

She spent that day and night with such thoughts and was persuaded to live not because of herself but because of her baby. Plangon came the next day. At first she sat there dejectedly, projecting a sympathetic demeanor.

---

78. "before . . . discovered": A fainter echo of the Thucydidean phrase found earlier at 1.14.6.

79. A swift, maneuverable ship with rowers sitting in three banks. It was the standard warship of fleets at the dramatic date of the novel.

Neither of them said a word. But after a long while Plangon asked, "What have you decided? What do we do? There's no time to waste."

Callirhoe could not answer right away because she was crying and upset, but eventually she said, "I'm opposed to it, but the child betrays me. Plangon, do what's best. I'm just afraid that even if I submit and let him have his way with me, Dionysios will look down on me because of my present circumstances, and, since he'll think of me more as a concubine than a wife, he won't raise the child I bear.* Then I'll be giving up my fidelity for no reason."

The words were barely out of her mouth when Plangon interrupted. "I'm ahead of you there, too. I've come up with a plan because I now care more for you than for my master. We've got to put our faith in Dionysios' character since he's a good man, but I'll still make him swear an oath, even if he is master. We can't be too careful. And you, child, have to trust him once he's sworn his oath. I'm off to present him with your terms."

Book 3

[1] Having failed to obtain Callirhoe's love and no longer able to stand it, Dionysios decided to starve himself to death. He wrote his last will and testament with instructions for his funeral, and in it he begged Callirhoe to come to him, even if only after his death. Plangon wanted to go in to see her master, but his valet had orders to admit no one and stopped her. While they were arguing outside his door, Dionysios heard them and asked who was making the fuss. His valet said that it was Plangon, and Dionysios replied, "It's a bad time for her to be here"—he no longer wanted to see even a reminder of his desire—"but tell her to come in anyway."

She opened the door and said, "Master, why are you wearing yourself out with grief, as if you've failed? Yes! Callirhoe invites you to marry her. Change your clothes from black to white. Make sacrifice. Receive your bride, the woman you love."

Dionysios was taken aback by the shock, and a mist poured down over his eyes.[80] Utterly drained, he presented the very image of death.

---

80. "a mist . . . his eyes": A slight modification of a Homeric formula (*Iliad* 5.696, 16.344, 20.421; *Odyssey* 22.88) echoed elsewhere by Chariton (1.1.14, 2.7.4, 3.9.10, and 4.5.9).

Plangon shrieked, causing a commotion, and throughout the whole house the master was mourned as if he was dead. Not even Callirhoe was dry-eyed when she heard this. So great was everyone's grief that even she wept for Dionysios as a good man.*

At last he eventually came out of it and in a weak voice said, "Which god is playing tricks on me, wanting to turn me back from the road that lies before me? Did I really hear this, or was it a dream? Callirhoe is willing to marry me? When she didn't even want me looking at her before?"

Plangon was standing nearby and said, "Stop torturing yourself for no reason. Quit disbelieving your own good blessings. I'm not fooling my master. Callirhoe sent me as her ambassador to negotiate the marriage."

"Then negotiate," said Dionysios, "and tell me her exact words. Leave nothing out and add nothing. Just remember them exactly."

"This is what she said: 'I am from the leading family in Sicily. Although I have fallen on hard times, nevertheless I still retain my pride. I have lost my country, my parents—the one thing I have not lost is my nobility. So if Dionysios wishes to keep me as a concubine and gratify his own desire, I will hang myself before I surrender myself to being raped like a slave. But if he wishes to have me as his lawfully wedded wife, I for my part am willing to become a mother so that Hermocrates' line will have a successor. Dionysios must consider this matter—not alone and not quickly, but with his friends and family. I don't want anyone to say to him later, "Are you raising children born from a slave woman and dishonoring your house?" If Dionysios isn't willing to become a father, let him not be a husband either.'"

These words inflamed Dionysios more, and he conceived a misplaced hope[81] that she loved him in return. Stretching forth his hands to heaven, he said, "O Zeus and Helios,[82] I pray that I see a child from Callirhoe—then I will think myself* more blessed than the Great King. Let's go to her. Lead me there, my sweet Plangon, you faithful slave, you!"

[2] Running upstairs, his first instinct was to fall at Callirhoe's knees. He nevertheless got himself under control and sat down calmly. "My lady," he said, "I have come to you to thank you for saving my life. I

---

81. "and he conceived . . . hope": A reminiscence of Thucydides 2.51.6, which Chariton references more closely later at 6.9.3, where he also uses it of Dionysios. The original context is the absurd hope of the survivors of the plague at Athens that they would henceforth be immune to all diseases.

82. Helios was the sun god.

would never have forced myself upon you against your will. In fact, I had resolved to die if I couldn't have you. But thanks to you, I've been brought back to life. Although I'm most grateful to you, I do actually have one point of criticism: you didn't trust that I would take you as my wedded wife for the production of children[83] in accordance with Greek laws. If I weren't in love, I would never have prayed for such a marriage. I guess you had me pegged as a madman who thinks a noble-born woman is a slave and the descendant of Hermocrates is unworthy to be my own son. 'Consider the matter,' you say. I have considered it. Are you afraid of my loved ones? You are the one I love most of all! Who will dare to call a child of mine unworthy when he has a grandfather even greater than his father?"

He said that with tears in his eyes, then came close to her. She blushed and gave him a shy kiss. "You I trust, Dionysios, but I distrust my fortune. It has caused me to fall from greater blessings before. I'm afraid that my luck hasn't yet changed for the better. So, even though you're a good and just man, you should call on the gods to witness. Not for your sake, but for the sake of your fellow citizens and your relatives. That way no one can ever give you nasty advice about me—they'll know you've sworn an oath. A woman alone in a foreign country is an easy thing to despise."

"What sort of gods do you want me to swear by?" he asked. "For I am ready to swear,[84] were it possible, by climbing up to heaven and putting my hand on Zeus himself."

"Swear to me," she said, "by the sea that brought me to you, by Aphrodite who showed me to you, and by Eros who is giving me away as a bride."

That was agreed upon and quickly done.

His passion goaded him on and permitted no putting off of the marriage, for the ability to satisfy one's desire is a difficult thing to control. But Dionysios was a man of culture, and though he was overwhelmed by a storm and his soul was drowning, he nevertheless compelled himself to hold his head up, as it were, above a great wave of emotion.

He thought about it in these terms. "Am I going to marry her out here in the middle of nowhere as if she really was a slave? I'm not such

---

83. "for the production of children": A formula found several times in Athenian New Comedy (e.g., Menander, *Dyscolus* 842).

84. "For I am ready to swear": The opening of the sentence is perhaps an imitation of a phrase from the end of Demosthenes, *Contra Calliclem* 35. One might also compare Isaios, *Pro Euphileto* 10 (again from the end of the speech).

an ingrate that I won't have a ceremony to celebrate my wedding to Callirhoe. I must honor my wife from the start—and it gives me some assurance regarding the future. Rumor is the fastest thing in the world. She travels through the air and nothing blocks her path. She's why it's not possible to keep something that's beyond belief a secret. She's already running, taking the novel tale to Sicily: 'Callirhoe's alive! Tomb-robbers opened her grave, took her, and sold her in Miletos.' Any time now triremes from Syracuse will sail here and General Hermocrates will demand his daughter back. What are you going to tell him? 'Theron sold her to me.' But where *is* Theron? And even if I convince him I'm telling the truth, I've received stolen goods from a pirate. Practice your defense speech, Dionysios. You might be delivering it before the Great King. It would be best, in that case, to say, 'I don't remember how, but I heard a free woman was visiting the area. I married her, legally and publicly, in the city, and she agreed to the marriage herself.' With this argument I'll also be more likely to persuade my father-in-law that I'm not unworthy of the marriage. Endure a short wait, my soul, so that you might enjoy for a longer time a secure pleasure. I'll be in a stronger position for the trial if I act before the law as a husband and not as a master."

He made up his mind and summoned Leonas. "Go to the city. Make magnificent preparations for the marriage. Let flocks of animals be brought in. Have food and wine brought in by land and sea. I've chosen to throw the city a public feast."

The next day, after carefully making all the arrangements, Dionysios made the journey by carriage. But Callirhoe he ordered to be brought in the evening by boat—since he was not yet ready to show her to the people of the city—to his house, which was right on Docimos Harbor. Plangon was trusted with the job of caring for her. Before she left the countryside, Callirhoe first prayed to Aphrodite. After she went into the temple, she asked everyone else to leave and spoke to the goddess as follows.

"Mistress Aphrodite, should I rightly criticize you or thank you? When I was a maiden you united me with Chaireas, and now you are giving me as a bride to another man after him. I would never have agreed to swear oaths by you and your son if this baby here"—she gestured to her belly—"had not betrayed me." She continued, "I beg you. Not for me. For this child. Make sure my deceit stays a secret. Since the baby doesn't have his real father, let him pass for Dionysios'. When he grows up, he can find his true father."

As she walked from the sanctuary to the sea, the sailors caught sight of her and were gripped with fear since they thought Aphrodite herself was coming to get aboard. As one they moved to kneel in reverence.

Due to the fervor with which they rowed, the ship sailed into the harbor faster than it takes to tell.

First thing in the morning[85] the entire city was covered in garlands. Everyone sacrificed in front of their own house, not just in the temples. There was gossip about the identity of the bride. Because of the woman's beauty and the lack of information about her, the common people were convinced that a Nereid had risen from the sea or that a goddess had come from Dionysios' estate—the latter was what the sailors were saying. The one thing they all wanted was to see Callirhoe. The crowd packed together around the temple of Concord,[86] where it was the tradition for the city's grooms to receive their brides.

It was the first time since her funeral that Callirhoe had gotten dressed up. Once she had decided to get married, she came to think of her beauty as a stand-in for her country and family. After putting on a Milesian dress and a bridal garland, she faced the crowd. Everyone shouted, "Aphrodite is getting married!" They spread cloth of royal purple in her path and threw down roses and violets. They sprinkled perfume as she walked. No one, young or old, was left inside the houses—even the harbors themselves were empty. There was so little room that some of the crowd climbed up onto the roofs.

On this day too, however, that resentful divinity once more bore his grudge. I will tell you how a little later. First, I want to tell you what had been happening in Syracuse during this time.

[3] The tomb-robbers had not done a careful job of closing the tomb. After all, it was night and they had been in a hurry. Chaireas waited until exactly the crack of dawn[87] and came to the spot. His excuse was that he was bringing flowers and libations, but in reality his intention was to kill himself. He could not bear to be parted from Callirhoe and thought that death was the only thing that could soothe his grief. When he arrived, he found the stones had been moved and the entrance exposed. He was thunderstruck at the sight and, because of what had happened, he was overcome by a terrible inability to act.

Rumor the messenger swiftly reported the incredible news to the Syracusans, and everyone ran down to the tomb. No one dared to go inside before Hermocrates gave the order. The man sent inside gave a

---

85. "First thing in the morning": A Thucydidean phrase. See the note earlier at 2.3.4, where Chariton also uses it.

86. The Greek goddess Homonoia, the personification of "oneness of mind" and civic harmony.

87. "waited . . . dawn": This phrase is taken from Thucydides 2.3.4.

complete and precise report. The fact that the dead girl was not inside seemed unbelievable, so Chaireas himself then decided to go in. He wanted to see Callirhoe again even as a corpse. Though he searched the tomb, he was unable to find anything. Full of doubt, many people went in after him, but all were overcome by helplessness, and one of the bystanders said, "The grave goods have been stolen, the work of tomb-robbers. But where is the dead girl?"

The crowd was full of many different theories, but Chaireas looked up to heaven and raised his hands. "Which one of the gods was my rival in love? Which one has taken away Callirhoe and keeps her now with him against her will, compelled by a fate too strong for her? That's why she died so suddenly! So she wouldn't suffer any illness! That's the way Dionysos took Ariadne from Theseus and Zeus took Semele.[88] Perhaps I was married to a goddess and didn't know it, and she was too good for the likes of me. But even so she wouldn't have had to leave the world of mortals so quickly, or by means of such a charade. Thetis was a goddess, but she stayed with Peleus, and he had a son with her,[89] while I have been abandoned at the height of my love.

"What is to become of me? What am I to do now that my luck's run out? Kill myself? And who would I be buried with? After all, I had this hope in my adversity, that if I couldn't have a shared bedroom with Callirhoe, I would find a shared grave with her.

"I'll give you my reason for living, mistress. You are forcing me to go on living, for I shall look for you across land and sea, and, if I am able, I will climb up to the sky. I beg this of you, my lady: do not flee from me."

At this the crowd broke out in lamentation, and everyone began to sing a dirge for Callirhoe as if she had just died. Triremes were launched immediately and many men split up to conduct the search. Hermocrates personally scoured Sicily and Chaireas North Africa. Some were sent to Italy, and others were ordered to cross the Ionian Sea.[90]

---

88. When Theseus abandoned Ariadne, she was rescued by the god Dionysos, and some versions of the myth specify that she was abandoned in accordance with the wishes of the god Dionysos, so that he could marry her. Semele, a princess of Thebes and mother of Dionysos, was tricked by Zeus' wife Hera into asking Zeus to appear in his immortal form. She died instantly. Chariton seems to imply here that Zeus did so of his own volition.

89. Achilles, who was the son of the immortal Nereid Thetis and the mortal hero Peleus.

90. The sea between southern Italy and Greece; it is not connected to the region of Ionia.

Human intervention was entirely powerless, but Fortune brought the truth to light—Fortune, without whom no deed is accomplished, as one may learn from what happened.

After the tomb-robbers had sold their hard-to-sell merchandise—the woman—they left Miletos and made for Crete, having heard reports that it was a large and prosperous island. They hoped it would be easy to sell the rest of their cargo. But a strong wind took them off course and drove them into the Ionian Sea, and there they afterwards wandered on empty waters. Thunder and lightning and a long night came upon these godless men, Providence's demonstration that earlier they had had a good voyage because of Callirhoe. Time and again they came close to a swift death, but the gods did not release them from their fear and drew out their shipwreck. Land would not receive these godless men, and after being at the sea for a long time[91] they faced a shortage of necessities, particularly water. Their ill-gotten wealth was of no help to them[92]—they were dying of thirst surrounded by gold. Slowly they came to regret what they had had the presumption to do and hurled accusations at each other now that everything had gone wrong.

So all the rest of them were dying of thirst, but Theron was cunning in this crisis too—he was filching water, robbing his fellow robbers. He thought he was pulling a fast one, but it was the work of Providence. She was actually saving the man for tortures and crucifixion. The trireme carrying Chaireas encountered the ship as it drifted, at first keeping its distance in case it was a pirate ship. But after it became clear that there was no one at the helm and it was simply moving erratically with the motion of the waves, one of the men on the trireme shouted, "It has no crew! No reason to be afraid. Let's pull up alongside and solve this mystery."

The helmsman—it was him because Chaireas was below deck with his head covered, weeping—agreed to this plan. Pulling alongside, they first called to those onboard. When no one answered, one of the men from the trireme went aboard and saw nothing—nothing but gold and corpses. He relayed this to the sailors. They were ecstatic, thinking themselves fortunate to have found a treasure at sea. Chaireas asked what the cause of the commotion was, and when he found out, even he wanted to see the strange sight.

---

91. "after being . . . time": The wording is reminiscent of Thucydides 7.12.3, which is also recalled later at 3.4.9.

92. "wealth . . . to them": The wording and thought are close to Aeschylus, *Persae* 842. See note to 1.9.3 earlier.

Recognizing the grave goods, he tore at his clothes and gave a loud, piercing shout: "Oh, Callirhoe! These are your things. This is the crown I put on your head. Your father gave you this. Your mother gave you that. Here's your wedding gown. The ship has become your tomb, but although I can see your belongings, where are you? Of everything in the tomb, your body is all that's missing."

Theron heard this and lay still like one of the corpses—he was, in fact, half-dead. He was determined not to make a sound or move since he had a pretty good idea of what was in store for him. People are, however, by nature creatures that love life and do not abandon, even in their final misfortunes, hope of a change for the better—the god that created us planted the seed of this deception into all of us so no one would run away from a life of hardship.[93] Accordingly, the first word out of the mouth of Theron, who was overwhelmed by his thirst, was: "Water!"

After they brought him some water and he had received all the care he needed, Chaireas sat down next to him and asked, "Who are you people? Where are you sailing from? Where did you get this stuff? And what have you done with the woman who owns it?"

Theron regained his composure and, clever man that he was, said, "I'm from Crete.[94] I was sailing to Ionia to find my brother, who's soldiering there, when I was left behind in Cephallenia[95] by the crew of the ship I was on. They departed ahead of schedule. Then I got on this ship when I got lucky and it came sailing through. We were driven off course to this sea by strong winds, and then we were becalmed for a long time. Everyone else died of thirst. I alone was saved because of my piety."

After listening to this story, Chaireas ordered the ship to be towed behind the trireme all the way back to the harbors of Syracuse.

[4] Rumor, however, being naturally swift, got there first, particularly eager on this occasion to report so much incredible news. Everyone ran down to the shore and various emotions were combined: people wept, marveled, asked questions, disbelieved answers. The strange tale shocked them to the core. When Callirhoe's mother saw the grave goods of her daughter, she wailed, "I see everything, but you alone are missing.

---

93. "life of hardship": A phrase with a tragic ring. Compare Sophocles, *Oedipus Coloneus* 91 and the so-called Critias fragment, though it is also found in Attic comedy.

94. Upon his return to Ithaca in the *Odyssey,* the disguised Odysseus weaves a series of lies in which he claims to be from Crete. Cretans were generally thought of as inveterate liars.

95. An island off the west coast of mainland Greece with ties to Odysseus.

What strange tomb-robbers! They kept the clothes and the gold with them. The only thing they stashed away was my daughter!"

The beaches and harbors echoed with the sound of the women striking themselves in mourning. They filled both land and sea with lamentation. Hermocrates, used to taking charge as a general and a master of practical affairs, said, "We shouldn't pursue this matter here. We ought to hold a more conventional hearing. Let's go to the assembly. Who knows? Perhaps we even need to select jurors."

His entire word was not yet spoken[96] and already the theater was full—the women,* too, took part in this assembly. The citizens sat there in suspense. The first to come before the assembly was Chaireas, wearing black, pale, disheveled, just as he had been when he followed his wife to her grave. He was unwilling to mount the speaker's platform and stood just below it. At first he wept for a long while and was unable to speak despite his desire to. The crowd shouted, "Courage! Speak!" Eventually he looked up and spoke.

"The present occasion should be more about grieving than speechifying. But I'll speak and go on living, forced by necessity, until I find out about Callirhoe's disappearance. That's why I sailed from here and made my journey—whether it was one of good fortune or bad, I don't know. You see, I spotted a ship adrift in fair weather, hampered by a storm all its own and swamped amidst a calm. Surprised, we got close. I thought I was looking at my poor wife's tomb. All her things were there—except her. Oh, it was full of bodies, but they all belonged to others. This one man, whoever he is, we found half-dead among them. I revived him with all care and saved him for you."

Some public slaves,[97] meanwhile, brought Theron in chains into the theater, along with a procession that suited him: right behind him were a wheel, a catapult,[98] fire, and whips—Providence awarding him the prizes for his exertions.

When he had taken his place in the middle of the theater, one of the magistrates asked him, "Who are you?"

"Demetrios."

"From?"

---

96. A Homeric phrase (*Iliad* 10.540 and *Odyssey* 16.11) found also in Chariton at 7.1.11.

97. These functioned as police, jailers, and executioners.

98. It is unclear whether this was a repurposed siege weapon of that name or another implement inspired by and named after one, but "catapults" as instruments of torture appear also in 4 *Maccabees* 8.13.

"Crete."

"What do you know? Tell us."

"When I was sailing to see my brother in Ionia, I was left behind by a ship. Then I got on another ship that was passing through. I thought they were merchants at the time, but now I suppose they were tomb-robbers. After being at sea for a long time,[99] all the others died from a lack of water, but I alone have been saved because I've never done anything wicked in my life. Syracusans, you are a people famed for your compassion. Do not prove yourselves more cruel to me than thirst and sea were."

He spoke movingly, and the crowd was filled with pity. Perhaps he would have persuaded them, maybe even persuaded them to give him passage home, if some god taking vengeance for Callirhoe had not begrudged him his unjust persuasion—it would have been the wickedest of judgments for the Syracusans to be persuaded that the man had been saved because of his piety when he was the only one saved because of his *impiety* so that he could suffer even greater punishment. Someone sitting in the crowd recognized him and quietly told the people around him, "I've seen this guy before walking around in the harbor here."

What he said was then passed along quickly to more people and someone shouted, "He's lying!" Then all the citizens turned around and the magistrates ordered the man who had spoken first to come down. The fisherman's accusation was more convincing than Theron's denial, and immediately they called for the torturers and they used whips on the fiend. They burned and cut him, but he held out for a long time. He almost triumphed over the torture, but conscience is strong in all of us, and truth is all-powerful,[100] and though it took a good long while, eventually Theron confessed and began his tale.

"I saw riches put in a tomb and I gathered pirates. We opened the grave and found the dead woman still alive. We stole everything and loaded it into our ship. We sailed to Miletos, where we sold only the woman. We were taking the rest of the stuff over to Crete when we were driven off course into the Ionian Sea by the winds. What happened to us then, you've seen for yourself."

---

99. "After being . . . time": The wording is another echo of Thucydides 7.12.3. See Chariton earlier at 3.3.11.

100. "truth is all-powerful": This is fashioned after a line in a fragment of a lyric poem found on papyrus, attributed variously to Simonides or Bacchylides (P.Oxy. 2432). The portion of the poem that is preserved expresses the sentiment that moral virtue is difficult to achieve. For the phrase compare also Bacchylides, fr. 14.4–5 Snell.

He told them everything except the name of the person who had bought Callirhoe.

At his words, joy and pain were felt by all—joy because Callirhoe lived, pain because she had been sold. Theron received the death sentence, despite Chaireas' pleas that the man should not be killed yet. "That way," he said, "he can come with me* and show me the people who bought her. Take into account the compulsion I'm under. I'm pleading on behalf of the man who sold my wife."

Hermocrates blocked this eventuality by saying, "It would be better to face a more laborious search than that our laws be broken. I beg you, Syracusans, remember my service as general and render your gratitude for my victories toward my daughter. Send emissaries for her. She is a free woman—let's get her back."

The words were barely out of his mouth when the people shouted, "Let's all sail!" and the majority of the council stepped up to volunteer.

"I thank you all for this honor, but two envoys from the people and two from the council should do, and Chaireas will sail as the fifth," said Hermocrates.

This resolution was made and ratified, and then the assembly was called to a close. A large part of the crowd followed Theron as he was taken away. He was crucified in front of Callirhoe's tomb, with a view from his cross of the sea over which he had carried as a prisoner Hermocrates' daughter, a woman not even the Athenians had captured.

[5] The others thought it best to wait for the sailing season and to set out at the first sign of spring, for it was then still winter and they felt it was simply impossible to cross the Ionian Sea. But Chaireas was impatient to go. Because of his love he was ready even to build a raft and throw himself into the sea to be carried along by the winds.[101] Out of respect for him and, especially, for Hermocrates, the envoys certainly did not want to delay, so they prepared to sail. The Syracusans sent out the expedition at public expense so that this too would add to the mission's grandeur. They launched the flagship, which was still carrying the victory standards, and when the day of departure came, the people ran down to the harbor, not just men, but women and children too. Mixed together were tears, prayers, groans, encouragements, fear, bravery, pessimism, and optimism. Chaireas' father, Ariston, who was being carried because he was extremely old and ill, threw his arms around his son's neck and hung onto him.

---

101. Perhaps a reminder of the raft Odysseus builds in the fifth book of the *Odyssey* to leave Calypso's island and return to Penelope on Ithaca.

There were tears in his eyes as he said, "Why are you abandoning me now, my child? I'm old, half-dead. Clearly I'll never see you again, so wait just a few days for me to die in your arms. Bury me and then go."

Chaireas' mother held onto his knees and said, "I beg you, my child, do not leave me here alone, but load me onto the trireme. I'm not a heavy piece of cargo! And if I do turn out to be too heavy, you all can throw me into whatever sea you're sailing across." As she spoke, she tore open her clothes and exposed her breasts to him, and said, "Child, respect these and pity me if ever I offered you the comfort of my breast."[102]

Chaireas broke down in tears at the pleas of his parents and threw himself overboard into the sea, wanting to die so that he could avoid the choice between searching for Callirhoe and distressing his parents. The sailors quickly dove in and eventually pulled him out. Then Hermocrates dismissed the crowd and ordered the helmsman to go ahead and set sail already.

Another deed of friendship, and not an ignoble one, also occurred. Chaireas' friend Polycharmos did not right away make an appearance with everyone else. He had even told his parents, "Sure, Chaireas is a friend, but not such a good one that I'd risk my life with him. So I'm going to steer clear of him until he sails." But when the ship moved away from the shore, he bade them farewell from the stern so they could no longer keep him from going.

Once he was out of the harbor, Chaireas faced the open water and said, "Sea, lead me on the same course you took Callirhoe on. I pray to you, Poseidon,[103] either that she return* with us or that I do not return here without her. If I can't bring my wife back, I'm more than willing to be a slave with her."

[6] A favorable wind came up behind the trireme, and it ran along, practically on the track of Theron's ship. It took them the same number of days to get to Ionia and they anchored at the very same promontory on Dionysios' property. The others were exhausted, and after disembarking, they saw to getting a bit of rest by pitching tents and preparing a meal. But Chaireas, with Polycharmos at his side, took a look around and said, "How can we find Callirhoe now? I'm really afraid that Theron lied to us and that her luck ran out and she's dead. But if she really has been sold, who knows where? Asia's a big place."

---

102. "respect these . . . my breast": A citation of Homer, *Iliad* 22.82–83, when Hecabe tries to keep Hector from facing Achilles.

103. God of the sea.

In their wandering they came to Aphrodite's temple and decided to show reverence to the goddess. Falling at her knees, Chaireas said, "Mistress, you first showed me Callirhoe at your festival. Now return to me the one you favored me with."

While his head was raised, he saw next to the goddess a golden statue of Callirhoe, an offering of Dionysios. His knees gave way, as did his dear heart.[104] A wave of vertigo hit him and he collapsed. The temple attendant saw him and brought him some water.

When she had revived him, she said, "Take heart, my child. The goddess has astonished many others besides you. She makes appearances and shows herself clearly. But this is a sign of great blessing. Do you see the gold statue? This woman was a slave, but Aphrodite has made her the mistress of all of us."

"Who is she?" asked Chaireas.

"She is mistress of this estate, my child. The wife of Dionysios, the leading man of Ionia."

When Polycharmos heard this, he, being a man with his wits about him, did not let Chaireas say anything else. He helped him to his feet and got him out of there, not wanting their identities to be discovered[105] until they had a chance to give serious thought to everything and come up with a plan of action. While the attendant was nearby, Chaireas said nothing. He forced himself to keep quiet, although tears burst forth from his eyes of their own accord. But after he went off a ways by himself, he threw himself to the ground and said, "Kindly sea, why did you save me? So that I could have a good voyage and see Callirhoe as the wife of another? That's something I hoped would never happen, not even if Chaireas died. What am I to do now that my luck's run out? I was hoping to get you back from a master. I believed that with the ransom money I could persuade the man who bought you, but now I've found that you're rich, perhaps even royalty. I would've been so much happier if I'd found you a slave. Am I supposed to go up to Dionysios and say, 'Give me back my wife!'? Who says that to a married man? But even if I ran into you, I couldn't approach you or even greet you as a fellow citizen, that most routine of courtesies. I'd probably be in danger of being put to death for seducing my own wife!"

Polycharmos tried to comfort him as he made this lament.

---

104. "His knees . . . dear heart.": A citation of a formula from Homer, seen earlier at 1.1.14.

105. "to be discovered": The phrasing is inspired by Thucydides, though this is a looser echo than those earlier at 1.14.6 and 2.10.8.

[7] In the meantime Dionysios' estate manager Phocas spotted the battle-ready trireme and was rather apprehensive. Getting in good with one of the sailors, Phocas found out from him the truth of who they were, where they came from, and why they were making their voyage. Then he realized that the trireme was bringing a great disaster for Dionysios, who would not survive being separated from Callirhoe. Since he loved his master, he wanted to forestall the danger and snuff out a war that might not have been big or even between whole countries, but which would affect Dionysios' house alone.

For this reason he got on a horse and rode to a Persian fort and reported that an enemy trireme had slipped through, perhaps on a scouting mission, perhaps also lying in wait before a pirate raid. He said it was in the king's interest that it be captured before it could do any harm. He convinced the barbarians, and once they were ready for action, he showed them the way. In the middle of the night they attacked. They hurled fire onto the ship and destroyed it. They captured all the survivors and took them back to the fort in chains. The prisoners were divided up, and Chaireas and Polycharmos begged to be sold to the same master. The man who got them sold them in Caria,[106] where, wearing heavy shackles, they worked on the estate of Mithridates.[107]

Chaireas appeared to Callirhoe in a dream. He was in chains but wanted to approach her, though he was unable to. In her sleep she gave a loud and clear shout, "Over here, Chaireas!" That was the first time Dionysios had heard Chaireas' name. His wife was distraught and he asked her, "Who was the man you were calling?" Her tears betrayed her, and, unable to contain her grief, she gave voice to her emotion.

"An unfortunate person. The man I married as a girl. He is no more fortunate in my dreams, for I saw him in chains. Oh, you poor thing, you died looking for me—the chains reveal your death—but I live in the lap of luxury, lying on a golden bed with another husband. But it won't be long before I come to you. Even if we couldn't enjoy each other's company when we were alive, we'll have each other after death."

Dionysios heard these words and experienced a swirl of opinions. Jealousy took hold of him because Callirhoe loved Chaireas even when he was dead, but a fear that she would kill herself also gripped him. On the whole, he was encouraged by the fact that his wife thought her first husband was dead, for she would not abandon Dionysios now that

---

106. The inland region to the east of Miletos.

107. An abrupt introduction for a character who will be more fully identified later in 4.1.7.

Chaireas was no more. So he comforted his wife as much as he could and watched her closely for several days to make sure she did not do herself any serious harm. She was diverted from her grief by a hope that perhaps Chaireas was alive and her dream had been wrong. Her pregnancy was an even more effective diversion, for in the seventh month after her marriage she gave birth to a son, supposedly Dionysios', but really Chaireas'.

The city threw a festival and envoys came from all over to share the Milesians' delight at the growth of Dionysios' family. Overjoyed, Dionysios agreed to Callirhoe's every request and declared her the mistress of his house. He filled the temples with dedicatory offerings and provided a feast for the whole city with his sacrifices.

[8] Anxious that her secret would be divulged, Callirhoe requested freedom for Plangon, the only one who knew that she had come to Dionysios already pregnant. That way she could claim her loyalty not only because of her inclination but also because of her rise in station.

"I'll happily reward Plangon for her service in love," said Dionysios, "but we are making a mistake if we honor our servant and do not properly thank Aphrodite, in whose temple we first saw each other."

Callirhoe replied, "I want that even more than you do since I owe her a greater debt of gratitude. Right now I'm still confined to bed, but let's wait a few days until it's safer and then go to the country."

She recovered swiftly from the delivery and grew more striking and lovely, no longer a girl, but now a woman. When they got to the estate, Phocas had prepared magnificent sacrifices because a large crowd had come with them from the city. As he began the great sacrifice, Dionysios said, "Mistress Aphrodite, you are responsible for all of my blessings.[108] From you I have Callirhoe. From you I have my son. I am a husband and a father, thanks to you. Callirhoe was enough for me, sweeter than country and parents.[109] But I love my child because he has bound his mother to me more securely. He is my guarantee of her affection. I beg you, mistress, keep Callirhoe safe for me and our son safe for Callirhoe."

The crowd of people standing around gave a shout of approval and showered them with enough roses, violets, and whole garlands to fill the sanctuary with flowers.

---

108. "responsible . . . blessings": The words reverse the meaning of those uttered by Callirhoe at 2.2.6 earlier in imitation of Lysias 1.7. See also Chariton 4.2.7 and 6.6.4.

109. "sweeter . . . parents": See 2.11.1, where the same citation of Homer, *Odyssey* 9.34 appears.

Dionysios had delivered his prayer with everyone listening, but Callirhoe wanted to speak with Aphrodite privately. First, she took her son in her arms and it was the most beautiful sight ever seen—like none a painter ever painted, or a sculptor ever sculpted, or a poet ever told, until now. For none of these artists has ever portrayed Artemis or Athena carrying a baby in her arms.[110] Dionysios wept with joy when he saw this and quietly bowed in reverence to Nemesis.[111]

Callirhoe told only Plangon to stay with her and sent the rest on ahead to the villa. When they were gone, she stood near Aphrodite and held up the baby in her hands.

"Mistress, I am grateful to you for this child—*not* for myself. I would've felt grateful to you for myself if you'd kept watch over Chaireas. But you have given me the exact likeness of my beloved husband, so you haven't deprived me entirely of Chaireas. Grant me that my son be more fortunate than his parents[112] and like his grandfather. May he too sail on a flagship, and when he is in a battle at sea, may someone say, 'Hermocrates' grandson is greater than he.' His grandfather will be happy to have someone to succeed him in valor. We, his parents, will be happy even if we are dead. I beg you, mistress, give up your grievance against me. I've suffered enough misfortune. I've died, I've come back to life, been taken by pirates, lost my country, been sold, and become a slave. And I think of my second marriage as weighing upon me more heavily than those other things. But to make up for all of it, I ask a single favor from you, and through you from the rest of the gods. Keep my fatherless child safe for me."

She wanted to say more, but her tears stopped her.

[9] After waiting a bit, she called for the priestess. The old woman came and asked, "My child, why are you crying in the midst of such blessings? Why, even foreigners show reverence to you as a goddess! Yesterday two handsome young men who were sailing by came here. One of them saw your statue and nearly breathed his last. That's how famous Aphrodite has made you!"

This struck Callirhoe's heart. Like a woman possessed, she fixed her eyes on the priestess and cried, "Who were the foreigners? Where were they sailing from? What did they say to you?"

---

110. Because the two were virgin goddesses.

111. Nemesis is the personification of divine retribution. Dionysios is praying that his supreme happiness will not be followed by a commensurate disaster.

112. "be more . . . parents": A not uncommon sentiment, but this looks as though it gestures back, in particular, to Homer, *Iliad* 6.479 and Sophocles, *Ajax* 550–51.

Alarmed, the old woman at first stood there speechless, but eventually she answered, "I only saw them. I heard nothing."

"What did they look like? Try to remember their faces."

The old woman could not tell her accurately, but Callirhoe suspected the truth anyway, for what people want to be true, that is what they believe to be true.[113] Looking at Plangon, she said, "My unfortunate Chaireas might have come here as he wandered. So what became of him? Let's look for him, but let's do so discreetly."

When she went to Dionysios, she told him only what she had heard from the priestess, for she knew that love is naturally curious and that Dionysios would investigate what had happened for himself. That is exactly what occurred. As soon as he found out, Dionysios was filled with jealousy. He did not have the slightest suspicion that it was Chaireas, but he was afraid that someone in the countryside was secretly plotting to seduce his wife. Her beauty made him suspicious and scared of everyone. And he was afraid not just of the plots of mortal men, but he thought that perhaps a god had descended from heaven to be his rival in love. So he summoned Phocas and questioned him.

"Who were the young men? Where were they from? Were they rich and handsome? Why were they worshiping my Aphrodite? Who told them about her? Who let them?"

Phocas concealed the truth, not because he was afraid of Dionysios, but because he knew that Callirhoe would destroy him and his family when she found out what had happened. When he denied that anyone had visited the area, Dionysios, unaware of why he was lying, suspected that Phocas was part of a more serious plot against him. He flew into a rage and asked for whips and a wheel to use on Phocas—and not just him, but he summoned everyone on the estate, convinced he was looking into a case of adultery.

When Phocas realized how much trouble he was in* regardless of whether he spoke or kept silent, he said, "Master, I'll tell you—and only you—the truth."

Dionysios dismissed everyone else and said, "Now we're alone. No more of your lies. Tell me the truth, even if it's bad."

"It's not bad at all, master," said Phocas. "I bring you news of great blessings. If it starts out a little gloomy, that's no reason for you to feel agony or misery. Just wait until you hear the whole story. It has an ending that's a happy one for you."

---

113. "what people . . . be true": Demosthenes, *Olynthiacs* 3.19, which Chariton also references in a slightly different form at 6.5.1.

This news set Dionysios on edge and he hung on his every word. "Don't wait! Tell me, already!"

Then Phocas began to speak. "A trireme arrived here from Sicily with Syracusan envoys to demand Callirhoe back from you."

Dionysios could have died when he heard that, and night poured down over his eyes.[114] He had a vision of Chaireas standing there and dragging Callirhoe away from him. Laying there, his appearance and color were that of a corpse.[115] Phocas had no idea what to do. He did not want to call anyone, since that would mean there would be a witness to his secrets. He managed to revive his master gradually and told him, "Don't worry. Chaireas is dead. The ship has been destroyed. There's no reason to be afraid anymore."

These words instilled life into Dionysios, and gradually he came back to himself. He asked in detail about everything, and Phocas told him about the sailor who had revealed to him where the trireme was from, why they were sailing, and who they were, as well as the trick he had played on the barbarians and about the night, the fire, the destruction of the ship, the killing, the chains.

Dionysios lifted a cloud or shadow off his soul, so to speak, and embraced Phocas. "You are my benefactor! You are my true protector, the one I most trust with my secrets. Thanks to you I have Callirhoe and our son. I wouldn't have ordered you to kill Chaireas, but I don't blame you for having done it since your crime was motivated by love of your master. In one way you were careless, though. You didn't dig around to find out whether Chaireas was one of the dead or one of the prisoners. You should have looked for his body. He would've had a burial, and I would've had a better reason not to worry. As it is now, because of the prisoners I can't relax and enjoy my good fortune. We don't know where any of them were sold."

[10] He told Phocas to go ahead and openly talk about most of what had happened but to keep quiet about two matters, his own trick and the fact that there were some men from the trireme who survived. Dionysios went to Callirhoe with a gloomy look on his face and then called in the peasants he had co-opted into his scheme* so that his wife, when she found out what had happened, would then come to accept with more certainty that she had lost Chaireas.

---

114. "night . . . his eyes": A slight modification of a Homeric formula (*Iliad* 5.696, 16.344, 20.421; *Odyssey* 22.88) echoed elsewhere by Chariton (1.1.14, 2.7.4, 3.1.3, and 4.5.9).

115. "appearance . . . corpse": The phrase may have been suggested by the same words at Menander, *Aspis* 345.

They came and told her everything they knew. "Barbarian pirates came out of nowhere during the night and attacked and burned a Greek trireme that had anchored the day before at the promontory. When day came, we saw blood in the water and bodies floating on the waves."

The woman tore her clothes when she heard this. She struck her eyes and cheeks and ran off to the room she had first gone into after being sold. Dionysios gave free rein to her emotion, afraid there would be a distasteful scene if he went to her before she was ready. He ordered everyone to leave but told Plangon to stay by her so she would not do herself any harm. When Callirhoe was alone, she sat on the floor and poured dust over her head. Tearing out her hair, she began the following lament.

"I had prayed to die either before you or with you,[116] Chaireas. There's no doubt that I must die, even if it will be after you. What hope is left to keep me alive? Unfortunate though I was, up until now I could think, 'I'll see Chaireas one day and tell him everything I've suffered on his account. It will make him honor me more. How full of joy he'll be when he sees our son!' Now it's all been rendered pointless, and I've got the child on top of it all. Without a father he's just another addition to my troubles. Aphrodite, unjust goddess, you alone saw Chaireas, but you didn't show him to me when he came. You delivered his handsome body up to the hands of pirates. You didn't pity him, though it was your fault he was making this voyage. Who could pray to such a goddess, one who[117] killed her own suppliant? You didn't help during that fearful night you watched a handsome young man, a lover, get murdered right next to you. You deprived me of my companion, my fellow citizen, my lover, my beloved, my husband. Return him to me, even if only his body. I grant that we were born the unluckiest people in the world, but what crime did the trireme commit that barbarians had to burn it? Not even the Athenians defeated it! Now our parents are sitting by the sea, waiting for us to sail home. Whenever they see a ship far off, they say, 'Chaireas is coming with Callirhoe!' They're preparing our marriage bed. They're decorating a room for us, though we don't even have a tomb. Foul sea, you brought Chaireas to Miletos so he could be killed, and me so I could be sold."

---

116. "to die . . . with you": This may be an echo of Plato, *Symposium* 180a1–2.

117. "Who could . . . one who": The beginning of this question is a citation of Euripides, *Heracles* 1307–1308.

Book 4

[1] Callirhoe passed this night in lamentation,[118] mourning for Chaireas though he was still alive.[119] She had just nodded off when she dreamed that she saw a band of barbarian pirates carrying torches, a trireme being set on fire, and herself helping Chaireas. As he watched his wife wearing herself out, it pained Dionysios to think that her beauty might somehow be diminished as well, but he thought it could only help his own love if she accepted with certainty that she had lost her first husband. So, wanting to demonstrate his love and his generosity, he said to her, "Get up, my dear, and prepare a tomb for the poor man. Why do you worry about what is impossible while ignoring what is indispensable? Imagine he was here, telling you, 'Bury me so that as soon as possible I may pass beyond Hades' gates!'[120] Even if the unfortunate man's body hasn't been recovered, still, we Greeks have an old custom of honoring with tombs even those who have disappeared."[121]

He quickly won her over since his advice was to her liking. The idea made an impression on her, and her grief subsided. Rising from her bed, she began to look for the place where she would have the tomb built. She settled on a spot near Aphrodite's temple so the people there might have a monument of love.

But out of jealousy Dionysios did not want Chaireas to be so close, and he had been saving this spot for himself. At the same time he also wanted something to occupy her thoughts, so he said, "My dear, let's go to the city. There, in front of the city, let's build a tomb high enough to be seen for miles, so that from the open sea it may be conspicuous to men.[122] Miletos has excellent harbors, and even Syracusans often come to anchor in them. That way your munificence will become known also among your fellow citizens."

---

118. "Callirhoe . . . in lamentation": The opening words of this book recall the closing sentence of the first book of Xenophon's *Anabasis* 1.10.19.

119. "mourning . . . still alive": The words here imitate Isocrates' description, in his *Encomium to Helen* 25, of the legendary Athenian youths who were sent to their deaths in the Minotaur's labyrinth, "mourned though they were still alive."

120. "Bury me . . . Hades' gates": A citation of Homer, *Iliad* 23.71, where the spirit of Patroclos appears to Achilles.

121. Chariton plays with elements from Euripides' *Helen* here. In that play the action hinges on Helen holding funeral rites for Menelaos, who is actually still alive. To do so she convinces the Egyptian king that it is "a custom among the Greeks" (1241) to perform a ceremony for those who die at sea.

122. "so that . . . to men": A citation of Homer, *Odyssey* 24.83.

Callirhoe liked his proposal but restrained her eagerness for the moment. Once she arrived at the city, however, on a high spot on the coast she began to build a tomb in every way like her own in Syracuse—in plan, in size, and in richness of decoration. This one, like the other, was for someone who was alive. No expense was spared and many hands worked on it, so it was completed quickly. Then Callirhoe replicated the funeral that had been held for her. A day was set and announced in advance, and not only did the people of Miletos come for the funeral, but so did nearly the whole population of Ionia. There were even two satraps who took this opportunity to visit, Mithridates[123] the satrap of Caria, and Pharnaces[124] the satrap of Lydia[125] and Ionia. Ostensibly they came to honor Dionysios, but really they came to see Callirhoe.

The woman's fame was great throughout Asia, and the name Callirhoe had gone inland to reach the Great King—farther than the names of Ariadne or Leda.[126] On this occasion she was found to exceed even her reputation, for she appeared in mourning black, her hair loose, her face radiant. Her arms and lower legs were bare and she seemed to surpass those "white-armed" and "fair-ankled" goddesses in Homer.[127] No one there was unmoved by her scintillating beauty. Some turned their faces as if a sun-ray fell on them, others actually knelt in reverence to her. Even children were not immune. Mithridates, the governor of Caria, fell slack-jawed, like a man unexpectedly hit by a stone from a sling. His attendants eventually had to lift him up and help him along.

A statue of Chaireas modeled on the seal stone in Callirhoe's ring was led in procession, but though this image was quite beautiful, no one looked at it with Callirhoe present. She alone mesmerized the eyes of all.

How could anyone fittingly tell how the procession ended? When they came near the tomb, the men carrying the bier put it down, and Callirhoe climbed on it by herself, embraced and kissed the statue, and said, "You buried me first in Syracuse. Now it's my turn to bury you in Miletos. It's not just that we suffer misfortunes that are serious— they're unbelievable. We've buried each other, but neither of us even

---

123. For the Greeks this was a typical Persian name. It was held by, among others, one of Cyros' companions in Xenophon's *Anabasis*.

124. Another typical Persian name held by several important historical figures.

125. The inland region to the east of central Ionia.

126. Leda was in Greek myth a lover of Zeus and the mother of Helen of Sparta.

127. In the *Iliad* Hera is frequently referred to as "white-armed Hera" and several goddesses are "fair-ankled" in the Homeric poems.

has the other's body. Resentful Fortune, even in death you've denied that we might be covered together by the earth.[128] You've driven even our corpses into exile."

The crowd broke out in lamentation,* and everybody pitied Chaireas, not because he was dead, but because he had lost a wife like her.

[2] While Callirhoe was burying Chaireas in Miletos, Chaireas was slaving away in chains in Caria. As he dug, he was quickly wearing himself out physically because many things were weighing on him: beatings, neglect, his chains, and, even more than these, his love. A certain slender hope[129] that he would perhaps one day see Callirhoe would not let him die, though he wanted to.

When Polycharmos, Chaireas' friend who had been taken captive with him, saw that he was unable to work and was being beaten and cruelly abused, he spoke to their foreman. "Give us a separate section all to ourselves. That way the laziness of the other prisoners won't be counted against us. The two of us by ourselves will do our own share of the work every day."

The foreman agreed and gave his permission. Since Polycharmos was physically strong and not a slave to that harsh tyrant Eros,[130] he did practically both their shares by himself, happy to take a larger part of the work if it kept his friend alive. Such was their plight as at last they realized what it meant to lose their freedom.[131]

The satrap Mithridates returned to Caria a different man than the one who had set out for Miletos, now pale and thin as if he had a piercing, hot wound in his soul. Melting with love for Callirhoe, he doubtless would have died if he had not obtained the following relief.

Some of the workers shackled with Chaireas—there were sixteen of them cooped up in a dark little cell—broke through their chains at night, slit the foreman's throat, and then ran for it. They did not make it because the dogs barked and gave them away. After they were caught, they were all bound more securely in wooden stocks for that night.

At daybreak the estate manager went and informed his master of what had happened. Mithridates neither saw the prisoners nor listened to any

---

128. "covered . . . earth": The wording is from Xenophon, *Cyropaideia* 6.4.6.

129. "A certain slender hope": This echoes Aristophanes, *Knights* 1244, which is cited as proverbial by later sources.

130. "tyrant Eros": For Eros as tyrant compare Euripides, *Hippolytos* 538 and *Andromache* fr. 136 and Plato, *Republic* 573b7 and 573d4.

131. "at last . . . freedom": A citation of Aeschines, *In Ctesiphontem* 157 (also imitated earlier at 2.3.6).

defense but immediately ordered the sixteen cellmates to be crucified. They were brought forth bound together by their feet and necks, each of them bearing his own cross. The men in charge of the punishment added this gloomy public spectacle to the strictly necessary penalty as an example to frighten the other slaves. As he was led away with the others, Chaireas said nothing, but Polycharmos, when he picked up his cross, said, "Callirhoe, it's your fault we're going through this. You're responsible for all our troubles."[132]

When the estate manager heard him say this, he thought some woman had been in on the crime. So that she could also be punished and an investigation made into the plot, the manager quickly took Polycharmos off the chain that bound the prisoners together and took him to Mithridates. He was sitting alone in a garden, depressed, painting a picture of Callirhoe in his mind as she had been when he had seen her in mourning. He was entirely absorbed in that thought and was none too happy to see his servant.

"Why are you bothering me?" he asked.

"I had to, master," the estate manager said. "I've discovered the source of their daring crime, and this damned guy knows a nasty woman who helped commit the murder."

Mithridates furrowed his brow when he heard this and gave Polycharmos a dangerous look. "Tell me the name of the woman who knew about this and was your accomplice in your crimes."

Polycharmos said that he did not know since he had not been involved in any way in what had happened. Whips were called for and fire brought and implements of torture were readied. One of the men grabbed him bodily and said, "Tell us the name of the woman, the one you admitted was the 'cause of your trouble.'"

Polycharmos said, "Callirhoe."

The name struck Mithridates, and he thought the fact that the woman had the same name was a bit of bad luck. He was no longer willing to eagerly pursue the interrogation, afraid that he might at some point be forced to sully that most pleasing name. His friends and servants, however, were urging him to investigate the matter more carefully, so he said, "Have Callirhoe come here."

Then they beat Polycharmos and asked him who she was and where they could go get her. The poor man did not know what to do, but he was unwilling to falsely accuse some woman. "Why are you wasting your time by making such a big deal about finding a woman who isn't

---

132. "responsible . . . troubles": The third echo of Lysias 1.7. See Chariton earlier at 2.2.6 and 3.8.3 and later at 6.6.4.

even here? I was talking about Callirhoe of Syracuse, the daughter of the general Hermocrates."

When Mithridates heard this, he turned bright red, and a sweat built up inside him. At one point a tear slipped out of his eye in spite of himself. That made Polycharmos stop talking and baffled everyone else who was there.

Eventually Mithridates managed to pull himself together and said, "What's your connection with that Callirhoe? And why did you mention her name when you were about to be executed?"

"It's a long story, master, and it won't do me any good at this point. I won't bother you by rambling on about it. It's not really the right time for it. Besides, I'm afraid that if I take too long, my friend will go before me, and I want to share his death, as well."

The anger of those who heard this reversed direction as their feelings switched to pity. Of all of them Mithridates was the most moved, and he said, "Have no fear. You won't be bothering me with your story. I have a compassionate heart. Don't worry. Tell me everything and leave nothing out. Who are you? Where are you from? How did you get to Caria, and why were you in chains on a digging crew? Above all, tell me about Callirhoe and who your friend is."

[3] Polycharmos began his story. "We—the two prisoners—are Syracusans. The other young man was once the outstanding man in Sicily for reputation, wealth, and good looks. I, on the other hand, was no one special, just a friend of his from school. We left our parents and sailed from our country. I came because of him, while he came because of his wife. Her name is Callirhoe. Thinking she was dead, he had given her a splendid funeral. But tomb-robbers had found her alive and sold her in Ionia. This information was given to us by Theron the pirate when he was being tortured in our public assembly. So the city of Syracuse sent a trireme and envoys to try to get the woman back. While the ship was anchored at night, barbarians burned it. They killed many, but tied up my friend and me and sold us here. We were trying to bear our misfortune with composure, but some of our fellow prisoners, men we didn't know, broke their chains and committed murder. On your orders we were all being taken to be crucified. My friend wouldn't blame his wife even when he was about to die, but I couldn't help mentioning her and saying she was the cause of our troubles since we'd set sail because of her."

The words were barely out of his mouth when Mithridates shouted, "You mean Chaireas?"

"Yes, my friend Chaireas," said Polycharmos. "But I beg you, master, order your executioner not even to separate our crosses!"

Tears and groans followed his story, and Mithridates sent all his men after Chaireas so they could get him before he died. They found the others already hung up, but Chaireas was just going up on his cross. Still far away, they all shouted different things. "Spare him!" "Get down!" "Don't hurt him!" "Let him go!" The executioner checked his eagerness, and Chaireas came down from the cross disappointed—he had been happy to escape a miserable life and an unhappy love.

He was led off and Mithridates met him on the way and embraced him. "Brother! Friend! With this impressive but inappropriate silence of yours you almost tricked me into committing an impious deed."

He immediately ordered his servants to take the young men to the bathhouse and to take care of their physical needs. He also ordered them, once the men had washed, to dress them in nice Greek cloaks. Mithridates himself invited some friends to a dinner party and made sacrifices in thanks for Chaireas' rescue. The drinking went on for a long time, the hospitality was pleasant, and there was no lack of good cheer.

As the festivities proceeded, Mithridates, warmed by wine and love, said, "Chaireas, I don't so much pity you for the chains and cross, but because you've lost such a beautiful wife."

Stricken, Chaireas shouted, "Where did you see my Callirhoe?"

"Yours no longer," said Mithridates. "She's the lawful wife of Dionysios of Miletos. Now they have a son too."

When he heard that, Chaireas could not restrain himself and threw himself at Mithridates' knees. "I beg you, master, give me back my cross! You're torturing me worse by forcing me to go on living after telling me a story like that. Faithless Callirhoe, you are the most unholy of all women! I was sold into slavery because of you. I dug. I bore a cross. I was handed over to an executioner. Meanwhile you lived in luxury and celebrated a marriage while I was in chains. It was not enough that you became another man's wife while Chaireas was still alive—you also became a mother!"

Everyone began to weep and the party turned into a gloomy drama. Mithridates alone was happy at this turn of events, conceiving a certain lover's hope since he would now be able to talk and do something about Callirhoe while seeming to help a friend. "For the moment," he said, "let's break things up—it's nighttime now. But when we're sober tomorrow, let's think things over.[133] We'll need more time to give this our full consideration."

---

133. A sly reference to Herodotus' claim (1.133) that Persians deliberate over important matters first drunk and then, on the next day, sober.

After that he got up and ended the party. He retired as he usually did but made it known that the young men from Syracuse were to be taken care of and have their own room.

[4] That night was full of anxieties for them all, and no one could sleep. Chaireas was angry, Polycharmos was trying to comfort him, and Mithridates was taking pleasure in the expectation that, like a contestant who has drawn a bye in the athletic competitions, if he waited while Chaireas and Dionysios fought it out, he would walk off with the prize of Callirhoe without breaking a sweat.[134]

The next day, when the matter came up for discussion, Chaireas thought he should head to Miletos right away and demand his wife back from Dionysios, for Callirhoe would not stay there once she had seen him.

"If it were up to me," Mithridates said, "I'd say go ahead. I don't want you to be apart from your wife even one more day. You should never have left Sicily. Nothing bad should ever have happened to the two of you. But now that Fortune, who loves novelty, has arranged this gloomy drama around you, you must give very careful consideration to what comes next. Right now you're in a rush because you're motivated by your emotions rather than your reason. You're not at all looking ahead to what's going to happen. Alone and a foreigner, you're going off to the big city. Your goal is to take from a rich man—the leading man in Ionia, in fact—his wife, who is bound particularly closely to him. How exactly are you going to persuade him? Your Hermocrates is far away. So is Mithridates. They're your only two allies. They're in a better position to mourn you than help you. I'm also afraid of your luck in that place. You have already suffered terribly there, but that experience will one day seem golden to you.* Miletos was kinder then. You were put in chains, but survived. You were sold, but sold to me. But which of the gods will be able to save you now if Dionysios learns that you're plotting against his marriage? You'll fall into the hands of a tyrannical rival. Maybe he won't even believe you're Chaireas, though you'll be in more danger if he does think you're really you. Are you the only one who doesn't know the nature of Eros? This god delights in deceits and tricks! I think it would be best for you to gauge your wife's reaction by letter. See if she remembers you. See if she's willing to leave Dionysios or wishes to prosper the

---

134. In ancient combat sports such as boxing, when there were odd numbers of competitors, one would "draw a bye" and sit out a round. This rest period while the other athletes tired themselves out often assured an easy victory.

house of him who weds her.[135] Write her a letter. Let her regret. Let her rejoice. Let her seek you out. Let her summon you to her. I'll come up with a plan to get the letter to her. You go and write it."

Chaireas was persuaded, and when he was alone in a quiet place, he tried to write the letter but was unable because his tears were pouring out and his hand was shaking. But after weeping for his misfortunes, he eventually began to write the following letter:

"To Callirhoe from Chaireas. I'm alive—alive thanks to Mithridates, my benefactor, and, I hope, your benefactor also. I was sold in Caria by barbarians, the ones who burned my fine ship, the flagship, your father's. The city sent an embassy on it for you. I don't know what happened to the rest of our fellow citizens, but my friend Polycharmos and I were saved by our master's pity when we were about to be killed. But though Mithridates did me all these services, he undid them all with the pain he caused me when he told me about your marriage. Being human, I expected to die, but I didn't expect you would get married. I beg you, change your mind! I pour out offerings of tears and kisses over my words. I am your Chaireas, the man you saw when you as a maiden made your way to Aphrodite's temple, the one you lay awake for. Remember our wedding chamber and the mystical night on which we first had experience of each other, you of your husband, and I of my wife. But I was jealous. That's what happens to people in love. But I've made it up to you. I've been sold. I've been a slave. I've been in chains. Don't hold a grudge against me for that rash kick. For you I've even been put up on a cross, uttering not a word of reproach in your direction. So if you were still to remember me, my sufferings mean nothing. But if you feel otherwise, you'll be sentencing me to death."

[5] He gave this letter to Mithridates, and Mithridates gave it to Hyginos, his most trusted servant, the one he employed also as the administrator of all of his property in Caria, and he revealed to him his own love as well. In fact, he himself wrote a letter to Callirhoe in which he pointed out his goodwill and solicitude toward her because he had saved Chaireas for her sake. He advised her not to spurn her first husband and promised her that he would come up with a strategy for them to be reunited so long as she too approved of this idea. He sent three servants with Hyginos, as well as rich gifts and a great deal of money. To allay suspicions the rest of the servants were told that he was sending these things to Dionysios, but he ordered Hyginos to leave the

---

135. "wishes to . . . her.": A citation of Homer, *Odyssey* 15.21.

others behind when he got to Priene.[136] Hyginos was to make his way alone to Miletos disguised as an Ionian (he could speak Greek) to scout things out. Then, when he had figured out how he would handle the situation, he was to bring the men in Priene to Miletos.

He went off and started to carry out his orders, but Fortune did not opt for an outcome in line with the intended one. Instead, she kicked off a series of greater troubles. When Hyginos left Priene for Miletos, the slaves, now left alone and deprived of their leader, began to live the high life with all that money. In a small city full of Greek nosiness, strangers spending a lot of money drew everyone's attention. Unknown individuals indulging themselves in luxury, the townspeople decided, were certainly thieves and doubtlessly runaway slaves. So the general of the city[137] went to their hotel, made a search, and discovered money and extravagant clothing. Believing it to be stolen property, he questioned the slaves about who they were and where the goods had come from. Afraid of being tortured, they divulged the truth, that Mithridates the governor of Caria had sent gifts to Dionysios, and they produced the letters as proof.

The general did not open the letters because they were sealed on the outside. Instead, he gave them to some of his men and sent everything, including the slaves, to Dionysios, believing that he was doing him a favor. Dionysios happened to be entertaining the city's most eminent citizens. It was a splendid dinner party. At just about this point a flute was playing and the sound of people singing could be heard. In the midst of this someone handed him the letter:

"Bias,[138] general of Priene, sends greetings to his benefactor, Dionysios. Gifts and letters were being brought to you from Mithridates, governor of Caria. Some good-for-nothing slaves were ruining them, so I arrested them and sent them on to you."

Dionysios read this letter out in the middle of the banquet, taking pride in the princely gifts. He ordered the seals to be broken and began to read the letters. Then he saw it: "To Callirhoe from Chaireas. I'm alive." His knees gave way, as did his dear heart,[139] and then darkness

---

136. A city just to the north of Miletos.

137. *General* (*strategos*) in many Greek cities was a title applied to the highest civil official rather than to one with strictly military functions.

138. A bit of a joke. Bias of Priene was a sixth-century BC philosopher and one of the legendary "Seven Wise Men" of Greek tradition.

139. "His knees . . . heart": The beginning of this sentence is a citation from Homer, seen earlier at 1.1.14 and 3.6.3.

poured down over his eyes.[140] Still, even though he fainted, he kept his grip on the letters, afraid that someone else would read them. There was an uproar and people ran to him, and he came around. Fully aware of his calamity, he ordered his servants to carry him to another room. He pretended he just wanted to get a bit of rest.

The party broke up gloomily—the spectacle of an apparent attack put a damper on their spirits. Dionysios, when he was alone, read the letters over and over again. He was overcome by various emotions: anger, despair, fear, disbelief. He could not believe that Chaireas was alive. That was, after all, the last thing he wanted. Instead, he suspected it was some adulterous scheme of Mithridates, who wanted to seduce Callirhoe with hope for Chaireas.

[6] The next day Dionysios had closer watch kept on his wife so that no one could approach her or tell her any stories of what had happened in Caria. He himself came up with the following plan to get revenge. It just so happened that Pharnaces, the satrap of Lydia and Ionia, was in town at the time. He was considered the most important of the officials sent by the king to the coastal regions. Dionysios went to him—they were friends—and asked to speak with him privately. When it was just the two of them, Dionysios said, "Master, help me and yourself! Mithridates—the most evil man alive, a man who bears you a grudge— although he is my guest-friend,[141] is plotting against my marriage and has sent letters of seduction, as well as money, to my wife." He then read out the letters and explained Mithridates' scheme.

Pharnaces was happy to hear what he had to say, perhaps partly* because of Mithridates (there was a fair amount of friction between them because their territories were adjacent), but more because of love. Yes, he too burned with love for Callirhoe, and it was because of her that he visited Miletos so frequently and invited Dionysios and his wife to dinner so often. So he promised to help in whatever way he could and composed a letter for the king's eyes only:

"Pharnaces, satrap of Lydia and Ionia, sends greetings to his master, the King of Kings, Artaxerxes. Dionysios of Miletos is your slave, loyal and devoted to your house, as his ancestors were. He was complaining bitterly to me because Mithridates, the governor of Caria, is trying to

---

140. "darkness . . . his eyes": A slight modification of a Homeric formula (*Iliad* 5.696, 16.344, 20.421; *Odyssey* 22.88) echoed elsewhere by Chariton (1.1.14, 2.7.4, 3.1.3, and 3.9.10).

141. Guest-friendship was the formalization of close reciprocal ties that bound two individuals in a ritualized relationship of hospitality and obligation.

seduce his wife, though he is his guest-friend. This has the potential
to bring great disrepute to your government, and, more importantly,
unrest and upheaval. Every misdeed of a satrap is to be condemned, but
especially this one—Dionysios is one of the most powerful of the Ionian
Greeks, and the beauty of his wife is so famous that we will not be able
to keep the insult under wraps."

When this letter was delivered, the king read it out to his friends
and sought their counsel about what he should do. Different opinions
were put forward. Those who resented Mithridates or wanted to replace
him as satrap thought that the king should not turn a blind eye to
a plot against an eminent man's marriage. Those with more tolerant
personalities or who held Mithridates in esteem—and he had many
defenders—were not pleased with the idea of a noble man being arrested
on the basis of slander.

Since these opinions were evenly divided, the king put off his delib-
eration of the matter and made no decisions that day. When night fell,
he was overcome with revulsion as he thought about the threat to the
decency of his kingdom, but also with caution about what was going to
happen—Mithridates, he thought, was starting down the road of ignoring his authority. So he became determined to summon him to trial.
Another impulse urged him to send also for the beautiful woman. In his
solitude, night and darkness became his counselors and reminded him
of the part of the letter about her, and a rumor that a certain Callirhoe
in Ionia was the most beautiful woman also roused him. That was the
one thing he found fault with Pharnaces for—he had not included the
name of the woman in his letter. Uncertain whether another woman
could possibly be even more beautiful than the one in the rumors, he
decided to send for the wife as well.

He wrote to Pharnaces: "Send Dionysios, my slave from Miletos.
Send his wife along too."

To Mithridates he wrote: "Come and prove that you did not plot
against Dionysios' marriage."

[7] Mithridates was stunned by this and baffled about the source
of the accusation until Hyginos returned and told him what had happened with the slaves. And so, betrayed by the letters, he considered
not making the journey inland. Instead, he would capture Miletos and
kill Dionysios, the man responsible. Once he had gotten Callirhoe, he
would revolt from the king. "Why be so eager to place your freedom
into a master's hands? Perhaps you'll even prevail if you stay put.* After
all, the king is far away and he has worthless* generals. And even if he
should break faith,* nothing worse can happen to you. In the meantime,

do not give up the two finest things: love and power. Authority is a glorious shroud,[142] and death with Callirhoe sweet."

While he was still making these plans and preparing for rebellion, a messenger came with word that Dionysios had set out from Miletos and had Callirhoe with him. This was more painful for Mithridates to hear than the command summoning him to the trial, and he lamented his misfortune. "Am I to continue waiting? Hoping for what? Fortune is forsaking me on every side. Perhaps the king will take pity on me since I've done nothing wrong. And if I have to die, I'll get to see Callirhoe again. And if I have Chaireas and Polycharmos with me at the trial, they won't just be on my side—they'll also be witnesses."

He gave orders for his whole retinue to accompany him, and then he set out from Caria, confident that he would be found innocent of wrongdoing. As a result his people sent him on his way not with tears, but with sacrifices and pageantry.

And so Eros was dispatching both this first company from Caria and also a second from Ionia. The latter was more notable, for its beauty was both more remarkable and more regal. Rumor ran ahead of the woman, announcing to everyone that Callirhoe was coming—that famous name, that great achievement of nature, like Artemis or golden Aphrodite.[143] Report of the trial also increased her renown. Whole cities turned out to meet her, and the people who came thronged the roads to get a look. Everyone thought that the rumor did not do the woman justice. The more they congratulated Dionysios, the worse he felt, and the magnitude of his good fortune made him more miserable, for as an educated man he was well aware that Eros is capricious—this is why poets and sculptors outfit him with bow and fire, the lightest and least stable of things.

Dionysios kept thinking of old stories of all the infidelities of beautiful women, and so everything frightened him. He saw everyone as a rival in love—not just his opponent in the trial, but the very judge himself—and as a result he also regretted so rashly telling Pharnaces about it, when he could have been sleeping with his beloved.[144] Keeping watch over Callirhoe in Miletos was nothing like trying to do so in the whole of Ionia, but he managed to keep his secret until the end, not revealing

---

142. "Authority . . . shroud": Modeled on a well-known phrase from Isocrates, *Archidamus* 45, "tyranny is a fine shroud."

143. "like Artemis or golden Aphrodite": A citation of Homer, *Odyssey* 17.37 and 19.54.

144. "when he could . . . his beloved.": This is a citation of Menander, *Misoumenos* A9 (Sandbach).

to his wife the reason for their journey.* His explanation was that the king had sent for him because he wanted to consult him about affairs in Ionia. Callirhoe was distressed to travel so far from the Greek sea, for she thought of herself as being near Syracuse so long as she could look upon the harbors of Miletos, and she also had Chaireas' tomb there as a great source of comfort.

Book 5

[1] How Callirhoe, the most beautiful woman, married the most hand-some of men, Chaireas, after Aphrodite arranged the marriage; how out of jealousy Chaireas struck her and she was thought to be dead; how, after she was buried in a lavish funeral and then regained consciousness in the tomb, tomb-robbers took her away from Sicily at night, sailed to Ionia, and sold her to Dionysios; Dionysios' love, Callirhoe's faithful-ness to Chaireas, her being forced to marry because of her pregnancy, Theron's confession, Chaireas' journey in search of his wife, his being captured and sold into slavery in Caria with his friend Polycharmos; how Mithridates discovered who Chaireas was when he was about to be executed; how he was eager to reunite the lovers with each other, but Dionysios discovered his plans through some letters and accused him to Pharnaces, who made an accusation to the king, and the king sum-moned them both to a trial—these things have been described in the preceding narrative.[145] I will now tell the rest of the story.

Callirhoe coped well with the journey through Syria and Cilicia[146] since she could hear Greek spoken and look upon the sea that led to Syracuse. However, when she reached the Euphrates River, beyond which lies a vast continent, the gateway into the bulk of the king's territory,[147] then longing came over her for her country and family, as well as despair of ever going back. She stood on the bank of the river,

---

145. "these things . . . preceding narrative": Books 2, 3, 4, 5, 7 of Xenophon's *Anabasis* are prefaced with recapitulations that end with these words. Chariton is manifestly imitating this feature here (and also at the beginning of Book 8 later).

146. Syria was bounded on the east by the Euphrates, and Cilicia was the region to the west of Syria (in the southeast corner of Asia Minor). Callirhoe would thus have traveled through Cilicia before Syria on her way eastward.

147. "into the bulk . . . territory": A phrase taken word-for-word from Thucydides 2.48.1.

ordered everyone to withdraw except for Plangon, the one person she trusted, and began to speak.

"Resentful Fortune, so insistent on waging war on one woman, you shut me up alive in a tomb, and then you got me out—not because you pitied me, but so you could hand me over to pirates. The sea and Theron share responsibility for my exile. I, the daughter of Hermocrates, was sold and, far worse than slavery,* someone fell in love with me, so I had to marry another man though Chaireas still lived. Even this you now begrudge me. You no longer keep me in exile in Ionia. That was a foreign land you allowed me, but a Greek one, where I took great comfort because I was near the sea. Now you are casting me out of the very air I know, and I'm a world away from my country. You've deprived me of Miletos just as you earlier did Syracuse. I'm being taken beyond the Euphrates and, though a girl from an island, I'm being imprisoned in the furthest reaches of barbarian lands where the sea does not extend. Now what sort of ship am I to hope will come sailing from Sicily? I'm also being torn away from your tomb, Chaireas. Who is supposed to pour out libations for you, my dear departed? Bactra and Sousa,[148] that's where I'll live from now on and die. I'll cross you just once, Euphrates. I'm not so much afraid of the length of the journey as I am afraid that someone will think me beautiful there too."

As she said this, she kissed the ground. Then she stepped onto the ferry and made the crossing. Now, Dionysios had a large retinue since he was making the richest possible show of his means for his wife, but their treatment by the local inhabitants made their journey even more regal. The people of one town would escort them to the next, and satraps delivered them to the next in line—her beauty won over everyone. Another hope, that the woman would gain great power, also burned inside the barbarians, and because of this each was eager to give her hospitality or to curry favor with her for the future in whatever way they could.

[2] So that was how things stood with them. Mithridates, on the other hand, was traveling the quicker route through Armenia.[149] More than anything else he was concerned that the king would also find fault with him for following in the woman's footsteps,[150] but he was

---

148. Bactra (modern Balkh in Afghanistan) and Sousa (modern Shush in Iran) were important and well-known cities in the interior of the Persian empire.

149. The Persian Royal Road ran from Sardis in Lydia overland to Sousa in the east and provided quicker travel than the coastal route taken by Dionysios and Callirhoe.

150. "concerned . . . the woman's footsteps": The phrasing derives from Xenophon, *Anabasis* 3.1.5.

also eager to get there first and prepare his defense for the trial. When he arrived in Babylon[151]—that is where the king was in residence—he passed that day quietly in his quarters (all the satraps have individual lodgings assigned to them). The next day, however, when he went to the king's doors, he greeted the Persian Peers[152] and also Artaxates, who was the most important and powerful eunuch in the king's court. First he honored him with gifts and then he said, "Make an announcement to the king: 'Mithridates, your slave, has come to refute* the accusation of some Greek person and to show reverence.'"

A little while later the eunuch came back out and replied, "It is the king's hope that Mithridates is innocent, but he will pass judgment when Dionysios has also arrived."

Mithridates then departed after bowing in reverence. When he was alone, he called for Chaireas and said to him, "I'm on trial, charged with trying to restore Callirhoe to you. That letter you wrote to your wife? Dionysios says that *I* wrote it and supposes that he has proof that I wanted to seduce her because he believes that you're dead. Let him go on believing that until the trial, when you can make a surprise appearance. This is how I'm asking you to repay the favor I did you. Don't reveal yourself! You need to wait to see Callirhoe or find out anything about her."

Chaireas agreed—reluctantly—and, though he tried to hide his tears, they streamed down his cheeks.[153] "I'll do what you've told me to," he said, then went off to the room where he was staying with his friend Polycharmos. He threw himself on the floor and tore his clothes; taking dark dust in both his hands, he poured it over his head, sullying his fair countenance.[154] Then, weeping, he said, "We are close, Callirhoe, but we cannot see each other. You're doing nothing wrong, for you don't know that Chaireas is alive. I, on the other hand, am the most ungodly person in the world. I've been ordered not to see you, and I, too much in love with life, coward that I am, submit to the tyranny of it all. If someone had ordered you to do that, you wouldn't have gone on living."

---

151. A major city in the Persian empire, south of modern Baghdad.

152. Persian nobles of the highest rank.

153. "though he tried . . . cheeks.": An imitation of Xenophon, *Cyropaideia* 6.4.3 (imitated earlier by Chariton at 2.5.7).

154. "taking . . . countenance.": Another citation of Homer's *Iliad* (18.22–24), when Achilles learns of the death of his friend Patroclos. Compare Chariton 1.4.6 for an earlier and fuller citation.

Polycharmos tried to comfort him. In the meantime Dionysios was also near Babylon, and Rumor went to the city ahead of him, spreading word to all that a woman was coming, the likes of whom the sun did not look upon anywhere on earth, a beauty not mortal but divine. Barbarian culture is by nature woman-crazy,[155] and the result was that every house and every street was filled with anticipation. Word got as far as the king himself, and he asked Artaxates the eunuch if the woman from Miletos had arrived.

For a long time his wife's celebrity had been a source of insecurity for Dionysios, and now that he was about to enter Babylon, he grew more aggravated. He groaned to himself, "Dionysios, we're not in Miletos anymore. That was your city, and you could keep on guard against schemers. You were too impulsive! You didn't think about what would happen. Now you're taking Callirhoe to Babylon? Where there are so many more men like Mithridates? Menelaos couldn't keep watch over Helen in straitlaced Sparta. No, a barbarian shepherd[156] won out over him, though he was a king. There are many Parises in Persia. Can't you see the risks? Can't you see where this is headed? Cities have been coming out to meet us. Satraps have been paying court to us. She's already gotten conceited, and the king hasn't even seen her yet. Well, my one hope of salvation is to keep my wife hidden. She'll be safe if she can't be seen." Having made this calculation, he mounted his horse, left Callirhoe in the carriage, and drew the curtain closed.[157] Perhaps things might have gone the way he wanted if the following events had not occurred.

[3] The wives of the most important Persians came to Stateira,[158] the king's wife, and one of them said, "Mistress, a Greek girl is on the march against our women, who* everyone has, since olden times, admired for their beauty. There's a risk that the reputation of Persian women will come to an end in our time. We'd better get busy figuring out how not to be beaten by this foreign woman."

The queen laughed, disbelieving the rumor, and said, "The Greeks are full of it. And they're poor. That's why they're so impressed by the

---

155. "woman-crazy": The word Hector castigates Paris with in Homer, *Iliad* 3.39 and 13.769.

156. Paris, prince of Troy.

157. "drew the curtain closed": The language of the last part of this sentence is modeled on that of the scene in Xenophon, *Cyropaideia* 6.4.11, in which Abradatas takes his leave from Pantheia. See also Chariton 5.3.10.

158. The name of several historical Persian women (including two queens, the wives of Artaxerxes II and of Dareios III).

insignificant. They talk about Callirhoe being pretty in the same way they say Dionysios is rich. So let one of us be seen with her when she enters the city. That'll put an end to the penniless slave."

They all knelt in reverence to the queen and expressed their admiration of her idea. At first, as if from one mouth they cried out,[159] "If only it were possible for you to make an appearance, mistress!" But after that they could not agree on anything and began to name those women most famed for their beauty. There was an election, just as in an assembly, and Rhodogoune[160] was selected. She was the daughter of Zopyros and the wife of Megabyzos[161] and a very celebrated beauty. What Callirhoe was to Ionia, Rhodogoune was to Asia. The women took her and dressed her in fine clothes, each of them contributing something of her own to the outfit. The queen donated bracelets and a necklace.

Then, after they had outfitted her well for the contest, Rhodogoune made her appearance, giving the impression that she was there to welcome Callirhoe. She had a perfectly suitable excuse for this since she was, in fact, the sister of Pharnaces, the man who had written the king about Dionysios. All of Babylon poured out to get a look, and the people formed a huge crowd at the city gates. Rhodogoune waited in the most conspicuous spot, surrounded by attendants like a queen. There she stood, lovely, proud, practically throwing down the gauntlet. Everyone looked at her and said, "We've won! Our Persian woman will put an end to the foreigner. Let her show herself, if she can. Let the Greeks find out they're full of it!"

Just then Dionysios showed up, and when he was told that Pharnaces' kinswoman was there, he leapt down from his horse, approached her, and made his greeting. She blushed and said, "I wish to welcome my sister," and at the same time drew near the carriage. Callirhoe could not very well remain behind the curtain after that. Reluctantly, his voice full of embarrassment, Dionysios asked Callirhoe to come out. At once everyone strained not only their eyes but their very souls and practically

159. "as if . . . cried out": The military and political language here make this very likely an echo of Aristophanes, *Knights* 670, where the members of the Athenian council, worked into a frenzy over the price of anchovies, wrong-headedly cry for continued war. Compare a similar phrase in Plato, *Republic* 364a1.

160. An attested name of several Persian noblewomen (a daughter of Xerxes I, for example).

161. The names, though not the details of the relationships, come from Chariton's reading. A Zopyros, son of Megabyzos, is mentioned several times in Herodotus, Ctesias, and Thucydides.

fell over one another, each wanting to catch a glimpse before anyone else and get as close as possible.

Callirhoe's face shone forth, and it dazzled everyone's eyes, like a bright light suddenly appearing in the depths of night.[162] Stunned, the barbarians knelt in reverence and no one noticed that Rhodogoune was even there. Recognizing her defeat, Rhodogoune was unable to leave but unwilling to be looked at, so she slipped behind the curtain with Callirhoe, surrendering herself to the superior force to be carried away captive. The carriage moved forward with the curtain closed, and the people, no longer able to see Callirhoe, kissed the vehicle instead.[163]

When the king heard that Dionysios had arrived, he ordered Artaxates the eunuch to relay to him the following message: "Since you make accusations against a man entrusted with an important office, you ought not to have delayed. But I will not hold this against you because you were traveling with your wife. I am at present celebrating a festival and am busy with the sacrifices. I will hear the case thirty days hence." Dionysios knelt in reverence and departed.

[4] Preparations for the trial were being made on both sides as if for the greatest of wars. The barbarian public split into two factions. All those of the ruling class backed Mithridates, for he was originally from Bactra and had moved to Caria only later. On the other hand, Dionysios had the favor of the common people, for they thought that he had been injured contrary to the laws through a plot aimed at his wife—and, more importantly, what a wife! The harem of the Persians[164] was not uninterested in the matter either, and there too passions were divided. Those that prided themselves on their beauty were jealous of Callirhoe and wanted her to be humiliated by the trial. But the bulk of them were jealous of the other local women and prayed for the foreign girl to have honor heaped upon her.

Each of the litigants thought victory was already his. Dionysios put his confidence in the letters that Mithridates had written to Callirhoe using Chaireas' name—he did not for one minute suppose that Chaireas

---

162. "like a bright . . . of night": This comparison of Callirhoe's beauty is inspired by Xenophon, *Symposium* 1.9, where Autolycos' beauty affects those around him "like when a light shines in the night."

163. "kissed the vehicle": This is an echo of Xenophon, *Cyropaideia* 6.4.10, where Pantheia kisses the chariot of Abradatas, who is riding off to war in his chariot (see also Chariton 5.2.9).

164. The phrase here appears to be a colorfully exotic way of collectively referring to "the women of Persia" rather than a reference to the harem of the king alone.

could actually be alive. Mithridates was able to produce Chaireas, and so he was convinced nothing could go wrong.* Still, he pretended to be frightened and summoned advocates. His intention was to make his defense more spectacular through the element of surprise.

In those thirty days the Persians, men and women alike, talked about nothing but this trial; so much so that, if truth be told, all of Babylon was a courtroom. Everyone thought the delay was too long—even the king himself, not just the other people. What Olympic games or Eleusinian nights[165] ever generated such anticipation?

When the designated day arrived, the king took his seat. In the palace there is a special chamber, distinguished both in size and appearance, which is set aside as a courtroom. In the middle of this sits a throne for the king, and on either side of him chairs for his friends and all those who, by virtue of their rank and services, are leaders of leaders.[166] In a circle around the throne stand captains, commanders, and the most highly valued of the king's freedmen. As a result, in speaking of this council one might well say, "and the gods seated by Zeus' side met in council."[167] Those on trial are brought in amidst an atmosphere of fearful silence.

On this day Mithridates came in first, at dawn, escorted by friends and family, and looking not too happy or cheerful, but rather pitiful as suits a man giving an account of himself. Dionysios came in after him. He was dressed in Greek fashion with a Milesian robe and was gripping the letters in his hand. Brought forward, they knelt in reverence. Then the king ordered the clerk to read the letters, both the one from Pharnaces and his own reply, so that his fellow judges could find out how the case had come about.

After the king's letter was read out, a loud exclamation of approval broke out among the crowd as they admired his self-restraint and sense of justice. When silence was restored, it was up to Dionysios, the accuser, to begin, and all turned their eyes to him. But Mithridates preempted him and said, "Master, I am not trying to give my defense speech ahead of time. No, I am aware of the order of things. But all of the necessary parties have to be present for the trial before the speeches.

165. A reference to the initiation rites into the Eleusinian Mysteries at Eleusis near Athens. This was a cult of international importance in the Greek world.

166. "leaders of leaders": It sounds here almost as though Chariton is inventing a Persian title along the lines of the well-known "King of Kings." He perhaps also had in mind the phrase "officers of officers" from Thucydides 5.66.4.

167. A citation of Homer, *Iliad* 4.1

So where is the woman that we're having this trial about? You thought her necessary in your letter, and you wrote for her to come, and she came. You cannot allow Dionysios to hide away the crux and root of the whole business."

Dionysios objected, "It is just like an adulterer to drag another man's wife before a crowd against her husband's will when she herself is neither the accuser nor the defendant. Now, if she had actually been seduced, then it would be necessary for her to be present to give an account of her actions. But as it is now, you laid your snares for a woman who did not even know it was happening, and I am calling my wife neither as a witness nor as a supporter. So why is it necessary for her to be here when she has no part in the case?"

What Dionysios said was technically correct, but he convinced no one—they all wanted to see Callirhoe. When the king proved too embarrassed to give the order, his friends brought up his letter as a pretext, for she had been summoned as a necessary party. "How does it make any sense," one of them said, "for her to come from Ionia and be in Babylon but not be present?"

Now that it had been ruled that Callirhoe also needed to be present, Dionysios—who had said nothing to her earlier but had all along kept the reason for their journey to Babylon a secret—was alarmed at the prospect of bringing her suddenly into the courtroom without any idea of what was going on. Anger was his wife's likely response at finding out she had been tricked, so he requested a recess until the next day.

[5] And so they adjourned on that day, and Dionysios went back to the house. Being a rational and cultured man, he addressed his wife with words as convincing as possible in the situation, coolly and calmly going through every detail. To be sure, Callirhoe did not listen without shedding a few tears, but she wept a great deal at the name of Chaireas and was appalled about the trial.

"That was all I needed to complete my misfortunes," she said, "to go to court. I've died. I've been buried. I've been robbed from my tomb. I've been sold. I've become a slave. Look, Fortune—now I'm on trial too! It wasn't enough for you to unjustly accuse me to Chaireas. No, you've also made it look like I'm cheating on Dionysios! The first time you topped off your slander with a tomb; this time it's a king's courtroom. I'm the scandal of Asia *and* Europe! How will I face the judge?[168] What sort of things will I have to listen to? Treacherous beauty, that's why you were

---

168. "how . . . the judge": Literally, "With what eyes will I look upon the judge?" A recollection of Demosthenes, *In Aristogitonem* 1.98.

given to me by nature—so that you could get your fill* of false accusations against me. Hermocrates' daughter is on trial and she doesn't have her father to support her. Everyone else prays for goodwill and kindness when they go into court. Not me. I'm afraid that the judge is going to end up liking me."

With such lamentation she spent that whole day feeling depressed, and Dionysios was even worse off than her. When night fell, she had a dream in which she saw herself as an unmarried girl in Syracuse entering the sanctuary of Aphrodite, leaving to go back home, seeing Chaireas, then her wedding day, the whole city garlanded, herself being escorted by her father and mother to the groom's house. She was just about to kiss Chaireas when she bolted awake from her dreams, called for Plangon (Dionysios had gotten out of bed much earlier to prepare his case), and told her about the dream.

Plangon said, "Take heart, mistress, and be happy![169] You had a good vision. You will be freed of all worry, for as you saw things in your dream, so will it be in real life. Go off to the king's courtroom as if you were going to Aphrodite's temple. Remember who you are. Regain the beauty you had on your wedding day."

As she spoke, she dressed and adorned Callirhoe, and Callirhoe had a spontaneous improvement of her mood, believing she had foreseen what was going to happen.

At dawn it was standing room only near the palace and the streets were packed all the way beyond the city limits. Everyone was gathering, supposedly to listen to the trial but really to see Callirhoe. Previously she had surpassed all other women in beauty, and now she seemed to surpass even herself. She entered the courtroom, just as the divine poet says Helen appeared to those "around Priam and Panthous and Thymoites,"[170] the elders of the city. When she appeared, she created a silent wonder, and all prayed to lie beside her in bed.[171]

If Mithridates had had to speak first, he would not have been able to find his voice, for it was as if on top of his old wound he received another, more violent blow.*

[6] But it was Dionysios who spoke first: "I am grateful to you, sire, for the honor you have paid to me, to the faithfulness of this woman here, and to the marriages of all. You did not look the other way when a

---

169. "Take heart . . . happy": An allusion to Xenophon, *Cyropaideia* 6.4.10 (Abradatas encouraging Pantheia).

170. A citation of Homer, *Iliad* 3.146, when Helen appears on the walls of Troy.

171. "and all . . . in bed": A citation of Homer, *Odyssey* 1.366 and 18.213, describing the suitors' reaction to Penelope.

private citizen was the object of a plot by a man in a position of power. No, you summoned that man to trial so you could punish his immorality and depravity in my case, and provide a deterrent in other cases.

"The crime, it turns out, warrants a greater penalty because of who committed it. For Mithridates was not my enemy, but my guest and my friend. He plotted to get what was mine. And not just any old possession, but that which is more valuable to me than my body and soul—my wife. And he is someone who, if anyone else had perpetrated this against me, should have been the one helping me out, not just for my sake as his friend, but for your sake as his king. For you entrusted to him the most important office, and he has shamed it by proving to be unworthy of it. Moreover, he has betrayed the one who trusted him with the position.

"Mithridates' appeals, his power, his preparation for this trial—I am fully cognizant that we are not on equal footing here. But I have confidence, sire, in your sense of justice and in the laws, which you preserve for all equally. For if you were going to let him get away with it, it would have been far better not to have summoned him at all. Prior to this, everyone was afraid to go on trial, because their immorality would be punished. However, if someone is tried before you and is not punished, in the future they will think they have nothing to fear.

"My argument is clear and concise. I am the husband of Callirhoe here. I have already had a child with her. I was not her first husband, but she had another before, named Chaireas, long dead. He even has a tomb back home in Miletos. Mithridates came there and saw my wife—all perfectly proper since he was our guest. But in what followed he acted neither as a friend nor as a self-controlled, decent man—the sort you want those to whom you entrust your cities to be—but he showed himself to be debauched and autocratic. Becoming aware of my wife's faithfulness and her love for her husband, he decided it was impossible to persuade her with words or money, so instead he came up with a devious plot that could not fail to win her over—or so he thought.

"He pretended that her first husband, Chaireas, was still alive and fabricated letters in his name and sent them to Callirhoe via some slaves. But your divine Fortune, sire, appointed a good man,* and the providence of the other gods caused the letters to be uncovered. You see, Bias, the general of Priene, sent the slaves with the letters to me, and I, upon discovering the plot, informed Pharnaces, the satrap of Lydia and Ionia, and he informed you.

"That is the story of the affair about which you are sitting in judgment. The evidence is inescapable, for one of two things must be true: either Chaireas is alive or Mithridates has been proven an adulterer. After all, he cannot even deny that he was unaware that Chaireas was dead. No, he was in Miletos when we raised the tomb for that man. He joined us in our mourning. But when Mithridates wants to seduce another man's wife, he can raise the dead!

"I will end by reading the letter that this man sent from Caria to Miletos with his own slaves. Take it and read what it says: 'From Chaireas. I am alive.' Let Mithridates exonerate himself by proving *that*. Consider, sire, just how brazen an adulterer has to be when he is even willing to forge a letter from a dead man."

Dionysios' speech moved his listeners, and right away he had their vote. Infuriated, the king gave Mithridates bitter, severe looks.

[7] Then, completely unfazed, Mithridates said, "I beg you, sire, since you are a just and compassionate man, not to condemn me before you hear the arguments of both sides. And do not let this Greek here, who has cleverly concocted false accusations against me, be found more convincing in your eyes than the truth. I am aware that his wife's beauty gives weight to suspicions against me, for it will seem perfectly believable to everyone that a man would want to seduce Callirhoe. But I have lived the rest of my life in moderation, and this is the first accusation that I have had leveled at me. Even if my lusts were really so uncontrollable, the fact that you have entrusted so many cities to me would have reformed me. Who is such a fool that he would choose to lose such great advantages for the sake of a single pleasure, and such a reprehensible pleasure at that?

"Besides, if I were actually aware of having done something wrong, I could just have the case dismissed as inadmissible. Dionysios is not bringing this accusation on behalf of a wife who is legally married to him. No, he bought her when she was up for sale, and the law of adultery does not cover slaves. Let him first have the registration of her manumission read into evidence, and then and only then let him talk about marriage.

"You, Dionysios, have the gall to call 'wife' the woman that Theron the pirate sold to you for a talent after *he* kidnapped her from her tomb? 'Well,' he says, 'she was free when I bought her.' In that case, that makes you a slave trafficker, not a husband.

"No matter. I will now defend myself against you as if you were her husband. Pretend her sale was her wedding and the price you paid was her dowry. Let the woman from Syracuse be considered a Milesian for today.

"Sire, know that I have not wronged Dionysios either in his capacity as husband or master. First of all, he charges me not with a seduction that happened, but one that was *going* to happen. He cannot say anything about actual acts, so he reads out worthless notes. But the laws exact punishments for deeds.

"You show a letter. I could say, 'I did not write it. That is not my handwriting. Chaireas is looking for Callirhoe. So put *him* on trial for adultery.' 'Fine,' he says, 'but Chaireas is dead, and you tried to seduce my wife by using the name of the dead man.' Dionysios, you're challenging me in a way that won't do you any good. I swear it. I'm your friend and guest. Drop the indictment for your own benefit. Ask the king to dismiss the case. Retract your accusation. Say, 'Mithridates is guilty of nothing. I accused him wrongly.' If you persist, you'll regret it. You'll end up condemning yourself. I warn you: you will lose Callirhoe. The king won't find that I'm an adulterer—he'll find *you* are."

He fell silent at the end of this speech, and everyone looked back at Dionysios, wanting to know whether, given a choice, he would drop the indictment or stand his ground. They themselves had no clue what in the world the riddle posed by Mithridates meant, but they supposed that Dionysios knew.

But he was also in the dark and never would have suspected that Chaireas was alive, so he said, "Say whatever you want. You won't trick me with your funny business or your barely credible threats.* Dionysios will never be found to be making a false accusation!"

Picking up from there,[172] Mithridates raised his voice and, as though receiving divine inspiration, said, "Gods of the royal house, both above and below the earth, aid a goodly man who has many times prayed righteously and sacrificed lavishly to you! Render unto me the deserts of my piety now that I am falsely accused. Lend me the use of Chaireas, even if only for this trial. Appear, dearly departed spirit! Your Callirhoe calls you! Stand right here in the middle, between me and Dionysios, and tell the king which of us is the adulterer!"

[8] As he finished speaking, right on cue, Chaireas himself came forward. When Callirhoe saw him, she cried out, "Chaireas, are you alive?" and started to run to him, but Dionysios held her back and got between them and would not allow them to embrace.

Who could fittingly describe that scene in the courtroom? What poet has brought such an incredible story on stage? You would have thought you were in a theater filled with every sort of emotion. It all happened at once: tears, delight, amazement, pity, disbelief, prayers. They congratulated Chaireas, celebrated with Mithridates, grieved with Dionysios, were at a loss about Callirhoe. She stood there utterly bewildered and speechless, just looking at Chaireas, her eyes wide open.

---

172. "Picking . . . there": Perhaps an imitation of Homeric language, used also in 1.7.6 and 8.7.9.

I think that at that moment even the king would have wanted to be Chaireas.

Between all rivals in love, conflict is expected and can break out for any reason at all. In the case of these two, the prize was in plain sight and ignited their rivalry with each other, so much so that they would have come to blows if it had not been for the reverence they felt toward the king.

"I'm her first husband," Chaireas said.

"I'm a more steadfast one," Dionysios replied.

"How so? I never divorced my wife, did I?"

"No, you buried her."

"Show me the divorce decree."

"You can see her tomb."

"Her father gave me her hand in marriage."

"She gave herself to me."

"You don't deserve Hermocrates' daughter."

"You deserve her less after being in chains on Mithridates' estate."

"I'm demanding Callirhoe back!"

"And I'm keeping her."

"You're in possession of another man's wife."

"You killed yours."

"Adulterer!"

"Murderer!"

As they argued back and forth like this, everyone else listened and quite enjoyed themselves. Callirhoe stood with her eyes downcast, loving Chaireas, feeling sorry for Dionysios.

The king dismissed everyone from the room and consulted with his friends, no longer about Mithridates, who had proved his innocence beyond a shadow of a doubt, but about whether he ought to hand down a ruling regarding the woman. Some thought that the dispute did not fall under the royal purview. They assured him, "It was natural for you to hear the accusation against Mithridates since he was a satrap," but pointed out that everyone involved now was a private citizen. But most gave the opposite advice, both on behalf of the woman's father, who had proven himself quite useful to the king's house, and because the king was not transferring the trial from another jurisdiction to his own—it was more or less a part of the case he was already judging. They were not willing to admit the real reason—it was hard for those who saw Callirhoe's beauty to tear themselves away from it.

The king called back those he had sent out and said, "As for Mithridates, I find him not guilty. Tomorrow, after receiving gifts from me, he can leave for his own satrapy. As for Chaireas and Dionysios, each is to argue the legal claims he has to the woman. It is my obligation to take care of the daughter of Hermocrates, the man who defeated the Athenians, the archenemies of me and Persia."

When the verdict was announced, Mithridates knelt in reverence, but the other two men were overcome with confusion. The king noticed their perplexity and said, "I am not forcing you to speak now. I will allow you to prepare and then come to trial. I am granting a five-day recess. In the meantime my wife Stateira will take custody of Callirhoe. It is not fair to have the woman come to court with a husband if she is coming to court to have it decided who her husband is."

Then they left the courtroom, all of the rest despondent, but Mithridates alone happy. He received his gifts, stayed the night, and set out at dawn for Caria more renowned than before.

[9] Eunuchs collected Callirhoe and took her to the queen without giving any advance notice. When the king sends someone, there is no announcement. So Stateira was surprised to see Callirhoe, and she bolted up off the couch, thinking Aphrodite, a goddess she especially honored, was appearing to her in a vision, but then the other woman knelt in reverence. The eunuch took note of the queen's consternation and said, "This is Callirhoe. The king has sent her so that she might be under your protection until the trial."

Stateira was pleased to hear this and let all feminine rivalry drop away. The honor of the responsibility disposed her more kindly to Callirhoe since she was thrilled at having her entrusted to her care. She took her by the hand and said, "Take heart, my dear,[173] and stop crying. The king is a good man. You'll have the husband you want. After the trial you'll be married with greater honor. But go and get some sleep now. From what I can see, you're worn out and your spirit is still shaken."

Callirhoe was happy to hear this since she longed for peace and quiet. When she lay down and they let her rest, she put her hands to her eyes and said, "Did you really see Chaireas? Was that my Chaireas, or have I been deceived about that too? Maybe Mithridates produced a phantom for the trial. They do say there are sorcerers in Persia.[174] No, Chaireas talked, and he really seemed to know about everything he said. But then how could he stand not to hold me in his arms? We parted without even kissing each other!"

---

173. "Take heart, my dear": The first of several reminders of the Persian soldier's words to Pantheia at Xenophon, *Cyropaideia* 5.1.6 (telling her Cyros will marry her).

174. The famed *magoi*.

While she was going through this in her mind, she heard footsteps and the loud voices of women—all of them were hurrying to the queen, thinking it was a great chance for them to see Callirhoe.

But Stateira said, "Let's leave her be. She's feeling poorly, and we have five days to see her and listen to her and talk to her."

They left disappointed, but returned at sunrise the next day. On each of the subsequent days they did this so eagerly that the population of the king's house swelled. Even the king visited the women more frequently, supposedly to see Stateira. Extravagant gifts were sent to Callirhoe, but she accepted them from no one, maintaining the attitude of a woman who has suffered adversity—sitting dressed in black, with no makeup or jewelry on—all of which just made her more radiant. When the queen asked her which husband she would prefer, she said nothing in response but just wept.

That was Callirhoe's situation. Dionysios, meanwhile, was trying to bear his misfortunes valiantly, relying on the equanimity of his nature and the discipline of his education, but such unbelievable misfortune was enough to break even the bravest of men. He burned more fiercely than he had in Miletos. In the beginning stages of his desire he had been a lover merely of her beauty, but by this point many things fueled the fire of his love—intimacy, having children together, kindness, lack of gratitude, jealousy, and, above all, the unbelievable turn of events.

[10] All worked up, he shouted, "What Protesilaos[175] is this who's come back to life to oppose me? Which of the gods below the earth did I offend to find myself with a dead man as my rival in love? A man whose tomb *I* built! Mistress Aphrodite, you double-crossed me after I built a shrine for you on my property and made so many sacrifices to you. Why did you show me Callirhoe when you weren't going to let me hold on to her? Why did you make me a father when I wasn't even a husband?" Then he took his son in his arms and tearfully said, "My poor son, I used to think it was good fortune that you were born, but now I think it's bad. Your mother bequeathed you to me as a memento of ill-starred love.

"You're just a little boy, but surely you can sense some of the misfortune your father is going through. We've come on a terrible journey. We shouldn't have left Miletos. Babylon has destroyed us. I've been beaten

---

175. In myth, Protesilaos was killed after being the first Greek hero to set foot on Trojan soil during the Trojan War. He was allowed by the gods to return from the underworld to spend time with his wife, whom he had married just before setting out.

in the first case, which Mithridates turned around against me. And I'm even more afraid of the second case—this time the danger is greater, and the preliminaries to the trial have robbed me of hope. Without so much as a hearing I've had my wife taken away from me, and now I've got to compete for her with another man. What's worse, I don't know which of us Callirhoe wants.

"But you could find out, son. She's your mother. So off with you now. Go beg on your father's behalf. Cry. Kiss her. Say, 'Mommy, my daddy loves you!' But no accusations! What's that, slave?[176] They aren't allowing us to enter the palace? How terrible tyranny is! They're keeping a son from visiting his mother as an ambassador for his father!"

So while Dionysios spent the time leading up to the trial waging a battle between love and reason, Chaireas was inconsolably overcome with grief. Pretending to be sick, he told Polycharmos to go see Mithridates off since he had helped them both.

When he was alone, he tied a noose and got ready to hang himself with it. "I would be dying happier," he said, "if I were going up on that cross that was set up for me back when I was falsely accused as a slave in Caria. In that case I would be departing this life mistakenly believing that I was loved by Callirhoe. As it is now, I've lost not only my life but even the comfort of death. Callirhoe saw me, but she didn't come to me, didn't kiss me. I was standing right there, and she was worried about the feelings of another man. There's nothing for her to feel bad about. I'll preempt the trial. I won't wait around for a humiliating conclusion. I know that I'm no match for Dionysios. I'm foreign. I'm poor. The underdog from the get-go.

"May you be happy, dear wife.[177] Yes, I call you wife even though you love *him*. As for me, I'm going away and won't interfere with your marriage. Be rich. Live the high life. Enjoy the luxury in Ionia. Have the husband you want. But now that Chaireas is truly dying, I'm begging you for one last favor, Callirhoe. When I'm dead, visit my body and, if you can, weep. I will consider this even better than immortality. Get up close to my gravestone and say—and I don't care if your husband and child can see—'Now you're truly gone, Chaireas. Now you're dead. I was going to choose you in the presence of the king!' I'll hear you, my wife. Perhaps I'll even believe you. You'll increase my honor with the

---

176. The slave here is specified as the *paidagogos,* a servant put in charge of a male child.

177. "May you . . . wife": The words may derive from Euripides, *Helen* 163.

gods below. Even if in the house of Hades men forget the dead, yet will I even there remember you, dear one."[178]

He made that lament, then kissed the noose and said, "You are my comfort, my support. Victory is mine because of you. You have loved me more than Callirhoe."

As he was climbing up and putting the noose around his neck, his friend Polycharmos came back in. Unable to console Chaireas any longer, he had to physically restrain him as one would a lunatic.

And then the day of the trial was upon them.

Book 6

[1] Now that the king was only one day away from rendering his decision about whether Callirhoe should be the wife of Chaireas or Dionysios, all of Babylon was on tenterhooks. As they talked to each other at home and met people on the streets, people were saying, "Tomorrow is the wedding of Callirhoe. Who will the lucky man be, do you think?"

The city was split down the middle. Chaireas' backers argued this way. "He was her first husband. He married her when she was a girl, and they were mutually in love.[179] Her father gave him her hand. Her country buried her, he didn't leave her, and she didn't leave him. Dionysios didn't buy her, and he didn't marry her. Oh, the pirates put her up for sale, but it wasn't legal to buy her because she's a free woman."

Dionysios' backers countered this way. "He got her away from a band of pirates when she was going to be killed. He gave a talent to save her life. First he saved her, then he married her. When Chaireas married her, he killed her—Callirhoe should remember her tomb. And the greatest thing in favor of Dionysios' winning is that they have a child together."

Those were the arguments of the men. The women, meanwhile, were not just setting forth their views, but actually giving advice to Callirhoe as if she was there. "Don't let the man you married as a maiden slip away.

---

178. "Even if in the house . . . .dear one": Slightly adapted from Homer, *Iliad* 22.389–90, where Achilles has just killed Hector but cannot forget his friend Patroclos, earlier killed by Hector, and the second verse is "yet will I even there remember my dear comrade."

179. "and they were mutually in love": Literally, "her loving he loving," a reminiscence of Euripides, *Iphigeneia in Aulis* 75, describing Paris carrying off Helen.

Choose the one who loved you first, the one who's from your hometown, because that way you'll also see your father again. If you don't, you'll live as an exile in a foreign land."

But their counterparts said, "Choose your benefactor, the one who saved you, the one who didn't kill you. What if Chaireas gets angry again? Another tomb? Don't desert your son. Honor the father of your child."

You could hear so many people talking it over like this that you might have said all of Babylon was a courtroom.

That night was the last before the trial. The king and queen lay in bed thinking very different thoughts. She was praying for the day to come quickly so she could be rid of her somewhat burdensome charge—the woman's beauty was depressing when it could be compared side by side with her own. She was also suspicious of the king's flurry of visits and unusual sociability. Earlier he had rarely come into the women's quarters, but from the moment she had Callirhoe in there with her, he made routine visits. Even in the middle of their conversations she caught him glancing at Callirhoe on the sly, his eyes stealing looks at her, drawn there as if they had a mind of their own.

While Stateira was looking forward to the day with pleasure, the king felt very differently and lay awake all night long, now lying on his side, now again on his back, now on his stomach,[180] turning it over in his mind. "The day of judgment is here. I was reckless when I granted a short recess. So what I am going to do tomorrow? Callirhoe will go away to Miletos or Syracuse for good. Unlucky eyes of mine, you have only one more chance left to enjoy the loveliest sight in the world. After that, one of my slaves will be more fortunate than I.

"Think about what you have to do, my soul. Come to your senses. You have no one else to give you advice. Eros himself is a lover's advisor. First, make a choice for yourself. Who are you? Are you Callirhoe's lover or arbiter? Don't fool yourself. You're in denial, but you're in love. You'll be convicted on this charge more definitively when you cannot see her. Why are you willing to cause yourself grief? Your ancestor, the Sun, has chosen this creature for you, the loveliest of those under his gaze. Are you going to drive away the god's gift? Am I so very worried about Chaireas and Dionysios, my lowly slaves, that I'm rendering judgment about their marital status while I, the Great King, am performing the duties of a matchmaker like some old woman? But I fell over myself to

---

180. "now . . . now . . . now on his stomach": A citation of Homer, *Iliad* 24.10–11, where the words describe the sleepless anguish of Achilles.

accept the case, and everyone knows it. I'm particularly worried about what Stateira must think. Well then! Don't reveal your love and don't let the case come to a conclusion! It's enough for you just to see Callirhoe. Put off the trial. Even a regular judge is permitted to do that."

[2] When day arrived, the servants prepared the royal courtroom as the people flocked to the palace. All of Babylon was astir.[181] At the Olympics one can see the athletes arriving at the stadium escorted by crowds of fans—that is just how it was with Chaireas and Dionysios. The elites of Persian society surrounded Dionysios, the common people Chaireas. There was no end of prayers and shouts for each man from his supporters, who called out, "You're the better man! You'll win!" But the prize was not wild olive, or apples, or pine,[182] but the greatest beauty, over which even the gods would have contested.

The king summoned the eunuch Artaxates, the most powerful man in his court, and said, "The gods of the royal family have appeared to me in a dream and demanded sacrifices. I must discharge my religious duties before anything else. I want you to make a proclamation. All Asia is to celebrate a holy month of thirty days and is not to conduct any legal or business affairs."

The eunuch announced the king's directive, and immediately the whole city was full of garlanded crowds making sacrifices. Flutes trilled, pan-pipes warbled, and the sound of singing could be heard. Incense was burned in doorways, all the city streets turned into a celebration, and the savor of meat rose heavenward, entwined with the smoke.[183] The king furnished the altars with lavish sacrifices. For the very first time he even sacrificed to Eros and earnestly begged Aphrodite to intercede for him with her son.

While everyone else was in this festive mood, three people alone were troubled—Callirhoe, Dionysios, and, even more than these two, Chaireas. Callirhoe could not openly express her grief in the palace, but she would softly and discreetly sigh and curse the festival.

Dionysios cursed himself for ever leaving Miletos. "Stubborn fool! Now you'll have to deal with the disaster you brought on yourself.

---

181. "was astir": The verb here may be recollected from Herodotus 7.1.2.

182. These are the prizes for victory in the Olympic, Pythian, and Isthmian athletic games, respectively. The apples were added as prizes in the Pythian games at some point in or a little before the early first century AD. If future discoveries allow us to date this change precisely, that would provide us with a date after which Chariton must have been writing.

183. "the savor . . . the smoke": A citation of Homer, *Iliad* 1.317.

There's no one to blame but you. You could've held on to Callirhoe even with Chaireas alive. You were in charge in Miletos. There was no way the letter could've been given to Callirhoe without your say-so. Who would have seen her? Who would've gotten close to her? But you went and threw yourself into the middle of your enemies. If only it was just yourself—but now the one thing you have that means more to you than your own soul is at risk. Thanks to that, battle is brewing all around you. You idiot! Do you still* think that Chaireas is your opponent in this trial? You've made your master your opponent in love. Now the king is even seeing dreams, and the gods are demanding sacrifices from him when he already sacrifices to them every day! What shameful behavior for someone to keep putting off the trial when he has another man's wife in his house and for a man like that to call himself a judge!"

That was the lament of Dionysios. Meanwhile, Chaireas, who had absolutely no desire to go on living, would not touch food. His friend Polycharmos tried to keep him from starving himself, but Chaireas just said, "On the outside you seem like a friend, but really you're my greatest enemy in the world. While I'm being tortured, you keep me from doing anything, and you like to watch while I'm being abused. If you were really my friend, you wouldn't begrudge me my freedom when I'm being persecuted by a cruel god. How many chances at good fortune have you lost for me? I would've been happy if I'd been buried with Callirhoe in her tomb in Syracuse. But *you* kept me from dying then, even though I wanted to, and you robbed me of a happy reunion. Maybe she wouldn't have abandoned my body and left the tomb. But even if she had, I'd be lying there and would've avoided what came after: being sold, pirates, chains, the cross, and the king, who's worse than the cross. Sweet death! If I'd died, I wouldn't have heard about Callirhoe's second marriage.

"And you also destroyed a perfectly good chance for me to starve myself after the trial. I saw Callirhoe, but I didn't go to her. I didn't kiss her. What a strange thing—it's hard to believe there's a trial to decide if Chaireas is Callirhoe's husband! But the envious god isn't even letting that trial, such as it is, come to a conclusion. In both dreams and in real life the gods hate me."

With that he made a move for his sword, but Polycharmos grabbed his hand and did everything but tie him up to keep him safe.[184]

---

184. "made a move for his sword . . . safe": In Xenophon, *Memorabilia* 4.2.17, taking a sword from a suicidal friend is noted as an example of just behavior.

[3] The king called the eunuch, who was the person he most trusted in the world. At first he displayed some embarrassment in front of him, but when Artaxates saw that he was blushing deeply and wanted to say something, he asked, "Master, what are you hiding from your slave? I am on your side, and I can keep a secret. What has happened that could be so bad? I am so worried that a conspiracy—"

"A conspiracy, all right," interrupted the king, "and a vast one. Not a conspiracy of men, but of a god. I used to hear what Eros was like in myths and poetry, how he ruled all the other gods, even Zeus himself. Even so, I refused to believe that anyone could lord it over me in my own court. But the god has me beat. He has lodged powerfully and tenaciously in my soul. And while it's a hard thing to admit, in truth I have succumbed to him."*

As he spoke, he became so choked up with tears that he was unable to go on. He fell silent, and Artaxates immediately understood the source of his wound. Of course, he had had his suspicions before, aware of the fire that was smoldering. And, for that matter, he was absolutely certain that with Callirhoe around, the king could not have fallen in love with anyone else. All the same, Artaxates feigned ignorance.

"What sort of beauty," he asked, "can overcome your soul, master, when all beautiful things are subject to you—gold, silver, clothes, horses, cities, whole nations? You have countless beautiful women, not least Stateira, the most beautiful woman under the sun, whom you alone enjoy. Abundance puts an end to love. Unless, that is, one of the goddesses has descended from heaven or a second Thetis has emerged from the sea. After all, I am certain even goddesses desire your company."

"You may be onto something when you say that this woman is one of the gods," the king replied. "Her beauty is too great to be human. Only she doesn't admit it. She's pretending to be a Greek woman, a Syracusan. That too is a mark of her deception. I mean, she doesn't want to be caught in a lie by saying she's from one of the cities in our empire, so she sets the story she tells about herself on the other side of the Ionian and Mediterranean seas. She used the trial as a pretext to get to me. *She* arranged this whole drama. I'm surprised at you when you call Stateira the most beautiful woman in the world. You've seen Callirhoe! So we must figure out how to alleviate my distress. Leave no stone unturned to see if, in fact, it is possible to find a remedy."

"This remedy you are asking for, my king, has already been discovered both among Greeks and barbarians," the eunuch said. "There is simply no remedy for love aside from the very one that is loved. This is precisely the point of that celebrated oracle: 'The very one who wounded is the one who will heal.'"[185]

The king became indignant at what he said. "Do not ever so much as suggest that I seduce another man's wife. I abide by laws that I set for others and by the justice that I practice before everyone. Do not think for one moment that I have lost my self-control. I haven't fallen so low."

Afraid that he had gone too far, Artaxates turned the discussion to flattery and said, "Your thoughts are exalted, my king. Do not apply to your love the same treatment that other men do, but rather the stronger and greater cure of struggling with yourself. Master, you of all people are capable of overcoming even a god. Distract your soul with every pleasure. You especially enjoy hunting above all. Why, I have known you to take such delight in it that you can spend an entire day hunting without eating or drinking.[186] It is better to take up your time with hunting than to be at the palace, close to the fire."

[4] The king liked the idea, and a magnificent hunt was proclaimed. Both the Persian nobles and the elite members of the rest of the army rode out on horseback, dressed in their regalia. They were all a sight to behold, but the most illustrious of all was the king himself. He sat astride a very beautiful and tall Nisaean stallion outfitted with a golden bit; the cheek-pieces, frontlet, and breastplate were also made of gold. The king was dressed in Tyrian purple[187] (the fabric was Babylonian) and a headdress[188] dyed the color of hyacinths.[189] He wore a golden short sword on his belt, carried two javelins, and had a quiver and bow—of extremely expensive Chinese workmanship[190]—slung over his shoulder. He sat there resplendent (a characteristic effect of love is a fondness for

---

185. An oracle delivered to Telephos, a mythical king wounded by Achilles' spear during the lead-up to the Trojan War. The rust from the spear point provided the cure for his wound.

186. "without eating or drinking": A recollection of Xenophon, *Cyropaideia* 7.5.53.

187. The people of Tyre produced an expensive scarlet dye associated with royalty.

188. A *tiara*, the headdress restricted to the Persian king.

189. The distinctive color is a detail taken from Abradatas' helmet-plume in Xenophon, *Cyropaideia* 6.4.2.

190. Chinese goods had made their way into the Greco-Roman world for quite some time, but the word used here for the Chinese is attested in other literary works only from the first century BC on, in both Greek and Latin (aside from a single doubtful instance). This gives us some idea of an early boundary for dating Chariton, but the lack of attestation of a word is a weak basis on which to build such a case.

dressing up). He wanted Callirhoe to see him in the midst of all this, and as he rode out through the whole city, he kept looking around to see if she was watching the procession.

The hills filled quickly with men shouting, men rushing, dogs barking, horses neighing, and beasts on the run. The intensity of that commotion would have distracted Eros himself, for there was delight mixed with distress, joy mixed with fear, and pleasant danger. But the king saw no horse, though there were so many horses galloping around him, and no beast, though so many were being chased, and he heard no dog, though so many were barking, and no man, though all of them were shouting. He saw only Callirhoe, even though she was not there with him, and he heard her, even though she was not speaking to him, for Eros had come on the hunting trip with him. And, being a god who loves to win, when Eros saw the king was trying to fight him off and had come up with what he thought was a good approach, the god turned his own strategy against him. The very thing that was supposed to cure him Eros used to set his soul on fire. The god got inside his head and said, "It would be so great to see Callirhoe here, her dress belted high, exposing her calves, her arms bare, her face flushed, her bosom heaving, truly like the Archer Artemis moving over the mountain—lofty Taygetos or Erymanthos—delighting in boars and swift deer."[191]

Picturing that in his imagination, the king burned more fiercely < . . .

. . . >[192] and when he said that, Artaxates interrupted, saying, "Master, you have forgotten what's happened. Callirhoe has no husband. The trial to decide who she's supposed to marry is at a standstill. Remember: you are in love with a widow.[193] Don't worry about the laws—they apply to marriage. And don't worry about committing adultery—there has to be a husband as the injured party first before you can have the adulterer who causes the injury."

---

191. "like the Archer . . . deer": A citation of Homer, *Odyssey* 6.102–104.

192. < . . . > is used in this translation to indicate a lacuna, or gap, in the text where we have lost something and where I do not follow Reardon, the latest editor of Chariton, or otherwise feel confident in any scholarly reconstructions. Sometimes there is no indication other than unusual phrasing (a "jump" in thought) or disrupted syntax that leads us to believe something has dropped out. The manuscript at this point presents a nonsensical text and a gap, in which the king must have spoken to Artaxates. The extent of the missing material is impossible to determine, but it may have been only a few sentences.

193. A legalistic argument hinging on the idea that Callirhoe has no husband until the king decides who her husband is.

The king was pleased with the argument because it was right in line with his desire. Putting an arm around the eunuch, he kissed him and said, "I knew there was a reason I honored you before all others! You have my best interests at heart and protect me well. Now go and bring Callirhoe. I give you only two commands. Do not bring her against her will or bring her openly. I want you to win her over and keep it a secret."

Immediately word was passed along that the hunt was over, and everyone started heading back. The king, buoyed by his hopes, rode to the palace as happy as if he had bagged the finest prey. Artaxates, for his part, was happy because he thought that he had taken on a job that would please the king* and that he would in the future hold the reins of royal power, with both the king and Callirhoe grateful to him, especially Callirhoe. From the perspective of a eunuch, a slave, and a barbarian, he judged* the task an easy one. He had no experience of a noble, Greek spirit, especially not that of Callirhoe, who was faithful and full of love for her husband.

[5] Waiting for a good opportunity, he approached her and took her aside. "My lady, I have brought you a treasure of great blessings, and you will need to remember my good service. I am confident you are a person who repays favors."

At these opening words, Callirhoe became overjoyed. By nature what people want to be true they believe to be true,[194] so she thought she would soon be restored to Chaireas and was eager to hear about it, promising the eunuch she would repay him for the good news.

He began again, starting with a preamble. "My lady, you are blessed with divine beauty, but you have reaped no particularly great or impressive benefit from it. Your world-famous good name has until today found you neither a worthy husband nor a worthy lover. Oh, it's found two for you, all right. One is a poor islander and the other is a slave of the king. What great or splendid thing have you gotten from them? What fertile land do you possess? What valuable jewelry? Which cities do you govern? How many slaves kneel in reverence to you? Babylonian women have maidservants richer than you. But you have not been left entirely out in the cold. The gods have been looking out for you. That is why they brought you here, devising the trial as an occasion for the Great King to see you. Here is the first piece of good news for you: he liked

---

194. "By nature . . . to be true": Demosthenes, *Olynthiacs* 3.19 (also referenced at Chariton 3.9.3 in a slightly different form).

what he saw. In addition, I bring you up in conversation with him and say nice things about you in his presence."

That last bit he added because it is normal for any slave, when he talks to someone about his master, to insert himself into the discussion, thinking of the advantage he can gain for himself from the association.

His words immediately struck her heart like a sword, but she pretended not to understand and said, "I pray the gods remain favorable to the king, and he to you, since you are both taking pity on a woman who has suffered misfortune. Let him, I beg, free me from my worry quickly by concluding the trial so that I will no longer impose on the queen either."

The eunuch thought he had been unclear about what he wanted and that the woman had not understood, so he began to speak candidly. "That is precisely your good fortune, no longer to have slaves and paupers as lovers but the Great King, who has it in his power to give Miletos itself as a gift, or the whole of Ionia, or Sicily, or other even larger countries. So sacrifice to the gods and count yourself blessed. Do what you can to please him more, and when you are rich, remember me."

At first Callirhoe had the urge to rip out the eyes of the man trying to prostitute her, but since she was a cultured and coolheaded woman, she quickly considered where she was, who she was, and who was talking to her. She modulated her anger and put on an act for the barbarian after that.

"I certainly hope I'm not crazy enough to think that I'm worthy of the Great King! I'm no more suitable than the maidservants that Persian ladies keep. I beg you, please mention me no more to your master. You see, if he isn't already irritated at you, he will get angry with you after what you're doing now, when he figures out that you tried to set up the master of the world with Dionysios' slave. I really am surprised that such an intelligent man as you has failed to recognize the king's kindheartedness. He's not in love with a woman who has suffered misfortune—he's taking pity on her. Anyway, let's stop talking. I don't want anyone to spread rumors about us to the queen."

She hurried off, but the eunuch stood there, mouth open in astonishment. Having been raised under a powerful tyranny, he was under the assumption that nothing was impossible, not only for the king, but also for himself.

[6] Left all by himself and denied the courtesy of a reply, he went away full of countless emotions, angry at Callirhoe, distressed for himself, fearful of the king. Perhaps the king would not believe that he had talked to her at all, even if unsuccessfully. He would look like he was intentionally failing in his mission in order to ingratiate himself with

the queen. And he was afraid that Callirhoe would tell the queen about their conversation. Stateira would then be offended and come up with some awful plan against him for not only supporting the king's love, but also for taking an active role in it.

While the eunuch tried to work out how he could tell the king what had happened without getting in trouble, Callirhoe, when she was by herself, said, "I prophesied this. Euphrates, you're my witness. I predicted that I would never again cross you. Farewell, father, and you, mother, and Syracuse, my country. I will never see you again. Now Callirhoe is really dead. I left my tomb, but not even Theron the pirate will be bringing me out of another one again.

"Treacherous beauty, you are responsible for all my troubles.[195] Because of you I was carried off. Because of you I was sold. Because of you I married another man after Chaireas. Because of you I was brought to Babylon. Because of you I went to court. You've delivered me to so many things: tomb, pirates, sea, slavery, trial. And as far as I'm concerned, the worst is the king's love. And I haven't mentioned the king's anger yet. Yet, I think I'm more afraid of the queen's jealousy—Chaireas could not control his, and he's a man and Greek. She's a woman and a barbarian queen, so how will it affect her?

"Come on, Callirhoe, think up some brave plan, something worthy of Hermocrates. Kill yourself! Only not yet. So far you've just had the one encounter with a eunuch. If things get any rougher, then you'll have your chance to show your faithfulness to Chaireas when he's there to see it."

The eunuch did go to the king, but he hid the truth of what happened from him. He pretended that there had been no good opportunity and the queen was watching closely so he had not been able to talk to Callirhoe. "Master, your orders to me were to make sure that I was discreet. This was a very proper instruction since you have assumed the most august role of judge and want to be held in high esteem among the Persians. Everyone praises you for this very reason. But the Greeks are whiners and gossips. *They* are the ones who are going to turn this business into a public scandal—Callirhoe out of eagerness to brag that the king is in love with her, Dionysios and Chaireas out of jealousy. Besides, it is not worth it to hurt the queen. Not for a foreign woman whose beauty has been exaggerated by the trial."

---

195. "responsible . . . troubles": The fourth echo of Lysias 1.7. See earlier allusions at 2.2.6, 3.8.3, and 4.2.7.

He threw in this retraction in the hope of making the king forget about his love for Callirhoe, as well as to free himself from a difficult task.

[7] He succeeded in persuading him for the short term, but later, when night came, the king's love flared back up and made him think of what Callirhoe's eyes were like and how beautiful her face was. He sang the praises of her hair, her walk, her voice, the way she had entered the courtroom, the way she stood, how she talked, how she kept silent, how she blushed, how she wept. He lay awake through most of the night and got just enough sleep to see Callirhoe in his dreams.

In the morning, he summoned the eunuch and said, "Go and keep an eye on her the whole day. Surely you'll find a chance to talk to her without being seen, even if just for a few moments. If I'd wanted to satisfy my desires through force and with everyone knowing about it, I had guards for that."

The eunuch knelt in reverence and promised to do so (nobody can say no when the king gives an order). He knew that Callirhoe would not give him an opening and would steer clear of conversation with him by intentionally spending time with the queen. Wanting to deal with this, he blamed not the woman being guarded but the one doing the guarding by saying, "Master, if you are in agreement, send for Stateira and tell her that you have something you wish to discuss with her in private. That way her absence will give me a chance to approach Callirhoe."

"Make it happen," said the king.

Artaxates went to the queen and knelt in reverence, saying, "Your husband summons you, mistress."

When Stateira heard this, she knelt in reverence and hurriedly went off to see the king. Noting that Callirhoe had been left alone, the eunuch took her by the right hand as if he was fond of Greeks and full of compassion, and led her away from the crowd of maidservants. She knew very well what was going to happen and instantly grew pale and fell silent, but she went along with him anyway.

As soon as they were alone, he said to her, "You have seen how the queen kneels in reverence and runs off when she hears the name of the king. Yet you, her slave, do not accept your good fortune, nor does it please you that he requests the pleasure of your company when he has the power to order it. But I hold you in high esteem, and so I did not inform him of your lunacy. Just the opposite—I told him yes for you. You have a choice of which of two roads you want to take.[196] I will lay

---

196. "You have . . . to take": An allusion to Herodotus 1.11.2.

them out for you. Give in to the king, then get really wonderful gifts and the husband you want. Obviously he is not about to marry you himself—you will just be offering him passing gratification. If you do not give in—well, you know what the king's enemies suffer. They are the only people who long for death but cannot have it."[197]

She laughed at his threat and said, "It won't be the first time I'll have suffered something terrible. I'm an expert in misfortune. What can the king dole out that's worse than what I've suffered? I was buried alive! A tomb is more confining than any courtroom. I was handed over to pirates. At present I am suffering the worst evil of all—I cannot see Chaireas, even though he is here."

That statement gave her away, for the eunuch was naturally astute and realized that she was in love.

"You are the most idiotic woman alive! Do you rank Mithridates' slave above the king?"

It infuriated Callirhoe to hear Chaireas being put down, and she said, "Watch what you say, *sir*. Chaireas is a noble man, the leading citizen of a city that even the Athenians could not conquer—and they defeated your Great King at Marathon and Salamis."[198]

As she said this, she released a flood of tears, and the eunuch pressed her harder.

"You have yourself to blame for how slow things are going. Now, what could you do to get the judge to be favorable so that you can also get your husband back?* Chaireas would probably not even know what you did, and if he does find out, he will not be jealous of his superior. He will think you even more precious for having pleased the king."

He added that last bit not because of Callirhoe but because he actually believed it. All barbarians are completely awestruck by the king and consider him the manifestation of a god. But Callirhoe would not have welcomed marriage with Zeus himself nor chosen immortality over a single day with Chaireas.

Unable to make any headway, the eunuch said, "My lady, I am giving you time to reflect. Think not only about yourself, but also about Chaireas, who risks dying by the cruelest possible means. After all, the king will not allow himself to be surpassed in love."

He left, but the last thing he had said made a powerful impression on Callirhoe.

---

197. "who long . . . have it": A recollection of Xenophon, *Anabasis* 3.1.29.

198. Marathon (490 BC) and Salamis (480 BC) were the most famous victories of the Athenians during the Persian Wars.

[8] Fortune very soon put a stop to all reflection and discussion of love, having plotted a story full of quite novel events. Messengers came* to report that Egypt was in revolt and fielding a large army.[199] The Egyptians had killed the royal satrap and appointed one of their own as king, and he, marching out from Memphis,[200] had passed Pelousion[201] and was now overrunning Syria and Phoenicia.[202] The cities could no longer resist, as if a flood or inferno was flowing past them.

The king was disturbed by the news and the Persian people terrified. Despair gripped all of Babylon. Then the rumormongers and seers began to claim that the king's dream had foretold what was going to happen. The usual sorts of things began to happen, and people said and did everything one would expect in the context of a sudden war. A great upheaval[203] gripped all of Asia. The king accordingly summoned the Persian Peers and all the leaders of the subject nations who were in the city. It was his normal practice to consult with these men about important affairs. He asked them about the current situation, and everyone had a different recommendation to make. What they all agreed on was that they needed to move quickly and not, if they could help it, lose even a single day. They had two reasons. First, they would keep their enemies from growing stronger, and second, they would raise the morale of those on their own side by showing them that help was close at hand. If they delayed, everything would go entirely the other way. Their enemies would disdain them, thinking them frightened; their own people would capitulate, thinking themselves abandoned. They also pointed out that it was a great stroke of luck for the king that this occurred not in Bactra or Ecbatana[204] but had happened in Babylon,

---

199. Egypt frequently rebelled against Persian domination. Scholars have attempted to determine whether a single such historical revolt lies behind Chariton's fictional rebellion, but the question remains open.

200. A little south of modern Cairo, Memphis was a major administrative center and for much of antiquity the capital of Egypt.

201. The city on the eastern edge of the Nile Delta that marked the borders of Egypt proper.

202. The coastal region along the east coast of the Mediterranean that roughly corresponds to parts of Lebanon and Israel today.

203. "A great upheaval": The phrase recalls Thucydides' description of the Peloponnesian War as the "greatest upheaval" (1.1.2).

204. Modern Hamadan in Iran, this was the old capital of Media and one of the Persian royal residences.

close to Syria. All he had to do was cross the Euphrates and he would be right on top of the rebels.

So the king decided to march out with the forces he currently had at his disposal and send messengers in all directions with orders for the army to muster at the Euphrates River. Now, it is a very simple matter for the Persians to get their forces into the field.[205] From the time of Cyros, the first king of Persia, there has been a system governing which of the subject nations had to send cavalry for war and how many they had to provide, which had to send infantry and how many troops, which were to send archers, how many ordinary and scythe-wheeled chariots[206] each people had to send, how many elephants were to be sent and from where, and how much and what sort of material from whom. Everything can be gotten ready by everybody in the same amount of time it would take one man to get ready.[207]

[9] On the fifth day after the news arrived the king marched out of Babylon. By a general order of mobilization all the men of military age accompanied him, and Dionysios too was one of those who set out. He was an Ionian, and it was not possible for any Persian subject to stay behind. He had outfitted himself in armor of the finest quality and had formed a quite respectable contingent from the men with him. He positioned himself in a conspicuous place toward the front, and he made it clear that he was going to commit some act of valor, just as one would expect from a naturally ambitious man who, furthermore, did not think of bravery as incidental but as one of the finest virtues. In that situation he also had some misplaced hope[208] that if he proved himself useful in the war, he could dispense with the trial and receive his wife from the king as a reward for his battlefield exploits.

The queen did not want Callirhoe to be brought along, and for that very reason she neither made mention of her to the king nor asked what his instructions were regarding the foreign woman. In the same vein, Artaxates too kept silent because he was not sure it was the right thing,

205. Xenophon, *Cyropaideia* 8.5.2–16 (imitated verbally by Chariton in 6.8.7), contains a description not of the mobilization of Cyros' army, but of its order of marching, and this may be the inspiration for the current passage.

206. Scythe-wheeled chariots are described in detail in Xenophon, *Cyropaideia* 6.1.28–30, and mentioned elsewhere in that work.

207. The thought of the concluding sentence is clearly derived from two similar sentences in Xenophon, *Cyropaideia* 8.5.4 and 8.5.5.

208. "he also had . . . hope": The wording comes from Thucydides 2.51.6, also imitated by Chariton at 3.1.8.

with the king facing danger, to bring up his amorous amusement—that
is what he told himself, anyway, but in truth he was as happy as a man
escaping from a wild beast. He was even grateful for the war, it would
seem to me, because it interrupted the king's passion, which had been
sustained by lack of anything better to do.

The king, however, had not forgotten Callirhoe. No, even in that
indescribable chaos,[209] memory of her beauty entered his mind, though
he was too embarrassed to say anything about her to anyone—he did not
want to appear so completely immature by bringing up a pretty girl in
conversation during a major war. When his urge became overpowering,
he said nothing directly to Stateira, and he also did not approach the
eunuch, since he was all too aware of the secret of his love. Instead, he
came up with the following plan.

There is a custom that both the king himself and the Persian nobles,
when they are going to war, take with them wives, children, gold, silver,
clothes, eunuchs, concubines, dogs, tables, and all their lavish wealth
and luxury.[210] After summoning the official in charge of this, the king
began with a lot of preliminaries. Then he gave instructions about everything else. He explained how every detail should be handled. Last of all,
with an expression on his face that would not betray him, he mentioned
Callirhoe, as if it was a matter of little importance to him.[211]

"Oh, that woman, the foreign one I agreed to hear the case about?
Have her travel with the other women."

And so that is how Callirhoe ended up leaving Babylon, and she was
quite happy about it, for she assumed that Chaireas would also be leaving. War, she thought, brings many unforeseen events and changes for
the better for the unfortunate—maybe if peace came quickly, the trial
could be concluded without having to come back to Babylon.

---

209. "in that . . . chaos": A citation of Xenophon, *Cyropaideia* 7.1.32, also imitated
later in 7.4.9.

210. This seems to expand the statement in Xenophon, *Cyropaideia* 4.2.2, that "most
of those who inhabit Asia go on campaign" with their wagons and families, though it is
particularly the Hyrcanians, not the Persians, who are referenced there.

211. "it was . . . to him": A citation from Plato, *Phaedrus* 235a.

Book 7

[1] When everyone was leaving with the king to fight against the Egyptians, no one told Chaireas what he was supposed to do. He was not the king's subject and was, in fact, the only free man in Babylon at that time. He was pleased since he assumed that Callirhoe was also staying, so the next day he went to the palace looking for his wife. When he saw the palace closed up and many guards at the gates, he went around the whole city looking high and low. As if on the edge of sanity, he kept pestering his friend Polycharmos with questions. "Where's Callirhoe? What's happened? I mean, she can't have marched off to war too."

Unable to find Callirhoe, he began to search for Dionysios, his rival in love, and came to his house. A man came out and in all apparent sincerity* told him exactly what he had been coached to say. Dionysios, it turns out, wanted Chaireas to lose all hope of marrying Callirhoe and not stay around for the trial, so he had devised the following scheme. When he departed for the battle, he left the man behind to give Chaireas the news that because the Persian king needed allies, he had sent Dionysios to collect an army to fight the Egyptian king and, in order to secure his loyal and eager service, he had rewarded him with Callirhoe.

When Chaireas heard this, he immediately believed it, for a man in the midst of misfortune is easy to deceive. He tore his clothes and pulled out his hair, and as he beat his chest, he said, "Faithless Babylon, what a terrible host you've been. You hold nothing for me. And what a great judge. Turns out he's pimped out another man's wife. A wedding in wartime! And here I was, preparing for the trial, completely convinced that I would get to present my case. But I've lost by default, and Dionysios didn't have to utter a word to win.

"Well, his victory won't do him any good. Callirhoe won't go on living, not now that Chaireas has survived and she's separated from him. Sure, she was fooled the first time, but that was because she thought I was already dead. So what am I waiting for? I should be killing myself in front of the palace, spilling my blood on the judge's door. The Persians and Medes[212] need to know what kind of verdict their king has rendered here."

Polycharmos saw that he could not provide consolation in the face of the disaster and that Chaireas could not be saved. "You're my best

---

212. The Medes were a people closely related to the Persians and incorporated early into their empire. So close was the association in the Greek mind that *Mede* could function as a synonym for *Persian*.

friend," he said, "and I tried before to keep your spirits up. I managed
to stop you from getting yourself killed many times. But now I think
you've got the right idea. In fact, I'm not only not going to *stop* you,
I'm now actually ready to die *with* you. But we have to figure out what
would be the best way to go, because the way you're thinking of . . . well,
it will cause some criticism of the king and make him think twice about
how he acts in the future, but it's hardly payback for what we've suffered.
Seems to me that the death we settle on once and for all should be used
as an opportunity for us to get our revenge on the tyrant. It would be
great if we could do something that would hurt him enough to make
him really regret it all, and at the same time to leave behind a glorious
story for future generations of how two Greeks got back at the Great
King when he wronged them, and how they died like men."

Chaireas replied, "So how can just the two of us, poor foreigners that
we are, hurt the master of such great and numerous nations when we
have seen that he wields great power? He's got bodyguards, and then
he's got bodyguards in front of his bodyguards. So, let's say we do kill
one of his men, or we set some of his property on fire. He won't even
notice the damage."

"You'd be right if there wasn't a war going on. But now we know
that Egypt has revolted, Phoenicia has been captured, and Syria is being
overrun. The war is going to hit the king before he even crosses the
Euphrates. So it's not just the two of us—every ally the Egyptian king
brings is one for us. The same goes for every weapon, every piece of
equipment, every trireme. We'll be able to use another man's army to
achieve our revenge!"

His entire word was not yet spoken[213] when Chaireas gave a shout.
"Let's do it! Let's go! I'll use the war to make my judge pay!"

[2] They set out quickly in pursuit of the king, pretending that they
wanted to join his campaign. They hoped by this pretense to cross the
Euphrates without running into trouble, and so they caught up with the
army at the river, infiltrated the rearguard, and followed along. When
they got to Syria they went over to the Egyptian lines, and the Egyptian
king's guards took them into custody and questioned them about their
identity, since they did not look like messengers and were suspected of
being spies instead. Then they really would have been in serious trouble
if one of the men—a Greek, as they found out by chance—had not
understood what they were saying. They asked to be taken to the king,

---

213. "this entire word . . . spoken": A Homeric phrase (*Iliad* 10.540 and *Odyssey* 16.11)
found also in Chariton earlier at 3.4.4.

because they were bringing him something that would give him a great advantage.

When they were brought to him, Chaireas said, "We are well-born Greeks from Syracuse. This man came to Babylon for my sake, because he is my friend, and I came because of my wife, the daughter of Hermocrates. Perhaps you've heard of a certain Hermocrates, the general who defeated the Athenians in a naval battle?"

The Egyptian king nodded, there being no nation that had not heard of the catastrophe the Athenians suffered in the Sicilian war.

"Artaxerxes has treated us as a tyrant would," Chaireas continued, and then told the whole story. "So here we are, offering ourselves to you as faithful friends, two men with the strongest motives for courage: desire for death and for revenge. As far as my misfortunes go, I'm already dead. I continue to live for one reason, to harm my enemy. May I not die without struggle or glory, but after doing a great deed of which even posterity will hear."[214]

The Egyptian king was pleased to hear this. Taking his right hand, he said, "You've come at the perfect time for both you and me, young man!"

Immediately the king ordered his men to give them armor and a tent. It was not long before he made Chaireas a companion at his table,[215] then made him one of his advisors too, for the young man showed both prudence and courage, and loyalty as well, fully equipped as he was with an excellent nature and training. His eagerness to defeat the Persian king spurred him on and made him stand out, as did his desire to prove that he was not to be looked down upon, but worthy of respect.

Very soon he performed an impressive feat for all to see. In most ways success had come easily to the Egyptian king. He had taken Coele Syria[216] by storm and brought it under his control. Phoenicia was in his

---

214. "May I not . . . posterity will hear.": Chaireas quotes Homer, *Iliad* 22.304–305, Hector's words before his attack on Achilles, which leads to his own death.

215. *Homotrapezos,* "table companion," seems to be something of an official position. The word's use here might also raise the connotations of a glorious death, for in Xenophon's *Anabasis* 1.8.25–27, it is Cyros' "so-called *homotrapezoi*" who charge with him against the king when he is struck down, and in *Cyropaideia* 7.1.30, as Abradatas charges to his death in an attack against the Egyptian king, he is joined in his attack by "both his companions and *homotrapezoi.*"

216. Coele ("Hollow") Syria is the modern Beqaa Valley of Lebanon, but the name could apply more broadly to the region south of Syria proper.

power, with the exception of Tyre.[217] But the Tyrians are naturally a very warlike people, and they want to maintain their reputation for bravery so that they will not seem to dishonor Heracles, the most important god among them, to whom they almost exclusively dedicate their city.[218] They also have confidence in the natural defenses of their locale, the city being situated in the sea, with only a narrow causeway connecting it with the mainland to prevent it from being an island[219]—like a ship at anchor, with the gangway lowered to the shore.

So from any direction it was easy for them to repel the Egyptian king's attack. They were protected from his land force by the sea, one gate being enough to hold the infantry off, and from the naval assault by walls and harbors, the city being strongly fortified and locked up tight as a house.*

[3] With all the surrounding cities in enemy hands, only the Tyrians spurned the Egyptians, maintaining their goodwill and loyalty toward the Persian king. This rankled the Egyptian king, and he called a council—the first time he had invited Chaireas to one of their planning sessions. The king gave a speech.

"Allies—yes, I call you allies, for I would never refer to my friends as 'slaves.' You can see the straits we're in. Like a ship that's had a fair voyage for a long time, we've hit a headwind, and the impregnable city of Tyre is holding up our progress. The king's almost upon us, as we've found out. So what should we do? It's not possible to take Tyre, but we can't bypass it either—it's like a wall between us and the whole of Asia, blocking our way.

"I think it's best for us to withdraw from here as quickly as possible, before the power of the Persians reinforces the Tyrians. If we're caught in enemy territory, we've got real trouble. But Pelousion is well fortified. Once we're there, we don't have to worry about Tyrians or Medes or anyone else in the world. The desert is impenetrable, the way in is narrow, the sea is under our control, and the Nile is Egypt's friend."

Silence and despair descended on them all after the king's timid words. Chaireas alone dared to speak.

---

217. The resistance of Tyre, one of the most important Phoenician cities, and the subsequent events around the siege of it are modeled on historical events from the conquest of the region by Alexander the Great.

218. The Phoenician god Melqart was identified by the Greeks with their Heracles.

219. "to prevent . . . island": The phrase is a reversal of Thucydides' description of Sicily (6.1.2), which had only a narrow stretch of sea to "prevent it from being mainland."

"King—yes, I'm addressing you as king, for you truly are one, unlike the Persian, who's the lowest of the low. It breaks my heart to hear you thinking about retreating right at the moment of victory. We win if the gods want us to, and we'll take not only Tyre, but Babylon too. War is full of obstacles,[220] but the last thing you should do is try to avoid them. No, you have to attack them, always keeping your good hope in front of you like a shield.[221] These Tyrians that are laughing at you now, I'll bring them to you—naked and in chains. If you don't believe me, fine. Leave. But send me on a suicide mission first. Because as long as I'm alive, I won't be joining any retreat. And if you want to go on no matter what, leave me the few men who will volunteer to stay. And we two, Polycharmos and I, will fight, for we have come with a god on our side."[222]

Everyone was too ashamed not to agree to Chaireas' proposition, and the king, amazed by his spirit,[223] gave him permission to take as large a contingent of handpicked men from the army as he wanted. Chaireas did not make his choice right away, but mingled with the men in the camp and told Polycharmos to do the same. First, he tried to find out whether there were any Greeks in the camp. When it turned out that there were many mercenaries, he selected the Spartans, Corinthians, and other Peloponnesians,[224] and he also discovered about twenty Sicilians. When he had three hundred men, he spoke to them.

"Greeks! The king authorized me to pick out the best soldiers in the army. I picked you. After all, I too am a Greek. I'm a Dorian from Syracuse. We have to be better than the rest—not just by having better ancestors, but by showing greater bravery. I've gotten you together for a mission, and I don't want anyone panicking about it. We're going to find it both doable and easy, more difficult to think about than to carry out. The same number of Greeks stood up to

---

220. "War . . . obstacles": Chaireas' declaration is a citation from Xenophon, *Hipparchicos* 4.8, a professional manual for cavalry commanders.

221. "attack. . . like a shield": This is a modified citation of Demosthenes, *On the Crown* 97.

222. "And we two . . . with a god on our side.": A slight adaptation of Homer, *Iliad* 9.48–49, where Diomedes responds to Agamemnon's call for a Greek retreat by declaring that he and Sthenelos will fight against Troy alone.

223. "the king, amazed by his spirit": Perhaps a distant echo here of Ctesias fr. 1b (*FGrHist* 688 F 1b). See also Chariton 2.5.9.

224. These are all Dorian Greeks by ethnicity, as are the Syracusans, and had been arrayed against Athens in the Peloponnesian War.

Xerxes at Thermopylai.[225] And there aren't five million Tyrians, just a few. And their strategy depends on defiance and boasting, rather than on courage and good judgment. They need to find out how much better Greeks are than Phoenicians!

"I don't have my heart set on being commander. No, I'm ready to follow whoever wants to lead you. He'll find I can follow orders,[226] because I'm not out for glory for myself. I want it for all of us."

"Be our commander!" they all shouted.

"I'm commanding willing men," he said, "and you're the ones who've granted me my position. That's why I'm going to try to do everything possible to make sure you don't regret giving me your support and loyalty. For the present, with the gods' help you will become honored and admired, as well as the wealthiest men fighting on our side. For the future, you'll get an undying name for courage, and just as all sing the praises of Othryadas* and his three hundred or Leonidas and his three hundred,[227] so too will they proclaim the glory of Chaireas and his three hundred!"

The words were barely out of his mouth when every one of them cried out, "Lead the way!" and every one of them rushed off to get his equipment.

[4] After having them dress in their very finest armor, Chaireas led them to the royal tent. When the Egyptian king saw them, he was startled, supposing that he was looking not at men he knew but different ones. He promised them great rewards, and then Chaireas spoke.

"We'll take your word on that.[228]* And you need to keep the rest of the army ready to go, and don't advance against Tyre until we have it* under control, get up on the walls, and call you in."

"May the gods make it so," the king said.

---

225. Three hundred Spartans led by King Leonidas formed the heart of a force that resisted the invading Persians (whose numbers were wildly exaggerated in Greek sources, as the next sentence shows) in 480 BC. Leonidas and his men were ultimately wiped out.

226. "He'll find . . . orders": This recalls the thoughts of Clearchos and Xenophon in Xenophon, *Anabasis* 1.3.15 and 3.1.25, respectively; compare also *Anabasis* 6.1.29: "Know well that if you choose someone else, you'll not find me working against him."

227. Both Othryadas and Leonidas were famed Spartan commanders of contingents of 300 men from Herodotus' *Histories*. Othryadas (Herodotus 1.82) commanded the Spartans at the battle of Thyreai, Leonidas the Spartans at Thermopylai (Herodotus 7.138–239).

228. "We'll take . . . that": The wording comes from Xenophon, *Cyropaideia* 5.4.33.

Chaireas bunched his men together as he led them to Tyre so that there would seem to be far fewer of them. It really was a matter of shield pressed against shield, helm against helm, man against man.[229] At first they were not even noticed by the enemy, but when they drew near, the men on the wall spotted them and pointed them out to their comrades inside the city. The idea that they could be hostile was the last thing on their minds. Who would have thought that such a small group of men was coming against the impregnable city when the entire Egyptian army had not even been bold enough to ever attack it? When Chaireas and his men got near the wall, the Tyrians asked who they were and what they wanted.

Chaireas answered, "We're Greek mercenaries. We were fighting for the Egyptian king, but he not only didn't pay us our wages, he even planned to kill us. So we've come to you. We want to work together to get back at our common enemy."[230]

One of the Tyrians reported this to those inside, and the commander opened the gates and came out with a few men. Chaireas killed him first, then laid into the others, and he smote on all sides, and an awful groan arose from the Tyrians.[231] Each of them struck down a man,[232] like lions falling on an unguarded herd of cattle. Wailing and lamentation filled the whole city, and though few could see what was going on, everyone was panicking, and a chaotic mob[233] poured through the gate, wanting to get a look at what had happened. That was what most contributed to the destruction of the Tyrians, for those inside were trying to force their way out, and those outside were trying to escape back in[234] while

229. "shield pressed . . . against man": A word-for-word citation of Homer, *Iliad* 13.131 and 16.215, which were widely cited and mentioned in rhetorical manuals.

230. An elected general taking a city and doing so by deception is one of the just behaviors described in Xenophon, *Memorabilia* 4.2.15.

231. "smote on all sides . . . arose from them": Technically a citation of Homer, *Iliad* 21.20 (Achilles slaughtering Trojans), but a very similar line appears also in *Iliad* 10.483 ("he [Diomedes] slew on all sides . . . " rather than "smote"), where it is followed by the simile "like a lion attacking sheep without a shepherd"—which may have inspired part of the next sentence in Chariton.

232. "Each of them . . . a man": These words recall the description of a sack of a city in Aeschylus, *Seven Against Thebes* 340–41.

233. "chaotic mob": The phrase comes from Isocrates, *Panegyricus* 150, a passage that insists that barbarian peoples under Persian rule cannot produce good soldiers.

234. "trying to escape back in": The wording here is reminiscent of the description of the fighting during Cyros' capture of Babylon in Xenophon, *Cyropaideia* 7.5.26 (compare also *Cyropaideia* 7.5.29).

being struck and stabbed[235] by swords and spears. As they ran into each other in the confined area, they gave their killers just the opportunity they needed—it was not even possible to close the gates because of the bodies piling up between them.

In that indescribable chaos[236] Chaireas alone kept a cool head. After he forced his opponents back and got inside the gates, he jumped up onto the walls with nine of his men and from the top gave the signal to call the Egyptians. Faster than it takes to tell they were there. Tyre was taken.

After the capture of Tyre everyone was busy celebrating. Chaireas alone neither made sacrifice nor wore a garland.

"What good does a victory celebration do for me if you're not here to see it, Callirhoe? I'll never wear another garland, not after our wedding night. The way I see it, either you're dead, and it would be sacrilegious to wear one, or you're actually alive, but then how can I celebrate and feast without you?"

So that was how things stood with them. The Persian king, meanwhile, had crossed the Euphrates and was hurrying as fast as he could to engage the enemy. He had learned that Tyre was in enemy hands and was worried that Sidon and all of Syria would be next, because he could see that his enemy was now evenly matched with him. Accordingly he made the decision to travel not with his full retinue but pared down to the essentials so nothing would limit his speed. He took only the core of his army, leaving those who were too old with the queen, along with the baggage, clothes, and royal treasure. And now that the whole land was filled with tumult and confusion and war had reached the cities as far as the Euphrates, he thought it safer to keep them out of harm's way on Arados.[237]

[5] Arados is an island three and a half miles off the mainland, with an ancient temple of Aphrodite on it. The women could live there in complete security, as if they were at home. But when Callirhoe saw Aphrodite's statue, she went and stood in front of it. At first she wept silently, rebuking the goddess with her tears, but eventually she found her voice.

---

235. "struck and stabbed": The words are from Xenophon, *Anabasis* 3.1.29.

236. "In that indescribable chaos": A citation of Xenophon, *Cyropaideia* 7.1.32, which Chariton also imitated earlier at 6.9.5.

237. Modern Arwad, Syria. It was one of the three most important Phoenician cities in the Persian period (with Tyre and Sidon). No other source mentions it as a particularly important cult site of Aphrodite (or her Phoenician equivalent Astarte).

"Ah, now it's Arados. A little island instead of big Sicily, and none of my friends or family are here. Enough, mistress! How far will you carry on your war against me? If I really offended you in the worst possible way, you have exacted vengeance on me. If you really thought my unlucky beauty deserved punishment, well, it has led to my downfall. The one misfortune I had left to experience was war, and now I have. Compared with my current surroundings, even Babylon was kinder to me. There Chaireas was near. But now he is surely dead. There is no way he would go on living after I left. But I can't ask anyone what's happened to him. All are strangers. All are barbarians, envious and hateful. And the ones who love me are worse than the ones who hate me. Mistress, reveal to me whether Chaireas is alive."

The words were barely out of her mouth before she departed. Rhodogoune, the daughter of Zopyros and wife of Megabyzos (both her father and her husband were noble Persians), came and offered her comfort. She had been the first of the Persian women to meet Callirhoe when she entered Babylon.*

When the Egyptian king heard that the Persian king was nearby and ready for battle on land and sea, he called Chaireas and said, "I haven't had a chance to repay you for your first triumphs yet—I mean putting Tyre in my hands. But I've called you here to talk about what comes next so that we don't lose the gains we already have, which I fully intend to share with you. Yes, Egypt is enough for me—Syria will be your realm. So let's think about what needs to be done. The war is coming to a head on both land and sea, and I'm giving you the choice of whether you want to command the army or the navy. I would think you'd be more at home on the sea,[238] since you Syracusans even defeated the Athenians, and today your struggle is against the Persians, who were defeated by the Athenians. You have at your disposal Egyptian triremes, and they are both stronger and more numerous than the Sicilian ships. You ought to imitate your father-in-law Hermocrates at sea!"

Chaireas answered, "Any danger is welcome to me. I will undertake this war for you and against my greatest enemy, the Persian king. But along with the triremes give me my three hundred men."

"Take them and as many others as you want," he said.

Immediately his word became reality, for their need was urgent. The Egyptian king went to meet the enemy with the land force while Chaireas was appointed admiral of the fleet. At first the fact that Chaireas was not

---

238. "more at home on the sea": The wording derives from Thucydides 7.70.8, the climactic sea battle between the Athenians and Syracusans.

campaigning with them lowered the morale of the soldiers, for by this point they thought the world of him and expected great things from him as commander—it was as if a strong body had lost an eye. But the men of the fleet were lifted up in their hopes and filled with pride that they had the bravest and finest man as their commander. They did not make plans on a minor scale,[239] but captains, helmsmen, sailors, and soldiers alike all busied themselves to see who could be the first to demonstrate his enthusiasm before Chaireas.

That very day battle was joined on both land and sea. The Egyptian army held out for a long time[240] against the Medes and Persians, then, overcome by sheer numbers, they capitulated. The Persian king was in the saddle, in pursuit.* The race was on—for the Egyptian king to reach safety in Pelousion, and for the Persian king to catch him before he got there. Perhaps he might have made it too, if Dionysios had not performed a remarkable feat. He had exerted himself magnificently in the clash, always fighting near the king so that the latter could see him, and had been the first to rout the men who were ranged against him.

Then as the Egyptian's flight grew long, stretching to several days and nights, Dionysios saw that his king was upset about it, so he said, "Master, don't worry. I'll keep the Egyptian from escaping if you give me some handpicked cavalry."

The king commended him and granted his request, so Dionysios took five thousand men, covered two days' march in one, and fell upon the Egyptians during the night by surprise, taking many of them prisoner and killing even more. The Egyptian king was still alive when they caught up to him, but he killed himself, and Dionysios delivered his head to the king.

When the latter saw it, he said, "Dionysios, I am having you registered as a Benefactor[241] to my house, and now I also grant you the sweetest reward of all, the one you most of all desire: Callirhoe as wife. War has rendered the verdict. You have the most beautiful prize bravery can win."

Dionysios knelt in reverence and thought himself equal to the gods,[242] convinced that now he was beyond question Callirhoe's husband.

---

239. "They . . . scale": A verbatim citation of Thucydides 2.8.1.

240. "held out . . . time": The wording here may look back to Thucydides 4.44.1.

241. A formal title in Persia.

242. "thought . . . the gods": Perhaps a reminiscence of Plato, *Phaedrus* 258c2.

[6] That was what was happening on land. At sea, Chaireas won such a convincing victory that the enemy fleet could not rival him.[243] The Persians neither awaited the ramming attack of the Egyptian triremes nor made any sort of stand at all. Instead, some of their ships were immediately capsized, and Chaireas captured some intact with their crews after they were driven ashore. The sea was filled with the wrecks of the Medes' ships.

But the king was not aware of his navy's defeat at sea, and Chaireas likewise did not know of the Egyptians' defeat on land, each of them thinking that his side had been victorious on both elements. So on the same day as his naval victory, Chaireas landed on Arados, ordered his ships to encircle the island and secure it < . . . >[244] so that they could provide an explanation to their master.

They gathered the eunuchs, female servants, and the less valuable slaves into the marketplace, for it was quite spacious. But there were so many of them that they ended up sleeping not just under the colonnades but also out in the open. They took anyone of any importance into a building in the marketplace where the city government usually conducted business. The women sat on the ground around the queen,[245] neither lighting a fire nor tasting any food. They were convinced that the king had been captured and the Persian empire lost, and that the Egyptian king was victorious everywhere.

That night, both most welcome and most grievous, covered Arados. The Egyptians rejoiced to be rid of war and Persian slavery, but the Persian prisoners were expecting shackles and whips and rapes and killings and—most humane of all—slavery. Stateira laid her head on Callirhoe's lap and wept, and Callirhoe gave the queen great comfort inasmuch as she was a cultivated Greek and not unversed in troubles.

Then the following happened. The Egyptian soldier that had been entrusted with the job of guarding those in the building realized that the queen was inside. Because of the innate veneration barbarians feel toward the name of royalty, he did not dare approach her, but he stood near the door, which was closed, and said, "Take heart, mistress.[246] Until now the admiral hasn't known that you are locked up here with

---

243. "fleet could not rival him": The wording echoes Thucydides 6.17.8.

244. There is a gap here that obviously described how Chaireas secured the island. Whether it is short or extensive is impossible to say.

245. "The women . . . queen": Reminiscent of Xenophon, *Cyropaideia* 5.1.4.

246. "Take heart, mistress": A reminder of the Persian soldier's words to Pantheia at Xenophon, *Cyropaideia* 5.1.6 (telling her Cyros will marry her).

the prisoners. But when he finds out, he'll treat you with kindness. He's not only brave, but also < . . . >[247] he'll make you his wife.[248] He's naturally fond of women."

When she heard this, Callirhoe let out a loud wail and began to tear at her hair. "I am truly a prisoner-of-war now. Better kill me rather than promise me that. I will not submit to marriage.* I pray for death! They can stab and burn me all they want. I won't get up from here. This spot is my tomb. And, if your commander is as humane as you say, he can do me this favor: he can kill me right here."

He begged her again, but she would not stand up. Instead she covered her head, collapsed onto the ground, and lay there. This gave the Egyptian pause, since he did not dare apply force. At the same time, he was unable to persuade her, so he turned around and went to Chaireas looking glum.

When Chaireas saw the Egyptian, he said "Was it just someone trying to steal the best part of the plunder?* Well, they won't get away with it!"

The Egyptian said, "There hasn't been any trouble. No, it's just that I was ordered to get the woman I found onto a ship,* but she doesn't want to come. She's thrown herself on the floor, and she's asking for a sword and wants to die."

Chaireas laughed at that and replied, "Not exactly the world's smoothest character, are you? Don't you know that a woman falls for appeals, compliments, and promises, and that she's particularly susceptible when she thinks a man's in love with her? You probably tried physical force and insults."

"No, master," the Egyptian replied. "I've tried everything you said— twice over, in fact, since I lied and told her that you would marry her. That really got her angry."

Chaireas said, "Obviously I have great charm and appeal if she rejects and despises me before she's even seen me! But the woman's spirit seems quite impressive—so, no one is to force her to do anything. Leave her

---

247. There seems to be a large gap in sense at this point. Perhaps as much as a page of the original is missing. The most likely reconstruction is that the Egyptian reports to Chaireas that the Queen is among the prisoners, as is an extraordinarily beautiful woman (Callirhoe). Orders are given to load up the plunder and prisoners, but Callirhoe refuses to go. The Egyptian soldier tries unsuccessfully to persuade her to go but has no luck. He praises Chaireas (without mentioning his name) and eventually goes so far as to promise that Chaireas will marry her, which is where we pick up again.

248. As Pantheia is chosen to be Cyros' wife in Xenophon, *Cyropaideia* 5.1.6.

to live as she has chosen to. After all, if anyone should honor chastity, it's me. Perhaps she's even mourning her husband."

Book 8

[1] How Chaireas supposed that Callirhoe had been awarded to Dionysios and wanted to take revenge on the king and had gone over to the Egyptian king, how he was appointed admiral and was victorious at sea, and how after his victory he took control of Arados, where the king had put his wife and his whole retinue for safekeeping, along with Callirhoe—these things have been described in the preceding narrative.[249]

Fortune was preparing to do something not only unbelievable, but also grim. Chaireas was not going to realize that he had Callirhoe and was about to take the wives of other men and carry them off on his triremes, leaving behind on the island only his own wife—not sleeping, like Ariadne, nor to be married by the god Dionysos, but as plunder for his own enemies. But Aphrodite thought this went too far. By this point she had softened her views on Chaireas. Earlier she had been bitterly angry because of his inappropriate jealousy. Although he had received from her the most beautiful gift,[250] such as not even Paris Alexander* had received, he had responded to her favor with outrageous behavior. But now that Chaireas had amply defended himself to Eros by wandering amidst countless sufferings from west to east, Aphrodite took pity on him. And since she had originally been the one to make a couple of the two most beautiful people, she wanted to restore them to each other now that she had hounded them across land and sea.

I think that this last book will prove the sweetest to my readers, for it will provide catharsis for the depressing occurrences in the earlier books. No more piracy or slavery. No more courtroom or battlefield. No more suicide, war, or conquest, just true love and lawful marriage. So I will

---

249. Compare the summary at the start of Book 5. Both are clear imitations of the summaries present in the manuscripts of Xenophon's *Anabasis* at the start of Books 2, 3, 4, 5, and 7.

250. "he had received . . . gift": For Helen and Callirhoe compared as gifts of Aphrodite, see Chariton earlier at 2.6.1. The wording here likewise suggests the same lines of Euripides, *Iphigeneia at Aulis* (178–81).

tell how the goddess brought the truth to light and revealed them to each other when they were unaware.

It was evening, and a lot of the spoils still remained to be loaded, so Chaireas wearily got up to make the arrangements for the voyage.

When he got to the marketplace, the Egyptian said to him, "In there's where the woman is, sir. The one who wasn't willing to come but is starving herself. Maybe you'll be able to convince her to get up. After all, why should you leave behind the most beautiful part of the spoils?"

Polycharmos too was in favor of his suggestion, since he wanted, if it was somehow possible, to get Chaireas to fall in love again to help him get over Callirhoe.

"Chaireas, let's go in," he said.

When Chaireas stepped across the threshold and saw her lying there with her head covered, his soul was immediately unsettled by the way she breathed and held herself, and he was filled with suspense. He certainly would have recognized her if he had not been so certain that Dionysios had recovered Callirhoe.

He quietly approached and said, "Take heart, my lady,[251] whoever you are. We will not force you to do anything. And you will have the husband you want."

The words were barely out of his mouth when Callirhoe recognized his voice. She unveiled herself and both called out at the same time, "Chaireas!" "Callirhoe!" They fell into each other's arms, then lost consciousness and collapsed.

Polycharmos too was at first speechless at the incredible turn of events, but after a while he said, "Get up! You've recovered each other! The gods have fulfilled the prayers of both of you, but remember that you're not back home—you're in enemy territory, and you need to take care of this situation first so no one can ever separate you again."

As he shouted this, they heard him like people drowning in a deep well can barely hear a voice from above. They slowly came to their senses. Then after looking at each other and kissing, they fainted again—and did this a second and third time. They said the same thing: "I have you, if you really are Callirhoe!"—"if you really are Chaireas!"

Report spread that the admiral had found his wife. Not a soldier remained in his tent, nor a sailor on his trireme, nor a watchman in his house. From all directions they gathered, saying, "What a lucky woman! She's got the best-looking husband."

---

251. "Take heart, my lady": A reminder of the Persian soldier's words to Pantheia in Xenophon, *Cyropaideia* 5.1.6, telling her that Cyros will marry her.

But when Callirhoe appeared, no one said anything else in praise of Chaireas—all of them turned their eyes toward her as if she was the only one there. Proudly she made her way through the crowd, Chaireas and Polycharmos on either side as her honor guard. The men of the army tossed flowers and garlands at them, and wine and perfume were poured in their path. The sweetest parts of war and peace were combined: a victory celebration and a wedding.

Chaireas had been regularly sleeping on a trireme and working hard day and night. But after this, he turned everything over to Polycharmos and, without even waiting for night, went to the royal bedchamber (in every city there is a special room set aside for the Great King). There was a gilded bed there with sheets of Babylonian cloth dyed with Tyrian purple.

Who could describe that night? How full of stories it was! How full of tears but also kisses! Callirhoe began her tale first, telling how she revived in the tomb, how she was taken out by Theron, how she sailed, how she was sold. Chaireas wept as he heard all of this, but when she got to Miletos in her story, Callirhoe fell silent in shame. Chaireas started to slip back into his natural jealousy, but she calmed him down with the news of their son.

Without waiting to hear it all, he asked, "Tell me how you came to be on Arados. Where did you leave Dionysios? And what happened between you and the king?"

First off, she swore that she had not seen Dionysios since the trial, and that while the king had been in love with her, she had had nothing to do with him, not so much as a kiss.

"Then it was wrong and hotheaded of me," Chaireas said, "to do such awful things to him when he wasn't harming you at all. You see, when I lost you, I felt my only option was to go over to the other side. But I haven't disgraced you—I have filled land and sea with victories!"

He told her about everything in detail, proud of his victories. And when they had had enough tears and tales, falling into each other's arms, gladly they turned to the rite of their old bed.[252]

[2] During the night an Egyptian of some importance arrived at the island, disembarked from his ship, and urgently asked where Chaireas was. He was taken to Polycharmos but said that his message was top secret, for Chaireas' ears alone, and that the matter he had come about was extremely urgent. Polycharmos prevented him from going in to

---

252. "gladly they . . . bed": A citation of Homer, *Odyssey* 23.296 (Odysseus and Penelope after their reunion).

see Chaireas for a long time. He did not want to bother him at such a bad time, but when the man kept pressing, Polycharmos cracked open the door to the bedroom and let Chaireas know about how insistent he was.

Like a good general, Chaireas said, "Tell him to come in. War brooks no delay."

The Egyptian was brought in and, since it was still dark, stood near the bed.

"You need to know that the Persian king has destroyed our Egyptian king. He has sent part of his army to Egypt to get the situation there under control. All of the rest of his forces he's leading here, and he'll be here any minute. He knows that Arados has been captured. He's worried about all the wealth he left behind here, but he's really in agony about his wife Stateira."

Chaireas leapt up when he heard this, but Callirhoe held him back.

"You haven't even thought about what we're facing. So where are you hurrying off to? If you publicly announce this, you'll cause a great war for yourself as soon as everyone finds out and discipline breaks down. If we fall into the king's hands again, it'll be worse for us than it was the first time."

He came around quickly to her advice and left the bedroom with a plan in mind. Grabbing the Egyptian by the hand, he called the whole army together and spoke.

"Men, we are victorious also over the Persian king's land forces! This man has brought us the good news, along with a letter from the king of Egypt. We are to sail as quickly as possible where he orders us to go. All of you need to pack up and get on board!"[253]

After he said this, the trumpeter sounded the call for withdrawal to the ships. They had loaded the plunder and prisoners the day before, and nothing was left on the island except what was too heavy or of too little value. They untied the mooring cables and weighed anchor, and the harbor was filled with noise and commotion, everyone busy with something. Chaireas went from ship to ship and passed along a secret order for the ship captains to put in at Cyprus. He pretended that they needed to capture the island by surprise while it was still undefended.

Sailing with a favorable wind, the next day they landed at Paphos, where there is a temple of Aphrodite.[254] After they dropped anchor but

---

253. Deceiving an army under one's command to prevent loss of morale is another of the just behaviors described in Xenophon, *Memorabilia* 4.2.15.

254. Paphos was thought to be the birthplace of the goddess.

before anyone left the ships, Chaireas sent his heralds to offer a formal peace with the inhabitants. When they had accepted this, he had his entire force disembark and honored Aphrodite with dedicatory offerings. Many animals were collected as sacrifices, and he threw a feast for the army.

While he was considering what to do next, the priests announced that the sacrificial omens had been auspicious. Taking courage from that, he called the ship captains and his three hundred Greeks, as well as all the Egyptians he could see were favorable to him. He spoke as follows:

"Comrades and friends, you've been my partners in great successes, and I find peace is finest and war safest in your company. We know firsthand that by sticking together we were victorious at sea. We are faced with a life-or-death situation and need to determine how to ensure our future safety. I have to tell you that the Egyptian king has been killed in battle, and the Persian king is everywhere master on land. We've been cut off, surrounded by the enemy. So does anyone recommend we go to the king and just throw ourselves into his hands?"

They immediately shouted that that was the last thing they should do.

"So where do we go? Everywhere is hostile to us, and it's not even a good idea for us to put our faith in the sea anymore, now that the land is in enemy hands. I mean, we can't *fly* away."

That was met with silence until a Spartan, a kinsman of Brasidas[255] who had been exiled from Sparta under severe pressure, was the first to get up the courage to speak.

"Why are we looking for a place where we can escape from the king? We've got sea and ships. Both can take us to Sicily and Syracuse, where we wouldn't have to fear the Persians—or the Athenians for that matter."

Everyone applauded his speech, but Chaireas pretended to be the only one not to agree, using as his excuse the length of the voyage. Really, though, he was testing to see whether they were sure about the decision.

When they kept pressing urgently for it and were ready to sail right then, he said, "Well, Greeks, you've got a good plan, and I thank you both for your support and loyalty. With the gods' help I'll make sure you don't regret it. But there are a lot of the Egyptians here, and it's not a good idea to force them to come along if they don't want to. Most

---

255. Brasidas was one of the most successful Spartan commanders during the Peloponnesian War until his death in battle.

of them have wives and children, and they wouldn't be happy to be separated from them. So I want you to spread out through the army and quickly ask each of them so we only take with us the ones who want to go."

[3] While his order was being carried out, Callirhoe took Chaireas by the hand, led him off by himself, and asked, "What's your plan, Chaireas? Are you going to take Stateira and the beautiful Rhodogoune to Syracuse?"

Chaireas turned bright red and said, "I'm not taking them for me. I'm taking them as servants for you."

Callirhoe exclaimed, "I hope the gods won't drive me so out of my wits that I'd have the queen of Asia as my slave! Especially not when she was my host! If you want to do something nice for me, send her to the king.* After all, she kept me safe for you, as if she had taken in her brother's wife."[256]

"There's nothing I wouldn't do if you wanted me to," answered Chaireas. "You're the mistress of Stateira and of all the plunder and, above all, of my soul."

Callirhoe happily kissed him, and immediately he ordered his aides to take her to Stateira. The queen happened to be with the noblest of the Persian women in the hold of a ship, having absolutely no idea what had happened, not even that Callirhoe had gotten Chaireas back. There was a heavy guard around her, and no one was allowed to approach her, or see her, or tell her anything of what was being done. When Callirhoe arrived at the ship with the captain escorting her, there was an immediate panic and tumult as everyone ran around.

Then someone whispered to someone else, "The admiral's wife is here."

Stateira gave a deep, heavy sigh and tearfully said, "Fortune, you have saved me for this day, so that I, the queen, might look upon a mistress. Maybe she's come to see what her new slave is like."

At that she started up a lament, and knew at that moment what captivity is like for people of noble birth. But the god caused a rapid reversal, for Callirhoe rushed in and embraced Stateira.

"Be glad, Queen. Yes, you are still a queen and will always remain so. You have not fallen into enemy hands, but into those of your dear friend, the woman you helped. My Chaireas is the admiral! Anger at the king for how long it was taking to get me back made him the Egyptian

---

256. "she kept me . . . brother's wife": A very close imitation of Xenophon, *Cyropaideia* 6.4.7 (Pantheia to Abradatas about Cyros).

admiral. But he's finished with that and has become reconciled to you. He is no longer your enemy. Come now, my dear friend. Get up and depart happily. You too must get your husband back. Yes, the king is alive, and Chaireas is sending you to him! Rhodogoune, you get up too. My first friend among the Persian women! Go to your husband. The same goes for as many of the other women as the queen wishes. And remember Callirhoe."

Stateira was stunned when she heard these words, able neither to believe nor disbelieve them. But Callirhoe's demeanor was such that she did not seem to be playing a cruel joke amidst great misfortunes, and the urgent situation was forcing them to do everything quickly.

Now, there was among the Egyptians a man named Demetrios, a philosopher and a friend of the king. He was advanced in years and the most educated and virtuous of all the Egyptians.

Chaireas summoned him and said, "Although I wanted to take you with me, I'm instead making you my representative in a serious matter. I'm sending the queen to the Great King, and I want you to take her. This will give you greater honor in his eyes and soften his attitude toward the others."

With that, he appointed Demetrios commander of the ships that were going back. For though everyone wanted to go with Chaireas and preferred him to their homelands and children, he chose only the twenty finest and largest triremes to accompany him, since he was going to be crossing the Ionian Sea. Onto these he loaded all the Greeks that were there, and as many Egyptians and Phoenicians as he knew to be ready for action. Many of the men of Cyprus also embarked as volunteers.

Everyone else he sent home, distributing shares of the plunder to them so they would return happily to their families as more notable men than when they had left. No one who asked for something from Chaireas failed to get it.

Callirhoe took all the pieces of the royal wardrobe to Stateira, but she refused to accept them.

"Adorn yourself with them," Stateira said. "Royal clothing suits a figure like yours. You should have them so that you can give gifts to your mother and make dedications* to your city's gods. Besides, I left more than this back in Babylon! And may the gods grant you a fair voyage and safety and that you might never be separated from Chaireas again. You've treated me justly in every way. You've displayed an excellent character, one that matches your beauty. The king put into my care a lovely charge."

[4] Who could describe that day? So many things happened, and they offered such strong contrasts—people making vows and saying

goodbyes, rejoicing and grieving, giving each other orders, writing to the folks at home. Chaireas too wrote the following letter to the king.

"You were going to decide the outcome of the trial, but now I've won before the fairest judge of all—war is the best arbiter of who is stronger and who weaker. It has not only restored my wife to me, but has also given me yours as well. But I have not imitated your foot dragging. No, I'm returning your wife to you quickly, without your even asking for her. She is safe and sound and has remained a queen even in captivity. But I want you to know that it's not me sending you the gift, but Callirhoe. We ask a favor in return: reconcile with the Egyptians. It is, as you know, fitting for the king to show greater mercy than anyone else. Besides, you'll get soldiers who love you, for they've chosen to remain in your service rather than accompany me as friends."

That was Chaireas' letter. Callirhoe decided that she owed it to Dionysios to write as well, and that this was the right thing to do. This was the only thing she did without Chaireas around—aware of his innate jealousy, she went out of her way to keep it a secret. Taking a small tablet, she wrote:

"Greetings from Callirhoe to Dionysios, her benefactor—benefactor because you saved me from pirates and slavery. Please, I beg you, don't be angry. I am with you in spirit through the son we have in common. I entrust him to you to raise and educate in a way worthy of us. Do not let him experience a stepmother. You have not only a son, but also a daughter. Two children are enough for you. Marry them to each other[257] when he grows up and send him to Syracuse so he can see his grandfather too. Greetings to you too, Plangon! I have written this to you with my own hand. Farewell, good Dionysios. Remember your Callirhoe."

After sealing the letter, she slipped it into the folds of her dress. When it was at last time for everyone to get aboard their triremes and set sail, she gave her hand to Stateira and took her onto her ship. Demetrios had set up the royal canopy on the ship, curtaining it off with purple Babylonian fabrics embroidered with gold.

As she was getting the queen settled on her couch with a great deal of fuss, Callirhoe spoke to her.

"Farewell, Stateira. Think of me and write to me often in Syracuse— nothing is hard for the king. I'll let my parents know how grateful I am to you, and I'll tell the gods of the Greeks as well. I trust you to take care of my son, since you liked seeing him. Think of him as a replacement ward in my place."

---

257. Half-siblings by different mothers could marry.

As she said this, her eyes filled with tears and set the women to weeping. As she was about to leave the ship, Callirhoe leaned a little closer to Stateira and with a blush handed her the letter.

"Give this to poor Dionysios. I'm trusting you and the king to take care of him. Console him. I'm afraid he'll kill himself now that he's been separated from me."

The women would have gone on talking and crying and kissing each other, if the ship pilots had not given the order for departure. Right before getting on board her trireme, Callirhoe knelt in reverence to Aphrodite.

"I thank you, mistress, for what is happening now. At last you have given up your anger toward me. Grant that I also get to see Syracuse. The ocean between here and there is large, and fearsome seas await me, but I'm not afraid so long as you sail beside me."

Not a single one of the Egyptians got on board Demetrios' ships until they had said goodbye to Chaireas first. They kissed his head and hands, so strong was the emotion he inspired in them all. He let the other fleet sail first so that they could hear hurrahs mixed with prayers until they were far out to sea.

[5] While they were sailing, the Great King, who had defeated his enemies on land, was sending a man to Egypt to get the situation there safely under control. Meanwhile, he himself hurried to his wife on Arados. When he reached Tyre on the coast and was in the midst of offering victory sacrifices to Heracles, a messenger came with the news: "Arados has been plundered. There's nothing left. The Egyptian ships are carrying off everything on the island."

This news brought great sorrow to the king, since the queen had been lost. All the noblest of the Persians grieved, outwardly for Stateira, but each for his own sorrows[258]—this one for his wife, another for his sister, that one for his daughter, all for someone, each for his own. The enemy had sailed off, and they had no idea over what region of the sea.

The next day the Egyptian ships were spotted as they sailed in to Tyre. It was unclear what the real situation was, but the king's men were amazed to see them. They were even more baffled by the royal standard that was flying from Demetrios' ship, since this is usually flown only when the king is a passenger. This confused them, since they supposed that the ships were those of the enemy. Immediately they ran and reported to Artaxerxes: "Perhaps we're about to find out that someone

---

258. "outwardly . . . own sorrows": A citation of Homer *Iliad* 19.302, with Stateira's name substituted for that of Patroclos.

else is the new king of the Egyptians." The king bolted up from his
throne, hurried to the sea, and gave the watchword for commencing
battle. Of course he had no triremes, but he positioned his entire army
around the harbor, ready for battle.

Just as some were drawing their bows or getting ready to hurl their
spears, Demetrios realized what was happening and reported it to the
queen. Stateira emerged from the canopy and showed herself. Immediately
the soldiers cast aside their weapons and knelt in reverence.

The king could not restrain himself, but he was the first to jump
aboard the ship before it had even landed. He embraced his wife and
wept tears of joy.

"What god has returned you to me, beloved wife? Both parts are unbelievable: that the queen was lost and then, once lost, that she was found.
How is it that I left you on land and get you back from the sea?"

Stateira replied, "You have me as a gift from Callirhoe."

Upon hearing her name, the king received a fresh wound, as it were,
on top of his old one. He looked at Artaxates the eunuch and said, "Take
me to Callirhoe so that I can thank her."

"You'll hear all about it from me," said Stateira as they made their
way from the harbor to the palace. When they got there, she commanded everyone to withdraw except for the eunuch, who she asked to
remain. She explained what had happened on Arados and on Cyprus,
then finally gave the king Chaireas' letter. He read it and was filled with
countless emotions—anger because of the capture of his most prized
possessions, regret for having forced Chaireas to go over to the other
side, then gratitude, in turn, because < . . . >[259] he would not be able to
see Callirhoe again. Above all, he was gripped by jealousy.

"Chaireas is blessed and more fortunate than I."

When they were done relating their news, Stateira said, "Comfort
Dionysios, my king. Callirhoe asks you to do so."

Turning to the eunuch, the king said, "Have Dionysios come here."

He arrived quickly, eager with anticipation. He knew nothing of what
Chaireas had been up to and thought that Callirhoe had come with the
rest of the women and that the king was summoning him to give him
back his wife as a reward for his bravery. But when he came in, the king
explained to him everything that had happened from the beginning.

At that critical moment Dionysios really showed his dignity and
exceptional refinement. Like someone unfazed by a lightning strike

---

259. D'Orville, Chariton's first modern editor, posited a lacuna here, certainly correctly,
proposing something like "then gratitude, in turn, because <he had gotten the queen
back, but upset because> he would not be able to see Callirhoe again."

right in front of him, he listened to words more potent than a thunder-bolt: Chaireas was taking Callirhoe back to Syracuse. Despite this, he remained composed and did not think it safe to express his grief when the queen had been saved.

Artaxerxes said, "I would have given Callirhoe to you, if I could have, Dionysios, since you have shown nothing but support and loyalty to me. But since this is impossible, I am making you governor of all Ionia, and you will be appointed First Benefactor to the royal house."

Dionysios knelt in reverence and expressed his gratitude, in a hurry to leave and give himself the opportunity to cry. As he went out, Stateira discreetly passed him the letter.

He went home and locked himself in his room. Recognizing Callirhoe's handwriting, the first thing he did was kiss the letter. Then after opening it, he clutched it to his chest as if it was Callirhoe herself. For a long time he held it there, unable to read it because of his tears. When at last he had cried himself out, he started to read the letter. First he kissed the name "Callirhoe," and when he came to the words "to Dionysios, her benefactor," he said, "Alas! No longer 'her husband.' You were *my* benefactor, Callirhoe. What did I ever do to deserve you?"

He took pleasure from the apologetic part of the letter, and he read these words over and over, for it suggested that she had left him unwillingly—so vain a thing is love, and so easily it persuades one that it is requited! Then he saw his son and spoke to him, rocking him in his arms.[260]

"My child, one day you too will sail away to go to your mother. Yes, she herself has commanded it. And I'll live all alone, with no one to blame but myself. A singular jealousy has been my undoing—and you, Babylon."

With these words he began preparations for an immediate return to Ionia, finding great solace in the thought of a long journey, of ruling many cities, and of the images of Callirhoe in Miletos.

[6] That was the situation in Asia. Chaireas, meanwhile, made the voyage to Sicily successfully. Despite his great fear that a hostile god would attack him, a wind had been at his back the whole way, and with large ships he could cross the open sea. When Syracuse came into view, he ordered the captains to adorn the triremes and, since the weather was calm enough to do so, to sail in close formation. When the people in the city spotted them, someone said, "Ships are sailing in! Where are

---

260. "rocking him in his arms": Echoing Homer, *Iliad* 6.474 (of Hector and his infant son).

they from? No way they're Athenian, are they? Come on, let's report this to Hermocrates."

They relayed the information to Hermocrates quickly. "General, you must decide what you'll do. Should we close the harbors or put our own ships out to sea? We don't know if there's a larger fleet behind this one. Maybe the ships we can see are just an advance force."

Hermocrates rushed from the marketplace to the sea and sent out a boat to meet them. His messenger, when he got close, asked who they were.

Chaireas ordered one of the Egyptians to answer, "We are merchants sailing from Egypt. We carry cargo that will gladden the hearts of the Syracusans."

"Well, don't sail in all at once until we can determine whether you're telling the truth. I don't see any cargo ships, just long triremes that look like they've seen battle. So one ship can sail in. The rest have to wait outside the harbor without dropping anchor."

"That's what we'll do."

Chaireas' trireme entered the harbor first, with a canopy on deck completely covered with Babylonian curtains. By the time it docked, the whole waterfront was full of people. By nature a crowd is a curious thing anyway, and on that occasion they had more reasons than usual to congregate. They gawked at the tent and supposed there was some rich cargo inside, not people. Everyone made a different prediction about what it was, guessing everything except the truth. After all, it was unbelievable, convinced as they were that Chaireas was dead, to think that he could be returning alive amidst such splendor. Chaireas' parents, in fact, did not even come out of their house. Hermocrates had official duties to perform, but he was grieving, so while he was present, he stayed in the background.

As everyone strained their eyes in perplexity, the curtains were suddenly drawn aside: there was Callirhoe, reclining on a couch of beaten gold, dressed in Tyrian purple, and Chaireas, sitting beside her, in a general's uniform. A thunderclap has never so astonished the ears, nor lightning the eyes of those who saw it, a man finding a treasure of gold has never shouted as loud as the crowd did then, when without any warning they saw a sight more beautiful than words can describe. Hermocrates leapt up to the canopy and embraced his daughter.

"You're alive, child! Or am I wrong about this too?"

"I'm alive, father! Truly I'm alive now that I see you alive."

Tears of joy were shed by all, and while this was happening, Polycharmos approached with the rest of the triremes. He had the rest of the fleet from Cyprus entrusted to him because Chaireas wasn't able to spare even a moment for anything except Callirhoe alone. The harbor was soon full, looking just like it had after the naval battle against Athens—for these triremes, too, were sailing in from war covered in garlands, under the command of a Syracusan. The voices of the men at sea as they saluted the men on shore mingled with the voices of the men on shore, who returned the salute of the men at sea. Hurrahs and praise and prayers came thick and fast from each group to the other.

Then Chaireas' father arrived too. He was carried in because he was in a faint from his unbelievable joy. Chaireas' fellow ephebes and his friends from the gymnasium jostled each other in their desire to welcome him, and the women did the same about Callirhoe. They thought that she had grown so much more beautiful that you might truly have said that in looking upon her you were seeing Aphrodite rising from the sea.[261]

Chaireas went up to Hermocrates and his father and said, "Receive the wealth of the Great King."

Immediately he gave orders for a vast amount of gold and silver to be brought out. Then he displayed to the Syracusans ivory, amber and clothes, all kinds of raw materials and splendid art, and a couch and table belonging to the Great King. The result was that the whole city was filled not as it was before with Athenian poverty[262] after the Sicilian War, but—strangest thing in the world!—with Persian plunder in peacetime.

[7] With one voice the crowd shouted, "Let's go to the assembly!" They were eager to see and hear them. Faster than it takes to tell, the theater was filled with men and women both. When Chaireas came in unaccompanied, all of them, men and women alike, shouted, "Call Callirhoe in!"

Hermocrates indulged the people in this too and brought in his daughter. The first thing the people did was to raise their eyes to heaven and praise the gods, feeling greater gratitude for this day than they had for the day of their victory celebration. Then they applauded, sometimes in separate groups, the men cheering Chaireas and the women Callirhoe, sometimes all together, cheering them both. Chaireas and Callirhoe enjoyed the latter more.

They led Callirhoe out of the theater as soon as she had a chance to greet her country, since she was fresh from her voyage and ordeal.

---

261. The painting "Aphrodite Rising from the Sea" was a famous and much copied masterpiece by the fourth-century BC painter Apelles.

262. "Poverty" because Athens was poor in comparison with the Persian empire.

Chaireas, on the other hand, the crowd held back because they wanted to hear the whole story of his time away from home. He began at the end because he did not want to distress the people with the earlier, depressing parts. The people, however, were insistent. "We beg you to begin at the beginning. Tell us everything. Leave nothing out!"

Chaireas was reluctant, since he was ashamed that much had turned out contrary to his wishes, but Hermocrates assured him.

"Don't be ashamed at all, son, even if you're going to tell us things that are painful or bitter. The outcome has turned out brilliantly, and that overshadows everything that came before. What remains unspoken creates worse suspicion because of the silence itself. You are speaking to your country and parents. Their love for you both is perfectly equal.

"Now, the first part of your story the people already know. After all, they're the ones who joined you in marriage. How you unduly succumbed to false jealousy because of the plot of your rival suitors and struck your wife, we all know. And we know that she received a lavish burial when she appeared dead, and that you condemned yourself when brought up on a charge of murder because you wanted to die with your wife. But the people acquitted you because they recognized that it was an accident. What comes next—that Theron the tomb-robber tunneled into the tomb and found Callirhoe alive and loaded her onto his pirate ship with the grave goods and sold her in Ionia; and that you set out in search of your wife but did not find her, but encountered the pirate ship at sea and found all the other pirates dead from thirst but brought Theron, who was the only one still alive, into the assembly; and that he was tortured and crucified; and that the city sent a trireme and ambassadors to get Callirhoe; and that your friend Polycharmos of his own free will set sail with you—we know all that. Tell us what's happened since your departure from Syracuse."

Picking up from there,[263] Chaireas told his story.

"We sailed safely across the Ionian Sea and arrived at an estate belonging to a Milesian named Dionysios, the richest, noblest, most illustrious man in Ionia. He bought Callirhoe from Theron for a talent—fear not, she didn't become a slave! No, he immediately put the woman he had just purchased in the position of mistress of his house. He couldn't bring himself to force himself upon her because she was of high birth and he loved her, but he couldn't stand the thought of sending her back to Syracuse when he was in love with her.

---

263. "Picking up from there": Perhaps an imitation of Homeric language, found also in Chariton 1.7.6 and 5.7.10.

"But after Callirhoe realized she was pregnant with my son, she wanted to save our fellow citizen and the only way to do so was to marry Dionysios and trick him about the conception of the child so that it would look like he was Dionysios', and he would raise it as it deserved.

"Yes, men of Syracuse, one of your fellow citizens is being raised in affluence in Miletos by a noble man. I mean it—his lineage is noble and Greek. Let us not begrudge him his great inheritance.

[8] "I learned of these things only later. Right then I had landed on the estate. I had only seen a statue of Callirhoe in a temple, and I had high hopes, but at night some Phrygian bandits raided the coast. They burned our trireme and slaughtered most of us, but they tied up Polycharmos and me and sold us in Caria."

The crowd broke out in lamentation upon hearing this, but Chaireas said, "Please allow me to pass over what happened next. It's even more depressing than the first part."

The people shouted, "Tell us everything!"

He went on, "The man who bought us, a slave of Mithridates, the general of Caria, ordered us to work the fields in shackles. After some members of our chain gang killed the guard, Mithridates gave orders for us all to be crucified. I was taken off for execution, but when Polycharmos was about to be tortured, he said my name[264] out loud and Mithridates recognized it. He'd been a guest of Dionysios in Miletos and was present at Chaireas' funeral. You see, Callirhoe had heard what happened with the trireme and the bandits and thought I was dead, so she had a splendid tomb built for me. Right away Mithridates ordered me to be taken down from the cross—it was almost over for me by then—and made me one of his closest friends.

"He was eager to return Callirhoe to me and made me write a letter to her. Through the carelessness of his servant, Dionysios of all people got hold of the letter. He couldn't believe I was still alive, and he thought that Mithridates was plotting to take his wife from him, and he immediately sent a message to the king accusing Mithridates of adultery.

"The king agreed to hear the case and summoned everyone to his court. That's how we ended up traveling inland to Babylon. Dionysios took Callirhoe and made her the object of admiration and wonder throughout all of Asia, while Mithridates brought me along. When we got there, we participated in a grand trial before the king. Mithridates was immediately acquitted, but the king promised to hold a hearing

---

264. It was actually Callirhoe's name.

to decide whose wife Callirhoe was, Dionysios' or mine. For the time being, she was entrusted to the care of Stateira, the queen.

"Men of Syracuse, how often do you think I wanted to die, being kept from my wife? But Polycharmos saved me, my one true friend in everything. The king, you see, failed to hold the hearing because he was burning with love for Callirhoe. But he neither seduced her nor violated her, for Egypt by happy coincidence revolted and began a major war, the cause of my great blessings.

"The queen took Callirhoe with her, but I listened to a false report from someone who said that she had been handed over to Dionysios. Wanting to avenge myself on the king, I went over to the side of the Egyptian king and accomplished some mighty deeds. When Tyre could not be taken, I captured it myself, and after being made admiral, I defeated the Great King at sea and became master of Arados. That's where the king had put his queen for safekeeping, along with the wealth which you've seen. I could've made the Egyptian king master of all Asia if he hadn't been killed fighting when I wasn't with him.

"In the end I made the Great King your friend by bestowing upon him his wife and sending to the noblest of the Persians their mothers, sisters, wives, and daughters. I myself have brought the noblest Greeks here, as well as those Egyptians who wanted to come. Another fleet will come from Ionia—one of yours. And the grandson of Hermocrates will lead it."

Prayers from all followed closely on these words. Chaireas cut off the yelling and carried on speaking.

"Callirhoe and I proclaim before you our gratitude to my friend Polycharmos. He displayed support and absolute loyalty to us. If you all approve, let's give him my sister as his wife. He'll get a portion of the plunder as the dowry."

The people shouted in approval. "The people express their thanks to you, Polycharmos. You are a brave man and loyal friend. You have benefited your country. You are worthy of Hermocrates and Chaireas."

After this Chaireas resumed. "And these three hundred, Greeks all, my brave band. I beg you, grant them citizenship."

The people called out, "They deserve to be our fellow citizens! Let's take a vote on it!"

A decree to that effect was enacted, and the men took their seats and joined the assembly. Chaireas granted each of them a talent, and Hermocrates apportioned land to the Egyptians so that they could have farms.

While the citizens were in the theater, Callirhoe went to the temple of Aphrodite before going home. She took hold of the goddess' feet and lowered her face to them, her hair hanging loose. Kissing the statue's feet, she said, "Thank you, Aphrodite, for showing me Chaireas in Syracuse again, the place where by your will I saw him as a maiden. I do not blame you, mistress, for the things I have suffered. That was my fate. But I beg you, do not separate me from Chaireas ever again. Grant us a happy life and a death together."

So much have I written[265] about Callirhoe.

---

265. Because Chariton opens his work with language reminiscent of Thucydides' *History,* some have seen in this verb another nod to Thucydides' introductory sentence (1.1.1), where the same word appears.

An Ephesian Story:
Anthia and Habrocomes

Book 1

[1] There was in Ephesos a man named Lycomedes, who was one of the most powerful people there. This Lycomedes and his wife Themisto, who was also an Ephesian, had a son, Habrocomes, a prodigy of exceptional handsomeness. Looks like his had never been seen in Ionia[1] or any other land. This Habrocomes grew more handsome with every passing day, and his intellectual virtues blossomed alongside his physical beauty. He studied every cultural pursuit and practiced various arts, and his regular exercises were hunting, riding, and weapons training.

He was immensely popular with all the Ephesians, but also with those who lived in the rest of Asia, and they had high hopes that he would turn out to be an exceptional citizen. They treated the young man like a god, and there were even those who knelt in reverence and offered prayers when they saw him. The young man was quite egotistical, exulting in his intellectual accomplishments but much more so in his physical beauty. Anything at all that was called beautiful he despised as inferior. Nothing, not a sight, not a sound, seemed to him to measure up to Habrocomes. If he heard that a boy was handsome or a girl beautiful, he scoffed at whoever said it, since obviously they didn't know he was the only one who was beautiful.

In fact, he didn't even think that Eros[2] was a god. He rejected him entirely, considering him beneath notice. He said no one would ever fall in love or submit to the god unless they did so willingly.* If he happened to see a shrine or statue of Eros, he would laugh at it and announce that he was greater than any Eros, both in physical beauty and in power. And it was true. Wherever Habrocomes put in an appearance, no one looked at any statues or praised any paintings.

[2] Eros was irate at this. He's a god that loves to fight and grants no quarter to the proud. He began to look for a stratagem to use against the young man—yes, even the god thought he'd have a hard time capturing the young man. Arming himself and cloaking himself with all the power of love magic, he began his campaign against Habrocomes.

An asterisk (*) indicates that a technical note on a given passage of the translation of Greek text can be found in the endnotes.

1. The Greek region along the western coast of modern Turkey, of which Ephesos was one of the most important cities.

2. The Greek god of love and erotic attraction. Son of Aphrodite, goddess of love and sex.

There was a local festival of Artemis[3] going on. It was a little less than a mile from the city to the temple,[4] and all the Ephesian maidens, dressed in their finery, had to traverse the distance in a parade, as did all those ephebes[5] who were the same age as Habrocomes. He was about sixteen and a member of the ephebic corps, and he marched at their head in the parade.

A huge crowd made up both of many locals and many visitors had come to watch the parade. It was the custom in that festival, you see, for the maidens to find themselves husbands and the ephebes wives. The participants marched in ranks. First were the holy objects, torches, baskets, and incense offerings. After them were horses and dogs and gear for hunting and warfare, but most of all for peaceful pursuits. < . . .

. . . >[6] Each of them was dressed as if she was meeting a lover. Leading the contingent of maidens was Anthia, daughter of Megamedes and Euippe, both native Ephesians. Anthia's beauty was something to marvel at, far beyond that of the other girls. She was about fourteen years old. Her body was blossoming into beauty, and the stylishness of her look contributed greatly to her loveliness:[7] blond hair—most of it worn loose, a little tied up, all of it moving with the blowing of the breeze; lively eyes—radiant like those of a girl,* but unapproachable like those of a chaste woman; clothes—a purple dress, belted to fall at the knee, worn off the shoulder, with a fawn-skin wrap; equipment—a quiver fastened on, a bow, javelins in her hand, dogs at her heel.

---

3. A virgin goddess who was connected with young women, hunting, and wild areas. Ephesos was the site of the most well-known cult of the goddess in the Greek world, and her temple there was counted among the wonders of the world.

4. The distance ("seven stades," literally) is accurate but need not be from personal knowledge on the part of our author; Herodotus 1.26 mentions the distance in a famous description of a siege of Ephesos.

5. *Ephebes* were young men enrolled in a city's training system for citizens. Emphasis had originally been on military training, but soon a broader civic, social, and educational preparation became a regular feature and eventually eclipsed the earlier purpose.

6. < . . . > is used in this translation to indicate a lacuna, or gap, in the text where we have lost something, and I do not follow O'Sullivan, the latest editor of Xenophon, or otherwise feel confident in any scholarly reconstructions. Sometimes there is no indication other than unusual phrasing (a "jump" in thought, as here, where obviously the introduction of the girls is missing) or disrupted syntax that leads us to believe something has dropped out, though occasionally we have an actual gap in the manuscript.

7. The description that follows strongly resembles in detail the usual iconography of Artemis in Greek art.

Many a time the Ephesians had spotted her in the sanctuary and knelt in reverence in the belief that she was Artemis. On this occasion too when she appeared, a shout went up from the crowd. The spectators made all sorts of comments. Some of them were so stunned they said she was the goddess, others that she wasn't the goddess but had been made by her.* All of them offered up prayers and knelt in reverence to her. They remarked how blessed her parents were. "Anthia the beautiful!" was what all the spectators were talking about. And as the group of maidens passed, no one said anything except "Anthia."

But from the moment that Habrocomes showed up with the ephebes, despite how beautiful the sight of the maidens had been, everyone forgot about them as they caught a glimpse of Habrocomes. They turned their eyes to him and, astounded by the sight, shouted, "Habrocomes is so handsome! No one looks more like a handsome god than him!" Some also then added, "How great it would be if Habrocomes and Anthia got married!"

That was Eros warming up for his plan.

Soon the two of them began to hear word of each other, and Anthia longed to see Habrocomes, and Habrocomes, though until now unaffected by love, wanted to see Anthia.

[3] When the parade ended, the whole crowd went into the temple for the sacrifice. The order of the procession was broken up as men and women, ephebes and maidens, came together. Then the two saw each other—Anthia was captured by Habrocomes, Habrocomes defeated by Eros. He stared at the girl constantly. He wanted to stop looking but couldn't as the god held him mercilessly in his power.

Anthia had her own problems. She took in Habrocomes' beauty as it flowed into her wide open eyes and soon forgot the proprieties that apply to maidens. Oh yes, she would say things just so Habrocomes would hear them and bare what parts of her body she could so he would see them. He surrendered himself to the sight and became the god's prisoner.

Then the sacrifice was over and they were departing, upset and complaining about how quickly they had to leave. They wanted to keep looking at each other, so they kept turning around and stopping and found many excuses to linger.

They each arrived home, and that's when they realized how bad they had it. Both found their thoughts turning to how the other looked, and love blazed up in them. The rest of the day their desire grew, and when they went to bed they were instantly in turmoil. Their feelings of love were irresistible.

[4] Habrocomes took hold of his hair, tearing at it, and ripped his clothes.

"This is terrible! What bad luck! What's happened to me? Up until now Habrocomes was so manly, he sneered at Eros, he bad-mouthed the god—but now I've been taken prisoner. I'm beaten. I'm being forced to be a slave to a girl. Now I can see that someone is more beautiful than I am, and I'll admit Eros is a god.

"What a gutless coward I am! Can't I resist it? Won't I stay strong? Won't I be able to overcome Eros? I have to beat this god. He's nothing! Sure, there's a beautiful girl. So what? Anthia looks good to your *eyes,* Habrocomes, but she doesn't have to look good to *you.* Not if you don't want her to. That's it. My mind's made up. Eros will never get the best of me."

At this the god increased the pressure and dragged him along as he tried to resist, hurting him because he went unwillingly.

When the young man could hold out no longer, he threw himself on the floor. "You've won, Eros! You've raised a great trophy in your victory over the abstinent Habrocomes. Accept him as a suppliant and save him now that he has fled for protection to you, the master of everything. Don't turn a blind eye to me, but also don't punish my impudence for too long. I was still ignorant of your works, Eros. That's why I was arrogant. But give me Anthia now. Don't just be bitter to me because I opposed you—be a patron god to me because I'm surrendering."

But Eros was still angry and planned on exacting a great punishment from Habrocomes for his arrogance.

Anthia too was in trouble, and when she couldn't stand it any more, she pulled herself together in an attempt to hide things from those around her.

"This is not good. What's happened to me? I'm a girl in love, but I'm too young. I'm suffering weird pains that a good girl shouldn't feel. I'm crazy for Habrocomes—he's so handsome . . . but so conceited. How far will my desire go? Where will my trouble end? This man I love only thinks of himself, and I'm a girl who's constantly being watched. Who will I get to help? Who can I share all this with? Where will I see Habrocomes?"

[5] They lamented like this the whole night through and held before their eyes the way the other looked and imagined in their minds each other's appearance. In the morning, Habrocomes went to do his regular exercises, and the girl went to worship the goddess as she normally did. Their bodies were worn out from the night before, their eyes dull, their complexions altered. That was the situation for a long while, and they weren't getting any better.

During this period they spent their days in the goddess' temple, staring at one another. They were too afraid and ashamed to tell each other the truth. It got so bad, Habrocomes would groan and cry, praying pitifully when the girl was within earshot. Anthia's feelings were the same, but she was more deeply affected by her misfortune, because whenever she caught another girl or woman looking at him—and they *all* looked at him—she was clearly pained, afraid that Habrocomes would like one of the others more than her. They both prayed to the goddess in common—even though their prayers were the same, they didn't know it.

As time passed, the young man couldn't stand it any longer. By this point his body was a total wreck and his spirit in despair. It was so bad that Lycomedes and Themisto grew seriously worried. They didn't know what was happening to Habrocomes but were scared by what they saw.

Meanwhile, Megamedes and Euippe were in a similar state over Anthia. They could see her beauty withering away but no apparent reason for her plight. In the end they brought seers and priests to visit Anthia so they could determine how to fix what ailed her. They came and made sacrifices and poured all sorts of libations and recited formulas over her in barbarian languages. They explained that they were placating certain spirits and alleged that her suffering was caused by the gods of the underworld. Lycomedes and his family were also making a lot of sacrifices and praying for Habrocomes. But there was no relief for either one. Their love simply burned more hotly.

They both lay ill, in critical condition, expected to die any minute, unable to confess their misery. At last both fathers sent messengers to consult the god* about the cause of their illnesses and how to end them.

[6] Not far away is the temple of Apollo in Colophon,[8] a ten-mile trip from Ephesos by boat. This is where the messengers went and asked the god to prophesy truly. They had come for the same reason, and the god gave them in poetic form an oracle that applied to both. This was the poem:

> Wherefore yearn to know the end and start of illness?
> One illness holds both; the answer lies therein.
> I see terrible sufferings for them and endless troubles.
> Both will flee across the sea, driven by madness,
> will face chains among men with the sea in their veins.

---

8. An internationally important oracle of Apollo, the god of prophecy. The temple was just south of Colophon in the village of Claros on the coast northwest of Ephesos.

For both a tomb as bridal chamber and destructive fire.
And yet, after calamities, a better fate will they have,
and by the flows of the sacred* river for holy Isis,[9]
their savior, furnish rich gifts afterwards.

[7] When this oracle was delivered to Ephesos, the two fathers were immediately baffled and completely lost about what the danger was. They couldn't interpret the god's response. What was the disease? The flight? The chains? The tomb? The river? The help from the goddess? They thought about it a lot and felt it best to go along with the oracle as best they could by joining their children in marriage. They assumed that was the god's will from the prophecy. That was their decision, and they also made up their minds to send the couple away for a while on a trip after their wedding.

Then the city was filled with revelers and everything was covered with garlands. The upcoming wedding was the talk of the town, and the couple was congratulated by everyone, Habrocomes because he was going to marry such a beautiful wife, Anthia because she would get to share her bed with such a handsome young man.

When Habrocomes learned about the oracle's response and the marriage, he was overjoyed that he would have Anthia. He wasn't at all afraid of the prophecy. His feeling was that his current pleasure more than made up for any suffering. In the same way Anthia was pleased she would get Habrocomes and could not have cared less about the flight or the misfortunes, since she had in Habrocomes something to comfort her in all the troubles to come.

[8] When the time for the wedding came, vigils were kept and many animals were sacrificed to the goddess. Once these preparations had been completed and the night arrived (Habrocomes and Anthia thought everything took too long), they brought the girl to the bridal chamber. They held torches as they sang the marriage hymn and shouted their best wishes. Then they brought her in and put her in the bed.

The bridal chamber had been prepared for them: a golden bed covered with purple sheets, and over the bed a canopy of Babylonian fabric[10] had been decoratively embroidered—playing cupids, some of them serving Aphrodite (her picture was there too), some riding mounted

9. Though Isis was originally an Egyptian goddess, her worship began to spread through the Greek world in the Hellenistic period and eventually was firmly established in the Greco-Roman world.

10. Purple dye was an expensive commodity, and textiles from Babylon (south of modern Baghdad) were luxury items.

on sparrows, some weaving garlands, some bringing flowers. That was on one half of the canopy. On the other side was Ares.[11] He wasn't in armor but was dressed for his lover Aphrodite,[12] with a garland on his head, wearing his short cloak. Eros was leading him with a lit torch in his hand. That was the canopy under which they laid Anthia when they brought her to Habrocomes. Then they closed the doors.

[9] Mutual passion overcame them, and they were no longer able to speak to each other or make eye contact. They lay there at the mercy of pleasure, embarrassed, afraid, breathing heavily. Their bodies shook and their souls trembled, but after a long while Habrocomes got hold of himself and embraced Anthia. She began to cry, her soul sending forth the tears as visible proof of her desire.

"This is the night I've longed for more than anything else," Habrocomes said. "It's mine at last, after suffering so many nights before. Girl, you mean more to me than my life, and you are more fortunate than any woman in any of those old stories—you have the man who loves you as your husband. I pray that you can live with him your whole life as his faithful wife till death do you part."

He kissed her and tasted her tears, and they seemed to him a sweeter drink than any nectar, a more potent remedy for pain than any drug.

She had a few things to say to him. "Really, Habrocomes? You think I'm beautiful? You find me acceptable compared to your own beauty? You spineless coward! How much time did you waste while you were in love? How long did you do nothing? I know what you must have been suffering from my own misery. But who cares? Taste my tears. Let your beautiful hair drink up the draught of love. Let us join ourselves together and unite in love. Let us drench our garlands with each other's tears so they too can take part in our love."

She kissed him all over his face and pressed all his hair to her eyes and picked up the garlands. She joined her lips to his in a kiss. In the act of kissing every thought they had was passed from one soul to the other via their lips.

As she kissed his eyes, she said, "You two! How many times you tormented me! You were the first to apply love's sting to my soul. You were once arrogant but are now loving. You've served me well and guided my love straight to Habrocomes' soul. So I kiss you again and again and fix

---

11. God of warfare.

12. The joining of Ares and Aphrodite, goddess of sex and love, in a love affair goes all the way back to the eighth book of Homer's *Odyssey* and was a popular literary and artistic motif.

my eyes on you—my eyes are here to serve Habrocomes. May you never look at anything else. I pray you never show another beautiful woman to Habrocomes, and that I never think another man is handsome. Keep yourselves fixed on souls that you yourselves have set on fire. Make sure they stay that way."

They lay down, their bodies entwined, and enjoyed for the first time the labors of Aphrodite. They vied through the whole night with each other, ardently competing to see which one could show greater love.

[10] When it was day, they got up much more cheerful and in much better spirits now that they had enjoyed each other's beauty, which they had desired for a long time. Life was one big festival for them, and everything was full of celebrations. By this time they had even forgotten about the oracle. But fate hadn't forgotten. No, the god who had decided these things did not let them slip his mind.

After a little time passed, their parents decided to go through with their plan and send them away from the city. The couple would see another country and other cities and would, as much as they could, go along with the god's oracle by leaving Ephesos for a while.

Everything was prepared for their departure. There was a large ship, as well as a crew ready to sail. The supplies were put on board: lots of different outfits, plenty of silver and gold, and more food than they could eat. Before their departure there were sacrifices to Artemis, the whole city offered prayers, and everyone wept as if the children of the whole community were getting ready to leave.

The plan was for them to take a trip to Egypt, and when the day of their departure came, many slaves, both male and female, were put aboard. As the ship was about to put to sea, the whole population of Ephesos, along with many foreigners, came with torches and sacrificial offerings to see them off. At that point it hit Lycomedes and Themisto all at once—the oracle, their son, the trip—and they collapsed in despair. Megamedes and Euippe experienced the same emotions but felt more optimism, because they were concentrating on the end of the prophecy.

Then the sailors began to bustle about, the mooring cables were untied, the pilot took his place, and the ship started to move off. From those on the land and those on the ship a loud cry arose, mingled together. The former shouted, "Dear children, will we, your parents, ever see you again?" and the latter, "Parents, will we come back to you?"

There were tears and wailing, and everyone called loudly to their kin by name, leaving behind the name in each other's memories.

Megamedes took up a bowl and poured a libation, and as he did so, uttered a prayer loud enough for those on the ship to hear: "Children,

may you enjoy the greatest fortune and avoid the cruelties in the prophecy. May the Ephesians welcome you home safe and sound, and may
you regain your beloved country. If anything else were to happen, know
this—we will not go on living. We sent you on a journey that may be
ill-starred but is necessary."

[11] He would have said more, but his tears stopped him, and
they returned to the city while the crowd urged them not to worry.
Habrocomes and Anthia lay wrapped in each other's arms. So many
things ran through their minds, pitying their parents, missing their
country, fearing the oracle, fretting over the trip. The fact they were
traveling with each other made them feel better about all of it.

Traveling that day with a favorable wind, they made the crossing
and arrived at Hera's sacred isle, Samos.[13] After sacrificing there and
feasting, they offered many prayers to the goddess, then set sail the
following night.

Their voyage was very pleasant, and they spoke to each other frequently, asking, "Do you think we'll be able to spend our whole life
together?"

Once Habrocomes groaned loudly as he recalled his situation, and
said, "Anthia, you're more important to me than my own soul. I pray
we'll enjoy great fortune and stay safe with each other, but if in the end
it's fated for something to happen and somehow we become separated
from each other, let's make oaths to each other, darling. You swear you'll
remain faithful to me and not accept another husband, and I'll swear
that I won't marry another woman."

Anthia wailed loudly when she heard this. "Habrocomes, what convinced you that if I'm separated from you I'll ever think again of a
husband or getting married? I mean . . . me? Without you, I won't even
go on living in the first place. I swear it to you, by the goddess of our
country, great Artemis of the Ephesians, and by this sea that we cross
and by the god who made us completely crazy for each other: if I am
separated from you for even a little while, I will neither go on living nor
look upon the sun."

So Anthia swore, and Habrocomes made his oath in return, and the
circumstances made the oaths even more formidable.

---

13. A very short trip at a leisurely pace. Samos lies offshore to the southeast of Ephesos.
The Heraion of Samos was one of the most important temples in the ancient world, and
the goddess had been closely associated with the island since at least the time of Homer.
Hera was the wife of Zeus and the goddess of marriage.

Then the ship cruised past Cos and Cnidos, and the island of the Rhodians came into sight,[14] large and fair, and they absolutely had to make a stop there since the sailors said they needed to take on water and rest up since they were headed for a long voyage.

[12] The ship came to port in Rhodes, and the sailors got off. Habrocomes also left, holding Anthia's hand. All the Rhodians flocked to them, astounded by the beauty of the young couple. No one who saw them passed by in silence. Some said it was a visitation by the gods, others knelt in reverence and offered prayers. Soon the names Habrocomes and Anthia had crisscrossed the city, and the people made official public prayers on their behalf, sacrificed many animals, and held a festival in honor of their visit.

The pair toured the entire city and dedicated a suit of golden armor in the temple of Helios[15] with a poem engraved in memory of the donors:

> The foreigners dedicated to you these arms of beaten gold,
> Anthia and Habrocomes, citizens of sacred Ephesos.

After making this dedication, they stayed a few days on the island and then at the sailors' insistence set sail, now that their supplies were restocked. The entire population of Rhodes saw them off. At first they traveled with a favorable wind and were pleased with their progress. For that day and the following night they sailed along and covered some of the distance across the Egyptian Sea. The next day, however, the wind quit, they were becalmed, and their progress slowed. The sailors got bored, then broke out the wine and got drunk.

That was the start of the prophecy.

A woman appeared to Habrocomes in his sleep. She was fearsome to look at, taller than a mortal, and wearing crimson clothes. He saw her come near the ship and set it alight. The others were killed, but he swam safely away with Anthia. As soon as he saw this, he was upset and expected something terrible from the dream.

Something terrible did happen.

[13] As it turns out, some pirates had been moored next to them in Rhodes. They were Phoenicians[16]—lots of them, and tough—in a

---

14. Cos, Cnidos, and Rhodes are islands off the southwest coast of Asia Minor.

15. Rhodes was one of the few major cult centers of Helios, god of the sun.

16. Inhabitants of Phoenicia, the region corresponding to the coast of modern Lebanon. They had been famed among the Greeks from early times as sailors and merchants—and pirates.

large trireme[17] (they were berthed there under the pretense of carrying cargo). These men had learned that the ship was full of gold, silver, and slaves, plentiful and valuable. So they decided to attack, kill anyone who resisted (though they really didn't think they'd put up much of a fight), and take the rest to Phoenicia to sell along with the property. The leader of the pirates was named Corymbos. He was a young man, tall of stature, with a fierce look in his eye and his hair worn long and grimy.

After coming up with this plan, at first the pirates sailed nonchalantly near Habrocomes' group, but finally—it was around noon and everyone on the ship was lying down from boredom or drink, some sleeping, some lazing about—Corymbos and his men attacked them, rowing their ship with great speed (remember, it was a trireme). When they drew along-side, they leapt up onto the other ship. They were wearing armor and their swords were unsheathed.

Some of the passengers threw themselves overboard in terror and perished, while others were slaughtered trying to mount a defense. Habrocomes and Anthia ran to Corymbos the pirate, took hold of his knees, and said, "Take the money, master! And take us as slaves! Spare our lives and don't kill those who submit to you of their own free will. We beg you by the sea itself and by your right hand. Take us wherever you want. Sell us—we're your slaves. Just have pity on us and sell us to the same master."

[14] When Corymbos heard this, he immediately gave orders to his men to stop the killing.[18] He transferred over to his trireme the most valuable of the cargo, along with Habrocomes and Anthia and a few of their slaves. Then he set the other ship on fire, and all the rest of its passengers were consumed by the flames. He did this because he couldn't take all of them and it didn't seem safe.*

What a pitiful sight. Some were being taken away in the trireme while the others were burning in the ship. All of them stretched out their hands and lamented.

"Where are they taking you, masters?" the ones on the ship asked. "What land will you end up in? What city will you live in?"

The others answered, "How blessed you are! You're fortunate to die before you experience chains, before you see a life of slavery to pirates."

That's what they said as some were carried off and some burned.

---

17. A swift, maneuverable ship with rowers sitting in three banks. It was one of the standard warships of ancient fleets.

18. "gave orders . . . to stop the killing": The words may echo Thucydides 7.85.1.

At that moment Habrocomes' tutor, now an old man, dignified in appearance and pitiful because of his age, couldn't bear the thought of Habrocomes' being taken away. He threw himself into the sea and swam in an attempt to catch up to the trireme.

"My boy, why are you abandoning me, your old servant? Where are you going, Habrocomes? Kill me yourself and bury me! My luck has run out! What is there for me to live for without you?"

At last, having lost hope of ever seeing Habrocomes again, he gave himself up to the waves and died. That was what most aroused Habrocomes' pity. He stretched his arms out to the old man and implored the pirates to pick him up.

They, however, paid him no mind, and after a three-day voyage over open water they put to shore at the city of Tyre in Phoenicia,[19] where the pirates had their home base. They took them not to the city itself, but to a nearby estate owned by a pirate commander named Apsyrtos. Corymbos was his subordinate. He worked for him in return for a wage and a share of the spoils. During the time the voyage had taken, Corymbos had fallen in love—deeply in love—with Habrocomes, since he had seen a great deal of him on a daily basis. Spending so much time with the young man fanned the flame of his love even more.

[15] He didn't think he had a shot at winning Habrocomes over on the trip. He could see he was in bad shape from depression and also that he was in love with Anthia. At the same time he was sure that using force would be traumatic. He was afraid that the young man would do something terrible to himself. But when they landed at Tyre, Corymbos began to lose his patience. First, he treated Habrocomes kindly. He urged him to cheer up and provided him whatever care he needed. But the boy thought that Corymbos was just being nice to him out of pity, so Corymbos next took the step of telling Euxeinos, one of his fellow pirates, that he was in love. He asked him for his help and advice about how to win the young man over.

Euxeinos was happy to hear Corymbos' situation. He himself was deeply in love with Anthia and miserable. He told Corymbos how things stood with him and advised him to stop driving himself crazy and to take action.

"Think about it. It would be pretty awful for us to face danger and risk our lives and not have the right to enjoy what we've acquired with our hard work. We can ask Apsyrtos to give them to us as a special bonus."

---

19. Modern Sour, Lebanon. Tyre was one of the leading cities of Phoenicia.

Corymbos was in love, so Euxeinos had no trouble persuading him. They accordingly agreed to speak up for each other, Euxeinos to win over Habrocomes, and Corymbos Anthia.

[16] This whole time Habrocomes and Anthia were lying there in despair. They worried terribly about the future, talked to one another, and swore to stick to their pact. Then Corymbos and Euxeinos came to them. They said they wanted to talk to them individually about something. They took them each to a different place, one leading Anthia, the other Habrocomes. The couple's spirits were shaken, and they had the feeling this didn't bode well for them.

Euxeinos spoke to Habrocomes about Corymbos. "Young man, it's perfectly reasonable for you to be having a rough time in the face of your misfortune. You're a slave when you used to be free. You're poor instead of rich. But you need to chalk it all up to your fortune—give in to the destiny that controls you, and show affection for those who have become your masters.

"I have to tell you, there is a way for you to regain your prosperity and freedom if you'll be willing to comply with the wishes of your master Corymbos. He's deeply in love with you and is ready to make you master of all that is his. Nothing bad's going to happen to you. You'll be making your master more friendly to you.

"Think about the position you're in. No one can help you. This is a foreign land. Your masters are pirates. There will be no escape from punishment if you turn up your nose at Corymbos. What do you need with a wife and all that comes with one now? Why do you need a woman to love at your age? Forget all that. You need to keep your eyes on your master alone and do what he tells you to."

When Habrocomes heard this, he was instantly speechless and unable to find words to answer. He broke into tears and groaned as he saw how bad things had gotten for him.

"Master," he said to Euxeinos, "allow me a little time to mull it over, and I'll give you an answer about everything you've said."

Euxeinos went away. Corymbos had discussed with Anthia Euxeinos' love and her current bind. He told her she absolutely had to obey her masters. He promised her a lot if she yielded: lawful marriage, money, and a life of comfort. But she gave him a similar answer and asked for a little time to think about it.

Euxeinos and Corymbos waited together to see what answer they would get. They hoped they'd win Habrocomes and Anthia over without any trouble.

Book 2

[1] Habrocomes and Anthia went to the room where they spent most of their time and told each other what they'd heard. Throwing themselves to the floor, they wept and wailed: "Father! Mother! Beloved country! Friends and family!"

Habrocomes finally pulled himself together and said, "We're cursed. What's going to happen to us? We're in a foreign land. We're at the mercy of the violence of pirates. The prophecy is starting. Now the god is exacting his punishment for my arrogance. Corymbos loves me, and Euxeinos loves you. What trouble our beauty has caused for both of us! Is this what I kept myself pure for up till now? To hand myself over to a horny pirate and his shameful lust? What kind of life is left for me when I've lost my Anthia and become a whore instead of a man? No, I swear by the purity that has been my companion until now—I will not submit to Corymbos. I'll die first, and they can look at my pure corpse."

He cried as he spoke, and Anthia said, "What evils! How soon we're being forced to remember our oaths! How soon we're experiencing slavery! A man loves me and hopes to seduce me, come to my bed after Habrocomes, sleep with me, and satisfy his lust. Well, I pray I won't cling to life that much. I pray I won't be able to look upon the sun after I'm violated. Let's make up our minds once and for all: let's die, Habrocomes. We'll be with each other after death, and no one will bother us."

[2] That was their decision, but in the meantime Apsyrtos, the pirate boss, had heard that Corymbos' party was back and had brought in a fantastically rich haul. He came to the estate, saw Habrocomes and the others, and was astonished by their beauty. Thinking they'd bring a nice profit, he immediately demanded to have them. He distributed the rest of the money and items, along with all the girls that had been captured, to Corymbos and his pirates. Euxeinos and Corymbos relinquished Habrocomes and his party to Apsyrtos—grudgingly, perhaps, but out of necessity they did release them.

Euxeinos and Corymbos left, and Apsyrtos took Habrocomes and Anthia, as well as Leucon and Rhode, two of their slaves, and brought them to Tyre. The group's progress was quite a sight, and all marveled at their beauty. Barbarians who had never before seen such beauty assumed that they were looking at gods. They congratulated Apsyrtos for having acquired such fine slaves, and he took them home and turned them over to a trusted slave. He gave orders for them to be treated with care, because he'd profit greatly if he could sell them for what they were worth.

[3] That was the situation Habrocomes and his friends were in. After a few days Apsyrtos left for Syria[20] on other business, and his daughter Manto fell in love with Habrocomes. She was a pretty girl and old enough for marriage, though she fell far short of Anthia's beauty. After constantly spending time with Habrocomes she was captivated and frantic. She had no idea what to do. She couldn't get up the courage to talk to Habrocomes, because she knew he had a wife and she was sure she would never win him over. But she also couldn't talk to anyone from her own household out of fear of her father. That only caused her to burn hotter and suffer. When she could no longer stand it, she decided to confess her love to Anthia's companion Rhode, since she was a girl and about the same age. Manto thought that Rhode was the only one who would help her gain her desire.

Waiting for a quiet moment, she took the girl to the altar of the household gods and pleaded with her not to expose her. She made her swear oaths, told her about her love for Habrocomes, begged her to help, and promised many rewards if she did.

Before dismissing Rhode she said, "Remember, you're my slave. And keep in mind, if you wrong a barbarian, you'll feel her anger."

Rhode was caught in a serious dilemma. She loved Anthia and so didn't want to speak to Habrocomes, but she was terrified of the barbarian's anger. She decided it was all right to first share with Leucon what Manto had said to her. Rhode and Leucon were, in fact, a couple and were still together in Tyre.

When they were alone, she said, "Leucon, we're done for. We're not going to have our companions any more after this. The daughter of our master Apsyrtos is deeply in love with Habrocomes. She's threatening to do terrible things to us unless she gets him. So think about what we should do. It's dangerous to refuse the barbarian woman, but impossible to separate Habrocomes from Anthia."

Leucon's eyes filled with tears as he listened, expecting serious misfortunes to come from this. Eventually he pulled himself together and said, "Say nothing, Rhode. I'll take care of everything."

[4] He went to Habrocomes, who actually had nothing to do except love Anthia and be loved by her, and talk to her while listening to her talk. So Leucon came to them and said, "My friends, what are we to do? What's our plan, my fellow slaves? One of our masters thinks you're handsome, Habrocomes. Apsyrtos' daughter is aching for you, and it's a dangerous thing to refuse a barbarian girl in love. So figure out what

---

20. The region north and northeast of Phoenicia.

you want to do and save us all. Don't let us be crushed by our masters' anger."

Habrocomes was filled with anger and looked Leucon straight in the eye. "You're despicable! You're more of a barbarian than the Phoenicians here! You've got the gall to talk like that to Habrocomes? You tell me about another woman when Anthia's right here? I'm a slave, sure, but I know how to keep my word. They can do what they want to my body, but I've got a soul that's free. Let Manto make threats if she wants to about swords and ropes and fire and all the things that she can use on a slave's body—I'll never willingly hurt Anthia."

Anthia lay there, speechless in the face of their misfortune, unable to say a word. In time she eventually roused herself and said, "Habrocomes, you care for me, and I've no doubt that your love for me is uncommonly strong. But I beg you, who are the master of my soul, don't hand yourself over or fall victim to a barbarian's anger. Give in to our mistress' desire. I won't stand in your way. I'll kill myself. I'd just ask this of you: bury me yourself and give me a kiss when I'm dead and remember Anthia."

All this heightened Habrocomes' misery, and he had no idea what to do.

[5] While they were up to that, Manto, no longer able to put up with Rhode's foot-dragging, wrote Habrocomes a letter: "Greetings to the handsome Habrocomes from your mistress. Manto loves you. I can't stand it any more. I'm begging you for something that may be inappropriate for a girl but is necessary for a woman in love. Don't ignore me, and don't insult me, not when I have your interests at heart. If you give in, I'll persuade my father Apsyrtos to make me your wife, and we'll get rid of your current one. You'll be rich and happy. But if you refuse, think about what you'll suffer when the woman you've insulted gets her revenge. And consider what your friends will suffer when it's been proven they're partners and advisors in your arrogance."

She took this letter and sealed it, then gave it to one of her own maids who wasn't Greek and told her to deliver it to Habrocomes. He got it and read it and was upset by all its contents, but the part about Anthia particularly pained him. He kept that writing tablet, and wrote his reply on another one and gave it to the maid. It said this:

"Mistress, do what you want. Use my body as you would a slave's. If you want to kill me, I'm ready to die. If you want to torture me, torture me in whatever way suits you. I will *not* come to your bed. If you order me to, I won't obey you."

Manto got this letter and lost control. All her emotions became jumbled—hostility, jealousy, pain, and fear—and she thought about how to punish the man for his arrogance.

Just then Apsyrtos got back from Syria. He was bringing back with him a man named Moiris for his daughter to marry. When he showed up, Manto quickly arranged her scheme against Habrocomes. She pulled at her hair and ripped her clothes, then went to meet her father and fell at his knees.

"Pity your daughter, father! I've been insulted by a slave. The 'faithful' Habrocomes tried to take my virginity! And he plotted against you too by saying he loved me. You've got to punish him in a way that matches his horrible crimes. I'll kill myself before I let you betray your own daughter and hand her over to your slaves."

[6] Apsyrtos believed she was telling the truth, so he made no further inquiry into what had happened. He sent for Habrocomes and spoke to him.

"You wicked, foul man. You're just a slave, but you dared to insult your masters and tried to debase a maiden? Well, you won't get away with it. I'm going to punish you and I'll make your torture an object lesson to the other slaves."

Refusing to listen to so much as one word, he ordered his servants to tear Habrocomes' clothes off him, bring fire and whips, and beat him. It was a pitiful sight. The blows disfigured his whole body, unused as it was to slavish torture. All his blood poured out, and his beauty drained away. Apsyrtos also used painful restraints and fire on him and assiduously tortured and interrogated him as a demonstration to his daughter's fiancé that he would be marrying a chaste virgin.

While this was going on, Anthia threw herself at Apsyrtos' knees and begged him to spare Habrocomes. He replied, "No, I'm going to punish him even more for your sake. He's harmed you too—he loved another woman when he already had a wife." Then he ordered his men to throw Habrocomes in chains and lock him in a room without windows.

[7] So Habrocomes was chained in a cell, and an awful hopelessness filled him, especially because he wasn't allowed to see Anthia. He looked for many ways to die, but he found none because there were lots of men guarding him.

Apsyrtos went ahead with his daughter's wedding, and they celebrated for many days. It was pure grief for Anthia. Whenever she could talk the guards into allowing it, she would sneak in to visit Habrocomes and mourn their terrible plight.

Finally, when preparations for departing to Syria were being made, Apsyrtos sent his daughter ahead with many gifts. He gave her clothes from Babylon and a lot of gold and silver, and he also presented his daughter Manto with Anthia, Rhode, and Leucon. When Anthia found out about that and learned she was to be taken to Syria with Manto, she went as soon as she could to the prison and threw her arms around Habrocomes.

"Master, I'm being taken to Syria as a gift for Manto—put into the hands of the woman who is jealous of me! And you'll stay here in the prison and die pitifully without anyone at all to prepare your body for burial. Well, I swear to you by our shared destiny that I will remain yours both while I live and also if I have to die."

She kissed and hugged him, and hung on to his shackles and lay prostrate at his feet.

[8] Finally she left the prison, and he then and there threw himself to the floor, groaning and weeping. "Dearest father! Themisto, my mother! Where is that happiness I once thought I had in Ephesos? Where are the famous and admired Anthia and Habrocomes, that beautiful couple? She is being taken as a prisoner to some distant land, and I've been deprived of my one source of comfort. I'm going to die miserable and alone in prison."

Then sleep overpowered him and he had a dream. In it he saw his father Lycomedes dressed in black, wandering across the whole earth and sea. He came to the prison, loosed Habrocomes' bonds, and set him free from the cell. Habrocomes himself turned into a horse and traveled over a lot of land in pursuit of another horse, a female. He finally found the mare and became a human being again. After this dream, he got up and was a little more hopeful.

[9] So he was shut up in the prison, and Anthia was taken to Syria along with Leucon and Rhode. When Manto arrived with the others in Antioch[21] (that was where Moiris was from), she bore a grudge against Rhode and hated Anthia. Right away she ordered some men to load Rhode and Leucon on a ship and sell them as far from Syria as possible. As for Anthia, she hit upon the idea of marrying her to a slave, and the lowest sort of slave at that, a peasant goatherd, thinking to get her revenge on her in this way.[22]

She sent for the goatherd, who was named Lampon, and handed over Anthia. She told him to take her as his wife and ordered him to use force on her if she resisted. Anthia was taken to the country to be with the

---

21. Antioch, founded at the end of the fourth century BC on the eastern banks of the Orontes River, was by far the most populous and important city in Syria.

22. The motif derives from the myth of Electra, daughter of Agamemnon. In the version presented in Euripides' *Electra,* her mother and stepfather, who have slain Agamemnon, get her out of the way by marrying her to a farmer. Xenophon here goes Euripides one further by marrying his heroine to a goatherd, the lowest of occupations in the countryside.

goatherd, but when she arrived at the estate where Lampon herded his goats, she fell at his knees and pleaded with him to pity her and keep her pure. She explained who she was and told him about her previous good birth, her husband, and her captivity. Lampon took pity on the girl when he heard this, swore he would make sure she stayed undefiled,[23] and urged her to cheer up.

[10] On the estate with the goatherd, she spent all her time lamenting for Habrocomes. Meanwhile, Apsyrtos searched the room where Habrocomes had been living before his punishment. He came across Manto's letter to Habrocomes and recognized the handwriting. He realized he'd been unjustly punishing Habrocomes, so he immediately ordered him released and brought into his presence.

Habrocomes, having suffered horrible, heart-rending things, fell at Apsyrtos' knees. Apsyrtos made him get up and said, "Don't worry, young man. I condemned you unjustly. I was convinced by my daughter's story. But now I'm going to make you a free man instead of a slave. I'll make you the manager of my household, and I'll give you the daughter of one of my fellow citizens as your wife. Don't hold what happened against me—I wronged you, but I didn't mean to."

Habrocomes said, "Master, I'm grateful to you for discovering the truth and for rewarding my purity."

Everyone in the house was happy for Habrocomes and thanked the master on his behalf, but he himself was in complete misery over Anthia. Over and over he thought to himself, "What's freedom to me? And money? A job taking care of Apsyrtos' things? This isn't what I should be doing. I pray I'll find her whether she's alive or dead."

That was the situation he was in. He managed Apsyrtos' affairs and thought about when and where he would find Anthia. Leucon and Rhode, meantime, had been taken to the city of Xanthos in Lycia[24] (the city is inland from the coast). There they were sold to an old man who treated them with every kindness and thought of them as his children, for he had none of his own. They lived amidst abundance but felt bad about not being able to see Anthia and Habrocomes.

[11] Anthia was with the goatherd for a while, and Moiris, Manto's husband, regularly visited the estate and fell deeply in love with Anthia. At first he tried to cover it up, but in the end he told the goatherd about his feelings and promised him many rewards if he helped keep his

---

23. In Euripides' play, the farmer both pities Electra and leaves her virginity intact.

24. The chief city of Lycia (a region in the southwest of Asia Minor), a little ways inland on the river of the same name as the city.

secret. The goatherd accepted Moiris' offer, but because he was afraid of Manto, he went to her and told her about Moiris' love.

She got angry and said, "I am the unluckiest woman in the world! Am I going to take my rival with me everywhere I go? She's the reason I lost the man I loved in Phoenicia before, and now I'm in danger of losing my husband. Well, Anthia won't enjoy having Moiris think she's beautiful too. No, I'm also going to make her pay for what happened in Tyre."

She didn't make trouble right away, but when Moiris was out of town on a trip, she sent for the goatherd. She ordered him to take Anthia, lead her into the thickest part of the woods, and kill her. She promised him a reward for this. He felt sorry for the girl, but he was afraid of Manto, so he went to Anthia and told her what was in store for her.

She wailed and lamented, "Damn this beauty! It creates danger for the two of us wherever we go. Because of our unfortunate good looks, Habrocomes has died in Tyre and I'm going to die here. I beg you, goatherd Lampon, in the same way you've treated me with respect until now, if you do kill me, bury me in the ground right on the spot, even a dusting, and place your hands on my eyes and, as you bury me, call out Habrocomes' name over and over. That would be a happy funeral for me, with Habrocomes present."

The goatherd felt pity as he thought about committing the impious deed of killing such a beautiful girl who'd done nothing wrong. He took the girl but could not bring himself to kill her. "Anthia," he told her, "you know our mistress Manto ordered me to take and kill you. But I'm a god-fearing man and pity your beauty, so I'm willing to sell you someplace far from this land. That way Manto won't learn you're still alive and treat me even worse."

She grasped his feet and tearfully said, "Gods and ancestral Artemis, repay the goatherd for his good deeds!" She told him to go ahead and sell her.

The goatherd took Anthia off to the harbor, where he found some Cilician merchants and sold the girl. He took the money he got for her and went back to the countryside. The merchants took Anthia, put her aboard their ship, and started their trip to Cilicia[25] at night. They ran into a strong headwind, and their ship broke up. Some of them barely managed to make it to safety on a beach by floating on the ship's timbers. Anthia was with them. There was a thick forest in that place, and as they wandered in it that night, they were captured by Hippothoos the bandit and his men.

---

25. The region in the southeast corner of Asia Minor to the west of Syria. Its leading city and administrative center was Tarsos (now most famous as the birthplace of St. Paul).

[12] At this time a slave arrived from Syria bringing the following letter from Manto to her father Apsyrtos:

"You gave me away to a husband in a foreign land, and I gave orders that Anthia, the girl you gave me as a present along with the other slaves, go and live in the country. She was a troublemaker. My handsome Moiris is in love with her because he saw her all the time out at the country estate. No longer able to put up with it, I sent for the goatherd and ordered her to be resold in one of the cities in Syria."

When Habrocomes found out about this, he could no longer bear to stay there. Without telling Apsyrtos or anyone else in the house, he went in search of Anthia. Arriving in Antioch at the farm where Anthia had been living with the goatherd, he went to the goatherd Lampon, who Manto had given Anthia in marriage to. He asked Lampon to tell him if he knew anything about a girl from Tyre. The goatherd told him that her name was Anthia, that they'd been married, that he'd respected her chastity, that Moiris had fallen in love with her, what he'd been ordered to do to her, and that she'd gone to Cilicia. He also said that she was always talking about some man named Habrocomes. Habrocomes didn't say who he was but got up at dawn and rode for Cilicia in hopes of finding Anthia there.

[13] Hippothoos the bandit and his men stayed and celebrated that night, and the next day they busied themselves with their sacrifice. Everything—the statue of Ares, the firewood, some garlands—had been prepared. The sacrifice was supposed to happen in its customary way: the sacrificial offering, whether a person or an animal, they hung from a tree and threw javelins at from a distance. All those who hit it were thought to have had their sacrifice accepted by the god, and all those who missed would try to appease the god again.

Anthia faced being sacrificed in this way, but when everything was ready and they were about to hang the girl up, they heard the sound of the trees rustling and men's footsteps. It was the magistrate in charge of keeping the peace in Cilicia, Perilaos by name, one of the most powerful people in Cilicia. This man attacked the bandits with a large force and killed almost all of them but captured a few alive. Hippothoos was the only one able to grab his weapons and escape.

Perilaos got hold of Anthia and took pity on her after finding out the misfortune that she'd been about to suffer. In point of fact, however, his pity contained within it the seed of great misfortune for Anthia. He took her and the captured bandits to the city of Tarsos in Cilicia. The constant sight of the girl caused him to fall in love, and little by little Perilaos was captivated by Anthia.

When they got to Tarsos, he delivered the bandits to the lockup, but
doted on Anthia, for he had neither wife nor children but was very well
off. He told Anthia she could be Perilaos' everything—his wife, his lady
of the house, his children. At first she refused him, not knowing what
to do. But as he became more forcefully insistent, she grew fearful that
he'd resort to something more violent, so she agreed to marriage but
pleaded with him to wait for a short time, around thirty days, and to
keep her untouched. She pretended < . . . >. Perilaos consented and swore
he would keep her pure of intercourse until the time had lapsed.

[14] While she was in Tarsos with Perilaos, waiting for the day of
her wedding, Habrocomes was making the journey to Cilicia. Not far
from the bandits' cave (he had wandered off the direct route) he ran into
Hippothoos, who was wearing armor. But Hippothoos ran to him when
he caught sight of him, greeted him as a friend, and asked to become
his traveling companion. "I have no clue who you are, young man, but
I can tell by looking at you that you're a decent guy, and a brave one
too, and I'm pretty sure your wandering means you've been wronged.
So let's forget Cilicia and head for Cappadocia and Pontos.[26] They say
prosperous men dwell there."*

Habrocomes said nothing about his search for Anthia, but said yes
to Hippothoos when he insisted, and they swore oaths to cooperate and
stick together. Habrocomes was actually hoping to find Anthia in their
wide wandering.

They went back to the cave for that day to see if there was still anything left they could get, and they rested themselves and their horses
(Hippothoos had a horse hidden in the woods).

Book 3

[1] The next day they passed from Cilicia and made their way to
Mazacon,[27] a large and fine city in Cappadocia. Hippothoos' plan was to
recruit some strong young men from there and rebuild his bandit gang.

---

26. Cappadocia was the landlocked region directly north of Cilicia. Pontos was directly
north of Cappadocia on the south coast of the Black Sea.

27. This is the old capital of the Cappadocian kings. Xenophon uses a rarely attested
spelling; it is more usually Mazaca. In the first century BC it was renamed Caesarea
(hence its modern name Kayseri, Turkey).

As they passed through large villages, they had plenty of everything they needed, because Hippothoos knew how to speak Cappadocian and everyone treated him like one of their own.

Finishing the journey in ten days, they came to Mazacon and found a place to stay near the city gates. They decided to rest up there for a few days after their exertions. As they were feasting, Hippothoos gave a groan and broke into tears, and Habrocomes asked him why he was crying.

"My story's long and full of tragedy," he answered.

Habrocomes begged him to tell it and promised that he would recount his own. Hippothoos told his story, starting all the way at the beginning (it happens that it was just the two of them present).

[2] "I was born a citizen of Perinthos, a city near Thrace.[28] I am from one of the most powerful families there. No doubt you've heard how illustrious Perinthos is and how prosperous its men are.

"When I was in my youth there, I fell in love with a handsome young man. He was a young man of a local family and his name was Hyperanthes. I first came to love him when I saw him wrestling at the gymnasium, and I couldn't hold back my feelings. A local all-night festival was being held, and while it was going on, I went up to Hyperanthes and pleaded with him to take pity on me. The young man felt compassion for me when he heard this and promised me everything.

"The first steps in our love were kisses and caresses and, from me, plenty of tears.* At last we were able to get a chance to be alone together, and our closeness in age meant there were no eyebrows raised. We were together for a long time—really, truly in love with each other—until some god came to resent us.

"A man came from Byzantion (Byzantion is near Perinthos), one of the most powerful people there. He was full of himself because of his wealth and affluence. His name was Aristomachos. As soon as he set foot in Perinthos, as if he had been sent against me by a god, he saw Hyperanthes with me and was instantly captivated, marveling at the young man's beauty, which could've enticed just about anyone.

"Once he'd fallen in love, he couldn't keep his love in check. First he sent gifts to the young man. That got Aristomachos nowhere. Out of loyalty to me, Hyperanthes let no one get close to him. So the man won over Hyperanthes' father, a wicked man with a weakness for money. His

---

28. Perinthos (a coastal city) and the region of Thrace are just across the Hellespont from northwest Asia Minor. Perinthos is a few miles west of Byzantion (later Constantinople, modern Istanbul).

father gave Hyperanthes to him, ostensibly making him his student—
the man claimed he was well-versed in the art of rhetoric.

"He got him and at first kept him locked away. Afterwards he took
him to Byzantion. I followed them, not giving a thought to any of my
own affairs. I spent as much time with the young man as I could, but
that wasn't very often. A kiss was a rare thing for me to have and conversation hard to come by, for lots of people were watching me.

"Finally, I couldn't stand it any longer, and I got myself worked
up and went back to Perinthos. I sold everything I owned, took the
money, and went to Byzantion. I got a dagger (I had arranged this with
Hyperanthes), and at night I went into Aristomachos' house and found
him in bed with the boy. Filled with rage, I struck Aristomachos a fatal
blow.

"It was quiet, and everyone went on sleeping, so without further ado
I left stealthily and took Hyperanthes with me. I traveled all night to
Perinthos, immediately got on a ship without anyone knowing it, and
sailed for Asia. For a while the journey went well, but in the end when
we had gotten to Lesbos,[29] a strong wind slammed into us and capsized
the ship. I swam alongside Hyperanthes and supported him. This made
it easier for him to swim, but when night fell, the young man couldn't
go on. He grew exhausted from swimming and died.

"The best I could do was get his body safely to shore and bury him. I
spent a lot of time weeping and groaning, then took mementos of him,
managed to find a suitable stone somewhere, and set up a headstone on
his grave. In memory of the unfortunate young man I carved an epitaph,
which I came up with on the spur of the moment:

> Hippothoos set up for famed Hyperanthes this tomb,
>   unworthy of the death of a sacred citizen,
> a famous flower, whom once from land to deep a god
>   abducted as a great storm gusted on the sea.*

"After that I made up my mind not to go back to Perinthos. I went
through Asia to Great Phrygia and Pamphylia.[30] There, because I had
no way to make a living and was depressed at my misfortune, I turned to
banditry. At first I was a henchman in a gang, but in the end I organized

29. A large island lying outside of the Hellespont to the southwest, just off the coast of
western Asia Minor.

30. Hippothoos' itinerary is a little unclear, but he made his way inland eastward
(Phrygia is an interior region east of the Aegean coast and to the west of Cappadocia)
and then southward (Pamphylia lies on the Mediterranean coast west of Cilicia).

my own gang in Cilicia. It had quite a reputation until my men were captured not long before I saw you. So that's how my story turned out. But you, my friend, tell me your own. Obviously some strong compulsion makes you wander."

[3] Habrocomes told him he was from Ephesos and that he had fallen in love with a girl and married her. He described the prophecy, their trip, the pirates, Apsyrtos and Manto, his chains, his flight, the goatherd, and his trip as far as Cilicia.

When he was barely done speaking, Hippothoos gave a sympathetic wail. "O parents of mine! O country I'll never see again! O Hyperanthes, dearest to me of all! You, Habrocomes, will both see your beloved and, in time, get her back, but I'll never be able to set eyes on Hyperanthes again."

As he spoke, he showed Habrocomes the lock of the young man's hair he had with him and shed tears over it. When they'd both had enough of crying, Hippothoos turned to Habrocomes and said, "I almost forgot to tell you something else. Right before the capture of my gang, a beautiful girl who was lost showed up at our cave. She was the same age as you and said she was from your city. I didn't find out anything else about her. It was decided to sacrifice her to Ares. Everything had actually been prepared when the lawmen surprised us. I got away, but I don't know what happened to her. She was really beautiful, Habrocomes. Simply dressed. Blond hair. Lovely eyes."

When he was barely done speaking, Habrocomes gave a shout. "You've seen my Anthia, Hippothoos! So where can she have escaped to? What land is she in? Let's go to Cilicia and look for her there. She can't be far from the hideout. Please, by Hyperanthes, who meant more to you than your soul, don't decide to hurt me. Let's go where we can find Anthia."

Hippothoos promised to do all he could and said they should recruit a few men to be safe on the road.

That was what they were up to, planning to go back to Cilicia, but in the meantime the thirty days had run out for Anthia. Preparations were being made for Perilaos' wedding. Many animals were brought in from his country estates for sacrifice, along with an abundance of other provisions. Both his own household and the members of his extended family came to be with him, and many of his fellow citizens also joined in celebrating his marriage to Anthia.

[4] During the time that Anthia had lived in Perilaos' house after being rescued from the bandits, an old man from Ephesos had arrived in Tarsos. He was a physician, and his name was Eudoxos. While voyaging to Egypt he had been shipwrecked. This Eudoxos would go around to all

the reputable men in Tarsos and ask for clothes from some and money from others, explaining to each his misfortune. He came also to Perilaos and told him he was a physician from Ephesos.

Perilaos invited him in and took him to Anthia, thinking she'd be happy to see a man from Ephesos. She welcomed Eudoxos and asked whether he could tell her anything about her family. He said he knew nothing because of the length of time he'd been away from Ephesos, but this didn't make Anthia enjoy his company less, for she was reminded of those at home. People in the house had gotten used to him, and he visited Anthia all the time. He got from her anything he needed. He was constantly asking her to send him home to Ephesos, for it turned out he had a wife and children there.

[5] When all the preparations for the wedding had been made by Perilaos and the day was upon them, a lavish feast had been readied and Anthia had been dressed up in bridal finery. But she didn't stop crying day or night, and she kept picturing Habrocomes. She thought about everything at once: her love, her oaths, her city, her parents, how she was being forced against her will, her marriage. When she was alone and had a moment, she tore at her hair and said, "What an unfair and horrible person I am. I'm not living up to my side of the bargain with Habrocomes. To remain my husband he suffers chains and torture, and perhaps he's even dead. Meanwhile I put those things out of my mind and I'm about to get married, wretch that I am. Someone will sing the wedding hymn to me and I'll go to Perilaos' bed. No! Soul of Habrocomes, dearer to me than all else, don't feel any pain because of me. I'll never willingly hurt you. I'll come join you and remain your bride till death."

Then Eudoxos the Ephesian doctor came to see her, and she took him to a quiet room and fell at his knees and begged him not to breathe a word to anyone of what she was about to say. She asked him to swear by Artemis, goddess of their city, to help her in any way she asked. He helped her to her feet as she lamented. He told her to cheer up and swore he would do anything she wanted. She told him about her love for Habrocomes and her oaths to him and their agreement about being faithful.

"If I could be alive and get back my Habrocomes also alive, or if I could get away from here without being caught, I'd be busy figuring out how to do just that. But since he's dead and escape is impossible, and at the same time there is no way for me to submit to my upcoming marriage—I won't break the agreements I made with Habrocomes or ignore my oath—you've got to help me. You have to find a poison somewhere that will free me, ill-starred as I am, from my troubles.

"In return for this you'll receive many gifts from the gods. I'll pray to them many times for you before I die. And I myself will give you money and provide a way for you to get home. You'll be able to get on a ship and sail to Ephesos before anyone finds out. Once there, find my parents, Megamedes and Euippe, and tell them about my death and everything else about my travels. And tell them that Habrocomes is dead."

She then groveled at his feet and pleaded with him not to refuse her anything and to give her the poison. She produced twenty minas[31] and her own necklaces (she had plenty of everything, for she had access to all that Perilaos owned), and offered them to Eudoxos. He thought about it long and hard. Taking pity on the girl for her misfortune, wanting to go to Ephesos, and overcome by the money and gifts, he promised to give her the poison and went to get it.

While he was gone, she grieved deeply. She lamented for her youth, distressed that she was going to die before her time. Again and again she called Habrocomes' name as if he was actually there.

Then after a short time Eudoxos was back with a drug—not one that caused death, but one that induced deep sleep, so nothing would actually happen to the girl, but he could get money for traveling and then make it home safely. Anthia took it, thanked him profusely, and sent him away. He immediately got on a ship and set sail, while she looked for the right chance to drink the drug.

[6] It was night now and the bridal chamber was ready. The people who were assigned to the task came and picked up Anthia. She left tearfully and unwillingly and hid the drug in her hand. When she got near the chamber, the members of the household loudly sang the wedding song, but she let out a wail and wept. "This is just like when I was taken to Habrocomes, my first husband! Love's fire was our escort, and the wedding song was sung for a happy marriage. But now what are you going to do, Anthia? Will you wrong Habrocomes, your husband, the man you love, the man who died for you? I'm not so cowardly or frightened in the face of trouble. Let's get this over with once and for all. Let's drink the poison. Habrocomes must remain* your husband. I choose him, even if he is dead."

She was taken into the chamber, and then she was all alone. Perilaos was still celebrating with his friends. Pretending that she was really thirsty, she ordered one of the servants to bring her some water to drink.

---

31. The *mina* was a unit of currency, though not an actual coin, equivalent to 100 drachmas, the value of which varied across time and location in the Greek cities of the ancient Mediterranean.

When a cup was brought, she took it and put the drug in it when no one was around.

Tearfully she said, "Beloved soul of Habrocomes, look! I'm doing what I promised! I'm making the journey to join you. It's a sad journey but a necessary one. Receive me happily and allow me to share a happy life with you there."

She drank the drug. Immediately sleep overcame her, and she collapsed to the floor as the drug took full effect.

[7] When Perilaos came in, right away he saw Anthia lying on the floor and let out a shocked cry. There was a great commotion among everyone in the house and mingled emotions: grief, fear, shock. Some felt pity for the girl they thought dead, while others shared Perilaos' grief. They all lamented what had happened. Perilaos tore his clothes and collapsed on her body.

"My beloved girl, who left the man who loved her before the wedding. You were Perilaos' bride for a short time. What a bridal chamber I'll put you into—your tomb! Habrocomes is fortunate, whoever he was. He was truly happy, having gotten such gifts from the woman he loved."

As he lamented, he threw his arms around her and kissed her hands and feet. "Poor bride! Wife who was too unhappy!"

He had her prepared for burial, dressing her in fine clothes and a lot of gold jewelry. He could no longer bear to look upon her, and so when day came, he put Anthia on a bier (she lay there unconscious) and took her to the cemetery near the city. There he placed her into a mausoleum. He slaughtered many animals over the tomb and burned piles of clothes and other finery as offerings.

[8] When he finished the funeral rites, he was led back to the city by members of his household. Anthia, meanwhile, was left in the tomb and came to. She realized that the drug was not a fatal poison and groaned and wept.

"Oh, the poison fooled me! It stopped me from making a happy journey to Habrocomes. In the end, wretched in every way,* I've been frustrated even in my desire to die. But it's still in my power to remain here in the tomb and finish the job of the drug by starving myself. No one will take me from here. I won't look upon the sun. I won't go forth into the light."

She settled in to wait and bravely accepted death.

Then night arrived and some robbers came to the tomb. They had learned that a girl had been given a rich burial and that she had a lot of women's jewelry buried with her, as well as a lot of silver and gold. They broke open the doors of the tomb, went in, began to carry off the finery, and saw Anthia still alive. Figuring this meant a tidy profit, they made her get up and wanted to take her, but she groveled at their feet and pleaded with them passionately.

"Men, whoever you are, take all the finery that's here. Take everything they buried with me and carry it off. But leave my body. I am dedicated to two gods: Eros and Death. Allow me to devote myself to them. Please, by the gods of your own people, do not reveal me to the daylight. I have suffered misfortunes that deserve night and darkness."

But she couldn't persuade the robbers, and they took her from the tomb and led her down to the sea and put her on a boat and set sail for Alexandria.[32] While she was on the ship they took care of her and urged her to cheer up, but she thought about what serious trouble she'd gotten into again and lamented and mourned.

"Once more it's pirates and the sea. Once more I'm a prisoner but even worse off this time because I'm not with Habrocomes. What land will I end up in? What sort of men will I see? Not another Moiris or Manto or Perilaos. Not Cilicia again. If only I could go where I could see Habrocomes' tomb."

Every time she said this she began to cry, and though she wouldn't touch drink or food, the robbers forced her to.

[9] They finished their voyage after several days and put into port at Alexandria. There they unloaded Anthia and decided to sell her to some merchants once they had rested her up after the exhausting trip. Meanwhile, when Perilaos found out that the tomb had been robbed and the body taken, he felt intense, uncontrollable anguish.

As for Habrocomes, he continued his search and made inquiries to see if anyone knew of a foreign girl anywhere who had been arrested with bandits. After finding out nothing he returned exhausted to where they were staying. Hippothoos and the men had made dinner for themselves, and the others ate, but Habrocomes was utterly depressed. He threw himself on the couch and wept and lay there without eating a bite.

As they proceeded to their drinking, an old woman who was there named Chrysion began to tell a story.

"Listen, you foreigners, to a sad story that happened not long ago in the city. Perilaos, one of our most powerful men, was chosen to be the magistrate in charge of keeping the peace in Cilicia. He went out in

---

32. Modern al-Iskanderiyya. Founded by Alexander in 331 BC, the city became the capital of Egypt under the Greco-Macedonian Ptolemaic kings that ruled until the country came under Roman rule in 30 BC. It was one of the largest cities in the Mediterranean world.

search of bandits, took some into custody, and brought them in along with a beautiful girl. He persuaded her to marry him, but when everything was done with the wedding and she was going into the bridal chamber, either because she went crazy or because she was in love with another man, she drank poison she got from somewhere and died. That's how they say she met her end."

Hippothoos exclaimed, "That's the girl Habrocomes is looking for!"

Habrocomes could hear the story, but he wasn't paying attention to it because he was so depressed. But after a moment he came to his senses and bolted upright at what Hippothoos said.

"Well, that means Anthia's clearly dead, and maybe she's got a tomb here and her body is safe."

He asked the old woman Chrysion to take him to her tomb and show him her body.

She gave a groan. "That's the saddest thing of all for the poor girl. Perilaos did give her a lavish funeral and adorned her body, but some robbers found out about the grave goods. They broke into the tomb, stole the finery, and made the body disappear. There's an intense and wide-ranging search for them being carried out by Perilaos."

[10] Habrocomes ripped his tunic open and wailed loudly for Anthia, who had died nobly and faithfully, and had by ill fate been lost after death.

"Wait! What kind of robber is so passionate that he would desire you even when you're dead and steal your body? Just my luck! I've been robbed of your body, the one thing that would make me feel better. It's sealed: I must die. But first I'll be strong—that is, until I can find your body, embrace it, and bury myself with it."

As he lamented, Hippothoos and his men encouraged him to cheer up. Then they slept the whole night through while Habrocomes went on thinking about it all: Anthia, her death, her tomb, her disappearance. Then he couldn't stand it anymore, and without anyone seeing him (Hippothoos and the men were passed out drunk), he left the house as if he needed something. Leaving them all behind, he went down to the sea and by luck found a ship leaving for Alexandria. He got aboard and set out in hopes that in Egypt he would find the robbers who'd taken everything. An ill-starred hope guided him.

While he was sailing to Alexandria, day arrived, and Hippothoos and his men were upset that Habrocomes had left. After spending a few days resting up, they decided to go to Syria and Phoenicia to engage in a bit of banditry.

[11] The robbers, meanwhile, got to Alexandria and passed Anthia along to some merchants, getting a high price for her. The merchants

fed her expensive food and took care of her physical needs, all the while on the lookout for the man who would buy her for the right price.

There arrived in Alexandria from India a man of the royal house there, both to see the sights and to conduct some business. His name was Psammis. This Psammis saw Anthia at the merchants' place and, once he saw her, was captivated. He offered them a lot of money and took her as a maid. But now that a barbarian had bought her and admired her beauty, straightaway he set about trying to force himself on her and have sex with her.

At first she said she wouldn't do it, but in the end she came up with a story she told Psammis (barbarians are naturally superstitious): she said that at her birth her father had dedicated her to Isis until she was of marriageable age and that there was still a year to go. "If you violate a woman sacred to the goddess," she said, "she'll be angry with you, and her retribution will be harsh."

Psammis believed this, did reverence to the goddess, and kept his hands off Anthia.

[12] She was still being held under guard at Psammis' house in the belief that she was sacred to Isis when the ship with Habrocomes on it drifted off its course to Alexandria and went aground near the outlets of the Nile and "the Coast," as it's called.*

As the people aboard came ashore, some of the shepherds[33] there swooped down on them, seized the cargo, and put the men in chains. They led them by a long, deserted road to Pelousion, a city in Egypt.[34] There they sold them to various owners.

Habrocomes was sold to an old soldier (he was retired from the service) named Araxos. This Araxos had a wife, repulsive to look at, worse to listen to, and utterly lacking in self-restraint. Her name was Cyno.[35] This Cyno fell in love with Habrocomes the minute he was brought into the house and couldn't restrain herself for a moment. She was terrible in her love and in her desire to satisfy her lust.*

Araxos grew fond of Habrocomes and thought of him as his son, but Cyno would talk to him of having sex and beg him to give in, promising

---

33. These shepherds are presumably meant to recall the *boukoloi,* or cowherds mentioned in later literary and documentary sources. They inhabited remote portions of the Nile Delta, were not under the control of central authority, and had a reputation as violent brigands.

34. The fortified city on the eastern edge of the Nile Delta that marked the Egyptian frontier.

35. The name means "bitch" and is taken from Herodotus 1.110.

to marry him.* Habrocomes thought that was horrible, and so many things ran through his mind at once: Anthia, his oath, the faithfulness that had so many times before hurt him. But in the end, under strong pressure from Cyno, he said yes.

When night fell, thinking that she was going to have Habrocomes as her husband, she killed Araxos and told Habrocomes what she had done. He couldn't stomach the woman's brutality and went out of the house, leaving her behind and declaring that he'd never sleep with a murderer.

She regained her composure,* and as soon as it was day, she went to where the people of Pelousion were gathered, let out a wail for her husband, and said that their new slave had killed him. She carried on lamenting like this for a long while, and the populace thought she was telling the truth. They immediately arrested Habrocomes, put him in chains, and sent him on to the man governing Egypt at that time. He was being taken to Alexandria to be punished, after he was convicted of killing his master Araxos.

Book 4

[1] Hippothoos and his men set out from Tarsos and made their way to Syria. They overcame all opposition, and burned villages and killed many men. Advancing in this fashion, they came to Laodiceia in Syria[36] and took up residence there, no longer as bandits, but as tourists come to see the town's sights. Then Hippothoos made inquiries to see if he could by chance find Habrocomes. When that came to nothing, they rested up and traveled through Phoenicia. From there they went to Egypt, for they had decided to pillage Egypt.

They gathered a large gang of bandits and made the journey to Pelousion. Sailing on the Nile to Egyptian Hermopolis[37] and

---

36. A coastal city in southern Syria near the border of Phoenicia.

37. Not the larger Hermopolis in central Egypt but another city (modern Damanhur) of the same name thirty-three miles southeast of Alexandria in the western Delta. Hippothoos and his men would have traveled through various branches of the Nile in the Delta in a generally westward direction to arrive here, but a journey entirely by water was possible in antiquity.

Schedia[38] and then traveling inland along the river canal built by Menelaos,[39] they bypassed Alexandria and arrived in Memphis, the city sacred to Isis,[40] and then moved on to Mendes.[41] They took on some locals as accomplices and guides in their plundering. Passing through Taua,[42] they came to Leontopolis.[43] Then, going past several other villages, many of which they wiped out, they arrived in Coptos,[44] which is near Ethiopia.

They decided to do their plundering there, for a great many merchants traveled through the area on their way to Ethiopia and India. They had a band of five hundred men, and they seized the heights and occupied some caves with the intention of robbing those who passed by.

[2] As for Habrocomes, when he came before the governor of Egypt, the governor, knowing all about it—the citizens of Pelousion had written him about what had happened, both about Araxos' murder and that Habrocomes, who was a slave, had dared to commit such acts—made no further inquiries into the events and ordered his men to take

---

38. About seventeen miles southeast of Alexandria, just south of the modern town of Kafr el-Dauwar. It was situated on a branch of the Canopic canal, which connected Alexandria to the Canopic branch of the Nile. Its harbor controlled the flow of river traffic between the interior of Egypt and the city.

39. This Menelaos was probably the brother of King Ptolemy I with that name rather than the Greek hero from the Trojan War. The nearby *nome,* or administrative unit, was named after him, but no other source tells us he built this canal. The hero Menelaos was, however, connected closely to this region, and we have no way of knowing which Menelaos Xenophon was referring to.

40. A little south of modern Cairo, Memphis, which did have a substantial temple of Isis, was a major administrative center and served as Egypt's capital before the foundation of Alexandria. Hippothoos has turned, taken the canal from Schedia to the Canopic branch of the Nile, and then traveled south to Memphis, which sits at the base of the Delta.

41. The ancient city by that name (modern Tell el-Ruba near Mansura) is located in the eastern Delta.

42. Modern Tanta in the central Delta.

43. There are several cities by this name. The two likeliest candidates are modern Tell el-Muqdam in the central Delta and Tell el-Yahudiya in the southern Delta. Xenophon, if the text is to be trusted, has Hippothoos move from Pelousion west across the entire Delta almost to Alexandria, down to Memphis just south of the Delta, back up to the eastern Delta, back over to the central Delta, and then to Coptos in the south well away from the Delta.

44. Modern Qift. Major land routes east to the Red Sea made this an important trading center throughout antiquity.

Habrocomes and put him up on a cross. Habrocomes was speechless from his woes, but cheered himself about his death with the thought that Anthia was also dead.

The men assigned this task took him to the banks of the Nile. There was a steep bluff overlooking the river's flow. They set up the cross and hung him on it, tying his hands and feet with rope (that's how they crucify people there). Then they went off and left him. They assumed the man they'd fastened securely was going to stay put.

Habrocomes turned his face toward the sun[45] and looked at the waters of the Nile. "You are the god who loves mortals most of all. You control Egypt. Through you both land and sea have been revealed to all humanity. If Habrocomes has done anything wrong, may I both die a piteous death and, if a greater penalty exists, may I pay it. But if I have been falsely accused by a wicked woman, may the waters of the Nile never be polluted with the body of a man unjustly killed, and may you not look upon such a sight, the sight of a man guilty of no crime dying in your land."

So he prayed, and the god took pity on him. A wind suddenly began to blow, struck the cross, and scoured away the soil of the cliff where the cross had been stuck in. Habrocomes fell into the river and began to drift, with neither the water harming him, nor his bonds hindering him, nor wild animals hurting him—the river just carried him along.

Drifting, he came to the place where the Nile discharges into the sea, and there the guards got him out and took him as a fugitive from justice to the governor of Egypt. The governor was even more angry and convinced that Habrocomes was thoroughly wicked, so he ordered his men to make a fire, put him on it, and burn him to death.

Everything was ready, and the pyre was built by the mouth of the Nile. Habrocomes was put on it, and the fire was lit under him, but just as the flame was about to reach his body, he again made a brief prayer, which was all he could manage, to be saved from the difficulties he faced. Then the Nile rose in a wave and the water fell upon the pyre and put out the fire.[46]

Those who were there thought what had happened was a miracle, and they took Habrocomes and brought him to the governor of Egypt. They told him what had occurred and explained how the Nile had helped

---

45. Ra, the most important of the solar gods of Egypt, though his worship did not spread beyond that country's borders, was equated by the Greeks with their Helios.

46. This episode looks to be inspired by the story of the miraculous salvation of the Lydian king Croisos from a pyre, as recounted in Herodotus 1.87.

the young man. The governor was astonished when he heard what had happened and ordered him to be put under guard in the prison and to receive all due care, "until such time," he said, "as we ascertain who this individual is and why the gods care so much about him."

[3] So he was in prison. Meanwhile Psammis, the man who had bought Anthia, decided to leave for home and readied everything for the journey. He was going to have to travel further into Egypt and go to Ethiopia, where Hippothoos' gang was operating. Preparations were complete: a large caravan of camels, donkeys, and horses; a great deal of gold,* a great deal of silver, and a lot of clothing. He was also taking Anthia.

When she left Alexandria and came to Memphis, she stood before Isis' temple and prayed to her. "O greatest of the gods, until now I have remained pure because it was believed that I belonged to you, and I kept my marriage unsullied for Habrocomes. But now I'm going to India, far from the land of the Ephesians and far from Habrocomes' remains. So, either save me in my misfortune and return me to the still-living Habrocomes or, if it is absolutely fated for us to die apart, do this: allow me to remain faithful to his corpse."

After this prayer they set out on their journey. They had already passed Coptos and were crossing the Ethiopian border when Hippothoos attacked. He killed Psammis and many of those with him, and took his belongings, including Anthia as a prisoner. Collecting the haul, he took it to the cave assigned by the gang for storing their property. Anthia went in there too, but she didn't recognize Hippothoos, nor did Hippothoos recognize Anthia, and whenever anyone asked her who she was and where she was from, she wouldn't tell them the truth but would claim that she was a native of Egypt and that her name was Memphitis.

[4] So she was with Hippothoos in the cave hideout, and in the meantime the governor of Egypt sent for Habrocomes. He asked him about himself and learned his story. He took pity on his bad fortune, offered him money, and promised to get him to Ephesos. Habrocomes thanked him profusely for saving his life but asked to be allowed to return to his search for Anthia. He received many gifts, boarded a ship, and set out on a voyage to Italy to make some inquiries there about Anthia. The governor of Egypt, now that he had found out the truth about Araxos, sent for Cyno and crucified her.

[5] While Anthia was in the cave, one of the bandits guarding her fell in love with her. His name was Anchialos. This Anchialos was one of those who had come with Hippothoos from Syria (he was from Laodiceia). He was respected by Hippothoos, because he was bold and had a lot of influence in the gang. When he fell in love with Anthia, at

first he talked to her to try and seduce her. He thought he would win her over with words and then ask for her as a gift from Hippothoos. But Anthia rebuffed all his advances, and nothing fazed her, not the cave, not her bonds, not the bandit's threats. She was still saving herself for Habrocomes, though for all she knew he was dead.

As often as she could without being caught, she'd lament. "May I remain wife to Habrocomes alone, even if I must die, even if I have to suffer worse things than I've already suffered."

This made Anchialos even more miserable, and seeing Anthia during the day made him burn with love. Unable to stand it, he tried to force Anthia. One night when Hippothoos wasn't around, because he was off with the others engaged in a bit of banditry, Anchialos got up and tried to rape her.

There was no escape from this predicament, so she drew Anchialos' sword, which he had set down, and struck him. The blow was fatal—he had been fully bent over her trying to trap her beneath him and kiss her, and she brought the sword up against his chest and struck.

So Anchialos paid the right price for his foul lust, but Anthia grew frightened at what she'd done. She spent a lot of time thinking about what she should do. One minute she planned to kill herself, but she still had some hope Habrocomes was alive; the next she planned to escape from the cave, but there was no way to do that because she couldn't easily travel on the road and there was no one to show her the way. So she decided to stay in the cave and accept whatever fate had in store for her.

[6] She waited that night. She got no sleep but kept going over much in her mind. When day arrived, Hippothoos and his men came back and saw Anchialos dead and Anthia next to his body. They guessed what had happened but found out all the details by interrogating her. They were angry and decided to punish her and avenge their dead friend. They went over various things they could do to Anthia. One of them suggested they kill her and bury her with Anchialos, another that they crucify her. But Hippothoos was really sad about Anchialos and came up with a worse punishment for Anthia. He told them to dig a wide, deep pit and put her in it along with two dogs, the point being for the dogs to provide severe punishment for what she'd dared to do.

They did what he said and brought Anthia to the pit and < . . . >.[47] The dogs were Egyptian and particularly large and ferocious looking.

---

47. Text has dropped out, though it seems that little other than the introduction of the dogs was in the gap.

When they had been put in, the bandits covered the pit with large timbers and piled dirt on top of those—it wasn't far from the Nile[48]—and set Amphinomos, one of their men, as a guard.

This Amphinomos had already been captivated by Anthia, and so at that time he felt even more sorry for her and pitied her for her misfortune. He thought about how he could keep her alive and keep the dogs from troubling her. He would at regular intervals pry up the boards that had been put over the pit and throw down bread and provide water. By doing so he encouraged Anthia to take heart, and the dogs, as long as they were being fed, did nothing at all to her. In fact, after a while they became tame and gentle.

Anthia took a look at herself and thought about her current situation. "This is terrible! What an awful punishment I suffer: a pit, a prison, and dogs as my cellmates—though they're a lot nicer than the bandits. I suffer the same way you did, Habrocomes, for you once were in a similar situation, and I left you behind in a prison in Tyre. But if you're still alive, that's not so bad. Perhaps we'll have each other back one day. But if you're dead now, I cling to life for no reason, and the man up there, whoever he is, takes pity on me in my misery for no reason."

That's what she said, and then she lamented constantly. And so she was shut up in the pit with the dogs, and Amphinomos constantly kept the dogs docile by feeding them.

Book 5

[1] Habrocomes made the voyage from Egypt but did not actually get to Italy, because the wind drove his ship off course and led it off the direct route and brought it to Sicily. They came to port in Syracuse, a large and fine city. Once there, Habrocomes decided to go around the island and see if he could find out anything about Anthia.

He took a room by the shore in the house of an old man named Aigialeus, who was a fisherman. This Aigialeus was a poor man and a foreigner, barely subsisting on his fishing. He was happy to take Habrocomes in, and, being very fond of him, came to think of him as a son. Because they were so close, at one point Habrocomes told him

---

48. Presumably the point is that the earth will hide the pit from casual observers traveling on the river.

his story, letting him know about Anthia, his love, and his wandering. Aigialeus then began to tell him his own tale.

"Habrocomes, my boy, I am neither a Sicilian Greek nor a native Sicel. No, I'm a Spartan from Lacedaimon,[49] one of the most powerful men there and from a very wealthy family. When I was a young man and had just been enrolled in the ephebic corps, I fell in love with a citizen girl named Thelxinoe, and Thelxinoe returned my love. We met while the city was holding an all-night festival—a god was guiding us both—and enjoyed the delights that we got together to enjoy. We were together for a while without anyone noticing, and we swore to each other over and over that we'd stay together until death.

"But I guess some god resented us, and while I was still an ephebe, Thelxinoe's parents gave her in marriage to a local youth named Androcles—Androcles had also been in love with her. At first the girl put forward many excuses for delaying the marriage, and in the end she was able to meet with me and agreed to leave Lacedaimon with me by night.

"On the very night of her wedding we dressed as young men, and I cut Thelxinoe's hair short. Then we left the city, bound for Argos and Corinth.[50] There we took a ship and sailed to Sicily. When the Spartans found out we'd eloped, they condemned us to death. We lived here, barely able to make ends meet, but we were happy and felt we had everything we needed because we were with each other.

"Thelxinoe died here not long ago, and her body hasn't been buried. No, I keep her with me. I'm always kissing her and spending time with her."

As he said this, he led Habrocomes into the back room and showed him Thelxinoe. She was an old woman by now, but still looked like a beautiful girl to Aigialeus. Her body had been prepared for burial in the Egyptian fashion, for the old man was acquainted with this practice.[51]

"Habrocomes, my boy, I talk to her all the time, just as if she was alive. And I get on the couch with her and we eat together. And if I ever come in from a fishing trip tired out, she comforts me when I see her. The thing is, she doesn't look to me like she looks to you now. No, my

---

49. The territory of Sparta, the powerful city-state in the south of the Peloponnese in mainland Greece.

50. Old and important Greek cities north of Sparta in the Peloponnese.

51. Greek sources describe Egyptians keeping mummified bodies in their houses. For instance, Diodoros of Sicily (1.92.6) says that those too poor to afford tombs would build a new room in the house and keep the body there.

boy, I think of her as she was in Lacedaimon, as she was when we eloped. I think of the all-night festival. I think of our pact."

When he was barely done speaking, Habrocomes let out a wail. "And you, unluckiest girl in the world! When will I find you, even if you are dead? Thelxinoe's body is a great comfort to Aigialeus in his life. Now I have truly learned that true love doesn't have any age limit. But I—I've been wandering all over land and sea, but I haven't been able to hear so much as a word of you. Miserable prophecy! Apollo, you are the god who delivered to us the harshest prophecies in the world. Now take pity on us and grant us the end of the oracle."

[2] As Habrocomes lamented in this fashion, Aigialeus tried to comfort him. Habrocomes went on living in Syracuse and eventually became Aigialeus' fishing partner. In the meantime, Hippothoos and his companions had established a large gang and decided to leave Ethiopia and try for bigger things. Hippothoos felt that robbing people one by one just wasn't enough unless he could also go after villages and cities. Taking his men and loading everything up (he had many donkeys and quite a few camels), he left Ethiopia, headed toward Egypt and Alexandria, and planned to pillage Phoenicia and Syria again.

He assumed Anthia was dead, but Amphinomos, the man guarding her in the pit, was in love with her and, because of his affection for her and her impending calamity, couldn't stand the thought of being dragged away from the girl. So he didn't follow Hippothoos. Instead, he hid himself in the crowd of other bandits and then concealed himself in a cave with the supplies he had managed to collect.

By nightfall Hippothoos and his men had reached an Egyptian village called Areia,[52] which they wanted to plunder. Amphinomos, meanwhile, dug open the pit, brought Anthia out, and tried to reassure her. She was still afraid and suspicious, so he swore by the sun and the gods in Egypt that he would keep her pure of intercourse until whenever she herself had been won over and was willing to sleep with him. Anthia put her trust in Amphinomos' oaths and followed him. The dogs were not left behind but, having grown friendly, were happy to come along.

They made it to Coptos. They decided to remain there for a few days until Hippothoos and his men had gone ahead on the road, and they made sure they had provisions for the dogs.

Hippothoos and his men attacked the village of Areia, killing many of the inhabitants, whose houses they put to the torch. But then they didn't follow the same route that had originally brought them south.

---

52. This does not correspond to any known locale.

Instead, they traveled on the Nile. They gathered all the boats from the villages they passed, then got on them and sailed to Schedia and Hermopolis. They disembarked there and traveled through the rest of Egypt along the banks of the Nile.

[3] Meanwhile, the governor of Egypt had learned about the events at Areia and about Hippothoos' bandit gang, including that they came from Ethiopia. He readied a large force of soldiers and appointed as commander one of his own relatives, Polyidos, a good-looking young man who was ready for action. Then the governor sent this force to attack the bandits. This Polyidos took his troops and engaged Hippothoos and his men near Pelousion, and immediately they fought a battle along the river banks and many fell on both sides. When night came, the bandits were routed, and all of them were killed by the soldiers, except there were a few who were captured alive.

Hippothoos alone, having thrown away his armor, escaped in the night and made it to Alexandria. There he evaded detection, boarded a departing ship, and sailed off. His one goal was to make it to Sicily, for he thought that was the best place to lie low and support himself, since he'd heard the island was large and prosperous.

[4] Polyidos didn't think it was enough just to defeat the bandits who had attacked, so he decided that he had to conduct a methodical search and clean up Egypt on the off chance that he might find Hippothoos or any of his men. He took one part of his force and the captured bandits (so that if one showed up, they could rat him out) and sailed up the Nile. He searched the cities and decided to go all the way to Ethiopia.

He got to Coptos, where Anthia was with Amphinomos. She happened to be back in the house when the captured bandits recognized Amphinomos and alerted Polyidos. Amphinomos was arrested and under questioning explained the situation with Anthia. When he heard this, Polyidos ordered her to be brought also. When she arrived, he questioned her closely about who she was and where she was from. She didn't tell him one word of the truth. Instead, she said she was Egyptian and had been captured by the bandits.

Polyidos then also fell deeply in love with Anthia, though he had a wife back in Alexandria. Once in love, at first he tried to persuade her by promising her great gifts, but in the end they left for Alexandria, and when they got to Memphis, he tried to use force on Anthia. She managed to get away and went to the temple of Isis, where she became a suppliant.

"Mistress of Egypt, you've helped me again and again. Now save me once more. Make Polyidos leave me alone. After all, my faithfulness to Habrocomes has been preserved through you."

Partly because Polyidos was afraid of the goddess, and partly because he loved Anthia and pitied her for her plight, he went into the temple by himself and swore never to use force on Anthia or insult her in any way, but to keep her pure for as long as she herself wanted. He was in love with her, he decided, and it was enough for him just to be able to look at her and talk to her. She believed his oaths and left the temple.

When they decided to rest up for three days in Memphis, Anthia went to the temple of Apis.[53] This is the most famous temple in Egypt, and the god gives prophecies to those who want them. After the petitioner approaches, prays, and asks the god a question, they leave, and the Egyptian children in front of the temple foretell—some of them in prose, some in poetry—everything that will come to pass.[54] So Anthia too approached and fell before Apis.

"You are the god who loves mortals most and takes pity on all foreigners. So have mercy on me also in my misfortune. Please proclaim a true prophecy about Habrocomes. If I am to see him once more and recover my husband, I'll wait and stay alive. But if he's dead, it's right for me also to depart this worthless life."

Moved to tears, she left the temple, and just then the children in front of the sanctuary were playing and shouting, "Anthia soon will recover Habrocomes her husband!"

When she heard this, she was heartened and offered a prayer to the gods. Right then they left for Alexandria.

[5] Polyidos' wife learned that he was bringing a girl home who he was in love with. Afraid that the foreign girl would possibly be preferred to her, she said nothing, but thought about how she could punish the woman she believed was plotting against her marriage.

Polyidos reported what had happened to the governor of Egypt and was at the camp dealing with the rest of the affairs that came along with his command. While he was away, Rhenaia (that's what Polyidos' wife

---

53. A bull god worshiped (in the form of a living bull) in Memphis but also of wider importance to the Egyptians. The Greeks combined him with Osiris and worshiped him as Serapis.

54. An authentic detail for a Greco-Roman audience. Pliny, *Natural History* 8.71, mentions crowds of Egyptian children singing to the Apis Bull on the rare occasions it emerged from its temple and becoming inspired to predict the future. Aelian, *De Natura Animalium* 11.10, reports a similar phenomenon and adds the detail that the boys foretell "in poetic meter." Dio Chrysostom *Orationes* 32.13 also supports the notion that Apis' oracular pronouncements worked through children. Plutarch, *De Iside et Osiride* 356e, remarks that Egyptians more generally believed that children had prophetic powers and attempted to gather portents from the utterances of children playing around temples.

was called) sent for Anthia, who was in the house, ripped her dress, and physically abused her.

"What a horrible woman, plotting against my marriage. It doesn't matter if Polyidos thinks you're pretty. This beauty of yours won't help you. Perhaps you could seduce bandits and sleep with a bunch of drunk young men, but you'll never get away with insulting Rhenaia's bed!"

She chopped off Anthia's hair, put her in chains, and handed her over to one of her trusted slaves named Clytos. She told him to put Anthia on a ship, sail to Italy, and sell her to the owner of a brothel.

"That way, my pretty girl," she said, "you can indulge your sluttiness to your heart's content."

Taken away by Clytos, Anthia wept and lamented. "Treacherous beauty! Unlucky good looks! Why do you keep on tormenting me? Why are you causing me so much trouble? Weren't the burials enough? The murders? The chains? The bandit gangs? Will I soon be standing in front of a whorehouse with a pimp forcing me to give up the faithfulness to Habrocomes that I've kept till now?"

She fell at Clytos' knees and begged him. "No, master, don't lead me to that punishment. No, kill me yourself. I can't handle a pimp as my master. You've got to believe me: I'm not used to sleeping around."

Clytos felt pity for her. So she was taken off to Italy, and Rhenaia told Polyidos when he got home that Anthia had run away, and he believed her based on what had happened before. Anthia landed at Taras,[55] a city in Italy, and out of fear of Rhenaia's orders Clytos sold her to the owner of a brothel. When the latter saw her beauty, which was unlike anything he'd ever seen before, he was sure he'd make a nice profit from the girl. She was exhausted from the voyage and Rhenaia's torture, so he let her recover for a few days. Clytos, meanwhile, returned to Alexandria and told Rhenaia what had happened.

[6] Hippothoos sailed over and landed in Sicily—not at Syracuse but at Tauromenion.[56] He started looking for a way to support himself. In Syracuse, now that a long time had passed, Habrocomes fell into depression and serious difficulty because he could neither find Anthia nor go back home. So he decided to take a boat from Sicily to Italy and travel up the peninsula. If he couldn't find anything he was looking for, he would make an unlucky journey from there to Ephesos.

By this point both their parents and everyone else in Ephesos were in deep sorrow because no message or letter had come from the couple.

---

55. Modern Taranto.

56. Modern Taormina.

They sent search parties in all directions. Unable to hold out against despair and old age, both sets of parents had ended their lives.

While Habrocomes was taking his trip to Italy, Leucon and Rhode, the companions of Habrocomes and Anthia, decided to sail to Ephesos. Their master had passed away in Xanthos and had left them everything, and it was a lot. They assumed that their masters had long ago made it home, and they themselves had had enough experience of misfortune during their time abroad. Loading all their property on a ship, they set sail for Ephesos. They made the voyage in a few days and arrived in Rhodes. There they learned that Habrocomes and Anthia had not made it home yet and that their masters' parents had died. So they decided not to head back to Ephesos but to stay there for a little while until they could find out something about their masters.

[7] After some time passed, the pimp that bought Anthia forced her to stand out in front of the brothel. He had dressed her up in fine clothes and a lot of gold jewelry and took her to show herself off in front of one of the cubicles.

She wailed loudly, "This is terrible! My earlier misfortunes weren't enough—the chains, the bandit gangs. No! Now I'm also being forced to whore myself. Beauty of mine, you deserve all the outrageous things that have happened to you. Why have you stayed with me when all you bring is trouble? But why do I lament like this? Shouldn't I be looking for a way to preserve the faithfulness I've kept till now?"

She was taken to her cubicle while the pimp alternately encouraged and threatened her. When she got there and stood out front, a crowd of men amazed by her beauty ran over, and many of them were ready to spend money on their lust.

In this impossible situation she hit upon a scheme to get herself out of it. She fell to the ground, went slack, and imitated those who suffer from the so-called "sacred disease."[57]

The bystanders felt pity, but also fear. They lost their appetite for having sex with her but did try to help her. When the pimp realized how bad things had gotten and resigned himself to the fact that the girl really was sick, he took her back into the house, put her in bed, and took care of her. When she appeared to have recovered, he asked her what had caused her illness.

---

57. Epilepsy, that is. To judge from legal texts, a common fear of buyers seems to have been that a slave suffered from a "hidden defect" such as this, which was not obvious upon initial inspection.

"Master," she said, "I wanted to tell you about my problem before and explain what happened, but I kept quiet because I was ashamed. But now I have no problem telling you everything—you already know all about my condition.

"When I was a girl, I wandered away from my family during an all-night festival and came to the grave of a recently dead man. I saw someone rise from the grave and attempt to hold me back. I tried to run away* and shouted. The man was fearsome to look at but his voice was much more horrible.

"At last when it was day, he let me go but struck me in the chest and said that he had afflicted me with this ailment.[58] From that point on I have suffered the trouble in different ways at different times. But I beg you, master, don't be angry with me. It's not my fault! You'll be able to sell me and not lose any of the money you paid for me."

The pimp was upset but excused her since this was happening to her through no fault of her own.

[8] So she was being cared for at the pimp's place as if she was ill. Habrocomes, meanwhile, set sail from Sicily and put in at Noucerion in Italy.[59] Without a way to make a living, he had no idea what to do. At first he wandered around searching for Anthia because she was the basis for his whole life and his wanderings. When he could find nothing (because the girl was in Taras at the pimp's!), he took a job with some stonecutters. The work was hard for him, since he was not at all used to putting his body to work on rough and strenuous tasks. He suffered and often lamented his fortune.

"Look, Anthia, here I am, your Habrocomes. I'm working at hard labor, and I've subjected my body to slavery. If I had any hope of finding you and of us living together in the future, that would cheer me up more than anything. But as it is, I'm probably out of luck, laboring away in vain, all for naught. And you, I suppose, have died, pining away for your Habrocomes. Yes, I am sure, my dearest, that you would never, either living or dead, completely forget about me."

So he was lamenting and suffering from his labors. Meanwhile Anthia had a dream as she slept in Taras. She dreamed she was with Habrocomes; she was beautiful and he was handsome. The time was

---

58. Anthia's account accords with popular knowledge of epilepsy in antiquity by indicating a supernatural cause and specifying the chest as an area that the ailment affected.

59. Properly Nouceria, the name of several cities in Italy. The only likely candidate among them is Nuceria Alfaterna, a city near the coast in Campania (modern Nocera Inferiore).

right at the beginning of their love, but another beautiful woman appeared and dragged Habrocomes away from her. At last, as he shouted and called her name, she bolted awake and the dream ended.

After she had this dream, she got out of bed and lamented, believing that what she had seen was the truth.

"This is terrible! I submit to all sorts of toil and go through all kinds of difficulties because of my bad luck. I find tricks no other woman could to preserve my faithfulness, Habrocomes. But perhaps another woman has caught your eye. That's what the dream is telling me. So why should I go on living? Why torment myself? Better to die and leave behind this painful life, to leave this offensive, dangerous slavery. Even if Habrocomes has actually broken his oaths, I pray the gods won't punish him, even a little. Maybe he's done it because he was forced to. But for me, the right thing to do is to die faithful."

As she lamented, she considered ways to die.

[9] In Tauromenion, Hippothoos the Perinthian at first had trouble because he had no way to make a living, but as time passed, an old woman fell in love with him. Compelled by his poverty, he married the old woman. After he lived with her for a short time, she died and left him her vast wealth and fortune. This consisted of a large troop of slaves, an abundance of clothes, and an extravagant supply of belongings, but he decided to sail to Italy and buy young slaves and maids, as well as a different set of belongings, one more suited to a rich man. Still, he thought all the time about Habrocomes and prayed to find him, and he cherished the notion of sharing with him his whole life and all his possessions.

He set sail and landed in Italy. With him went a young man from a very good family in Sicily. His name was Cleisthenes, and he shared all of Hippothoos' possessions because of his good looks.

In the meantime, Anthia seemed to have recovered, and the pimp decided to sell her, so he took her to the marketplace and displayed her to potential buyers. Just then Hippothoos was going around the city of Taras looking to see if there was anything nice to buy. He saw Anthia and recognized her and was astounded at the odds of it all.

He gave it a lot of thought. "Isn't this the girl that I once punished for the murder of Anchialos in Egypt by digging a pit and sticking dogs in there with her? So how did everything change? How did she survive? How did she escape from the pit? How was she saved against all expectations?"

He approached her as if he was interested in buying her, and when he was next to her, he said, "Girl, you're familiar with Egypt, aren't you? You had a run-in with bandits in Egypt, right? Didn't something else terrible happen to you in that land? Don't worry, you can tell me—I recognize you from that place."

When she heard "Egypt" and remembered Anchialos and the gang and the pit, she gave a wail and sobbed. Looking at Hippothoos (though she didn't recognize him at all), she said, "Stranger, I suffered a great deal in Egypt. Terrible things. I don't know who you really are, but I did have a run-in with bandits. But how do you know my story? How do you explain knowing me and my misfortune? I mean, I've gone through remarkable things worth talking about, but I don't have the faintest idea who you are."

When Hippothoos heard this, he was even more certain from what she'd said that she was who he thought she was. For the time being he said nothing, but after he bought her from the pimp, he took her to his place and tried to cheer her up. He told her who he was and talked about what had happened in Egypt. He also described how he had gotten away and become rich.

She asked for forgiveness and explained to him that she had killed Anchialos because he couldn't control himself. She also told him about the pit, Amphinomos, the taming of the dogs, and how she was saved. Hippothoos felt sorry for her. He was still unaware of who she was, and from his daily contact with the girl Hippothoos came to love Anthia. He wanted to sleep with her and promised her many things. At first she refused him, saying she wasn't worthy to share her master's bed, but in the end, as Hippothoos grew insistent and she no longer knew what to do, she thought it would be better to tell him all her secrets than break her promises to Habrocomes.

She told him about Habrocomes, Ephesos, her love, her oaths, her misfortunes, and her encounters with criminals, all the while wailing for Habrocomes. Hearing that she was Anthia and that she was the wife of his best friend in the world, Hippothoos gave her a hug, urged her to take heart, and told her about his friendship with Habrocomes. He kept her in the house and provided everything she needed out of respect for Habrocomes. He himself began a search to see if he could find Habrocomes anywhere.

[10] Habrocomes, meanwhile, at first worked laboriously in Noucerion, but eventually he couldn't stand the toil any longer and decided to get on a ship and sail for Ephesos. At night he went down to the sea, found a ship that was getting ready to shove off, got on board, and sailed back to Sicily. He planned to head from there to Crete and Cyprus, then Rhodes. From there he would go to Ephesos. He hoped during the long voyage to find out something about Anthia.

With his few provisions, he set out and made the trip. He first went to Sicily and found that his previous host, Aigialeus, had died. He poured libations at his grave and wept for a long time, then set sail again, passed through Crete, and came to Cyprus. He spent a few days there and offered prayer to the ancestral goddess of the Cypriots.[60] Then he set sail and came to Rhodes, where he took a room near the harbor.

By now he was close to Ephesos and thoughts of all the things that pained him came to mind—his home city, his parents, Anthia, and their slaves.

"How awful!" he groaned. "I'm going to arrive in Ephesos alone. My parents will see me without Anthia. Knowing my bad luck, I'll make a voyage in vain and I'll tell a story that perhaps won't be believed—I've got no one who shared what I went through. Be strong, Habrocomes! Stay alive long enough to get to Ephesos. Build a tomb for Anthia, mourn for her, and pour libations. After that you must join her."

He went around the city, distraught and depressed about Anthia and from his lack of provisions. This was during the time that Leucon and Rhode were living in Rhodes. They had made a dedication in the temple of Helios next to the golden armor that Anthia and Habrocomes had dedicated. They set up a pillar inscribed "For Habrocomes and Anthia" in golden letters. Also engraved were the names of the dedicators: "Leucon and Rhode."

Habrocomes came across this pillar when he came to pray to the god. He read it, recognized who had set it up and the loyalty of his and Anthia's slaves, and saw the armor nearby. Then he groaned loudly and took a seat by the pillar.

"I'm unlucky in every way! I've come to the end of my life only to be reminded of my own misfortunes. There's the armor I dedicated with Anthia. I set sail together with her from Rhodes, but now I've come back without her. If this pillar is the dedication of our companions for the two of us, what am I supposed to do now that I'm on my own? Where am I going to find my friends?"

Just then Leucon and Rhode showed up to pray to the god as they usually did. They saw Habrocomes sitting by the pillar and looking at the armor. They didn't recognize him, but they did wonder who would be hanging around the dedications of other people.

Leucon said, "Young man, what do you want? What are you doing sitting by dedications that have nothing to do with you. Why do

---

60. Aphrodite, who was said to have been born in Cyprus.

you mourn and lament? Why do you care about them? What's your connection with the people on this inscription?"

Habrocomes answered him, "They *are* mine! Dedicated by Leucon and Rhode for me, and I pray to see them again, second only to Anthia. I am the unfortunate Habrocomes."

Leucon and Rhode heard this and were immediately speechless. Coming to their senses little by little, they recognized him from his appearance, from his voice, from what he talked about, and from what he said about Anthia. They fell at his feet and told him their own story, how they made the journey to Syria from Tyre, Manto's anger, being sent away and sold in Lycia, the death of their master, their wealth, and their arrival in Rhodes.

Taking him with them, they brought him to the house where they were staying and offered him everything they had. They doted on him, took care of him, and encouraged him to cheer up. But nothing meant more to him than Anthia, and he mourned for her at every moment.

[11] While Habrocomes was living with their old friends in Rhodes, trying to figure out what he was going to do, Hippothoos decided to take Anthia from Italy to Ephesos to return her to her parents and find out something about Habrocomes there. He loaded all his possessions onto a large Ephesian ship, set sail with Anthia, and made a very pleasant voyage in a few days. He put in at Rhodes while it was still dark and found lodging near the shore with an old woman named Althaia. He had Anthia stay upstairs with their hostess, and he himself rested that night.

The next day they tried to arrange passage on a ship, but there was a magnificent public festival being celebrated by all the Rhodians for Helios. There was a procession and sacrifice, and the whole citizen body took part. Leucon and Rhode were there, not so much to participate in the festival as to see if they could find out something about Anthia. Then Hippothoos came to the temple with Anthia. She looked at the dedications and remembered everything that had happened before.

"O Helios, observer of the affairs of all mortals, in my misfortune you overlook me alone. When I first came to Rhodes, I worshiped you in my good fortune and made sacrifices with Habrocomes. I was considered happy then. But now I'm a slave instead of free, an unfortunate prisoner instead of blessed, and I'm going to Ephesos by myself and will show up to my family without Habrocomes."

She wept a great deal after this and asked Hippothoos whether she could take some of her hair, dedicate it to Helios, and offer up a prayer about Habrocomes. Hippothoos agreed, and she cut off as many tresses as she could. She took a convenient moment when everyone had left and made her dedication with the inscription: "For her husband Habrocomes Anthia dedicated her hair to the god."

After she had done this and prayed, she left with Hippothoos.

[12] Leucon and Rhode, who until now had been busy with the procession, arrived at the temple. They saw the dedications and recognized the names of their masters. At first they kissed the hair and lamented a great deal just as if they were looking upon Anthia. Finally they walked around to see if they could actually find her (the populace of Rhodes also would already recognize the names from the couple's earlier visit). They could find nothing that day and went home and reported to Habrocomes what was in the temple. His heart was moved by the strangeness of the situation, and he was hopeful that he would find Anthia.

The next day Anthia came back to the temple with Hippothoos because they could find no passage on a ship. She sat near the dedications and began to weep and moan. Just then Leucon and Rhode came in. They had left Habrocomes at home depressed about his situation. When they arrived, they saw Anthia. They had not yet recognized her, but they started putting it all together—her tears, the dedications, the names, the way she looked. In that way they recognized her little by little and fell at her knees, unable to speak. She wondered who they were and what they wanted, for she never would have expected to see Leucon and Rhode.

They recovered themselves and said, "Mistress Anthia, we are your slaves, Leucon and Rhode! The ones who shared your trip and your capture by pirates. What fortune has brought you here? Take heart, mistress! Habrocomes is safe, and he's here. He constantly laments for you."

Anthia was astonished at what they said but eventually came to her senses and recognized them. She embraced and kissed them and found out about Habrocomes' situation in detail.

[13] The entire populace of Rhodes came running when they found out that Anthia and Habrocomes had been found. Hippothoos was also there at the time. He was introduced to Leucon and Rhode and found out who they were. Everything was working out nicely for them except that Habrocomes didn't yet know of any of this.* Without further ado they ran to the house. When Habrocomes heard from one of the Rhodians that Anthia had been found, he raced through the middle of the city shouting "Anthia!" like a madman. He ran into Anthia and the others at the temple of Isis, with a large crowd of Rhodians following along.

When they saw each other, there was instant recognition—their souls had been longing for this. They embraced each other and collapsed to the ground. Many emotions overcame them all at once, pleasure, grief, fear, remembrance of what had passed, fear of what would happen.

The people of Rhodes cheered and shouted, calling upon the great goddess Isis: "Once more we see the beautiful Habrocomes and Anthia!"

Recovering themselves, the two got up and went into Isis' temple. They said, "Greatest goddess, we are grateful to you for saving us. Through you, goddess most honored of all by us, we have been reunited."

They prostrated themselves before the sanctuary and knelt before the altar.

Leucon and his friends then took them to the house, and Hippothoos moved his things into Leucon's house. They were ready to sail to Ephesos, and as they sacrificed and feasted that day there were many different stories from all of them about everything each had gone through and done. They kept the party going a long time, since they had been reunited after so long.

When it was already night, everyone else went to bed as they got tired—Leucon and Rhode, Hippothoos and the handsome Cleisthenes, the young man from Sicily who had followed him when he came to Italy, and Anthia went to bed with Habrocomes.

[14] When all the others had fallen asleep and there was perfect silence, Anthia embraced Habrocomes and wept.

"Husband and master, I've got you back after I wandered over so much land and sea, after escaping bandits' threats, pirates' plots, the pimps' outrages, chains, pits, clubs, drugs, and tombs. But Habrocomes, master of my soul, I've come to you just as I was when first I left for Syria from Tyre. No one persuaded me to stray. Not Moiris in Syria. Not Perilaos in Cilicia. Not Psammis or Polyidos in Egypt. Not Anchialos in Ethiopia. Not my master in Taras. No, I used every trick of faithfulness and have remained pure for you.

"And you, Habrocomes, did *you* stay true? Or did some other beautiful woman find greater favor than me with you? Or did someone force you to forget your oaths and me?"

As she said this, she kissed him continually.

"No!" Habrocomes said. "I swear to you by the day that we have desired and attained at long last that I found no girl beautiful, nor did it please me to look upon any other woman. No, you have your Habrocomes back as pure as you left him in prison in Tyre."

[15] All night long they made their cases to each other and easily convinced each other since that's what they wanted. When day came, they got on a ship, loaded all their possessions, and set sail. The entire

populace of Rhodes was there to see them off. Hippothoos also left with them and brought all his possessions, along with Cleisthenes. They made the voyage in a few days and put in at Ephesos.

The whole city had already learned they were safe, and when they disembarked, without further ado they immediately went to the temple of Artemis and offered many prayers. After sacrificing, they made several dedications, and most notably they dedicated to the goddess the written account of all they had experienced and done.

After that they went back to the city and built large tombs for their parents (it happens that they had died earlier from old age and despair). They themselves afterward lived their life with each other as if it were a festival. Leucon and Rhode were partners in everything with their old friends. Hippothoos, too, decided to live the rest of his life in Ephesos and finally went to Lesbos and built a large tomb for Hyperanthes. He adopted Cleisthenes as his son and lived in Ephesos with Habrocomes and Anthia.

This is the end of Xenophon's five books of *An Ephesian Story: Anthia and Habrocomes*.

SELECT BIBLIOGRAPHY

Introductory Bibliography to Chariton and Xenophon

The bibliography on the ancient novel is quite large now, and is rapidly growing larger every year. To prune this bibliographic thicket I have included here only works in English since the late 1960s, the period that marks the beginning of the modern revival of interest in these texts. I have also left out many of the more specialized scholarly works that will be of limited interest to general readers and students. I have particularly favored the inclusion of introductory books and essay collections (we are lucky to have many good ones in this area) and individual articles on Chariton and Xenophon whose titles make obvious their main concerns. No doubt I have accidentally left out something I ought to have included, and I certainly have left out much that by looser criteria would clearly belong, but the footnotes and bibliography of the studies here will aid in tracking down relevant additional references, particularly in other languages (of which there is much that is indispensable). Many of the edited collections in Section B will be particularly productive places to start.

A. Books on Chariton and Xenophon

Hägg, T. 1971. *Narrative Technique in Ancient Greek Romances: Studies of Chariton, Xenophon Ephesius, and Achilles Tatius*. Stockholm: Svenska Institutet i Athen.

Helms, J. 1966. *Character Portrayal in the Romance of Chariton*. The Hague: Mouton.

O'Sullivan, J. N. 1995. *Xenophon of Ephesus: His Compositional Technique and the Birth of the Novel*. Berlin/New York: Walter de Gruyter.

Schmeling, G. 1974. *Chariton*. Boston: Twayne Publishers.

———. 1980. *Xenophon of Ephesus*. Boston: Twayne Publishers.

Smith, S. D. 2007. *Greek Identity and the Athenian Past in Chariton: The Romance of Empire*. Ancient Narrative Supplementum 9. Groningen: Barkhuis.

B. Book-length Overviews of Ancient Fiction and Collections of Essays

(Articles from many of the collections listed here may be found in other sections of this Bibliography.)

Anderson, G. 1982. *Eros Sophistes: Ancient Novelists at Play*. Chico, Calif.: Scholars Press.

————. 1984. *Ancient Fiction: The Novel in the Greco-Roman World*. London: Croom Helm.

Branham, R. B., ed. 2005. *The Bakhtin Circle and Ancient Narrative. Ancient Narrative* Supplementum 3. Groningen: Barkhuis Publishing.

Brant, J.-A., C. W. Hedrick, and C. Shea. 2005. *Ancient Fiction: The Matrix of Early Christian and Jewish Narrative. Society of Biblical Literature Symposium Series* 32. Atlanta: Society of Biblical Literature.

Cueva, E. 2004. *The Myths of Fiction: Studies in the Canonical Greek Novels*. Ann Arbor: University of Michigan Press.

De Jong, I. J. F., and R. Nünlist, eds. 2007. *Time in Ancient Greek Literature*. Leiden/Boston: E. J. Brill.

Doody, M. A. 1996. *The True Story of the Novel*. New Brunswick: Rutgers University Press.

Goldhill, S. 1995. *Foucault's Virginity: Ancient Erotic Fiction and the History of Sexuality*. Cambridge: Cambridge University Press.

Hägg, T. 1983. *The Novel in Antiquity*. Berkeley/Los Angeles: University of California Press.

————. 2004. *Parthenope: Studies in Ancient Greek Fiction*. Copenhagen: Museum Tusculanum Press.

Harrison, S. J., M. Paschalis, and S. Frangoulidis, eds. 2005. *Metaphor and the Ancient Novel*. Groningen: Barkhuis Publishing.

Haynes, K. 2003. *Fashioning the Feminine in the Greek Novel*. London/New York: Routledge.

Heiserman, A. 1977. *The Novel before the Novel: Essays and Discussions about the Beginnings of Prose Fiction in the West*. Chicago/London: University of Chicago Press.

Hock, R. F., J. B. Chance, and J. Perkins, eds. 1998. *Ancient Fiction and Early Christian Narrative. Society of Biblical Literature Symposium Series* 6. Atlanta: Scholars Press.

Holzberg, N. 1995. *The Ancient Novel: An Introduction*. London/New York: Routledge.

Konstan, D. 1993. *Sexual Symmetry: Love in the Ancient Novel and Related Genres*. Princeton: Princeton University Press.

MacAlister, S. 1996. *Dreams and Suicides: The Greek Novel from Antiquity to the Byzantine Empire.* London/New York: Routledge.

Morgan, J. R., and R. Stoneman, eds. 1994. *Greek Fiction: The Greek Novel in Context.* London/New York: Routledge.

Panayotakis, S., M. Zimmermann, and W. Keulen, eds. 2003. *The Ancient Novel and Beyond.* Leiden/New York: E. J. Brill.

Perry, B. E. 1967. *The Ancient Romances: A Literary-Historical Account of their Origins.* Berkeley/Los Angeles: University of California Press.

Reardon, B. P. 1991. *The Form of Greek Romance.* Princeton: Princeton University Press.

———, ed. 2008. *The Collected Ancient Greek Novels.* 2nd ed. Berkeley/Los Angeles: University of California Press.

Paschalis, M., and S. Frangoulidis, eds. 2002. *Space in the Ancient Novel.* Groningen: Barkhuis Publishing.

Schmeling, G., ed. 2003. *The Novel in the Ancient World.* Rev. ed. Leiden/New York/Köln: E. J. Brill.

Swain, S., ed. 1999. *Oxford Readings in the Greek Novel.* Oxford/New York: Oxford University Press.

Tatum, J., ed. 1994. *The Search for the Ancient Novel.* Baltimore/London: Johns Hopkins University Press.

Whitmarsh, T., ed. 2008. *The Cambridge Companion to the Greek and Roman Novel.* Cambridge: Cambridge University Press.

C. Other Translations into English

Blake, W. E. 1939. *Chariton's* Chaereas and Callirhoe. Ann Arbor: University of Michigan Press.

Goold, G. P. 1995. *Chariton:* Callirhoe. Cambridge, Mass.: Harvard University Press.

Reardon, B. P. "Chariton." In Reardon 2008, 17–124.

Anderson, G. "Xenophon of Ephesus." In Reardon 2008, 125–69.

Hadas, M. 1953. *Three Greek Romances* (Longus, Xenophon of Ephesus, Dio Chrysostom). Garden City, N.Y.: Doubleday. Reprinted in W. F. Hansen, ed. 1998. *Anthology of Ancient Greek Popular Literature.* Bloomington: Indiana University Press, 3–49.

Henderson, J. 2009. *Longus: Daphnis and Chloe; Xenophon of Ephesus: Anthia and Habrocomes.* Cambridge, Mass./London: Harvard University Press.

D. Additional Select Bibliography

Alexander, L. C. A. 2008. "The Passions in Galen and the Novels of Chariton and Xenophon." In *Passions and Moral Progress in Greco-Roman Thought*, edited by J. T. Fitzgerald, 289–325. London/New York: Routledge.

Alvares, J. 1997. "Chariton's Erotic History." *American Journal of Philology* 118: 613–29.

———. 2000. "Perspective and Ideal in Chariton's *Chaireas and Callirhoe*." *Hermes* 128: 383–84.

———. 2001–2002. "Some Political and Ideological Dimensions of Chariton's *Chaireas and Callirhoe*." *Classical Journal* 97.2: 113–44.

———. 2002. "Love, Loss, and Learning in Chariton's *Chaereas and Callirhoe*." *Classical World* 95: 107–15.

Ascough, R. S. 1996. "Narrative Technique and Generic Designation: Crowd Scenes in Luke-Acts and in Chariton." *Catholic Biblical Quarterly* 58: 69–81.

Bakhtin, M. 1981. *The Dialogic Imagination.* Edited by M. Holquist. Austin: University of Texas Press.

Balot, R. K. 1998. "Foucault, Chariton, and the Masculine Self." *Helios* 25.2: 139–62.

Bowie, E. L. 1994. "The Readership of Greek Novels in the Ancient World." In Tatum 1994, 435–59.

———. 2002. "The Chronology of the Earlier Greek Novels Since B. E. Perry: Revisions and Precisions." *Ancient Narrative* 2: 47–63.

———. 2003. "The Ancient Readers of the Greek Novels." In Schmeling 2003, 87–106.

Chew, K. 2003. "The Representation of Violence in the Greek Novels and Martyr Accounts." In Panayotakis, Zimmermann, and Keulen 2003, 129–41.

Connors, C. 2002. "Chariton's Syracuse and Its Histories of Empire." In Paschalis and Frangoulidis 2002, 12–26.

Cueva, E. 2000. "The Date of Chariton's *Chaereas and Callirhoe* Revisited." *Classica et Mediaevalia* 51: 197–208.

Doody, M. 1996. *The True Story of the Novel.* New Brunswick: Rutgers University Press.

Doulamis, K. 2001. "Rhetoric and Irony in Chariton: A Case-Study from Callirhoe." *Ancient Narrative* 1: 55–72.

Edwards, D. R. 1994. "Defining the Web of Power in Asia Minor: The Novelist Chariton and His City of Aphrodisias." *Journal of the American Academy of Religion* 62: 699–718.

Egger, B. 1994a. "Women and Marriage in the Greek Novels: The Boundaries of Romance." In Tatum 1994, 260–80.

———. 1994b. "Looking at Chariton's Callirhoe." In Morgan and Stoneman 1994, 31–48.

Fusillo, M. 1999. "The Conflict of Emotions: A *Topos* in the Greek Erotic Novel." In Swain 1999, 60–82.

———. 2003. "Modern Critical Theories and the Ancient Novel." In Schmeling 2003, 277–305.

Griffiths, J. G. 1991. "Xenophon of Ephesus on Isis and Alexandria." In *Atlantis and Egypt; with other selected essays.* Cardiff: University of Wales Press, 68–91.

Hägg, T. 2004a. "*Callirhoe* and *Parthenope:* The Beginnings of the Historical Novel." In Hägg 2004, 141–61.

———. 2004b. "The *Ephesiaca* of Xenophon Ephesius—Original or Epitome?" In Hägg 2004, 159–98.

Hock, R. 2005. "The Educational Curriculum in Chariton's *Callirhoe.*" In Brant, Hedrick, and Shea 2005, 15–36.

Holzberg, N. 2003. "The Genre: Novels Proper and the Fringe." In Schmeling 2003, 11–28.

Hunter, R. 1994. "History and Historicity in the Romance of Chariton." *Aufstieg und Niedergang der Römischen Welt* II.34.2: 1055–86.

Johne, R. 2003. "Women in the Ancient Novel." In Schmeling 2003, 151–207.

Jones, C. P. 1992. "Hellenistic History in Chariton of Aphrodisias." *Chiron* 22: 91–102.

Kaimio, M. 1995. "How to Manage in the Male World: The Strategies of the Heroine in Chariton's Novel." *Acta Antiqua Academiae Scientiarum Hungaricae* 36: 119–32.

———. 1996. "How to Enjoy a Greek Novel: Chariton Guiding His Audience." *Arctos* 30: 49–73.

Kapparis, K. 2000. "Has Chariton Read Lysias 1 'On the Murder of Eratosthenes'?" *Hermes* 128: 380–83.

Konstan, D. 1994. "Xenophon of Ephesus: Eros and Narrative in the Novel." In Morgan and Stoneman 1994, 49–63.

———. 2007. "Love and Murder: Two Textual Problems in Xenophon's *Ephesiaca.*" *Ancient Narrative* 5: 31–40.

Kytzler, B. 2003. "Xenophon of Ephesus." In Schmeling 2003, 336–60.

Luginbill, R. D. 2000. "Chariton's Use of Thucydides' *History* in Introducing the Egyptian Revolt (*Chaereas and Callirhoe* 6.8)." *Mnemosyne* 53.1: 1–11.

Morgan, J. R. 1996. "The Ancient Novel at the End of the Century: Scholarship Since the Dartmouth Conference." *Classical Philology* 91: 63–73.

———. 2007a. "Chariton." In Brant, Hedrick, and Shea 2005, 479–87.

———. 2007b. "Xenophon of Ephesus." In Brant, Hedrick, and Shea 2005, 489–92.

Nimis, S. 1994. "The Prosaics of the Ancient Novels." *Arethusa* 27: 387–411.

———. 2003. "*In mediis rebus:* Beginning Again in the Middle of the Ancient Novel." In Panayotakis, Zimmermann, and Keulen 2003, 255–69.

Porter, J. 2003. "Chariton and Lysias I: Further Considerations." *Hermes* 131: 433–40.

Ramelli, I. 2007. "The Ancient Novels and the New Testament: Possible Contacts." *Ancient Narrative* 5: 41–68.

Reardon, B. P. 1969. "The Greek Novel." *Phoenix* 23: 291–309.

———. 1999. "Theme, Structure, and Narrative in Chariton." In Swain 1999, 163–88.

———. 2003. "Chariton." In Schmeling 2003, 309–35.

———. 2004. "Variation on a Theme: Reflections on Xenophon Ephesius." In ΕΓΚΥΚΛΙΟΝ ΚΗΠΙΟΝ (*Rundgärtchen*): *Zu Poesie, Historie, und Fachliteratur der Antike,* edited by M. Janka, 183–93. München/Leipzig: K. G. Saur.

Rife, J. L. 2002. "Officials of the Roman Provinces in Xenophon's *Ephesiaca*." *Zeitschrift für Papyrologie und Epigraphik* 138: 93–108.

Ruiz-Montero, C. 2003. "The Rise of the Greek Novel." In Schmeling 2003, 29–85.

———. 2004. "Xenophon of Ephesus and Orality in the Roman Empire." *Ancient Narrative* 5: 43–62.

Schmeling, G. 2005. "Callirhoe: God-like Beauty and the Making of a Celebrity." In Harrison, Paschalis, and Frangoulidis 2005, 36–49.

Schwartz, S. 1999. "Callirhoe's Choice: Biological vs. Legal Paternity." *Greek, Roman, and Byzantine Studies* 40: 23–52.

———. 2003. "Rome in the Greek Novel? Images and Ideas of Empire in Chariton's Persia." *Arethusa* 36: 375–94.

Selden, D. 1994. "Genre of Genre." In Tatum 1994, 39–64.

Sironen, E. 2003. "The Role of Inscriptions in Greco-Roman Novels." In Panayotakis, Zimmermann, and Keulen 2003, 289–300.

Smith, S. D. 2005. "Bakhtin and Chariton: A Revisionist Reading." In Branham 2005, 164–92.

Stephens, S. A. 1994. "Who Read Ancient Novels?" In Tatum 1994, 405–18.

Toohey, P. 1999. "Dangerous Ways to Fall in Love: Chariton 1.1.5–10 and 6.9.4." *Maia* 51: 259–75.

Trzaskoma, S. M. 2009. "Aristophanes in Chariton (*Plu.* 744, *Eq.* 1244, *Eq.* 670)." *Philologus* 153.2, 351–53.

———. Forthcoming 2010. "Chariton and Tragedy: Reconsiderations and New Evidence." *American Journal of Philology* 131.2.

———. Forthcoming 2010. "Citations of Xenophon in Chariton." In *The Greek Novel and the Second Sophistic. Ancient Narrative* Supplementum, edited by K. Chew and J. R. Morgan. Groningen: Barkhuis Publishing.

Watanabe, A. 2004. "The Masculinity of Hippothoos." *Ancient Narrative* 4: 1–42.

Wesseling, B. 1988. "The Audience of the Ancient Novels." In *Groningen Colloquia on the Novel* 1, edited by H. Hoffman, Groningen: Forsten, 67–79.

Whitmarsh, T. 2005a. "Dialogues in Love: Bakhtin and His Critics on the Greek Novel." In Branham 2005, 107–29.

———. 2005b. "The Greek Novel: Titles and Genre." *American Journal of Philology* 126: 587–611.

Zeitlin, F. 2003. "Living Portraits and Sculpted Bodies in Chariton's Theater of Romance." In Panayotakis, Zimmermann, and Keulen 2003, 71–84.

ENDNOTES

Callirhoe

Book 1

Pg. 3 . . . *of Aphrodite herself*　The manuscript specifies the "maiden [παρθένου] Aphrodite herself," which Hercher deleted as a repetition of the phrase "marvel of a girl [παρθένου]" in the preceding sentence. The paradox of a virginal Aphrodite, the goddess of sex and erotic power, may, however, be just the point, and Apuleius, in his Latin novel *Metamorphoses,* describes Psyche, the mortal heroine of a long inset fable, as a "second Venus endowed with the flower of virginity" (4.28).

Pg. 3 . . . *peoples on the mainland*　The manuscript literally reads "but also from Italy, the mainland, and the peoples in the mainland." Goold suggests that "mainland" here refers to the Balkan peninsula (or that portion of it which is called *Epeiros* or "mainland" regularly), but this seems unlikely. Plepelits ingeniously proposes that Chariton here uses Italy in an anachronistic and limited sense of only that portion of the peninsula immediately opposite Sicily, leaving "mainland" to cover the rest of Italy. My own feeling is that we are dealing with a simple textual error and delete the second καὶ thus: καὶ ἐξ Ἰταλίας [καὶ] ἠπείρου καὶ . . . "from mainland Italy and . . . " Cf. Posidonius fr. 310 Theiler ἠπείρῳ Ἰταλία. Other authors use ἤπειρος τῆς Ἰταλίας or ἤπειρος ἡ κατὰ Ἰταλίαν in the same sense.

Pg. 4 . . . *her father*　I translate Blake's restoration of "her father," though it is by no means certain. There is actually a gap in the manuscript, just where the name of the one who urged or ordered Callirhoe would have appeared. Other suggestions have included "Eros" and "a dream," but there are problems with all solutions proposed to date.

Pg. 4 . . . *this encounter*　Adopting Cobet's συνοδίαν.

Pg. 4 . . . *each could see the other*　Conjecturing ἵνα ἑκά<τερος αὐτῶν> ὀφθῇ, lit. "so that each of them would be seen." Chariton uses ἐκ. αὐτ. in the strong sense "both of them" at 5.4.3. This wording has the benefit of avoiding hiatus, the difficulty with the best suggestions to date.

Pg. 4 . . . *remarkable beauty meeting its match*　I translate my own conjectures in the genitive absolute *faute de mieux:* <θαυμασ>τοῦ κάλλους <συγ>γενεῖ συνελθόντος (or, possibly, <ὁμο>γενεῖ). Reardon 2004 prints an unsupplemented text.

Pg. 5 . . . *worthy of one another*　I translate my own suggestion of ἀλλήλων ἀξίοις for F's ἀλλήλων ἀξίως (which seems not to have been proposed before). Reardon prints

Reeve's ἀλλήλων ἄξιοι, which presumes the last words are a separate sentence: "They deserve each other!"

Pg. 5 . . . the crowd made room . . . to the girl   ἀπέλιπον, which, if it is not corrupt, has been generally taken in the slightly strained sense "made some room" with the crowd as subject, as here. The clause, however, most naturally reads "they left the crowd at the door," and it is possible either that Chariton has compressed the description of the wedding beyond the point of clarity or something has fallen out with a resulting gap. Maybe we have a lacuna just after "got her dressed," in which the wedding procession would have been described briefly.

Pg. 14 . . . "I'm alive!" and "Help!"   The text is corrupt at this point. I translate Hilberg's "ζῶ" βοῶσα, καὶ "βοηθεῖτε" without any certainty that it represents what Chariton wrote. Reardon obelizes the passage.

Pg. 16 . . . proof of their own guilt   Reading D'Orville's φώριον ("damning evidence") rather than F's φορτίον ("cargo, haul"), though D'Orville thought it only possible, not probable, and editors have not adopted it.

Pg. 17 . . . a life constantly on the move   Translating my own conjecture οὐδὲ γὰρ ἀκίνητον βίον ζῶμεν rather than the manuscript's ἀκίνδυνον ("In any case, the life we lead is a risky one," trans. Goold). The latter is defensible (and "life without danger" is a common phrase in Greek, whereas the conjecture is not), but it has caused doubts and does not seem to follow on what immediately precedes.

Book 2

Pg. 24 . . . The peasant women   An abrupt transition. A simple phrase such as "The next day" has perhaps fallen out at the start of this sentence.

Pg. 24 . . . took them off   The manuscript is seriously garbled in the preceding sentence, and the translation follows Renehan's reconstruction (the general sense is clear in any case). Three words in the manuscript, which Renehan is unable to work in and which Reardon marks as hopelessly corrupt, have also not been translated. Various solutions have been attempted.

Pg. 26 . . . Then Callirhoe said   The manuscript presents a problematic text here, and though there is a papyrus including this part of the novel, it has a gap here as well, preserving only Callirhoe's name. I follow Blake's reconstruction, though it is not likely to be absolutely correct in detail.

Pg. 31 . . . forced himself on?   I follow Jackson's deletion of ἄν, which Reardon retains ("whom not even Theron the pirate *would* have forced him on").

Pg. 31 . . . don't call me 'master.'   Conjecturing μή ⟨με⟩. Compare 7.3.2 for εἶπον in sense of "call."

Pg. 31 Feigning panic   The text as transmitted has Plangon in an actual panic, but it must clearly be feigned and I conjecture καὶ ⟨ὥσπερ⟩ περίφοβος, the ὥσπερ (or καθάπερ) having dropped out before the following περ-. Compare Leonas' feigned alarm in 2.4.6 (ὥσπερ τεταραγμένος).

Pg. 37 ... *the child I bear*   Conjecturing τὸ ἐξ ἐμοῦ γεννώμενον ("the child born from me," for the phrase compare 3.2.3) rather than the transmitted τὸ ἐξ ἄλλου γεννώμενον ("the child born of another man").

Book 3

Pg. 38 ... *a good man*   This sentence is corrupt in the manuscript ("For she was so great that even she wept for her husband Dionysios.") and I translate Reardon's suggestion, which is based on those of earlier scholars, though there is little reason to feel that it is correct in detail. Morel notes that, "It would be better to bracket the entire sentence altogether, as it is stupid and adds nothing to the previous sentence," but this goes too far.

Pg. 38 ... *think myself*   I think Cobet's <μοι> is probably right and translate it, though it is not strictly necessary.

Pg. 45 ... *the women*   Reading καὶ ⟨αἱ⟩ γυναῖκες with Gasda. The women of Syracuse normally are treated as a single unit, and the idea here is, I think, not that "some women" participated in this assembly but that "the women" did.

Pg. 47 ... *come with me*   It does not in essence affect the translation, but it seems likely to me that Chariton here probably wrote "ἵνα μοι" φησὶν "<συν>ελθὼν μηνύσῃ ...," the συν- dropping out after the similar -σιν, and I translate accordingly. The unaltered text would merely be rendered: "That way," he said, "he can come and show me who bought her."

Pg. 48 ... *that she return*   The verb "return" in this part of the sentence (doubled in the translation) is missing from the text.

Pg. 53 ... *trouble he was in*   Perhaps not οἷ καθέστηκε δεινοῦ but οἷ καθέστηκε <κιν>δύνου "how much danger he was in." Cf. Lucian, *Alexander* 55.27, Appian, *Iberica* 108.2.

Pg. 54 ... *into his scheme*   This portion of the sentence has suffered corruption. No satisfactory solution has been found, and I merely give what I think is an appropriate sense.

Book 4

Pg. 58 ... *broke out in lamentation*   Perhaps <ἐπὶ τούτοις> has dropped out here "<At this> the crowd broke out in lamentation ... " Cf. 3.3.7 and 8.8.2.

Pg. 62 ... *seem golden to you*   The text of the last part of this sentence is corrupt (as the next sentence may be).

Pg. 65 ... *perhaps partly*   Conjecturing τάχα μέν <τι> καὶ .... Cf. τάχα μέν τι καὶ ... τὸ δὲ πλέον at both Appian, *Punica* 12.86, and Josephus, *Bellum Judaicum* 5.534.

Pg. 66 ... *if you stay put*   Reardon obelizes the text after κρατήσεις: τοι ἅδε (sic) μένων. The sense is approximate.

Pg. 66 ... *he has worthless*   I translate D'Orville's φαύλους ("worthless") to cover a short gap of about five letters in the manuscript that Reardon leaves unsupplemented (probably correctly—D'Orville's suggestion provides an adequate sense but many others could be imagined).

Pg. 66 . . . should break faith   Reardon obelizes the verb ἀθετήσειεν. Its subject and precise sense are both uncertain here.

Pg. 68 . . . reason for their journey   The words "for their journey" are not in the text, but perhaps we ought to insert them, <τῆς ὁδοῦ> τὴν αἰτίαν (cf. the parallel passage at 5.4.13 where we have τὴν αἰτίαν τῆς εἰς Βαβυλῶνα ὁδοῦ).

Book 5

Pg. 69 . . . far worse than slavery   I translate δουλείας ("slavery"), Reiske's sugges-tion for the manuscript's φιλίας ("worse than love") or Abresch's ἀφιλίας ("worse than not being loved"), neither of which seems to make good sense.

Pg. 70 . . . come to refute   I do not follow Reardon's acceptance of Reeve's emenda-tion πάρεστιν ἀπολύσασθαι <θέλων> διαβολήν ("has come, wishing to refute the accusation"), which is unnecessary. This is a typical infinitive of purpose after a verb of motion—πάρειμι—so acts regularly; cf. the same construction in 8.3.5, πάρεστι . . . ἰδεῖν ("she's come to see").

Pg. 71 . . . against our women, who   The text is corrupt, probably beyond repair (Reardon obelizes). I translate here Blake's conjecture, which provides good sense, even if it is probably not correct in detail.

Pg. 74 . . . nothing could go wrong   The text is corrupt here, and I give merely a possible sense (roughly following Reiske's proposed emendation).

Pg. 76 . . . get your fill   The verb of this last part of the sentence ("could get your fill") seems to be corrupt and is obelized by Reardon. Others have tried various solu-tions, none satisfactory.

Pg. 76 . . . more violent blow   The text of the last clause is seriously corrupt, though the overall idea seems reasonably clear. I follow Jackson's somewhat radical surgery, but it seems unlikely to be ultimately correct, merely better than the other proposed suggestions.

Pg. 77 . . . a good man   The text here is very uncertain.

Pg. 79 . . . barely credible threats   I translate Cobet's <ἀν>αξιοπίστοις ("barely credible").

Book 6

Pg. 87 . . . Do you still   Translating my own conjecture of <ἔ>τι δοκεῖς, ἀνόητε, Χαιρέαν ἀντίδικον ἔχειν; instead of the manuscript's τί δοκεῖς . . . ; "Why do you think Chaireas is your opponent?"

Pg. 88 . . . succumbed to him   There is a short, unreadable sequence of a few letters at the start of this sentence in the manuscript. I follow Cobet in believing that we've lost nothing but an "and."

Pg. 91 . . . please the king   The text here is uncertain.

Pg. 91 ... *judged*   This word ("judged") is only partly legible in the manuscript.

Pg. 95 ... *get your husband back*   There is a textual corruption in this sentence. I follow Blake's text, which deletes the problematic words ἢ σχεῖν κάλλιον. Reardon believes the corruption is wider, and he may be correct in this.

Pg. 96 Messengers came   It seems unlikely that Chariton wrote ἧκον ἀπαγγέλλοντες. One would expect ἧκον ἀπαγγέλλοντές <τινες> (easier to explain the loss of the indefinite pronoun) or ἧκόν <τινες> ἀπαγγέλλοντες (the more usual order).

Book 7

Pg. 99 ... *in all apparent sincerity*   I vary from Reardon's text (where the manuscript's ἄκαιρος is printed with the obelus, indicating that it is corrupt) by accepting Abresch's ἀκέραιος.

Pg. 102 ... *tight as a house*   The sentence has been widely suspected of corruption. I have made a minor transposition of καὶ λιμέσι because the result sounds better to me than the transmitted text (which Reardon prints, though obelizing ἐκ τῆς θαλάσσης) rather than out of any certainty: τὴν μὲν πεζὴν στρατιὰν ἐκ τῆς θαλάσσης, ἀρκούσης αὐτῇ πύλης μιᾶς, τὸν δὲ ἐπίπλουν τῶν τριηρῶν τείχεσι καὶ λιμέσιν, ὀχυρῶς ᾠκοδομημένης τῆς πόλεως <καὶ> κλειομένης ὥσπερ οἰκίας.

Pg. 104 ... *the praises of Othryadas*   The manuscript has the name Mithridates here, obviously wrongly. D'Orville suggested as possible corrections both Miltiades, which Reardon prints, and with less conviction Othryadas (in the form Othryades). Reardon also must transpose the word "three hundred" or Miltiades cannot be right (he did not command 300 men). But I think the number is meant to be emphasized, and in that context Othryadas, who did command 300, is to be favored. On the other hand, Miltiades commanded Greeks against Persians (Othryadas was leading Spartans against other Greeks), and that speaks in favor of Miltiades.

Pg. 104 ... *your word on that*   Based on the parallel with the *Cyropaideia*, we ought perhaps read πιστεύομέν <σοι> in Chariton. The pronoun could easily have been dropped before the σύ that begins the next sentence.

Pg. 104 ... *until we have it*   For αὐτῆς ("it," i.e. the city) I wonder whether we ought to read τῆς πύλης ("the gate").

Pg. 107 ... *when she entered Babylon*   This last sentence has been suspected of being an explanatory comment that has made its way into the text, while the preceding one seems to be corrupt (the verb for "offered her comfort" is not in the text). The corruption may be deeper than has been suspected—the reintroduction of Rhodogoune with such fulsome language is exceedingly odd. We know who Rhodogoune is, and even if Chariton thinks we might have forgotten, why would he place so much emphasis here on her familial and marital ties?

Pg. 108 ... *saddle, in pursuit*   This sentence is corrupt, and several scholars have suggested that material has dropped out.

Pg. 110 ... *submit to marriage*   Perhaps read <ἄλλον> γάμον οὐχ ὑπομένω, "I will not submit to *another* marriage" (ἄλλον would have dropped out easily after the preceding ἐπαγγέλλου). Cf. 2.8.4.

Pg. 110 . . . *best part of the plunder*   The text of this sentence is problematic, and unlikely to be convincingly repaired unless through future discoveries we can somehow recover the material lost in the large gap earlier. Jacobs' <τί> τοῦτ' ἄλλο does not convince me, but his ἤ for ἦν seems promising.

Pg. 110 . . . *onto a ship*   The text of these two sentences is extremely (hopelessly?) corrupt. I've glossed over the difficulty—the inconvenient lacuna earlier makes it impossible to say whether any given appropriate sense is actually the correct one.

Book 8

Pg. 111 . . . *Paris Alexander*   Paris/Alexander is normally called by one name or the other, and Dawe prefers to delete "Paris" here as a gloss. This is an attractive suggestion.

Pg. 116 . . . *send her to the king*   Here I vary slightly from the text of Reardon, who prints D'Orville's intrusive supplement "<and Rhodogoune to her husband>" at the end of the sentence.

Pg. 117 . . . *and make dedications*   Reardon suggests that there is a small lacuna at the end of this sentence, or that τιθῇς ("so that you might give") has dropped out. I have translated the latter to cover the gap. The aorist θῇς would probably be more at home here and its loss easier to explain (καὶ πατρίοις ἀναθήματα θεοῖς <θῇς>). But it is hard to see why Chariton would have used the simplex, when the compound ἀναθῇς is expected. If Reardon is right that we have a gap, we might read καὶ πατρίοις ἀναθήματα ⟨ἀναθῇς⟩ θεοῖς.

Xenophon of Ephesos' *An Ephesian Story: Anthia and Habrocomes*

Pg. 131 . . . *they did so willingly*   The text of this sentence has suffered some corruption, but the sense is clear.

Pg. 132 . . . *those of a girl*   I vary from O'Sullivan by retaining the manuscript's κόρης. O'Sullivan adopts καλῆς ("beautiful woman's") because of Aristaenetus 1.10-7–8 (φαιδροὶ μὲν ὡς καλοῦ), but Aristaenetus would have had to change κόρης in any case because of the change of gender in adaptation, since κούρου would not have been an option for him.

Pg. 133 . . . *been made by her*   O'Sullivan supposes some words such as "like herself" have fallen out of the end of this sentence.

Pg. 135 . . . *consult the god*   I adopt Cobet's θεοῦ for the manuscript's plural.

Pg. 136 . . . *flows of the sacred*   Adopting Locella's ἱεροῦ "sacred" for Νείλου "Nile."

Pg. 141 . . . *it didn't seem safe*   The thought may be "safe *to try*" but the phrasing is abrupt. Perhaps we ought to read something like οὔτε ⟨φείσασθαι⟩ ἀσφαλὲς ἑώρα ("nor did it seem safe to leave them alive").

Pg. 152 ... *prosperous men dwell there*   I adopt Hercher's transposition of ἐκεῖ.

Pg. 153 ... *plenty of tears*   The text of this sentence is corrupt, but the general sense is certain.

Pg. 154 ... *gusted on the sea*   The text of Hippothoos' dedication is seriously corrupt in the second and third lines.

Pg. 157 ... *Habrocomes must remain*   I translate my own conjecture of <μ>εῖναι ("must remain your husband") for the manuscript's εἶναι ("must be your husband"), since loss of the μ is particularly easy after the preceding -μην of Habrocomes' name. Castiglioni suggested ⟨μόνον⟩ εἶναι ("must be your only husband"), comparing 4.5.3, but μόνον is there adverbial. The verb in 4.5.3, however, is μεῖναι, which seems appropriate.

Pg. 158 ... *wretched in every way*   Reading παντάλαινα with Jacobs for the manuscript's πάντα καινά.

Pg. 161 ... *"the Coast," as it's called*   I follow Hägg's deletion of καὶ Φοινίκης ὅση παραθαλάσσιος as an intrusive gloss, but even so the passage is clearly corrupt.

Pg. 161 ... *to satisfy her lust*   I vary from O'Sullivan's text here both in punctuation and by retaining the manuscript's ἐθέλειν.

Pg. 162 ... *promising to marry him*   The manuscript also has the words "and kill Arastos." I follow Konstan in deleting this phrase.

Pg. 162 ... *She regained her composure*   I follow the manuscript's ἐν αὐτῇ γενομένη, which O'Sullivan emends to ἐν ὀργῇ γενομένη ("growing angry").

Pg. 165 ... *great deal of gold*   Reading χρυσοῦ ("gold") with Locella rather than χρυσίου ("gold coinage").

Pg. 174 ... *tried to run away*   Reading ἀπέφευγον with Hercher rather than the aorist ἀπέφυγον ("ran away").

Pg. 179 ... *know any of this*   There is a slight corruption in the text here, but the general sense is clear.